THE BOOK OF MALACHI

THE BOOK OF MALACHI

T.C. FARREN

TITAN BOOKS

The Book of Malachi
Print edition ISBN: 9781789095197
E-book edition ISBN: 9781789095203

Published by Titan Books
A division of Titan Publishing Group Ltd
144 Southwark Street, London SE1 0UP
www.titanbooks.com

First Titan edition: October 2020
10 9 8 7 6 5 4 3 2 1

A CIP catalogue record for this title is available from
the British Library.

Printed and bound in the UK by CPI Group Ltd. CR0 4YY.

For David

MONDAY

My job is to check the plastic, see that it seals off the body parts, splays the flesh flat like faces against a windscreen. The vulnerability of a chicken is in the angle of their wings. If you pull them, the skin stretches, eases back. A newborn's legs have the same elastic, I have seen this at the refugee centre in Zeerust. Their skinny legs stay up against their stomachs, the skin on their thighs rumpled and loose. Now it is my job to see that the skin on the chicken's limbs is stretched and tucked to hide the hack marks. The machine must seal their pimpled skin, hide the tatters.

I know what they say about me at New Nation. One of my assistants, Beauty, is eighteen. She chews gum while she tears the plastic off the corrections, a perfect black grape, her chewing gum the pip.

'My granny's getting old, she asks me the same questions, she forgets. "How was your day, Nono?" Later, "How was your day?" I told her about you, Malachi. I said not a sound comes from your mouth.' Beauty smiles, her chewing gum stopped between her teeth. 'Do you know how we say we will keep a secret? We say, "Don't worry. I will make like Malachi."'

The phrase echoes in my head.

I am a successful mute. Malachi, well done.

1

*

My boss and I meet on the packing-office steps. We almost kiss, we both fall back.

'A woman was on the phone checking your psychometrics. A labour agent from Raizier Pharmaceuticals.' Lizet's face stays in the shadow, the sun colours her long neck yellow. 'I said you're always on time. You're . . . appropriate. I said you understand instructions. Nothing wrong with his brain, I said. But, you know, he doesn't communicate.' Her mouth wilts. 'The woman seemed pleased!' Lizet steps outside. 'Did you apply for something?'

I shake my head.

She checks my eyes for truth. Sighs, satisfied with the confusion she finds.

'About two hundred corrections. It's going to be a helluva day.'

All day I stroke the plastic back onto its track. I anticipate trouble, see it coming. My job is menial, but it doesn't show. The plastic leaves no calluses. It erases my fingerprints, smoothes my hand into a black silk glove.

I rinse off the static in my basin. Above it, the mirror has the skin disease mirrors get in gloomy rooms, dark spots that spread. In it, my hair is soft and knotted. My eyes are shallow sand at the edge of the Tantwa River. I have a cat's head, wide across the eyes, tapering to the chin. The mirror is so high, I can only see the slight lift of my top lip. I cannot see my teeth, miraculously unblasted, unchipped by molten blade or machine-gun butt. I cannot see my fine scar, smoothed by a volunteer plastic surgeon.

*

I rest on the bed I bought from a man who went to jail for stealing chickens. The mattress has two dents, hollowed for a man and a wife, a virgin ridge in the middle.

I can say that word now. Before, it would have meant a bolt through my body that ripped off my fingertips.

Virgin. Virgin. I would say, over and over in my mind as I pressed the wires to my testicles.

Virgin ridge.

Every twenty-four hours, I slip into the dent on the right. I take only the space I need, the air that I must breathe. At night, when the air is abundant, I run on the spot. I travel ten kilometres in the same place. In the morning, I go to the toilet in my shorts, drip two drops on the seat. Clean it. For breakfast I cook Jungle Oats in a small pan with no handle. I eat it with Huletts sugar and real butter. I am rich enough to buy butter.

I inhabit number twenty-nine in the long line of the men's hostel. They are stables, really, with a flush toilet in the corner. We peer over the top of the doors like dark horses at the scrappy grass. Beyond is a road pitted from rumbling trucks, bullies arriving with military frequency, carrying not men with weapons but live chickens with broken legs from being shoved into crates piled six storeys high. Now and then, a truck filled only with heads. I turn away.

I have seen decapitation. The head disengages as if the spine is nothing. A mere rumour.

3

TUESDAY

The Raizier agent lets my hand go, shocked by its silkiness.
'Susan Bellavista.'

Her cheeks are florid, her accent American. Her eyes are cornflower blue, pale petals crushed by hooves or running feet. The only signs of danger are her thick, languid fingers and her shoes, pressed together under the desk. They are polished and stiff, the grey of gunmetal. The leather climbs all the way up to the ankle bone.

'Malachi Dakwaa. I have a job for you.' The agent reaches for her tall, curved bag, red leather with a black handle. She splits it open like a carcass. Pulls out Africa, unfolds the map. Sixteen plastic squares knock staccato on the wood. She points at my country, coloured in pink.

'Which province are you from?'

I touch the province next to mine.

'Which village?' she asks.

A door shuts in my throat.

'Malachi, who did this to you?'

I see flying splinters, shattered school desks.

She tries a gentler way. 'Malachi, let me just say, what they did to you and your people . . .'

4

I push back the people clamouring, steal air through their limbs.

'You can correct it. Those monsters who kill with machine guns . . .' She checks to see if she has hit broken skin. Her words drift out of focus, refuse to hold on to the tail of the one in front. The agent's cinnamon breath disguises her predation.

'What we do on our medical programme is get these murderers to save lives.'

I blink, try to make her out against the sky.

'They can't harm you.' She watches me for signs of fear. 'No danger.' When she smiles, I see her eyeteeth are slightly grey. 'Malachi. Today is the luckiest day of your whole life.' Her fingers creep across the desk, her soft arms stick to the top. She wants to touch me.

'Do you want a tongue?'

My head snaps back, startled.

She nods. 'Raizier needs a new Maintenance Officer. As payment, they will graft a tongue for you.' She sews hasty stitches before her lips. 'I'm talking about the best surgeons alive.' She doesn't trust my English. 'The best medicine.'

A force surges up my throat, completes my stump. A phantom tongue. She sees it boasting there like an erection. She sees the cataclysm in my eyes.

I did not know I wanted it.

My foolish eyes bathe themselves in salt. I cry before this large peach skirt and her two stiff shoes.

God has decided I have been punished enough.

'Go home and think about it,' says Susan Bellavista.

I am a hungry animal, leading with my head as I gallop to the sound of my bullish breath. I will have a living, breathing tongue that can curl and lash and spit. A tongue that can tap the palate behind my teeth, suck air off my molars, make my Kapwa clicks. I am a broad-faced bull with a wet chest. I am Taurus in the *Times*.

My boss gives me the *Times* every week.

'Take it for your fires,' Lizet says.

Each of us has a drum outside our room, but I don't light fires, in case people come. I bring my lunch in the *Times*, vetkoek and jam, no evidence of it being read.

If people knew I could read, they would ask me about my father, my mother, my lover. They would say to me, 'Malachi, write a reply.'

Lizet is hunched forward like a chicken now, her shoulders flared to flap over her desk. 'Why-y-y?'

I turn up my hands, but there is nothing to read.

She throws her digital pen on the release form on her desk. It bounces and hits the blades of her solar fan. She doesn't laugh. 'No explanation.'

The stump of my tongue sinks into the floor of my mouth. *I'm going to be reconstructed*, I want to say. *Remade*.

Lizet waves a trembling hand with faint purple patches. 'You'll lose a month's pay. Why don't you wait?'

I let my head swing from side to side.

'Malachi. You're strange.'

A conviction, for slipping from her life like a loose page.

But she won't feel any difference in the weight. She will train someone new in two afternoons, someone who can smile and sing, perhaps talk of their love life.

I want to pick Lizet up, feel her pointed purple knees poking

6

my thighs. I want to squeeze her hard, implanted breasts against me and say, *Lizet, I will come back one day.* Then I will laugh and say, *Sorry for leaving you so suddenly.*

For seven years I have been her best quality controller, excellent with the automated plastic packing machine.

Only once did I have to electrocute myself for my boss. That day, she wore maroon high heels of soft leather with thin, crossed straps. It was not the shadow of her buttocks beneath her dress. I did not lust for the diamond that forms below a woman's bum. The problem was, my boss had perfect ankles.

Lizet will miss talking without causing offence.

'It's because you don't speak, Malachi. That's why you have such good eyes.'

She will miss my patronising shrug. *Whatever, Lizet.*

She took my silence as affection, which is strange when you think that I never, not once, made a single sound. Not even when the locals slapped me at the Nelspruit taxi rank.

'What's this? Makwerekwere.' An open-handed punch. 'What country are you from? Darkie!'

I showed my empty eyes, my open palms. For this I got a dislocated jaw, like a badly hung door.

WEDNESDAY

Today the agent's hair lifts up like a wig. She wears a loose woman's suit of baby blue. I check her feet under the desk. Her shoes are navy blue. On each ankle is a dark mark from pressing them together. Her hair follicles are black from constant chopping.

'You will be working offshore. On the sea?'

I nod.

'On a rig. It's like a boat, but it has . . . legs.'

I smile inwardly.

'Malachi.' A thread of cold threat coils in Susan Bellavista's voice. 'Confidentiality is the most important thing about this job. The consequences are very, very steep.' She taps the document with a clean nail. I give the plastic sheet a blank stare, but I read discreetly.

The organ is awarded on a leasehold basis. If the signee speaks of what he/she has witnessed, Raizier has the right to retrieve the organ without legal recourse.

'What this means, Malachi, is that if you ever talk about what you have seen, we will claim back your payment.' She waits. 'Do you understand me?'

I swallow some stinging spit.

8

'This is top-secret science,' Susan growls. She whips a digital pen from somewhere. 'Can you write your name?'

I hesitate.

'Just a mark?'

I grip the pen like it's a captured snake. I force its tip down near her fingernail, fight the reptile into a grim, deep *M*.

Susan lets go of her breath. There is a bitter triumph in the way she says, 'Good.'

I stop at the factory shop, buy a new radio for the deep sea. It will be my secret hardware. If they search me, they will see a radio for entertainment, not a strike that rips me inside out, a Molotov cocktail for my genitals.

I usually roll my clothes up tight like intestines but today I lay them flat in my suitcase, each pair of trousers, each shirt unfurled. I run my extra belt along the edge. My duvet, I roll up and tie tight. I bought it from Kashmir's with my first New Nation salary. It has feathers inside, the dead chickens' gift to me, perhaps for letting them spread their limbs on a polystyrene tray; not live crushed towards their own fat hearts, their cage cranking smaller every six hours. This is how fast they grow, their own fat cells shoving into each other, bruising their inflating heart that can do no other than punch back, pump.

I throw in the cheap yellow Nokia Lizet gave me for after-hours callouts. I dare not take any books. In a sudden spasm of longing, I tuck an ancient roller-gel pen into the suitcase lid, and a thin white pad made from real paper. I'll die without words, surely.

For fifteen years I have lied about my literacy, when the truth is I read any words that dare to float close. I read the plastic magazines dumped in the shallow bush – *Shutter Speed Photography*, *Cat Lover's Journal*, *S.A. Motorboat*. I read advertising flyers that truly fly in the wind. I read warning signs on everything, disclaimers. Ask me the ingredients on the Colgate shampoo bottle. In the bus I read long-distance over shoulders, so people think my fixed stare is vacant, perhaps autistic.

Every three months I take my suitcase on wheels to the Hospice shop in Nelspruit. I pack in thirty-six books from the waste crates in the corner, three books to read per week. I rattle the case over my threshold, shut the door with a double bang. In my locked room, my boxer shorts on to cover my shame, I read with my electric wires standing by.

Where will I hide those bodies now?

I have no choice but to light my first fire. A man is snoring two doors down. There is a whispering beyond, the whimper of a child. Someone else is smuggling what they love. No visitors are allowed overnight. Here at New Nation, the men sometimes sleep in the bush on cardboard sheets in order to cradle their children or make love to their wives. Tonight, the child in number eleven has two scared parents and two milky breasts. I know this from the uncertainty of his cry. His parents are risking their monthly income to touch the baby's face in the candlelight, play at being family in the hours between midnight and three a.m. when the chickens first feed.

I quietly pile some clods of chicken droppings into my fireplace. The chicken-shit flames crash silently towards the stars, envious of their silver. I drop the books in threes. They shrink and leave a fragile shell of black. Chimamanda Ngozi Adichie, Margaret Atwood, E.M. Forster. Louise Erdrich, Charles

Dickens, Kweku Adobol. Even *A Short History of Everything*. I let it burn alone. Whoof. It conspires towards silence, as if the pattern of civilisation and the jealous, obsessive energy of science were all only worth an exhalation. I am not joking. It was a definite sigh. The child cries in number eleven as if the flames are flicking his tiny feet. It is a swollen breast that muffles the child's shout. I hear it in the fullness of the silence. Some things I know because I am not living. I am listening.

It is three a.m. A late, late cremation.

THURSDAY

I wheel my case into and out of the ulcers on the road. When I look back there are men's eyes shining from every dark doorway. I breathe in, swing my case onto my head; keep a rough grip so I don't look too womanly. It throws a shadow over my eyes, brings a Bhajoan sun to my thighs – a sun which was, a moment ago, South African. I forget my audience, drop my hands from my suitcase. I wipe the strange tears from my eyes.

What are these? Why now?

The agent is waiting against a bullet-shaped BMW that looks like a huge, shining suppository. Susan's buttocks have warmed against the metal and spread.

'Ahhh!' her hips thrust off the car.

Relief ignites her eyes, illuminates the fluff on her orange trouser suit. Her suitcase is safely stored on the back seat, Scottish tartan. Next to it is a copper urn with a red ribbon tied around it. Susan clips open the boot. I don't dust off my suitcase before I lift it: I have so much to apologise for, it's better not to start. I'd have to apologise for the sweat I'm about to bring into her high-speed electric vehicle. And the fact that I won't make a single sound for seven hours.

Susan shuts the boot. 'Righty oh!'

I jerk my mouth into an awkward curve. That's me, for seven hours. I get in with my sweat.

Susan's brown suede boots take up the pedals like little leather men. We swing past the live man on stilts advertising Eddie's Gas.

'Here we go. Lesotho. The arse end of the world.' Susan glances sideways at me.

I save my laugh. One day, when I have my tongue, I will laugh out loud about driving through the arse end in a bulletproof suppository.

Susan tears open a Bar One and takes two huge bites, like it's a burger. She offers a chocolate to me, opens another one without apology.

'My next assignment is in China.' She taps the screen of her car media system. A man speaks gently, entreating us to speak Mandarin. Susan asks, 'Did you learn Mandarin at school?'

I press the air with my fingers and thumb.

'You're lucky. In those days they didn't bother with it in the US.'

I don't know about *lucky*, I'd like to say. In elementary school, they taught us the words you might need at a conveyor belt. Lift. Twist. Alternative item. Red light. Green. Later, our Mandarin teacher, Mr Li, began to groom the chosen few. We learned to say, 'Tell section seven to accelerate.' Or, 'You no longer have a job.'

After two hours in Susan's car, I could smoothly recite corporate management Mandarin. *How will we benefit from this arrangement? What guarantee can you give us? Do you have a digital privacy armour package? I have seen the sights, thank you.*

Susan leaves a fingernail space between the front of her vehicle and the bumpers before us.

'What's this?' she mutters. 'A Sunday drive?'

A slight shift causes a hard drift of the car to the right, a hurtle towards an oncoming car. A mere twitch slaps us back in front of three flatbed trucks, just missing a string of car comets.

Once, Susan glances at my cheek and starts to ask, 'That scar, was it from . . .?'

She ramps a blind rise, freefalls into a double-lane speed belt. Her question is a passing curiosity, dust from the recent past, part of the unremembered distance streaming behind us.

Susan doesn't look at the view, even when we get near Egoli with its repopulated mine dumps, their terraces glinting black, their fountains so high you can see the water evaporating. 'Shit heaps' they call them, the workers like me. The shit heaps glimmer with rim-flow pools. I learned the term in the surplus *Good Living* magazines that came to the refugee camp still in their wrapping. We flicked through pictures of solar-charged chandeliers, garden statues of Mr Mandela in his suit among the 'poor man's orchids' of the rich. There were wall-length sofas with floor connections for massage and warmth, photographed with huge house-cats fed on chicken intestines. *Positively Feline*, said the heading. One sofa had a young, live lion arranged across the back rest. Its golden eyes looked drugged, its body well fleshed like the lions Templeton Industries bred for the trophy hunters to prey on. The rogue lions, on the other hand, were skinny and wild, refusing a clumsy death at the hands of the panting, flaccid men who came all the way from America on jet planes to kill cats bigger than the ones that kneaded their pillows and meowed for tinned chicken.

No.

I shut my eyes. Why Bhajo? Why now?

*

Three hours from the city, the BMW slides past slow white figures on a golf course. A small white ball climbs the sky. A pale airport runway unrolls past the pressed green fields. Susan stops before a tall, gaunt guard. He meets my eyes once, sneaks a hostile shot. I know what it means. It means, Refugee.

'How are things, Matla?' Susan asks him.

'Problems with kids on motorbikes. Racing.'

'Brats,' Susan says.

The guard flicks the boom up like it's a toothpick. In the distance, three white helicrafts dip their noses at a white building.

Susan fetches her copper urn from the back seat, clamps a hand into my shoulder muscle.

'Don't let me down.'

As if, now that I've endured her chocolate farts and listened to her labouring through corporate Mandarin, now that I've sweated before impact perhaps five hundred times, we are friends.

I get out, embarrassed for Susan.

A pale hand waves from the door of the nearest helicraft.

I follow Susan's shoes, crushing loose pebbles like little sado-masochists; keep my eyes off the white beast looming before us. I was airlifted on a stretcher to a field hospital, they said, but I was deeply descending then, clawing towards death.

I am about to fly for the first conscious time in my life.

Susan climbs the five stairs. *Dragonfly, 554 FP*, it says on the underbelly.

'Malachi. This is Mr Rawlins.' Susan turns to the captain, 'Malachi's mute.' She drops her voice, murmurs, 'Not deaf and dumb.'

15

'Ah, good,' the pilot smiles like he is genuinely pleased for me.

He has sliding silver hair in a side parting, white chinos, a collared white shirt. His teeth glow white. He has a white film on his tongue too, perhaps from the coffee in his polystyrene cup. Susan gives Mr Rawlins the copper urn with the red ribbon, holds out her hand to me. 'Godspeed.'

She pounds down the stairs, swings her broad rear towards her too-thin BMW.

I drop into a seat, buckle up before the pilot tells me to.

Mr Rawlins leans across, taps the window. 'Watch out for golf balls.'

Is he joking? The pilot smells of tobacco smoke. The hairs in his nose are coated in nicotine. I need him to be perfect, but I am dismayed to see two small spots of sweat at his underarm seams. A second bad sign, apart from the fungus on his tongue. Mr Rawlins opens a tiny Perspex fridge filled with stumpy Coca Colas and nine pie packets with pictures of little pigs.

'All yours,' he says. 'It's a nine-hour flight. We cross a time zone, so we arrive the same day.'

One piggy pie for every hour of flying.

The pilot folds into his cockpit and lights up a cigarette. The alarm screams indignantly.

Is he crazy?

'Don't worry, the petrol tank is at the back.'

I cough loudly, twice. He touches a button. Some kind of vacuum sucks his smoke straight up. Mr Rawlins starts the engines and coasts gently out of the range of bad golfers and their hard, white balls abducted by the wind.

There is the sound of air escaping under terrible pressure. As we lift up, my body dives for the earth, yearning. The pilot takes off with a stream of smoke pulling from his head. Nine little pigs smile through the Perspex.

This must be what they call adventure.

As we rise I let my eyes drop through the glass, see the crowns of houses and upended skirts of trees. The Dragonfly erupts through the clouds with barely a sound, more like a hum, as if the thin vacuum that removes the man's smoke is keeping this craft in the sky.

After two hours, I am part of the Dragonfly. The machine breathes its mechanical breath through the soles of my sneakers as it takes me up to rub shoulders with the sun, fly within earshot of heaven, get the first whisper in. My fear is gone. The Dragonfly is taking me gracefully to a miracle of science. I will soon become a Raizier quality product.

Joy is fecund, but it rots easily. A dusting of old yellow appears on the rims of the pilot's white sleeves. Fluff forms, a gathering audience to our exhaustion. Several times I check my GPS on my timepiece but it says, *Aircraft Tracker Block On.* Mr Rawlins doesn't bother to speak to me, as if his words would be wasted on a mute.

The earth turns to heaving, sucking blue, but I would not call it a colour. It is a state, a plane, almost astronomical. I have seen the sea three times at Ladebi beach but this sea is as wilful as a seizure, as crushing as the unconscious mind. I would not call it blue.

After five more hours, the Dragonfly starts to slide from the sky. From a distance, the oil rig is a greedy creature crouched over its prey, covering it for consumption or mating. Closer, it's a piece of industry broken off, a floating block of factory, with cement beams and steel cylinders sinking into the water, rooting it, I can only hope, in the earth's core. Towers of criss-cross struts climb towards the sky as if someone was trying to build scaffolding to heaven. On the highest deck, a tall, round tower glitters near a landing ring. At the edge of the deck, an orange torpedo tilts down at forty-five degrees. A hi-tech lifeboat, ready to freefall into the sea.

As we fly closer, the sea smashes at the rig's metal legs, turns them into twigs to be snapped off with a careless slap before the water demolishes the rig, devours it without tasting. The Dragonfly descends.

I can swim. I can swim, I tell myself desperately.

The pilot does something astonishing. He works the controls with one hand and pulls his shirt over his head with the other. Mr Rawlins has unexpectedly big breasts. He covers them up with a perfectly pressed shirt, identical to the one in which he's spent nine hours sloughing skin. He clips down his mirror, combs his silver hair so it shines like the rotor blades through the window. He starts to brush his teeth, switching hands on the levers. He spits foam into his cup, speaks into the stiff wire on his cheek.

'Nadras tower, Dragonfly 554FP, seventy feet and descending. Landing estimated at thirty-five seconds.'

I grip my seat as the rig heaves to meet me. As the deep sea separates into green, grey, black, I see black fins like plastic, pricking curiously in the water beneath the rig.

Am I dreaming?

A pillow of wind tries to stop us from touching down. We find a second of surrender, dive the last ten metres.

We land more heavily than one would expect from a man with excellent hygiene and a silver side flick, a man who is too important to communicate with a mute.

* * *

A Chinese woman stands like a sculpture cut from pearly white rock. After hours of flying, all the pilot gets is a slight bow. Her eyes are so black the midday sun tints them magenta.

'Malachi Dakwaa.' She smiles out of custom rather than kindness. 'I am Meirong. The logistics controller on this project.' She is wearing a black dress, square at her neck. There are black radio devices clipped to her waist, which is impossibly slim. Nipped. Her shoes are low and black.

I brace against the faint rocking of the rig, keep my eyes off the pale, polished bump rising above her ankle strap. The hair on her head is simply black water. She nods. 'Come with me.'

Her flesh is shinier, more solid than I have ever seen. She is made of the same stuff as the life-size Buddha I saw in a garden shop once, but this woman is not the offspring of a gurgling teacher of joy without cause. She is the marble tree under which the fat man sat.

A black man steps from a huge old lifeboat with a torn-off roof. I want to duck away from his AK97, but I've taught myself to plant my feet, breathe before security personnel. The man's muscles are laid in thin, strong strips, I can tell by his easy flex on the slightly shifting surface. Metal jangles with each tread, as if his pockets are heavy with loose change. His eyes are as bleak as the surface of this rig.

Oh, God. His epaulettes.

My fists form into bone.

They bear the same sign as the ANIM. I suck air through my teeth, force my eyes to the devil-thorn insignia on his chest. *Nadras Oil*, it says. A barbed star with a right angle hooked to each tip.

A drilling emblem with a clockwise momentum, *not* the insignia of the devil who took my tongue.

'Malachi, this is Romano, our security officer.'

'Hello.' His voice is full-bodied, his only fat. 'Please give me your timepiece.'

I snap it off my wrist. He slides off the back, presses out the microchip.

'Turn around, please.' He pats every centimetre of my clothing. He pulls on rubber gloves. 'Open your legs.'

I refuse to move.

'Mr Rawlins gets it, too,' Meirong says.

The pilot sighs, presents himself for inspection. The machine-gun man slides his rubber hand into the pilot's trousers.

Meirong tries a personal touch. 'Romano's here to earn a heart for his little girl.' The man winces as if she has just sunk a thorn into his heart. I must remember – the logistics controller is manipulative.

I spread my legs. The tickle beneath my testicles sets off a knot of nerves, expecting electricity. I want to turn and hit him.

'Come, Malachi,' Meirong says. 'We must work right away. The prisoners are waiting.'

The murderers.

My heart dips, but I follow obediently. The Buddha in the garden shop was too focused on the pliancy of his toes, the expansion of his self as he bound a million universes into one locust swarm of love. He didn't feel the bony coldness of the tree.

Meirong marches past the tall, round tower towards a window-less steel edifice. She stops at a metal door halfway along the building. Lifts a key card from her breasts. Unlocks it.

*

It is not so comfortable, this factory ship. From the top I see narrow passages, sharp corners intended for servicemen, not polished pearls with supple skin. But Meirong pours herself down the steep stairs, suddenly a Chinese gymnast trained in sullen concentration, reserving her smiles for an outright win. I follow easily. I am a runner by night, luckily, my stomach is like steel. We are dropping down some kind of thoroughfare between the two wings of the rig, down narrow flights with skinny railings, our descent marked by bright, reliable rows of silver rivets punched against the sea. We move silently, two agile apes through the man-made trees.

Meirong pauses at a door to the right that says, *Private. Keep out.*

'Strictly out of bounds for maintenance crew.' Her eyes shoot black bolts. 'That's you.' She launches down again, stops at a door in the left wing. She speaks without even catching her breath. 'Here we are. Maintenance.'

The door emits a rusted screech. We walk along a corridor painted with thick yellow paint like congealed egg yolk. We pass some closed doors, then a room with benches and a table bolted to the metal floor. I glimpse two thin streams of sunlight filtering in near the roof, the only openings to the sky I have yet seen.

Further down the corridor, Meirong taps at a door. 'Your living quarters.'

She walks straight past any chance of leisure, leads me deeper into the building until I hear a low hum that might be the pressure of the sea. The sound gets louder, begins to ring like a soft, suppressed joining of voices. Just before the door at the dead end of the long corridor, Meirong swings up a set of spiral stairs.

At the top, computer screens cover two walls. The third wall is a window into falling space, the glass as thick as the crocodile tanks at the Tantwa River. Far, far below the yellow ceiling is a craving and a pulse; I sense it with the hairs at the back of my neck. I look away, try to focus on the screens, but my eyes refuse to understand the images I see – fluorescent light flung onto metal mesh, a sheen of human skin. That is all. I am not ready yet.

A young black man sits at a desk bristling with keypads and switches. His dreadlocks swing as he spins in his chair, jumps up to meet us. He has thick, wild eyebrows and an untidy patch of hair on his chin. His one eye is light brown, the other holds a splinter of green. His genes must be uneven. He grins.

'Ah, Malachi, how are you, man?'

I offer him a careful smile, lock my teeth behind my lips. 'I'm Tamboaga.' He glances at Meirong. 'From Zim.'

'Tamba's here for a kidney.'

His face becomes sombre. 'My brother's very sick.'

I nod in sympathy. Only then does the movement in the computer frames draw me in.

I gasp inwardly, try to understand the high-res pixels.

They are naked, all of them. An array of bent necks with long, dishevelled hair. They are all colours. A deep cocoa, here the ebony of the equatorial regions, here clay, here pink. Beards sprout on the men. A glimpse of black bush between their legs, tired and thick. A penis lolling, a breast swung to the side. Humans in cages.

Meirong says, 'Forty of them, sourced from prisons all around Africa. After three cycles, they go back to their justice systems. We grow the organs inside them for six weeks, give them two weeks to heal. We've done one harvest with this lot. We start again on Thursday.'

I trace the patterns on their skin from pressing on bare metal, the deeper, longer gashes with puncture marks where a needle has passed through and pulled tight. Stitches.

With horror I count the wounds on a huge black man. Two cuts per cycle. One to go in. One to come out. Will there be blood?

'Tamba runs the wiring and piping from up here.' Meirong points through the thick glass. 'Do you see how it works?'

Massive chains run inside steel tracks in the ceiling. Two rows of metal hooks dangle near the roof. Abbatoir hooks, but bigger.

I step towards the window, let my eyes plunge downwards.

Two rows of cages on curved cradles, bolted to the floor. Beneath each row, a twisted umbilicus of wires and pipes emerges from the floor, threads through the u-shaped cradles, drops away again.

I see no blood from this glass station. Beyond the thick mesh, all I see is the hair on their heads. I see shoulders, elbows. Here and there I see toes.

There are only a few women, but they are barely living. They will not waken my strange, sick libido.

'This is a very sophisticated system.' Meirong spins slowly, takes on a computer glow. She speaks with sincere pride. 'A Chinese engineer set it all up for us.'

Tamba rolls his eyes at me.

And me, Malachi? Naturally I am speechless.

At the bottom of the spiral stairs, the murmuring returns. I recognise the sound now: it is the muted pulse of a foreign crowd. At the refugee centre in Zeerust, the people sheltered beneath the hum, sipped their sugary orange drinks, unwrapped their bread with their fingertips as if it might take fright and fly.

It is only now I realise that the people on the screens were completely silent. The subjects were suffering in mime.

Meirong stops before the door at the dead end. Through the

steel, the wind of their breathing scrapes at the fine hairs in my ears.

'The last maintenance man was a failure.' Fury strikes her marble eyes. 'The recruitment agent fucked up. Listen carefully, Malachi. The first rule for you is no communication. If you communicate, you're out. And that agent,' contempt curls her top lip, 'will be fired.'

Now I see why Susan Bellavista was so excited by my inability to speak.

Meirong raises a key card, turns a tiny light green.

* * *

The inmates go quiet. I hear some whispers, a long, melancholic laugh. We are standing near the left-hand corner of the hall. The two rows of cages run towards Tamba's glass kiosk, high above, on the left.

Beyond the mesh I see skin and hair, shifting. Animal madness, broken, still slightly stinking from the mêlée. The huge hall mimics the pull and heave of the sea. The room is breathing. I hear the swish of natural electricity.

No. They are not real people. The cages are too cramped for them to even stand up. They have no t-shirts, no sun-tan lines, nothing to show they were once a banker, a bin collector, a mother, a physician. They have no bags, no phones, no buttons to brand them. Only nipples, sunken parts, the pathos of ribs. I glimpse soft vaginal lips, the sudden drop of a skinny buttock. A sad reminder of fat pouched on a man with loose stomach skin. Meirong shuts the door behind us.

'We keep them naked to avoid the logistics of clothes. And it's easier for hygiene.'

She walks a few steps, stops at a metal trolley. She picks up a long tool with twin blades, and next to it some kind of leather sheath reinforced with metal strips. A giant dog's muzzle or falconer's glove, with steel locks attached to it. Meirong digs a fingernail into the fabric beneath her breast, presses a switch on a device on her hip.

'Tamba, when did you last douse for lice?'

'It's been a while,' Tamba replies through her speaker. He presses a key. 'Yeah. Five days.'

Meirong nods grimly at him.

Tamba touches a switch. There is the hiss of nozzles unclogging. A soft mist drifts down from the roof. The sudden stink of pesticide as forty bodies cower and clench, try to escape it. There are some gasps, some words for God. Meirong leads me towards the cages, which, raised on their cradles, stand from my thighs to half a metre above my head. She waves her silver blades.

'It is your job to clip and clean their hands and feet. Also report signs of parasites, bleeding, things the cameras could miss.'

She points to a transparent tube leading into a cage at mouth level. 'Don't worry about nutrition. We record their intake.' She stops. 'Are you understanding all this?'

I nod twice to convince her.

'It's a twenty-four hour cycle. Their supplements speed up nail growth abnormally. And you won't believe what they get up to if you miss a clipping. They pick their wounds incessantly.'

She stops at the top of the two-metre wide aisle. Only now do I let my eyes sink behind the criss-cross wires. I was wrong about my libido.

The knees of these women will be my failing, with their smooth triangular caps, skin stretching over bone as they sit with bent legs.

25

In row two, a huge, ruined beauty sits with her knee dropped to the side so her private parts open like a dutiful flower. I look away so as not to be mistaken for a man with normal, lurid tastes. I swing my eyes from a white woman's finely hung collar bone, the way it dips, almost invisible, a mere shadow in the skin before it sinks into the roundness of her shoulder joint. I dream of my new radio beneath my tube of toothpaste, my aqueous cream, my Vaseline.

Meirong sighs. 'Masturbation is okay.'

I almost choke.

'We give them hormones to slow down their sex drive, but we can't go too far. Too much suppression slows cell growth. No penetration though, it's dangerous. Get Tamba to stop them.'

Does she mean a shock? My ears amplify the breathing, the shatter of a cough to my right.

Meirong turns to the sound, speaks into her device. 'Tamba, number one, what temp?'

'Umm . . . normal,' Tamba replies.

'Tell Olivia to check vitamins.'

The man's eyes tilt upwards, chestnut with golden flecks. His face is so gaunt his cheekbones are like steel pins placed under his skin. He has a long penis. It lies lethargic, untrimmed against the mesh. There is a single burn mark on the inside of the man's ankle.

Meirong points to the floor of the cage next to his. 'Those are the waste plates. They look like nothing, but they're very sensitive tools for measuring blood pressure, temperature, heart rate.'

An old woman sits with a full bum on the metal square, her legs, I am sorry to say, splayed. Her hair twists over her shoulder and drapes her groin in a long grey rope.

'The subjects slide them to the side and excrete into a tray.' Meirong's face assembles into sweet, pretty smugness. 'The waste is diluted with sea water and flushed away.'

I am relieved to see tiny numbers at the base of each cage. Meirong unlocks a rectangular hatch near the floor of cage three.

'Watch carefully, Malachi.' She clips the leather brace to the edges of the opening. Two pretty hands slide through the gap into the falconer's glove. Meirong pulls on the leather strap so it traps and separates the hands in one drag. The metal buckle bites the leather, squeezes the knuckles together. Meirong sinks her cutter beneath the nail of a little finger. 'This one's a husband killer.'

There is a snigger inside the cage. 'Only one, Miss China. You make it sound like there were a whole lot.' The woman has glossy black hair tangled in knots. Her skin is as white as the polystyrene trays we slapped the chickens onto. Her breasts are perfect, curiously tilting, their eyes innocent. She has a mouth like a fig, plush with a dip in the middle. Inside her mouth there is sweet wet flesh, seeds of salivary glands, soft pink papillae. I can't see them, but I know. The fig never disappoints.

We had a fig tree outside our hut. We watched every fruit grow, picked it at the first sign of pigeons.

I force my attention back to Meirong, sending a curve of nail flying against the mesh. The woman's arms and legs are notched with healed cuts, a peculiar scaling; a strange mutation of a mermaid. And she sits like a mermaid, her knees bent to the side, her feet tucked under her bum. The soles of her feet are pink from the pressure, her only colour besides her thick, fig lips and her nipples like a rabbit's nose. If you touched them they would retract. The fig splits, shows a dream of pink.

'In case you're wondering how I did it, I used a knife.'

Meirong smacks the buckle on the leather strap, loosens it. 'You're wasting your time, Vicki. This one can't speak.'

Vicki withdraws her hands. 'Can't or won't?'

Meirong steps back, delivers her high, triumphant line. 'Malachi has no tongue.'

Forty pairs of eyes slide down my jaw, find the place where my tongue should be rooted. I lift my chin, try to blur my eyes, but the black-haired woman starts a giggle that staggers and trots along the cage walls. Behind me, a mad guffaw blasts from a large man with curling black sideburns trying to creep into his mouth.

'Ah, Malachi.' The refrain starts with the rope-haired crone, who, up close, looks like Granny Elizabeth. She, too, looks like she could do with an alcoholic drink.

'Malachi-i-i . . .' More voices coalesce, broken by higher notes.

'Walk.' Meirong marches me between the cages like I am mounted on a trolley. She warns the prisoners, 'If anyone spits, you'll get ninety volts.'

A woman's imploring nipples press against the mesh, her hands against the cage making plump squares of skin. 'Malachi . . . Help me . . .'

They whisper, they wail with open palms. Men, most of them, their voices deep with a raw catch. Oh God, beseeching. Meirong turns at the end of the aisle, leads me back the way we came. She bangs on number forty, the last cage on our right.

'Josiah has killed over three hundred people.'

It is the man with coarse hair curling towards his teeth. He smiles at me. 'Malachi.' He savours my name like it is tender meat.

I want to run away as fast as my legs will carry me but I turn

28

my back on him, swallow my spit. I walk after Meirong, suddenly foolish in white, a ball boy at Wimbledon, my shirt too thin across my spine.

Meirong shuts the door, stares at me in the sudden, sucking quiet. 'Will you remember?'

The flames across my face, the agony that sent me into weeks of bloodless sleep.

'Will you remember, when they get like this?'

A cocktail of shame and rage in the guerrilla's eyes. Blood flowing like a river in the Tantwa watercourse, bodies arrested in the air then landing, weeping on the yellow linoleum.

'We deliberately left the sedative out of their morning feed.' There is not a nuance of remorse in her voice. She bows without a hint of respect. 'I think you've passed the test.'

She leads me up the spiral stairs to Tamba's observation station.

I ignore the flickering portraits on the wall, force my mind to register the piping diagram on Tamba's computer screen.

'We unclip the feed pipe when we winch the cages up,' Meirong says. 'As you can see, the irrigation is all done from above.'

Tamba notices my desperate composure. 'Hey brother, you need a rest.' He presses the switch on a printer, catches the sudden tongue of printed plastic.

'Keep it.' He hands me the picture.

But Meirong is not finished. She fixes on my useless mouth. 'The two of you must work out a system of signals. The agent said you had first aid?'

I nod. A requirement for supervisors, but I learned more from watching doctors fighting to save flesh, not rubber mannequins.

'Good. It's too bad you don't sign, but you'll have to try. For instance, Tamba, how would he say, "Administer shock"?'

'Umm . . .' Tamba thinks. He presses his wrists together, mimes handcuffs.

'Right. That's punishment. Got it?'

I nod. Meirong watches my hand hanging uncooperatively against my thigh.

'How would you say, "Check temp"?'

'It's okay.' Tamba tries to spare me. 'We'll work on it later.'

Meirong slings a red lanyard around my neck, anoints me. 'Your key card to the cultivation hall. Look after it.' She flicks her liquid hair. A black wave breaks. She melts down the spiral.

* * *

It is a short passage and three unexpected stairs to the canteen. I stumble down them, suddenly weak. A woman gets up from a table with long benches fixed to it, all of it bolted to the minutely swaying rig. Her two big teeth make me believe her wide smile.

'Hey, Malachi.' She is thin and planed like a corner of a wall, with a prominent nose and protruding throat. In the deep, unpractised silence, she shrugs. 'I'm here for my child.'

I glance at her arms, limp and hanging.

Meirong says, 'Olivia's baby boy needs lungs.'

'They're coming with this second cycle.' Olivia exhales, her breath catching on the deadline. Her eyes are filmed with salt. She locks her fingers, twists her empty arms inside out. 'I can't wait.'

Meirong waves at a trolley piled with white crockery. 'Come, let's eat. Janeé is going to be late.'

The food is alien-seeming on this planet of sea. The carrots are a deathly grey, but I am not surprised. The memory of roots and plants and transpiration already seems incredible this far out to sea. My lamb chop looks like it was carved and cooked a year ago. My potato took the heat then crumpled into its plastic skin.

'The food's good tonight,' Tamba says softly next to me. He laughs at my surprised twitch. 'Yeah, brother . . .'

Across from me, Olivia shines the arm of her fork for nearly a whole minute. She is jittery about the days to harvest, shallow-panting to the date. I puncture my potato tentatively. This is my warning. She is falling to pieces after only thirteen weeks. I chew doggedly, tell my queasy body that the subtle shifting of the rig is a mere fantasy. Next to me Tamba checks the growth on my chin, assessing, perhaps, how thick my beard could be. He stares at my cling-wrap hands, sniffs discreetly for an odour off me, but I am sanitised by salt air and Solo deodorant. I don't know what his story is, but Tamba is afraid of my black skin.

A woman sticks inside the door frame, forces her huge hips through the space. Her head is a plump pumpkin, her bum a plush double sofa on which two people could sit comfortably. She eyes me like she's trying to guess if my species bites. 'Malachi.'

I raise a hand to her, spoon some carrots in. As she sits, the joints of the bench surrender, then weakly fix.

'Janeé used to cook for hundreds in the Craymar fish factory,' Olivia says ingratiatingly.

Janeé's face comes gently alive. 'It was easy. After a few years, feeding a hundred people is the same as feeding ten.' Janeé mulches her food like a waste-disposal machine, drains a glass of juice the colour of blood. The bench almost levitates as she gets up.

'Thanks, Janeé,' Olivia and Tamba sing as she crashes our plates onto the trolley and rattles it over the threshold. Her bum bulges and slides. I almost hear the pop as she arrives on the other side.

Tamba clangs with me down the passage, shoves on the door to my living quarters. 'Here we go.'

It is a four-by-four yellow cell, painted lava thick. There are two beds against the walls.

'You're sharing with me.' Tamba grins. 'Sorry.'

My suitcase is already on one little bed, unzipped. Inside, everything is rumpled and rearranged. Tamba apologises on behalf of the bosses.

'They're serious about staying secret, dude. They trash our microchips. And their satellite shield is fifteen miles wide.'

They must have checked the lining of my case, my toothpaste, for what? I see it has been squeezed. I lift the jumble of my clothes. My radio is still there. The wires and the plastic plug. I think of the pretty bridge on the husband killer's foot. I check the wall socket. Two-pronged. Good. I sigh. My very first sound since I arrived. I push my suitcase off the bed and lie down.

'God, it's like a gift Janeé's got,' Tamba laughs. 'One thing's for sure, they didn't choose her for her cooking.' I feel him prying at my shut eyelids. 'She's here to earn arteries for her son. They say it's diabetes, but the truth is he's a smack addict.'

My eyes sneak open.

Tamba smiles, teasing me with the mystery. 'He doesn't qualify for a transplant but the thing with a cook is, you need extra insurance. Think about it, Malachi, if the cook gets pissed off . . .' He sprinkles air. 'She can poison you.'

I stare at him without intelligence.

'Do you wanna come and watch a movie?'

I shake my head.

Tamba backs out, dismayed by my meagre potential as a friend.

But I don't rest easily.

The old woman in the cage brings me the scent of yeast from Granny Elizabeth's palm beer. It brings me the shine of the crèche children's skin, the sweat on their palms as they clutched on to my mother – with me, her little prince, always closest to her heart.

I roll over, face the wall, try to stifle the memories.

I fastened my lips to her nipple until I felt brave enough to wrestle and yelp with the children my age, while she helped feed the new-borns with rubber teats.

The memories push up from the bottom of my spine, pass through the barbed wire around my heart. I roll into a ball, try to refuse them room at the inn. But they will not dissipate.

Cecilia worked night shift so she could be with me. She arrived home from the corn sheds and put me to her breast just as the sun was starting to sting her eyelids. There's no point in having a child if you didn't have time to love it, she said, and even then I knew she meant she would never leave me in a box to cry until my tears slowly dried in a factory crèche where I might as well be drip-fed. Where I would be lucky to get a turn to suck on hastily thrust rubber, thirty seconds to suck while my mother takes her slim place in the factory line, her elbows ticking, take, twist drop, hardly time to shift her weight to the other foot.

Sometimes my mother and Granny Amma would find a sliver of sun shining between the two crude fingers of the fibre-optic factory and speak of the politics of raising children who feel strong inside, not grow up to live on Granny Elizabeth's palm-beer oblivion. Sometimes my mother fell asleep against the wall of the crèche. We clapped her with our small hands.

She opened her eyes. 'Thank you! Ooh, it was the sun.' She shook her finger at the sun. 'Stop shutting my eyes!'

I press my face into my pillow, let my open eyes scratch against the pillowcase. I don't want to feel my mother's arms. The white pillow burns my eyeballs like the white, white sun on the corn fields of Krokosoe.

I jerk into a sitting position. I study the piping diagrams on Tamba's printed sheets, force the patterns into my short-term memory. I throw myself onto my back, dig my heels into my mattress. Tomorrow I must be stronger.

I flail towards sleep. Lying on this tiny bed, I can't deny the rocking of the sea. It sickens me, soothes me as I dive away from memories of love, tormented by my dread of the new day.

FRIDAY

Short sharp trumpet blasts shock me awake, a brass band gone mad. Tamba sleeps through it, his dreadlocks splayed on his white pillow. The burping sounds get louder. Tamba sits up and slaps at his wrist, silences the cacophony. He smiles at me.

'Frogs. Funny, right?' He falls back on the pillow. 'Agh,' he sighs, like he's just remembered I'm not going to be a huge amount of fun. He swings his feet to the floor. 'Let's go and get some breakfast. Meirong will be waiting. She's fucking never late.'

Tamba pees like a mule. He comes out of the bathroom with a wet face. Toothpaste fumes gather in the small room. I am seized by sudden panic. There is something I did not consider. How on earth will I get enough privacy to electrocute my genitals?

Tamba glances at his timepiece. 'Move it, Malachi. Seriously.'

There is a clack of plastic coat hangers as he throws on an orange t-shirt and jeans. Who cleans them, I wonder? It's been two days but it feels like two weeks since I washed myself. I slide open the concertina door, squeeze into the bathroom cubicle. I slip a new white shirt over my head, pull on a pair of black trousers. I look like some kind of steward.

'Must I wait for you?'

I slide the door open an inch, wave Tamba away. The first communication the poor man receives is me telling him to leave.

In the bedroom, I hook my radio to my belt. Sling Meirong's lanyard around my neck, add a touch of red.

Meirong sits in an office dress the colour of sour cream, irritated by my close shave with the clock. I take the place next to Tamba, lean back while Janeé slaps down my plate. My eggs are so greasy I can see my face in them. Romano the security guard takes the right-hand bench, his eyes strung with fine red capillaries. His fingernails are dirty, but I'm not the one to judge. I am like a dirty nail, all of me unclean.

Olivia asks, 'How did you sleep, Malachi?'

Tamba shows her mildly incredulous eyes. He answers for me, 'He died for twelve hours, right Malachi? You were history.'

I coax my oily egg onto my toast.

Meirong says, 'Malachi, Tamba says you two are set up with signs. Is everything agreed?'

I glance at Tamba, who's grinning obsequiously. I get away with a ghost nod, too imperceptible to qualify as a lie. I capture my egg, press it into a sandwich. In Bhajo we liked to eat with our hands, taste the food first with our fingertips.

'Is Mr Rawlins coming today?' Olivia asks.

'Eleven a.m.,' Meirong says. 'You'll know by lunchtime.'

Olivia sighs.

Tamba reassures her, 'Timmy's fine, Olivia. He's giving his granny a hard time.'

She shakes her head. 'He went into intensive care yesterday.'

'Ah, no.'

'Meirong only told me after supper last night.'

36

'I let you do your work first and eat a good meal,' Meirong snaps defensively.

Olivia sits with her hands in her lap, her tomato too red on her empty plate.

'Look, it's difficult, Olivia,' Meirong says. She waves the suffering away. 'All we can do is keep working.' She sweeps aside her black tea. 'Are the towels ready?'

Olivia nods her head.

'Malachi. Go with her, please.'

My tea is strong and sweet. I gulp some of it.

Tamba says quickly, 'Come to the surveillance room, Malachi. We'll run through what we practised.' His lie is as glib as the egg white still quivering on his plate.

Meirong nods. 'Call me if you need me. I've got to do security while Romano sleeps, then I've got lunchtime meetings.' Meirong checks her watch, a busy executive in the city. She slips off the end of the bench, leaving a drift of dismissive air.

I follow Olivia down the corridor, hover in the doorway of a room filled with large plastic tanks and rows of silver instruments. A pale pink fluid drips from glass tubes propped in rings that might hold toothbrushes. A pink infusion in a bulbous bottle says, *Sedative. Saturday.*

Olivia watches me studying her laboratory. 'It's got more equipment than Greyfield's radiation monitoring lab,' she says sadly. 'They didn't bother too much with safety. Do you know nuclear poisoning?'

I nod my assent.

'I left Timmy with an old lady so I could breast-feed him on my lunch break.' She picks up a metal bucket. 'She lived one road from the Greyfield gate.'

37

The chemical fumes from the bucket sting my eyes.

You were a good mother, Olivia. Really.

Olivia chokes, 'Timmy's lungs got blisters on them. Blisters.'

I don't know what to do with her guilt. A shrug would seem insensitive. I take the metal bucket, stand like a hotel steward in white shirt and black trousers. I wait until Olivia turns her grief-stricken back on me. I walk away from her pain, bearing towels for the hands and feet of the special guests.

I'm halfway up the spiral stairs when Tamba launches down them. I stagger back, hang on to the railing.

'Okay, quick. Temperature is like this . . .' He flicks mock sweat off his brow with his forefinger. 'Show me.'

I do it slowly, feeling foolish. I am unused to communicating. 'Shock, we know –' Tamba smacks his wrists together. 'Use fingers for cage numbers.'

I nod.

'For urgent, do this –' Tamba whips his forefinger against his middle finger, makes a smacking sound. It's the warning between children, *Ooh, you're in trouble now.*

'Do it, Malachi.'

I flick my fingers. They make a weak snap, but I feel like I've barked out loud.

'What else?' Tamba asks. 'Diarrhoea.' He waves from his waist towards the floor, signifying some internal flood.

I sweep my hands downwards. *Here he is, the diarrhoea.*

Tamba starts to laugh. 'That's a curtsey, not a shit.' He guffaws loudly.

My eyes squeeze to slits, but habit keeps my lips from separating. Do not laugh, Malachi. For God's sake, do not laugh.

Tamba stamps up the metal spiral, chuckling.

If I laugh I might tear open, release lava from the dark, broiling depths of me. I might kill people, cry a tsunami of tears. I raise the red lanyard from my chest, unlock the door to the prisoners.

* * *

Their heads turn my way like weeds to the sun. The husband killer murmurs something to the long-haired crone, who narrows her eyes thoughtfully. The man in cage one is watching me hungrily, his mind probing, rolling, landing on its feet. The beast in him is feline, an emaciated lion like the one Kontar tried to save. Across from him, the mass murderer spills sticky black ash.

I pick up the leather sheath and the long silver clipper, walk towards them. I lift the latch of the first cage, clip the sheath to the opening. I jab my hands at number one. A thrust, nothing dainty.

He gives me his fingers. I tighten the leather strap, sink the clipper beneath the nail of his little finger. Squeeze. The curve of nail falls like a frozen teardrop.

'I see they chose an angry man.'

His next nail snaps like a fragment of grief.

'My name is Samuel. I was a journalist, filming suicide bombers in Algiers. They blew up a market. It had nothing to do with me.'

There were children at that market, surely. I see the shattered fruit, the falling cigarettes.

He takes back his hands, lifts his feet into the leather sheath. I stare at the burn mark on his ankle. Was it a flying ember from a burning burka?

'Scooter burn,' he says. He watches me clip his feet. 'Don't

39

believe Meirong. We're not all killers. Some of us here don't even deserve prison, never mind this.'

A big talker, the journalist, trying to cover up his cowardice. But I see the shadows in his loquaciousness.

'Loquacious?' my father asked me.

'Talkative.'

He was testing my vocabulary in the hut.

'Ah, so this is what you are, Hamri,' my mother teased him.

To the Kapwa, it is not a noble trait; it is a wasted, worrying proclivity to prod at a subject like a cat playing with something dead.

'Loquacious,' she said. 'And there is no vaccination?'

'Cecilia,' my father answered sweetly, 'there are worse diseases.'

No. Not Hamri. Please.

I lift a white towel from the antiseptic, rub the day-old coating off the journalist's toes. I try not to stare. The supplements must speed up replication everywhere. It's not like he's been dancing barefoot on the deck. I loosen the strap, lock his wire prison. Start on the old woman who looks like Granny Elizabeth, who secretly milked the palms to make beer. Despite her withered flesh, the old woman's fingers are extraordinarily silky. I groom her hands, smooth like mine, fight the panic rising in me. I drop the towel in the stinking liquid, move on to the husband killer.

Her vagina is an oyster shut against the fluorescent sun. I press the clipper beneath her thumbnail, mother-of-pearl pink.

'It's true what Samuel says. Some of us are innocent.' She shrugs. 'Not me.' Something catches in her voice, a sliver of a sob wresting free.

My elbows suddenly become watery and weak. We have something in common, this hateful mermaid and I. We harbour in our minds the same terrible red. The white towel lifts brown off even the blindingly white Vicki. She sighs raggedly.

'I suppose I'm not as bad as Shikorina in number twenty. She killed her own children.'

Oh, please. Save me.

I work through eight prisoners, endure their whispers, their exclamations, their pleas for mercy. Ten years of New Nation keeps my hands steady as I wash away their impurities, trim their claws, ensure that their nourishment reaches their tongues. The ninth prisoner is dark and skinny, of Indian origin, I think. He is jabbering in a language that is foreign to me, his one front tooth missing. His one fingernail is black, like it has been hit with a hammer. Perhaps his victim bit him before they died, left a sign that he should go straight to hell, with no McDonald's stops.

I cut his crooked nails, refuse to look at him.

Dream creatures, all of them, in a sordid dream city. Let them babble, let them plead, I will not listen.

After twelve subjects, this job might as well be chicken maintenance. I remember the New Nation advertising pamphlets.

It is social in the cages. The chickens are kept warm and clean. Their comfortable quarters ensure they do no harm to themselves or other fowls.

I have, after all, not broken free of factory slavery, as my father so fervently wished for me.

'It is a waste, Malachi, of beautiful thinking. Factory work makes a desert of your mind.'

41

I mocked my father, with his poetry, 'But isn't there an infinity of yellows in the desert?'

'Crap!'

'Hamri!' my mother warned.

'It's crap. Words bring rain, lightning. Inspiration.' He implored, 'Never be content with the desert, please.'

'Hamri, stop pressuring him.'

My father was unusually assertive. 'Malachi. Words are water.'

I screw up my eyes.

Be gone, Hamri. Please.

An enormous black man inclines his head, as big as a mule's. 'Are you saving a loved one?'

If I had a tongue, I would bite it in surprise.

This man is so huge he could be Gadu Yignae, the first man who emerged from the bowels of the earth. The leather strap has to slide to the end of its length. I stare at his hands, the size of young chickens on growth hormones. I would not like to see the size of his fist.

I compress his huge knuckles, let the buckle teeth bite. Do a careless cut.

'Ouchie!'

A laugh ripples between my ribs. Where did he find that childish exclamation?

I blur my eyes, try to turn the giant into mist, but the huge man has cracked the dream horizon with his stupid expletive.

He sighs. 'I killed the ones I love.'

The dark side of love blasts through me.

'I shot my brother and my wife. He died inside her.'

His own blood. For love.

I sink to my haunches.

The giant is astonished. 'Malachi?'

Some prisoners start to jeer, 'Malachi-i-i . . .'

'Quiet!' the giant thunders.

The chanting fades into a sheepish twittering.

I grip the giant's thumb, shoot to my feet. I look up but Tamba is dipping his head to some music playing in his ears.

'Sorry if I shocked you. I can be very crude with the facts. I was a High Court judge for thirteen years.'

I whip away the brace, abandon the judge's gargantuan feet. Slam the hatch against his crimes of passion.

The cage next to the giant flushes. The prisoner shuts his waste plate.

'Taking strain, mate?'

It is a butter-coloured man, once fat. His old skin flares from his waist, rolls from his neck like a drooping Dilophosaurus. A jet of water rinses the remnants of his flabby bum. I attach the glove to his cage, fight the tremors still coursing through my system.

He stares balefully at the glove.

'I feel like a sheep or a pig, you know, having its trotters cut.'

Interesting that he used the word 'pig'. He shoves his hands into the glove. Even his fingers wear extra skin. His accent is rounded, warped like a boomerang. Australian, must be.

The man in the next cage is white and skinny, a tax consultant, perhaps, with allergies. He has faint red spots across his chest. I touch my button cautiously.

Tamba replies, 'Yes?'

I sign cage seventeen. Flick my fingers across my upper body.

'What, a rash?'

I nod.

'Olivia will mix some cortisone into his vitamins –'

I cut Tamba off. The white man has a nose like a beak and sharp blue eyes that could embed in your skin. He tugs on his skinny penis, a rude nervous tic.

I glare at his compulsive comforting.

He lets go of his penis and submits his hands to me. I am careful not to touch his skin. I clip through balloons of breath, hold and expel, use my last nerves to get to the end of the aisle.

In the last cage, the woman's eyes are wide, straining to see.

'Do you have my baby?' She smiles at some apparition. 'Will you play soccer with him? He loves the ball and he is not even three.'

Cage number twenty. This must be Shikorina, the one the mermaid spoke of. The woman who killed her children.

She has a pretty mouth, a pronounced M where the two halves of her top lip meet. M for mother. Her shoulders are broad, a crow's outstretched wings, her shoulder joints sharp and pricking. She has round bluish scars on her chest and her arms.

I lock the brace to her cage.

Her hands will not come through. Damn her.

She strokes a phantom head. 'Are you hungry, my love?'

My skin prickles at the back of my neck. The warmth of my mother's breath passes over me.

Someone says softly down the aisle, 'She drowned them. Three of them.'

No, please.

I hit the switch of my communication device. Tamba's forehead touches the glass. 'Number twenty being stubborn?'

Shikorina's long, sodden fingers drift into the brace.

44

'Watch that one's skin,' Tamba says into his microphone. 'She used to have lupus. They had to do a blood transfusion.'

I nod at Tamba, cut her sharp nails, this black bird of prey. I stare at the fingers that must have tangled in their hair, shoved their heads down while they thrust their little bums up. My empty stomach heaves. I rub the murderer's hands with detergent.

'Lunchtime, Malachi,' Tamba says through my speaker.

I squeeze out the soiled towels, throw them on the trolley. Leave the rolled virgin ones for after lunch. I try not to run towards the door.

One voice snaps free of the murmurings, flies high above them, 'I am innocent. Help me.'

I fumble for my key card, shut the door on the cry.

I slide my spine down the metal door. Twenty subjects' talons cut. Twenty to go. My fingertips are burnt white. My torso aches in places that might contain my heart, my lungs, my liver. I am a tumult of longing, of terror, after less than one day.

This is the Raizier price for being the chosen one.

* * *

Olivia's voice rings with a panic-stricken peal as Janeé bangs down our meatballs and spaghetti.

'My granny says our neighbours went to see Timmy in hospital. They're these gay guys next door.' She laughs desperately. 'They're like his uncles.'

Janeé has poured tomato sauce over the top, the colour of the paint bags they pop in cheap Nigerian movies. Too orange to be realistic.

I forsake Janeé's synthetic raspberry juice, pour myself a glass of water. Janeé's spaghetti rolls onto her fork and flies into her mouth at rhythmic intervals. I can almost hear the cymbals crash like in Zeke's Circus in Zeerust, who every year gave surplus tickets to us refugee children. The Nollywood blood bursts on her lips.

Come on, Malachi, it's fake ketchup, you stupid ass.

I can say ass, Father. If I mean a donkey.

Olivia is saying, 'I went clubbing with them once. Sjoe, I couldn't believe my eyes. All these guys in G-strings. Half a cap of MDMA in every drink. It was long before I was pregnant. I wouldn't have done it if . . .' Her voice fades away, her eyes drift to her little boy's ribs caving in, sucking for oxygen. She takes a mouthful, but it is a mistake. Olivia is too miserable to chew.

Tamba tries some flattery. 'You know, Malachi, Olivia was head-hunted by Greyfield Nuclear when she was still in college. She got top marks, didn't you, Olivia?'

Olivia swings her legs off the bench and hurries out with a meatball still in her mouth.

'Shit.' Tamba hits his head. 'It was the bloody job that did it.'

Janeé nods her big head sagely.

Tactless, I believe, is the right word for it.

Meirong prods her fork towards the doorway. 'Patch it up, please.'

Tamba sighs. He leaves a pile of spaghetti, trails out to go and say sorry to his friend.

Meirong smears her meatball in the sauce. 'You people really have to toughen up on this rig.' She races it around the track. 'I've had to look out for myself all my life. I was the second born. You know what that means.'

Janeé and I both stare at her blankly.

'In those days the one-child policy was very strict.' When the meatball has reached a good speed she tosses it between her lips. 'I grew up in an orphanage.'

Ah, I see. I have read about that policy. Poor Meirong was probably well schooled in politics and Chinese etiquette, but every day she waited for her parents to pay the fine and pitch up at the gate.

Poor, poor child. I study her surreptitiously. Where is that little kid?

Meirong catches the pity stealing over me. She gets to her feet, picks up a mountain of spaghetti from the tray. 'I've got to get this to Romano.' She turns to me, punishes me for guessing right. 'You've got seven minutes left, Malachi. Don't dally.'

I flick a piece of spaghetti hanging its head off my plate. I will neither dilly nor dally. I hesitate for a second, try a polite goodbye. I wave at Janeé, but I don't get it right.

I leave the scene of the Nollywood shoot-out.

My bravado dissipates with every step I take down the passage. At the door to the hall my heart kicks against my ribcage, tries to break free. I take a deep breath, raise the red lanyard. Open up.

* * *

I take up where I left off, cage number twenty-one, tune my ears to the roiling, rumbling sea. Very soon my ankles, my backbone protest against the relentless, repetitive bowing and straightening. Even my fingers hurt from sinking the metal semi-circle beneath each nail, and press, release, press, release. A human cutting-cleaning machine.

I groom four more prisoners, reach a man who is quoting from the Qur'an, I think.

'Al-Araf, verse number twenty-seven says we have made the evil ones friends to those without faith . . .' He taps his head. 'I had every verse here. But I am losing it.' The hands he offers me are misshapen, the flesh melted like wax. He sees me staring. 'Must I tell you what happened?'

It's the first time any of them have asked my permission. I can't help but listen.

'I was burning twelve hundred Bibles in a fire. I was making a . . .' he waves, but the English word eludes him. 'I am from Morocco, in the North. There we are Muslims.'

A glimmer of orange tongues leaps in his black eyes.

'This Catholic priest tried to stop me, but his robe caught the flames. I tried to roll him on the ground but he was big, he was . . .' His fiery eyes search the air for the English word. 'An accident, Malachi.'

I stare at the death branded into his skin. A dead priest, a man of the burning cloth.

He is lying, like the others. Of course he killed in cold blood. The only ones who have told the truth are the mermaid with the knife notches and the giant who killed his loved ones while they were making love. As I pull the brace away, the Moroccan's eyes are pools of sorrow. The ash of twelve hundred Bibles has doused the last sparks.

As I start on the next prisoner, I feel dark eyes driving into my crown. High above me, Meirong is standing in Tamba's glass kiosk, her pale arms folded like a communist boss. I compose myself to be precisely what she ordered. A mute man with no moods, no soft spots, as resilient as the little girl who grew up in an orphanage.

I clip the nails of a bald man of about fifty. He has a German accent. 'I was driving too fast, it was very misty . . .'

I squeeze my eyes shut, press on the clipper. Please.

My shelter comes from Bayira, singer of Kapwa songs. 'Mokaa, Mokaa . . .'

Don't cry, don't cry . . .

I deflect Meirong's sharp gaze with my springy hair, suck in my spit to hear Bayira more clearly. 'Mokaa ne komoka na danga . . .'

Don't cry, and let clouds rain in your mouth.

Bayira's chili stew was a rite of passage among the boys in our factory village. If you could eat a whole bowl you were ready to kiss a girl on the lips.

'Kafi fopaka nadyi . . .'

Bayira's voice vibrates within my eardrums, trembles in my chest. There is a cry in his voice, a grieving loss that says he would die right now for the love he sings of.

Bayira had fat, soft lips but when he sang they became acrobatic, fitted around the Kapwa vowels, retreated from his teeth when the consonants came.

Meirong is still at the glass, watching for weakness. Does this mean there is no camera to spy on the aisle?

I do a perfect job of the German hit-and-run, start on a woman's fingers.

When I turned fourteen I ate a whole bowl of Bayira's chili stew without weeping.

The men teased me, 'Whoo, Malachi. You are ready.'

I laughed and looked down at the fire, but I raised my eyes once to Araba's father. I wanted him to see I was nothing like my father, Hamri, who could not eat Bayira's chili without grabbing for a water glass and wheezing comically.

*

My blades slip from their position. The huge woman in the cage cries out in pain, 'Aaiee!'

Sorry, I would say, only because my parents taught me to never harm a woman.

The woman sounds grief-stricken. 'I miss Dominic.'

Dominic? Is this the name of the man before me?

The woman is dusky skinned, voluptuous. A dark-haired Amazon. She looks exactly like the huge painting on the bus in Nelspruit, an advertisement for a Tropika granadilla drink. The girl on the bus sucks on a plastic straw, throws dust on tiny men as the bus blunders past them. This one has a hungry mouth, a slight overbite.

'Dominic never ever hurt me,' she says petulantly.

Her hair is more suited to an asylum than a tropical island. One half is plaited in a straitjacket, the other half bursts free. She sits like an untrained child, her knees wide open.

Thank God I am not aroused by soft places. My only weakness now is soft, singing skin stretched over sculpted bone, the pretty architecture of a woman's skeleton. Women's bones are not so much a construction, no. They are a composition. A symphony of strength and vulnerability.

I clip the beauty's toes, tear my eyes from the skin on her ankles, as thin as the pages burnt by the Moroccan.

'Komoka na dango . . .'

Bayira saves me.

Near the end of the row, I glance up to see that Meirong has disappeared. The relief is like a slow tranquiliser through my elbows. I let my cutting glove hang.

The woman in the second-to-last cage has white teeth, white eyes as if she's on a diet of real cow's milk. Even her nails shine. Their half-moons are impossibly neat for someone with a ragged scar from ribs to pubis. Her toenails have received the same careful scraping.

Josiah the mass murderer reads my mind. 'Madame Sophie killed five girls with heroin. But she likes to keep her nails nice for the gentlemen.'

A hyena laughs behind me. I don't need to turn to know it is Vicki, the husband killer.

'Isn't Madame Sophie lovely, Malachi? Or Charmayne in number twelve. She's gorgeous, isn't she?'

'Vicki,' Samuel warns from cage number one.

'Charmayne was Dominic's favourite.'

'Vicki!' Samuel hisses.

I swing away from Madame Sophie, face the last cage.

Josiah slides his hairy hands into the leather glove.

'It's true what they say. I killed three hundred Seleka.'

In his eyes I see graves, hands begging for mercy.

'I was fighting for my people.' He pulls a hand free, wields a ghost machete. 'War is war.'

I swallow. Taste the metal of a blade. *Never.*

I pull the brace away, shaking. Let him pick holes in his greasy covering. Let the fungus bite and breed. I spin on my heel, walk towards the trolley.

'War is war!' Josiah bellows after me.

I lunge towards his cage, whip like a striking snake. I spit.

The prisoners gasp. I grab the morning's towels from the trolley, march towards the door. A growth coils in my belly like a cancer.

51

I have failed in my mission to be inviolable, silent. An excellent employee.

I have failed to be a mute man with no history.

* * *

I tear off my clothing, swing on the hot tap. I stand still in the shower, take the punishment. I need the heat to erase the bullets, scald my weakness.

'Geez, Malachi! You cooking in there?'

I spin the tap shut. The stillness grates against my raw skin.

'There's steam everywhere.' Tamba slides the concertina door open, sticks his head through.

I swing towards the wall, shield my private parts.

'You trying to kill yourself?' The door slides shut.

My skin starts to burn now. My scalp, my shoulders, my penis seared by acid rain. I open the cold tap and let it slap at my fiery skin. Take that, and be happy. Blanched, they would say in recipes.

The pain gives me a focus in the canteen. My hair sits uneasily on my head. It feels loose, like I've been scalped and left for dead.

'How was your first day, Malachi?' Olivia asks me. She is wearing a shining yellow tracksuit, as if the wall has swelled into a three-dimensional form. Tamba puts an arm around me, squeezes my shoulders.

Inwardly I scream.

'I'm sure he's fine now. He went and skinned himself.' Tamba laughs. 'It's like, bejesus, did you grow up at the hot springs or something?'

A light frown lands between Romano's eyes. Perhaps he has not seen the fake epoxy rock pools in the *Destination* magazine, with the busloads of tourists up to their chins, sloughing off the epithelial cells of their skin.

'Are the subjects freaking you out?' Olivia asks me.

I shake my afro, lie outright. Bald-faced, they call it. I pick up my knife and fork, tip them at forty-five degrees to what might be spinach. My curved wrists lie about two things. I am culturally white. I am mentally all right. I must find a way to cauterise my mind, become as lifeless inside as the pentagon of hake on the plate before me.

Meirong arrives to eat dessert with us, her cream dress crumpled from all her meetings. She stares at me appraisingly.

'Everything all right?'

I nod and scoop at my yellow pudding. It detaches from my bowl like a loose cornea. I spoon some into my mouth, refuse to show the weakness of my predecessor.

Was his name Dominic?

Meirong devours her pudding within seconds. She strokes her empty bowl with the back of her spoon, makes it sing. Is this some Eastern custom, I wonder?

'Is there any more caramel?'

Janeé shakes her head. 'Sorry.'

Meirong drops her spoon sulkily. 'Olivia, I'll meet you in the tank room before breakfast. We need to run through the special needs report before I give it to Doctor Mujuru.'

As she leaves, Romano rises to his feet.

Olivia says, 'Say hello to the stars for me, Romano.'

'And me,' Tamba adds mournfully.

'The security lights are too bright. I can hardly see them.'

When Romano has gone, Tamba nudges me. 'There's a games room upstairs. Do you wanna check it out?'

I offer him a horizontal movement of my head. Negative.

'Oh, come and play ping-pong.'

Another no for Tamba.

He hides his hurt with racism. 'Ping-pong, haww saww. Must be a Chinese thing.'

'I'll come,' Olivia says listlessly.

I watch Janeé jab her spoon into her caramel. I sense a yearning in her. *Ask Janeé*, I want to say. She might not be the one you would normally pick for sport but you never know, she might mop the floor with you in a ping-pong tournament.

The canteen empties, except for Janeé who packs the plates, one might say, indelicately. I nod gingerly at the cook. Walk my chafing, raw limbs towards my living quarters.

I need to read.

I am thirsty for words to escape into.

When I reach my room I hear the tap, tap of airtight plastic. Rifle shots in the distance, approximately twenty kilometres away – this is the volume of ping-pong through an acre of stainless steel. I sit painfully on Tamba's bed.

Ouchie, as the giant said.

Tamba's storage hatch is unlocked, a rusted Volkswagen sign dangling off an ancient key. I slide the door open, scratch through his things. I find a thin, red Kindle with Little Red Riding Hood on the cover. I open her cloak. Tamba's first favourite is a poetry book. *Riding White Clouds*. I click his second best. *Sun Prophet, Memoirs of a Psytrance DJ*. The cover is a naked torso of a man with wire tattoos coiling across his skin. His smile is transient, thin, his eyes unnaturally bright, even in black and white. It says he used to DJ in the Arizona desert, led ten thousand people into spiritual ecstasy.

I creep to the bathroom, shut myself in.

I sit on the toilet seat, my neck muscles tight against the sound of protracted gunfire pinging above me. I swipe the book to the middle, fall into the words like an addict.

When I cut molly with amphetamine it was like someone telling me I won the Lotto while I was getting head. But when I snorted MDMA straight, pure empathy and love built tiny houses inside me and sent waves of love children into the atmosphere . . .

My bum stings against the porcelain but I wallow in the words, grateful for the luxury.

I could feel my separate skin but my compressed kick drums fused us all into one, synchronised us . . .

The talk of chemical ecstasy calms me.

Tap tap. Tap tap tap. Olivia and Tamba are perfectly matched, two martyrs playing ping-pong, both of them missing the stars to bring back a pulsing, live gift to their loved ones.

Yet there is something about Tamba that does not quite fit. He is like the DJ in this book, a man without a long-term plan, *tickle me, let's dance, play ping-pong, haww saww*. I can't imagine him suffering this rig for a soulmate. I stare at the picture of the desert DJ, the barbed-wire art gouging his skin. Just like Kontar's scars, after he saved the lion cubs.

A rogue lioness dragged her cubs through the barbed wire at the factory wall. Kontar and I watched her cubs suck her dry until she was staggering. Kontar couldn't stand their mewling.

*

I shut down the Sun Prophet. But the razor thorns have already hooked into my memory.

My uncle burst through the dark doorway while I was sleeping.

'Kontar stole hippo meat from my storage drum. Where is he, Malachi? Tell me.'

I shook my head stupidly.

'Tell me!'

My father stepped between us. 'Malachi doesn't lie. Let's go and find him.'

I waited for their footsteps to fade beneath the distant night engines.

I ran out before my mother could catch my fluttering sleeve.

'Kontar!'

'Help me!'

The barbed wire lay tossed like tumbleweeds. Kontar's satchel was open in the long grass, chunks of hippo fat gleaming in the fluorescent light from the fibre-optic factory. I crouched down and peered into the wire tunnel. A skinny lion cub was licking Kontar's face, taking his ear softly between its teeth. The other cubs were balancing on the wire behind it, their paws bleeding. I flung a piece of hippo fat towards the dead lioness. The cubs scrambled back to the factory wall, whimpering. There was a terrible snarling as they tore into it. They must have been starving.

I ripped off my clothes, leopard-crawled into the tunnel.

'Aaaghh!' I cried as the pain arrived in stinging, hot rips. I back-tracked, rubbed a chunk of hippo fat down my arms, my legs, my belly. The barbed wire still tore my skin, but let me slither through.

*

I groan softly now, remembering. I force my attention back to Tamba's Kindle, scroll to the end of his list. *Basic Anatomy*. I click on the medical textbook, stare at the black diagrams of human skeletons. Clavicle, scapula, sternum. The scientific name for fingers is phalanges. A carpal is a wrist bone. Metatarsals are the bones in the centre of the foot.

The serrated steel tore my elbows as I pulled his trousers down his thighs, hooked them off his feet. I smeared the hippo fat on Kontar's legs as he hollowed his chest and slid his shirt over his head.

I shut the basic anatomy book.

I drop Tamba's Kindle on my pillow, take off my socks and shoes. I slouch on my bed, stare at my bare phalanges.

One lion cub caught the scent of our greasy skin and crept purposefully towards us. The others dipped after it, wincing with each step. I scrambled backwards, crying out as the wire clawed into me.

'Hurry!' Kontar begged me.

The barbs sank their teeth into my hips. They tore my underarms before I folded myself up and slithered past.

As Kontar and I stood up, the lion cubs burst from the tunnel. I grabbed the last chunk of fat and flung it to them. The cubs pounced on it, growling. We turned and sprinted.

When we reached the first rise, Kontar and I stopped to watch the cubs prowl and lick, circle and slink into the yellow corn as if they were made of it.

★

I stand up, undo my buckle. I slide my black trousers past my stinging thighs.

Kontar hugged me. 'Thank you, Malachi.'

He started towards their hut.

'No. Come to us!'

He stopped, shook his head. 'He will hurt my mother.'

My own mother cried out at the sight of me naked and torn up by razor blades.

'Father, you must help Kontar. Uncle's going to beat him.'

'Where is he?'

'Hurry, Father, run!'

'Go, Hamri.'

My mother used hot salty water to strip the hippo grease and clean the cuts. I kept my scream down to a whimper.

'Will Father save him, Mama?'

My mother said nothing.

I sink onto my back, balance on my raw shoulder blades. Above me is the sound of faint rifle fire. Tap, tap tap. A ping-pong marathon.

Hamri arrived home smaller, more yellow than I had ever seen him. His eyes slid past me to the shadows on the wall.

'If I fought him, he would have killed them.'

'No.'

His voice cracked. 'I don't know what he did to that child afterwards.'

'Stop him!' I jumped up and raced into the night. It was my mother who streaked after me and held me tight. My cuts began to leak through my clean shirt.

'Why doesn't someone stop him?' I cried. 'All the men can go together . . .'

'They won't. He's the only one with a hippo licence. He feeds everyone.'

I broke away, shouting, 'I'll stop him, I will!'

My mother whipped me close, pressed my kicking knees, my elbows deep into her belly. 'He'll kill you.'

My mother made me hold my tongue. But she could not stop the rotting malaise that grew within her son.

From the night of the lions, I was ashamed of Hamri. My father was too small, too yellow. Too weak for the monster that blocked out the light.

Kontar came to school squinting. He wore his long school shirt and trousers, even though it was sweltering. He rested his swollen head on his desk. He turned slowly from the waist for several weeks. His skull gradually returned to its usual shape, but Kontar stumbled all the time. My heart cried each time I saw him stop and consider a short jump from rock to rock.

The tap of the ping-pong stops. Or does it?

An echo haunts the air for nearly half a minute.

The Kindle. I pat the duvet. Where is it?

I drag the bed from the wall. I can't see it. I run my fingers against the floor. They hit something solid – ah! I tap the red X, shut the anatomy book. Shut the cloak of Little Red Riding Hood. I slip the Kindle back into Tamba's hatch, throw myself beneath my feather duvet. I face the wall just as Tamba's shoes stall at the door. He lets himself in and switches on his bedside light. He removes his shoes, then pees as if he's been drinking jugs of beer. Tamba tears his blankets back like the lid of a tin. He slides the door of his hatch, scratches for something. I feel the weight of his Kindle in his hands.

Will he smell me on the screen?

I control my breathing like a yogi.

Tamba begins to snore with the light on. I ease onto my back, cover my groin, an involuntary habit. My bed clothes feel as if they are woven from barbed steel.

Damn them.

Damn the prisoners for bringing my loved ones back to me. They called up my father, my cousin Kontar, the singer in our village, for goodness' sake. They hooked their toenails beneath my skin, dug their fingers in.

Somewhere between the moon and the sea a helicraft thrashes like an overhead fan.

Tomorrow I must be an unremembered dream; too ethereal for them to bite into, use my silent blood for sustenance.

Yes. Tomorrow *I* will be the ghost.

SATURDAY

My skin is still sore but, by some miracle, not torturous. An eerie whistling rises and falls miles above me. Is it the wind? I get dressed in a black shirt and pleated black trousers. Tamba breathes heavily in his sleep. He has an erection. I should wake him, but it would be a definite intrusion – enter stage left into a pornographic dream.

I slide the concertina door back with a deliberate bang, splash water on my face, still tingling from last night's scalding. I check the mirror. No redness. My hair growth is quite prolific, stubble like a burnt field after two days. I slap my chin with shaving foam, strip the new growth with a brand-new blade. I brush my teeth loudly. Check my timepiece. Ten to seven. I peep through the bathroom door. Tamba's white dome is still growing.

I remember those dreams from when I was fifteen, my narrow bed shielded by the red Chinese horse hanging between the beds, my skin still unmolested by voltage clips. Like Tamba, now so luxuriously, happily on his back, dreaming of a woman's hips fitting over him.

It makes me sick.

I retreat into the bathroom. I did not cross the sea to witness a stranger's wet dream.

I must be untouchable, remember. A ghost among the killers. I must float like a membrane across their retinas.

I catch my eyes in the bathroom mirror. They are too bright, too fraught. I draw a veil across them. Good. My eyes appear blind.

With these eyes I locate Tamba's big toe beneath the sheet. I give it a squeeze.

Tamba opens his eyes slowly. 'Shit.' He leaps to his feet like Meirong is after him with a gun. 'I need a piss.'

He groans as he tries to aim his heaven-thrust penis into the toilet. I have had more than enough of this gruesome intimacy. I dive through the door, hurry to the canteen.

Meirong is sitting in a bright red dress watching the doorway like a cash-in-transit guard. She has a briefcase at her feet and some emails printed on plastic sheets.

Olivia waves one at me, grinning. 'Look, Malachi. A message from my granny.'

'Malachi can't read,' Meirong says dourly. She eyes Olivia's precious email, her small hand itching to take it. 'Have you finished? I need to shred it.'

Olivia gives it to her reluctantly. 'My little boy's out of hospital,' she tells me. 'He's on a ventilator on the couch.' She laughs. 'Guess what happened, Malachi?' She reaches again for the sheet, but Meirong is already zipping it into her briefcase.

'Where is your roommate?' Meirong asks me.

This woman is emotionally stunted, she must be. I am hardly a normal citizen, but even I can read simple feelings. Olivia's fingers flutter to the table top. The doorway remains empty.

If I had a tongue I would say, *Tamba is waiting for his hardon to soften. Last time I saw him, he was trying to pee through a tree.*

Tamba sweeps in just then, his eyes innocently wide. 'Sorry,' he breathes. He lifts the top slice of toast, sets the pile teetering, like the atmosphere in this breakfast room. Tamba butters his toast lavishly.

'It's eleven minutes past, Tamba. Do you not care?'

Tamba floats his fried liver between them, drops it on his butter substitute.

'This is the third time,' Meirong says.

'Really?'

'Don't think there will be no consequence.'

'For God's sake, Meirong. Eleven minutes.'

Meirong leaves a Chinese-sized bite in her white toast, arrives on her feet. 'Olivia, I'll inspect your growth markers at ten.' She turns to Tamba and me. 'I want both of you on your jobs by half past.' Meirong strides through the door, choppy with indignation. Janeé almost crushes her on the other side. 'Janeé, please report to me if they stay late.'

When Meirong is gone, Tamba says under his breath, 'Stupid bitch.'

Janeé pours caramel-coloured tea from a silver teapot. The sound of a delinquent wind reaches my ears now. A shadow floats across the portholes above our heads. Yes. The clouds are racing. Romano steals in, grunts some Portuguese greeting. Eases his tired body onto the bench.

Olivia tells him, 'Timmy's hooked up to a ventilator day and night, but he's getting better. Guess how we know?'

Romano scoops half of the marmalade jar onto his toast. 'How?'

'He got off the couch and crawled to the glass cabinet. He turned

63

the key. I mean, he's only twenty months. He opened the blimming thing and he broke Little Bo Peep.'

There is a bewildered silence. Is this good news?

'It was my granny's best piece. It was, like, old china. Do you know what he did? He said, "Ahh, sha-a-ame."'

We wait.

'His first words, I mean except "Mama" and "Nana". "Ahh, sha-a-me."'

Romano's tired eyes reflect Olivia's pleasure. He talks with a huge piece of toast in his cheek. 'My little girl, she talked at one and a half years. My wife said, "Say Mae, say Mae."' Romano utters a laugh that has been soaked in pure love. 'She said, "Papai."'

Olivia chuckles. 'My granny stuck the Bo Peep together with superglue. I just wish . . . I just wish . . .'

I know what Olivia wishes. She wishes time would rush like a tidal wave, crush the pipettes, the poached eggs, the thousands of rivets and bring the day they carve out a pair of new lungs for Timmy.

Which prisoner is cultivating them, I wonder?

Janeé spoons three sugars into her tea, stirs vigorously. 'It's twenty-nine past,' she says meaningfully.

Tamba slashes at his liver with his butter knife. 'I take it your son is stable, Janeé? His veins?'

Janeé spills hot tea on her chin. She grabs for a serviette.

'They say if you're diabetic, sugar's like heroin,' he says spite-fully.

'Time to go,' Janeé says grimly. She collects the plates with a sur-prising quietness. It's amazing how guilt can make clumsy people delicate, turn noisy plate-crashers into nimble plate-stackers.

Olivia floats from the room, still delighted about Timmy. I bow slightly to Janeé, I suppose in pity. Follow Olivia out of the seething atmosphere.

In her laboratory, Olivia hands me my bucket of clean white towels. 'All strength,' she says, powerful now that her child is strong enough to break Little Bo Peep into pieces.

As I walk down the corridor, the sea lets loose a warning wave against the metal legs of the rig. Or am I imagining it?

Disappear, Malachi. Be a shadow in the wings.

My father used to make us enact our English pieces on the factory simulation mezzanine. Instead of our role-plays like, 'I am worried about the productivity over Christmas' or 'Section ten's figures are corrupted. Who is responsible?' Hamri nudged us onto the tiny, high stage to replace dry factory language with floral Shakespearian.

Be gone, Father.

I raise my key card from my heart, turn the red light green.

* * *

When I reach Samuel's cage, I can't help but stare at his nails. They are the same length as yesterday before I cut them. Those nutrients could grow a human in the same few days as a GM chicken. I put my bucket down, latch the leather glove to his prison.

Samuel doesn't even let me reach his little finger. 'Do you believe me, Malachi?'

He must be talking to himself. I do not exist.

65

'Do you understand my English?'

Second in the English Olympiad two thousand and twenty. Selected to work in America, Mister Journalist.

'Forget about me.' He inclines his head towards the old crone with the crocodile skin. 'Think about Eulalie. She's psychic, Malachi.'

The old woman smiles a wry, old smile.

'That means she can see things with her mind.'

I wipe the sweat from the skin between his fingers.

'She saw corpses buried in a swimming pool in Eritrea. Children.'

Oh, no. Help me.

A gust of wind beats the metal casing of this ship. I dig my thumb beneath the buckle, release Samuel's fingers.

'She told the prime minister's wife. The woman spoke out, so they poisoned her. They said it was Eulalie.'

Fuck off, monsters, this has nothing to do with me.

Sorry for swearing, Hamri.

I finish Samuel's feet, start on the old witch's astonishingly young fingers.

'Just look at him, Samuel,' the husband killer croons next to me. 'Such lovely smooth skin. He is better than us. A real victim.'

I groom the old crone's knobbly toes, set them free. I pick up my bucket, turn to the sarcastic mermaid.

Vicki hesitates for a second, surrenders her feet to me. 'Have you ever seen an angelfish, Malachi?'

I slice through a nail that has replaced itself overnight.

'My husband hooked one that day. It had these long, pretty wings, all the colours of the rainbow.' Her fingers touch the colours in the air. 'He chopped them off like they were just fins.' Her eyes have turned from black to a brooding violet. 'I got revenge for the angelfish.'

I release her feet, avert my eyes from the edge of her sternum, pressing through her skin like the beginnings of a fin. Vicki tucks her feet beneath her bum, her knees to one side. The Mermaid and the Angelfish. Charming.

What about the serrated scaling knife she stuck into her husband? I force myself to trim Vicki's pink fingertips. What about the red on the linoleum?

I wipe her slender hands with my white towel. As I pull the brace away, I catch a glimpse of the bone in her wrist, the tilt on the outer edge, the sweet, surprising rise. 'Carpal' is an ugly word. Vicki's wrist is the velvet inside of a bird's wing. A tremor passes through me, a tiny flight of my nervous system.

I lock Vicki's cage quickly, turn my back on her.

I work through six more prisoners, tune my ears to the crash of waves in the abyss below us.

'Al-Masihhh . . .' A quavery cry sinks into my senses. The voice is high, as cracked as the tar on a Kattra pavement.

The man's skin was once black, perhaps, but the years, perhaps decades without sunlight seem to be bleaching him yellow. Liverish, my father would have said, even though his own skin wore a Samwati tint.

The prisoner next to him laughs. 'Yassir says you are Jesus coming to heal him.'

This man is blacker than my viscose trousers. The two men are different-coloured twins with their hollow chests and long arms, but close up the dark man looks like an Ethiopian runner on the sports channel, his tendons laid on top of his skin like a topographic map showing crawling water courses, mountain contours.

'Actually, Malachi *must* be Jesus.' He chuckles affectionately. 'Remember, he cleaned the disciples' feet.'

Despite the rising fury of the sea, they calm me, these two. Their opposites express the conflict in me.

I work swiftly through two more subjects, tend to the toenails of a mad, happy man. It is the excitable Indian with one front tooth missing and one black thumb. What the heck is he so happy about? He thrusts one hand out as if he is asking for money, points to the gap in his teeth.

The Ethiopian laughs, interprets for me, 'Vihaan is asking for your tooth, Malachi.'

The Indian pinches his fingers, gives me a devilish grin. I clamp my teeth shut instinctively.

This is too ridiculous, the situation, for me to stay ghostly.

As I check his wiring and his pipes, he tugs hard at his mouth. A red trail of spit hangs from his fingers. A real tooth has come free.

'Hee heeee!'

I jam my thumb on my intercom.

'What?' Tamba's tone is as thick and bitter as vulture soup.

I bare my teeth, pinch at the air.

'Abscess? It can't be. There's a mouthwash in their vitamins.'

I shake my head, tug at my own teeth.

The Indian thrusts his tooth up proudly for Tamba to see, but the mesh must be blurring it.

I draw a computer screen, stab at my eyes to say, *Check your computer, stupid.*

Tamba swivels on his chair, his dreads floating like reeds of water-borne algae. 'He's pulling his teeth out. Wow!' Tamba grins through the window. 'Tell him to do another one.'

Very funny.

By now the hall is laughing as if the Indian and I are mime artists hired to entertain them for the afternoon.

Vicki shouts out mockingly, 'Call the tooth fairy, Malachi! Do you know her? I hear she's very sexy.'

Madame Sophie laughs across from her.

I pick up my bucket, feel the needle of Vicki's perspicacity driving into me. This woman senses something about me and sex.

When I reach the gigantic Gadu Yignae, he apologises like he is their caretaker, not me. 'Sorry, Malachi. They're just desperate to laugh. You must know the feeling.' He nods like we are some kind of compatriots.

I groom his huge hands, not plucked animals but the hands of a plaster god. His pubic hair curls in thick welts, like it is carved from rock.

They say Gadu Yignae led the people from the earth's core into the sunlight and built them a shelter beneath the trees, but a flash flood killed him prematurely.

The giant takes back his hands, pulls on a jagged scar across his chest. A bead of white fluid drips. 'You might as well tell Tamba. This sore has flared up again.'

How the heck does he know Tamba's name?

'Cage fifteen,' the giant advises me.

I press my intercom, panic for an instant. What was the signal for infection?

I touch my heart, make an imaginary incision. Let the stripe of my mouth turn down.

69

Tamba's mouth twitches. 'Wound not happy?'

I glare at him through the glass. Tamba pulls his head from the window before he succumbs to my extraordinary charm.

The giant gives me his hands, smiles at me kindly. 'That tongue of yours must have caused you a lot of suffering.'

For a moment, we are brothers sharing a similar hardship. I too was on an anaesthetic drip. I too died to human society, except for Lizet who resurrected me as a zombie very quick at detecting errors in the plastic wrapping machine.

I trim his huge, captive hands. An ancient memory lands as softly as a parachute.

My grandfather's huge hands clasped the sides of my head. 'A beautiful boy.'

Hamri spoke up bravely, 'He looks just like his mother.'

My grandmother stood up from her washing work, her hands dripping. 'Yes,' she said bitterly. 'Half Kapwa.'

Hamri spun around, pointed at his mother's hands, their pigment stolen by the chlorine bleach from rich people's white sheets. 'Look at *you*, Mother. Half white.'

My grandfather's hands were big enough to twist my head off my neck, but he sank back into his chair, scraping for raw breath.

We had to leave.

On the bus home, my father hugged me, his Kapwa baby. 'It's not the tribe that they hate, Malachi. It's the opportunity. They think we live in luxury. Do you see how the bosses divide us?'

Beneath my father's sigh ran a thick, ruined river. He fantasised about Utopia all the way home, but even at six years old I could sense the shadow of his guilt. Would a poet have left his parents

70

suffering in a rotten shack on a swamp? Would he have left his mother to peel her black skin; his father to bite for oxygen?

The giant with my grandfather's hands is asking me now, 'Conscious Clause, Malachi. Have you heard of them? They're the closest we've got to human rights.'

Actually, yes. An errant son of the head of the IMF started it. They assassinated him, but the movement has billions of mula behind it.

He nods at the rows of scarred human flesh. 'None of us signed for any of this.' He tries to capture my eyes. 'And I don't think you signed up to torture us.'

I lean into the clipper, pit my strength against his fingernails as big as Calabar pods.

'Remember Conscious Clause, if Raizier betrays you.' He drops his voice. 'Whatever you do, just don't fall in love like Dominic.'

My heart freezes in its cage. I breathe through dry ice.

'Be careful, boy.'

It feels as though the floor is sliding away beneath my feet.

The fat Australian is pressing against his cage, straining to hear. 'Did you say Dominic?'

'What are you going to do, Barry? Send all your men?'

The giant laughs hard enough to shake the Wapakwa Mountains. Barry flushes an extravagant pink.

The giant shackles his humour. 'Sorry, Barry, I take back that comment.' He withdraws his hands, gives me his monumental feet. His skin is slightly dry, as if the hammer and chisel have scattered rock powder.

Barry boasts to anyone who might be interested, 'They called me Farin Sarki in the oil basin. White King.' He glowers at the giant. 'And I didn't need a university degree for any of it.'

71

The giant nods, further assuaging the pink man's hurt. 'We're all the same here. All in the same big, ugly boat.'

'Exactly,' Barry says morosely.

The giant turns his back on Barry, confides to me, '*Off* the boat, not so. Some of us are dangerous criminals. Some are casualties of corrupt justice systems. Any democratic country would grant them asylum.' He ticks the names off on his fingers. 'Samuel. Andride. Eulalie. Lolie.' He pauses, considers. 'Vicki.'

The poisonous mermaid? Is he joking?

The giant sighs. 'Not me. I should still be in the Addis Ababa Penal Facility.'

Speaking of penile, his baby toe is the size of a small one. The giant waves at the prisoners, shakes his head sadly. 'This is not justice.'

It's like the rivets have popped in this metal universe, leaving me swimming in the ferocious sea. The giant was a High Court judge for thirteen years. How can I not believe him?

I dig my sneakers into the floor, move to the skinny man, whose rash has faded substantially. He has to let go of his limp penis to give his hands to me. I clip his nails mechanically, my thoughts sliding and slapping against my cranium.

What was that stuff about Dominic?

I release the skinny man's hands. They flutter instantly to his drooping treasure. The wind sends a sustained, high note through our metal seams.

What the heck *did* happen to Dominic? Now that I think of it, the entire rig is strangely silent about him, just as they are silent about this hurricane.

How will I get someone to speak of him?

A laugh curdles inside me. The irony of my frustration strikes even me, the man who vexes people every day with his silence.

I groom a young woman who looks like she has black liner on her eyes, the offspring of a cruel black cat. But her hands are small and soft. Childlike. I shift my eyes to my own smooth hand. Not real, a ghostly glove. I try to dissolve into mist, but Shikorina the child killer catches me and holds me under with her sucking, translucent eyes. For a moment I feel like I can't breathe.

Shikorina clucks sympathetically. 'Poor baby.'

I force myself to drop her hatch down, latch the sheath onto it.

Shikorina's hair is matted and moth-eaten. It is the madman's beard my father grew for two months to play the Earl of Gloucester in our production of *Hamlet*. I drag my eyes from it, but my memory bites me behind my knees, snatches pieces off my hips.

They shattered my father's hip.

Stop.

A gigantic wave rocks the foundations of the rig.

I fish out a white towel, pinch the ends. Scrub it roughly over her skin. The circular blueish marks on her arms and chest prove that she is not a gentle mother but a hideous, slimy creature that strangles its prey with anaconda knots. I throw her towel in the bucket, drop it on the trolley. I march from the hall of horror, slam the door behind me.

I suck some ordinary air, compose myself for human company. These hands before me are not gossamer gloves but bone and blood. I have got to find another way to get through the afternoon.

* * *

I must have had a psychic vision of the lunch to come. Janeé has served up piles of rice with pink tentacles in curry spice. I manage to take my seat at the table. I have never in my life seen an octopus except in ancient books, but Chincha told me once he found one on Ladebi beach. He said he put it in his bag, but it started to stink. His father made him throw it from the window of the bus and it landed on a man walking from church in a suit and hat.

Tamba bangs in and throws himself next to me. 'Geez, what's this? Monster of the deep? Did you wrestle this yourself, Janeé?' He laughs loudly.

Janeé chews her tentacles like she is feeding on Tamba's own chopped bits tossed with rice. Tamba pitches the pink pieces into a sighing heap. Somewhere the wind screams through thick sea salt while I glaze my eyes, pick out my rice, flick the grains into my mouth.

Janeé frowns. 'Don't you like octopus? Romano's got a net down at the shark pit.' She condemns me to a caste that has no taste for gourmet snakes, 'The bosses love octopus.'

Where the heck is the shark pit?

'We have the right to refuse, Janeé,' Tamba says. 'Not many other rights going around on this rig.'

Janeé glares at him. 'We are lucky to be here.'

'You're right, Janeé. We're fucking lucky.'

I get that feeling of tectonic plates shifting beneath my feet, continents splitting off and drifting out of sight. I try to find my footing, spoon in some oily rice. A coat of grease forms on the roof of my mouth. Sadly, I have no tongue to remove it.

Perhaps I should become slippery, slither away when the prisoners try to catch me, like Kontar and me when we wrestled near the river. We covered ourselves in red clay that made us so slick our hands slid off each other in useless, laughing swipes. The only way to win the wrestle was to pin the other boy to the ground, chest to chest until he surrendered.

Yes. This afternoon I will be nimble, fleet of foot. If they try to sink a tooth or diseased claw into me I will smear myself with clay, slide from their grip.

I swallow my last mouthful of rice. I slip off the bench, thank Janeé with a lubricated nod, leave with footsteps so slick I could be barefoot. Not even Olivia's false smile finds a place to stick.

'Cheers, Malachi,' she calls after me.

I drift through the wind screaming in a fit of fury. I raise the red lanyard, let the key card do its trick.

* * *

I slip through the door, pad past Shikorina, who is curled in a foetal position, staring. Her eyes try to cling to my shining clay, but they slide off the bank into her own dark bathwater.

I groom three more prisoners on the toes of my sneakers, ready to duck a flying punch, a spoken flame, a tilt of the floor in the metal hall. I release the feet of a red-haired man with orangutan arms and a contagion of freckles, pad to the next prisoner.

'Are you Bhajoan?'

I lock my head to my spine to stop it from snapping. The man looks my age; premature white hair at his temples.

'Were you perhaps a member of ANIM?'

The mud dries on me. Anger whips away my spit so my mouth feels like it is coated with bitter cocoa.

The prisoner nods. 'I am Andride. I was working with the ANIM soldiers from the Nachimale forest.'

My breath rasps through the powdery dryness.

'I was a trained social worker, but I taught them wood art.'

A roar rumbles in my chest. I jam the brace onto his cage, try to veil my hatred, but a machine-gun glint escapes my eyelids.

'The military shot down my whole woodwork class. Thirteen of them.' There is a hollow in his eyes, a vacancy left by his guerrilla friends. 'They blamed me.'

I pinch a half moon of flesh between the clipper blades. He talks like I am about to sever his fingers one by one. 'I was helping them, Malachi.' This is what the English call barking up the wrong tree.

I could pick neat, semi-circular holes in him for teaching murdering pigs to carve African figures for curio stalls in airports. I snatch away the clipper, unravel a white towel to its full length. I scrub the man's feet, half blind with fury.

Of course I have kept abreast of Bhajoan politics. The ANIM lost their war six years after I lost my whole universe. Of course I heard how the guerrillas tried to creep out and live among the factory communities, but the people lynched them for burning Kapwa workers as if they were imperialist assets, factors in production, not human beings who take their places on the factory floor for the sake of their children. Showing up every day in caps and overalls for the sake of love, *LOVE!* I want to scream.

If someone lit a match we would both burst into flames, Andride with his wooden carvings, me with the dry, caked mud on my skin.

But surely this man is lying. Surely he is guilty?

If so, this is one stupid irony, like a monkey's wedding, shining through the soaking rain. Irony like a monkey's bum, an unexpected bright blue.

I muse furiously about metaphors such as these, cut a trail of flying nails to the priest burner's disfigured fingers.

'Whosoever kills a soul, it shall be as if he had killed all mankind . . .'

The man is quoting from his disappearing Qur'an but he can't catch me, I am sealed in wet clay, as slimy and slick as the mud bream at the bottom of the Tantwa River.

'Allah forbids murder and I am his son. But do you know who the judge believed?'

In his eyes I see Bibles burning, their skin-thin pages melting faster than my own bargain books.

'The tourists in a big hotel looking through a window.' He shakes his head. 'Stupid, those tourists, you know those fat ones from the United States and Japan?'

His talk of fat tourists seems to relax him.

'Sometimes my elevator could only carry three.' His fingers cramp again, perhaps on the Catholic priest's vestments. 'He hung on to me. Please believe me.' His pleas gather speed down my slippery back, fly off to kingdom come.

As I cut and clean, the giant watches me with the eyes of my large grandfather, as if I was a familiar-looking boy from an alien tribe. I finish two more prisoners, make it without incident to the big beauty who entranced Dominic. I capture her handsome hands, glance up at the glass. Tamba is watching me closely.

Relax, Tamba. There is no danger of me falling in love with the girl on the side of the bus. Firstly, one-way love is just not possible.

Secondly, I have an FM radio waiting to shock my libido into subservience.

Still, I am careful to keep my eyes off the latent strength of her ankles. The glimpse of moist pink between her legs, of course, leaves me dead. I have never, ever had sex, but I have no interest in going into the bush. I have erased those erotic visions with electricity. The same applies to her nipples. They might just as well have been made at a rubber factory.

I groom Charmayne impassively, boast to the spy above, *See, this beauty does not move me.*

'It was the tallest office block in Bulawayo City. Worth fifty million to each of us.'

Her eyebrows soar in savage arcs – violent, somehow, in this end-of-tether atmosphere. Her half-tamed, half-rebel hair makes her look madder, more unkempt than the child killer, even.

'My partners fought like two goats. Pete slipped off the roof. He dragged Bongi with him –'

'Don't believe her.'

It is the Ethiopian runner with gnarled muscles that seem laid atop his skin.

Charmayne snaps, 'Were you there, Gibril?'

I see a skyscraper, scaffolding, those airborne eyebrows flying.

'Were you?'

The wind quietens suddenly, lets go of this ship. The whole hall seems to be holding its breath. Charmayne thrusts her feet into my glove. Her breasts shine with sweat, her nipples prickle with the effort of persuading me.

'I was happy with my thirty-three percent . . .' Her succulent lips form more sexless, corporate words, but still Tamba does not move from his window.

Charmayne drops her business talk, tries to suck me into her childhood. 'I grew up in a little room off a fire escape. My mother was a cleaner. Malachi?' Her eyes are a vat of swirling molasses. 'All I wanted in the world was to make my mama happy.'

I fall into Charmayne's hunger, up to my knees.

Vicki's titter slowly calls me back to my dignity.

I pick up my bucket, force my puny thighs down the aisle. This woman, beautiful enough to adorn a fleet of buses, is just a child who loves her mother as much as I loved mine.

I continue my work in a drunken, dream state. Madame Sophie, the brothel owner, watches me demolish the perfect curves of her toenails. She must have shaped them with her teeth. I glance at the hamstrings running behind her knees. Madame Sophie must be supple.

She shocks me from my reverie. 'They were heroin addicts *before* they came to me. They arrived at my door as weak as lambs, so I put them to bed. I washed them, dressed them, fed them . . .'

I stare at Madame Sophie. To my tired mind, she looks like a psycho nurse, with an eerie platinum colouring. I glance at her breasts. They don't even fit her.

Did she steal them from one of her drug addicts?

In the cage next to her, one half of Josiah's black moustache curls up. 'You *saved* them, Sophie.'

Madame Sophie tries to wrench her feet free. 'Quiet, Josiah.'

I release the strap, slam her hatch shut. I stare at Josiah's fingernails, crooked and filthy after only one night. Where has he been digging?

I will not cut the nails of this death-eating sadist. I will not touch this beast.

79

I leave the last towel rolled tightly beneath the limp, sullied ones. The clay on my skin cracks and leaves a shower of dry disgust as I walk to the door. Behind me I hear a high, quavery cry. It is Shikorina, mimicking her youngest child.

* * *

I shower at normal temperature, let the rain pound the clay from my eyelids. Thunder rumbles too close as I wash my armpits, cleanse my sweat.

It is right that these people suffer.

I lift my testicles, rinse my penis.

I see Vicki's elbows, their perfect little points nestling against her soft, scarred hips.

Damn it.

I squeeze my penis, test it. I feel not a stiffening but a kind of tension, an animal sensing an impending storm. The barometer is dropping.

I turn off the water, check my timepiece. I have no time to disassemble my radio and shock this treachery from me. I will have to do it after supper. Come hell or high water, I must find some privacy.

I leave my bucket at the door to Olivia's laboratory. As I turn into the canteen, I jerk to a halt. A massive tongue sits in the centre of the table, its skin rough and pimpled.

Thunder rolls like circus drums. Tamba arrives unceremoniously, shoves me into the canteen. Meirong glances at the atomic clock.

'In time,' Tamba says triumphantly. He throws himself onto the bench. 'Where's Olivia?'

'Staying late to mix hormones for the breakfast feed,' Meirong says. 'Malachi, I checked the day's records. You saw no problems with sexuality?'

I stare at the gigantic replica of what I am missing. Is this a joke at my expense?

Tamba follows my eyes. A laugh bubbles to his lips but he strangles it.

'Jesus,' he exhales under his breath.

'Malachi? Did you hear me? Any sexual issues? The hormone cocktail sometimes fades on day three.'

I drag my eyes from the platter, shake my head at Meirong. Negative. Meirong is too obsessed with her schedule to see the horror of the scene. She must be stupid.

I shut my eyes as Janeé descends with her carving knife. I want to dive to the floor and leopard-crawl through the door, but I lock my spine straight, float in perspiration, watch Meirong's lips move around her vowels.

'There's only the one subject we can't seem to stop from masturbating. Angus. He's not hurting himself, is he?'

Tamba answers for me. 'Uh-uh. But it's creepy. He's a sexual offender, isn't he?'

Meirong nods.

'I wouldn't like to be Malachi,' Tamba says.

They turn to look at me just as Janeé slams down a slice in front of me. I lift my utensils, swallow the resistance that has gathered behind my teeth. First the octopus, now the flesh cut from the mouth of a cow, complete with taste buds. The scientific word is papillae.

I saw so my knife sings against my fork. I part my teeth and slip the meat in.

I flail for my water, take a gulp.

'Take it easy, Malachi,' Tamba says. The green streak in his eye has grown dim, no longer mocking me. He points at the tongue in the centre of the table, accuses Janeé: 'A bit dumb of us. We didn't think, did we?'

Meirong suddenly gets the tongue thing. 'Ohhh.'

The final thread of Tamba's angry day seems to snap. He sags, lays his hands on the table for everyone to see.

'Meirong, do you think Olivia can help me out one more time tonight? The last time. I swear on my life.'

Meirong's red acrylic dress bristles with the same splinters that coat the rude tongue. 'No, Tamba. Definitely not.'

'Why-y?' Tamba whines like a small boy in the toy aisle.

'Do you think this is the right place to discuss this?'

Tamba stabs towards the door. 'Let's go then.'

Olivia shuffles into the canteen with new, tired lines drawn by her overtime. 'Hi everyone.'

Meirong's mouth has gone white. 'You, Tamba, are not going to ruin my career. A lot has gone wrong.'

Tamba speaks with a warrior stillness: 'Are you blaming me for Dominic?'

Meirong is shaking imperceptibly. I stare to make sure. Yes. Her lips are trembling.

'Only weaklings need sedatives to sleep,' she says.

'Shit. You're such a bitch.'

'That's it!' Meirong snaps. 'You're in for a disciplinary review.' She leaps off the bench. 'You'd better sleep tonight, Tamba. You're going to need it.'

Olivia wails, 'Stop fighting, you guys!'

Meirong flounces out.

'Please, Tamba,' Olivia begs. 'We're not here for us.'

I catch Tamba's shifty sleight of eye, his uneasy foot-shuffle beneath the table. Tamba is here for his own benefit, somehow I know this.

Just like me.

I sit accused in the presence of a meat souvenir.

My mother, my father, my friends all dead. I am all I have left.

Fuck. Shit. I would say it, Hamri. If I had a tongue.

Ragged white light streaks through the portholes near the roof.

Fuck. Shit. I have a right to be here only for me. I stand up, seething. Leave a cold, empty space on the bench behind me.

As I enter the bedroom, Tamba barges in after me. He punches the wall. 'Bullshit!'

There is blood on his knuckles. He thrusts out a finger. 'One sedative! One!'

I turn away from the smear of red on his knuckle. *For goodness' sake, Tamba. Stop the histrionics.*

'What am I supposed to do?'

Go and play ping-pong, you idiot. I slip into the bathroom, shut the concertina door between us.

'What are you, Malachi? Are you even human?'

Tamba's words blast through the soft partition, hit their target. A sob dislodges in me.

He talks through the plastic panel. 'Fuck. Sorry.'

Thunder smashes massive rocks together in the sky. I flush the chain unnecessarily, come out, glare at Tamba. He is licking the blood off his knuckles like a cat with a grazed paw. I catch a streak of pink on his tongue, strangely fat for a naturally lean person.

'Sorry,' he says again.

I see now Tamba's knuckles have a row of pale stars where his skin has repaired itself with thicker scar tissue. He sits on his bed, sighs. I drop onto my pillow, lift my aching legs for the first time today.

Tamba hooks a finger beneath his top lip, turns it inside out. 'See this, Malachi?' he lisps.

I peer closer. Tamba's gums are gouged with small, round potholes.

'Cocaine.' He lets his lip fall with a funny plop. 'I rubbed so much it ate my flesh, man, burnt right through.' Tamba turns his elbows inside out, shows me a massacre of sharp instruments. 'I popped all my veins first.' He pulls off his socks and shoes.

I blow out in disgust. 'Pphhh.' His feet smell like dead mouse.

'Sorry. My nostrils are nuked.' That makes a trio of apologies. Tamba props his foot on his knee, shows me a clutter of old punctures in his heels. 'Eventually I had to shoot up in my feet.'

I stare at the scattershot marks, groan inwardly. I have already showered, please. Don't smear your drug history on me.

'I shot MDMA to try and kick the glitter, but it didn't help. I worshipped the stuff.' Tamba waits, like I might drop his sins in a shopping basket and go and pay for them. But after what I've heard today, cocaine addiction is an angel's pastime.

'I'm not kidding you, Malachi, when you hit your peak, there's nothing between you and the old woman begging in the subway. You love her like she's your mother. It breaks through the walls, man. But when you crash . . .' He shakes his head, stares at the metal floor. 'You're the last man on earth.'

Of course I do not comfort him. I pick up Tamba's socks with the tips of my fingers, carry them to the bathroom.

'Oh, okay-y-y.' He sighs. 'I missed my shower yesterday.' Tamba gets to his feet listlessly, a different man to the groovy guy I met on Friday. This Tamba has pitted gums and needle scars on the heels of his feet. This one is too lazy to even wash his own skin. Most of all, this Tamba thinks he is a waste of breath. As he passes me on the way to the shower, our bodies don't touch, but a soft fur of compassion brushes against us.

I lie down on my mattress, exhausted. From morning to night, this has been a day of sinister surprises. The giant's comment about Dominic. Tamba's secret needle marks. Vicki's elbows, the way they lit a tiny flame in my charred libido. I glance down at my trousers. They peak infinitesimally.

Oh, no.

Tamba's shower is softly dripping. I hear the friction of his towel rubbing to and fro.

'Hey, Malachi, I just thought of something!' Tamba comes in, drips water from the loose eye of his foreskin. He pulls a yellow Samsung from the cabinet between our beds. 'They took my sim, I just use it to play games. But I was thinking in the shower, why the hell don't you talk like the deaf and dumb?'

I stare at him blankly.

He keys in three stars, unlocks the Samsung. He touches an icon, shows me the screen. A shimmering microphone flares and recedes.

'Have you tried this app where you type and it talks for you?'

A scary possibility throbs in my larynx.

'This one's called Glossia. I make it read books to me when I'm feeling lazy. I just load the text.' He taps the screen. 'Look. You can choose deep and sexy.' He types something, taps the top of a list. A suave American says huskily, 'Hey babe, you wanna dance with me?' Tamba grins mischievously.

I sit up, a hot fissure spreading across my chest.

Tamba tries another setting. An audacious chipmunk invites me to dance with it. Tamba laughs, shows me a row of sliding dials.

'Talking speed. Volume. Look, it goes from *Whisper* all the way to *Megaphone*.' He sticks his nail into a seam at the bottom of the phone. 'I've never appreciated this stuff, but look . . .' A tiny plastic disc comes free in his fingers. 'Have you seen this ear clip? You put it here like this . . .' It is cone-shaped on the other side, a bit like a golf tee. It is halfway to Tamba's ear when he realises his oversight. He hits his forehead with blunt force. 'Ah, shit! Sorry. I forgot. You can't read and write.'

My vocal chords tick as they cool inside my cartilage.

Tamba drops his eyes. Black guilt for certain, he suffers from the malady.

'I was just lucky. Education is something the Zim government kept up.'

I shrug as if I know nothing of such things. Tamba tosses his phone into the cabinet. He quickly forgets about the sorry illiterate staring at the space that just swallowed his Samsung. With the selfishness of a drug addict, he scratches for his Kindle, presses the on switch. I can tell by the backlit barbed wire that tonight he will be reading the Sun Prophet's desert memoirs.

Thunder splits the nearby sky.

One hit is all I need.

One hard knock to stop the sex from filtering into my veins, climbing scar by scar up Vicki's subtle wrist.

Like Araba's, as she sat so languid and still, her eyes loyal to my father's whiteboard. She wanted me too; the deep downstrokes of her writing told me so. She had the gift of composure, her skin like windless water, but she loved the Valentino books the girls read at school, each with the same purple strip but with a different black beauty, a different man in a suit with his collar loosened, kissing. I trailed my eyes across the classroom, cut Araba out of the backdrop with her one wrist hanging loose, her breasts pressed against the desk as she leaned into her untidy cursive. I returned to my *Macbeth* questions, hungry.

Tamba flings down his Kindle so it bounces on the bed. 'Man, this book just makes me feel worse!' He jumps to his feet, his face dark, washed thunder. 'This is a pharmaceutical ship, for God's sake.' He storms to the door. 'I'm going to try Janeé.'

Good. Go.

Watch out she doesn't feed you arsenic.

I listen to Tamba's feet stomping towards the cook. Then I roll off my bed, drag out my suitcase. I dig out my radio, try to pry off the back. Damn. I smash a corner against the metal floor. A triangle of black plastic flies against the wall. I hook my fingers into the crack. The plastic plate snaps off, baring its coloured wires. Brown, blue, yellow, running from positive to negative. I take a moment to admire the beautiful predictability of its nervous system.

I rip the brown from its copper pin. Jerk the blue loose. I stick my plug into the wall. A hundred and twenty volts. I unbuckle my belt roughly, shove the raw wires into my trousers.

I see Vicki's mermaid knees, lucent in the sunlight sifting through a green ocean.

I hit the switch. The rig catches fire in split delicious seconds, crashes me to the floor. There is a searing sensation between my legs; my spine becomes a tunnel of terrible flames. The pain rips me inside out as I sprawl, make no sound, clutch at my genitals.

I am nerves blown out. Black carbon flesh.

Slow footsteps pad along the corridor. I jerk the copper wires from my trousers, snort from the agony. I clamp the broken plate over the innards of the radio. Shut my suitcase with fingers that feel like prostheses. I roll onto my bed just as Tamba shuffles in with an overflowing teacup.

'Fucking chamomile.'

A few minutes ago Tamba's desperate, doleful look might have been funny, but I am fighting the aftershocks jittering in me. Tamba perches on the edge of his bed, sips his tea like a nephew of the long-deceased queen.

A drumming starts up, the syncopation of raindrops against the steel rig.

Tamba sighs. 'How the hell am I gonna get through the night?'

If I could, I would say, *Tamba, I know of something that would help you*. It has to do with leaping into an agonising blue fire then resting in the music of the cooling, the plucking of the electric current through your bloodstream.

Of course I do not offer Tamba my radio.

I slip into a sleep so lifeless I might as well be a fibre-optic cable burnt by a vicious power surge, then left to tie up a loose bumper or use as a noose to hang yourself. I sleep like I am litter, forgotten factory waste lying in the dust of Africa. Somewhere I am aware of the rain lashing this cold, steel earth. I hear Tamba moving about the room, pacing perhaps, but he is a mere pedestrian passing over me.

SUNDAY

I roll in the carbon-dark sand. Susan Bellavista's ankle boots crush me carelessly. A cool toothpaste breeze blows across my face.

'Malachi. Geez!'

My eyelids are sealed shut by heat. Susan nicks them open with a razor-thin blade. The eyes above me are bloody. Suspicious.

'Did you have a sleeping pill stashed in your bag? Get up. It's ten to seven.'

It is Tamba, waking me too late.

'Okay, look. You coming?'

I nod, vaguely surprised by the weight of my teeth. 'See you in the canteen.'

I lift my head like a patient recovering from a spinal tap. Arrange myself into a sitting position. I hear the soft hiss of electricity coursing through the wall next to me, but there is no sign of thunder or lightning. Last night's injury chafes against my sleeping shorts as I drag my suitcase from beneath my bed, open it. My fingers singe my radio. All I can face today is grey. Grey trousers, matte. A soft grey shirt with a floppy collar. As I slip on clean socks, my panic penetrates.

Get moving, Malachi. Do you want to lose your tongue?

I leave seven drops on the toilet seat. Too many.

I am a wasted, grey creature, but I am in time to meet Meirong at the door to the canteen. I step back, let her pass through. Today, Meirong is a one-woman dynasty in an emerald dress so silky it must have been spun at a silkworm factory. It ends just above the knees.

'Beautiful green,' Tamba says.

Meirong glares at him.

'Lovely colour,' Tamba says weakly. He must be trying to apologise for last night.

I take a seat next to my roommate.

'*Thank you*, Tamba, for saving my skin,' he coaches me softly.

What does he want me to do, repeat after him?

My tiny smile gives Tamba the courage to lie outright. 'I slept like a log. Whew, it's like I died. And you, Meirong?'

Meirong's eyes narrow. 'Why the red eyes?'

'Too much sleep.'

'Oh, yes?'

Tamba nods, lies again. 'Delicious oats, Janeé.'

Janeé tilts the rig as she takes her seat, uses her spoon like an earth-moving machine.

Across from me, Meirong pours too much milk on her oats. She scoops up an oat island and tips it into her tiny mouth.

'Romano, we need you to stay awake to watch a merchant tanker convoy until they are safely past. Five hours is our guess.' She turns to Olivia. 'Olivia, can you give Romano a stimulant?'

Romano shakes his head, 'Not for me.' He grates his spoon

across his plate, hunts for the food he has already eaten. Janeé heaves to her feet, produces a pot of oats as if from her bodice.

Romano sighs. 'Thank you, sister.'

We are like a badly matched family, clinging to the ordinary, eating oats as if we are not trespassing on the ocean. Today every member of this crew seems familiar and sweet. A warning tries to swirl up from the depths of me. Last night's electricity has stripped me of my fighting spirit. I suspect it might have killed some of my intelligence. How will I protect myself against the monsters I am about to walk among?

I must use this murky trepidation, stay in the grey. Let the subjects feel for me with their bony fingers and find only smoke, perhaps the light stink of electrocuted flesh. I have nothing to fear. Just as Romano can stay awake for another day, I can take a hundred and twenty volts of electricity, get dressed in five minutes and eat my oats as casually as the green Ming vase across from me.

Romano springs up on wiry thighs, stalks out as if leading reconnaissance into enemy territory.

Me, I leave three oats on my bowl for old time's sake. Drop it on the trolley.

'Wait for me, Malachi.' Tamba lifts his bowl to his face. 'Sorry guys, but –' He sucks his milk from his oats.

Meirong frowns as if silkworms are hatching in her dress.

'What?' Tamba smiles with a bitter, milky mouth. 'Isn't this how the Chinese drink their tea?'

Olivia giggles. I don't wait to see if Meirong cuts off his head.

* * *

I listen for the click, sidle inside with my smoke-damaged brain matter.

Samuel, the journalist, is even more loquacious than yesterday. As I fasten the falconer's glove to his cage he says urgently, 'There is no way we go back to jail. Did they tell you three cycles?' He shakes his head. 'We will never leave this rig.'

The smoke thins. I peer at Samuel's fingers, press my blades together.

'Not even our corpses. Look at these scars, Malachi. Can you imagine if they returned our bodies to our families?'

My eyes flick across the needle marks from sewing up Samuel's carcass.

'There would be an inquiry.'

His words shove through my deadened nerves.

'What I'm saying is, they're going to use us up. Then kill us.'

I squint through the smoke into his lion eyes.

'You've got to get hold of the Free Press. This is murder, Malachi. Not medicine.'

I buckle at the stricture in my chest. I hang over my bucket, wring out Samuel's towel. I struggle up again, clean his feet clumsily.

I check the pipes that bring Eulalie sustenance and take her waste away. I clip her milky nails, the only sign that her hands belong to an ancient hag. I feel her grey eyes stroking me, trying to peel my skin and spy beneath it. I smoke her out silently, a poisonous beehive. Move on to Vicki.

The mermaid's toes are unaccountably pink. There is something transparent, newborn about them. Ten little beads of flesh facing in, searching for their mother to suckle.

'It makes sense what Samuel says. It looks like they choose

prisoners that no one would miss.' She smiles sardonically. 'Look around, you'll see. They're the ones no one visits.'

'My father lives in London,' Samuel splutters. 'Otherwise he . . .' He trails off, wavery.

The mermaid shrugs, 'I couldn't care less.' She growls, 'I don't want my human rights.'

'It's mass murder, Vicki.'

A dry laugh cracks from Vicki.

'Mass murder of the mass murderers? Her evil sense of humour shuts her eyes, splits her fruity mouth open to show sharp, white pips. 'Samuel, that's funny.'

I release Vicki's toes, watch them clench with glee on her excretion plate. Hilarious, I agree. I should be laughing with the husband killer, rolling on the floor in happy apoplexy. But her mirth only makes me furious.

Mass murder of the mass murderers. This is what Samuel is accusing me of.

I slap Vicki's cage, make it ring. She recovers her breath, gives me her fingers. She smiles treacherously, as close to pretty as a living cadaver can be.

Watch out, Malachi. Get your skin back on, quickly.

I groom a string of prisoners, make it all the way to the Sudanese yellow man.

'Save us, Jesus,' he says in English. 'Thank you, Al Massih.' His tears roll off his skin, glitter on the mesh before vanishing.

What did he do that he is so sure of his salvation? Steal a red apple for his hungry son? The man's hysteria must be contagious, because three cages away, the tooth-pulling Indian starts chattering and pointing towards the sky. I lock the yellow man's cage, move to his friend, the pitch-black Ethiopian.

He gives me his hands woven with muscle. 'You're not Jesus, I know, but you're the only one we can pray to.'

I cut his fingernails, wipe his hands with a towel so white it draws his sins from deep inside him.

'I'll tell you the truth. I have nothing to lose. The soldiers from Eritrea stole our food aid from the desert, where the aeroplanes dropped it. They sold it in the city. They let our children eat sand.' He clenches his muscular fingers. 'We had to stop those soldiers with our bare hands.'

Oh no. Please.

I don't know how to feel, who to be. Jesus. Malachi. Pontius shitting Pilot.

Sorry for swearing, Hamri.

My nerves are repairing too quickly. I stare down the aisle. How the heck will I get through this long line of murderers?

And how do I forget a child's mouth filled with sand?

I must think of these people as slaughter animals. They are chickens, all of them. If Raizier is to murder them, this is their destiny. I work through two prisoners, cling desperately to my analogy. The fussing Indian in cage number thirteen is miming fire now, explosions. I throw open his metal hatch. He thrusts his feet through, but he waves wildly at the ceiling. A deranged chicken, that's what he is. He holds a wet finger to his nose, sniffs. He waves it towards me, entreats me to smell it. I capture his hands, hurry through the cutting as the Indian shouts a mad monologue to the roof.

What did he do? Drop bombs somewhere, and now expects revenge?

I wish I was deaf as well as dumb. Earplugs would be lovely.

I want to hit my button and beg Tamba for some. The madman yowls with frustration as I set his hands free. I latch his cage, check my timepiece. I spent four hundred and eighty-three seconds on him. I have begun to rise again. In a few days, this will be as easy as plastic-wrapping chicken.

I groom another prisoner without even blinking. Drop my bucket at the giant Gadu Yignae's feet. Judge James, Vicki calls him.

'Samuel's right,' he says in his rumbling baritone. He shakes his massive head. 'Raizier can't send us home in this condition.' A crease spreads like slow lightning across his brow. 'My guess is they'll say we died in jail of something like cholera or TB. They'll say it's too infectious to return our bodies.' He nods thoughtfully. 'They might keep our teeth.' He smiles for the first time, his teeth shining like a sculptor carved each one out of marble. 'Our first tool, our last proof. Built in.' The judge is beginning to sound like an impassioned dentist. But a deep anger rises to his reasonable eyes. 'I don't want to die like this.'

I wait for yesterday's tirade to come but he watches me with an expression of pity.

'It will ruin you, Malachi.'

The giant pulls his hands free. 'If you want to go to Conscious Clause, do you know what the crux of your argument should be?' He waves at the rows of chicken mesh. 'You had no idea you would be aiding and abetting the death of forty people.'

I rub his thick heels with shaking fingers.

'Bring me something, Malachi. I'll write it for you.'

I bang his wire hatch, lock it.

Aiding and abetting the death . . .

95

Antiseptic sloshes onto my white sneakers as if I am squirting urine.

I stumble away from the giant, flee to the fat Australian.

Confusion racks me like a fever as I groom his loose skin. A rushing sound inside my eardrums surges like the sea as I fumble through the skinny rapist, check his wires and his pipes.

But as I work through the next prisoner, I hear someone singing, 'Cula, Cula, Kuya kudi kunyi.'

Next door, the girl with kohl eyes is chanting a child's song under her breath. A mournful sound, somehow calming. The prettiest trace of guitar strings plays on each side of her spine as she hunches over her knees, wipes her face compulsively.

Andride, the social worker, asks softly behind me, 'She's singing in Luba. She's from the DRC.'

I tear my attention from the girl's architecture.

'They tortured Lolie to make her pull the trigger.'

I stare at the young woman brushing the sack off her face. Or was it a sheet of plastic?

'She was an excellent shot. The M23's best sniper.'

Together we watch the girl fighting for breath, over and over.

'She was ten.'

I bite on my breath.

He nods towards the giant. 'Judge James said she should never have been sentenced.'

There is a long, swollen oval protruding from the girl's abdomen. I hit the switch on my device.

'Yes?'

I touch my own stomach, spread my fingers to indicate a swelling.

Tamba assumes the worst. 'What? Burst appendix?'

I shake my head.

He shrinks with relief. 'Ah. Spleens. They're growing two in number seventeen because the cells graft so easily.' He chuckles unexpectedly. 'You know how they say, I nearly split my spleen?'

I wait in the presence of a crack killer with two spleens inside her belly.

'Never mind,' Tamba says mournfully. He clicks his microphone off, once again disappointed in me.

Lolie gives me her fingers, stares unblinkingly down the barrel at me.

How many hearts have those kohl eyes found through her rifle sights? How many spleens has she split with exploding copper sheaths? The girl is a brutal killer.

I cut Lolie's nails with steady, strong fingers. With each slotting of the blade in the interstice between skin and nail, with each slim half-moon that falls to the floor, I prove to Lolie that, crack shot or not, she is not the only one who can be accurate.

The skinny Indian is screeching now but I ignore the ruckus, move on to Shikorina.

Unlike the sniper, the child killer greets me with her arms open wide. 'My brother. Did you come on an aeroplane?'

Her smile is as warm and cherishing as a deep silky bath on a dusty afternoon. Her nails are soft and clear, they give way easily.

'Hear me, Kenneth,' she implores me. 'I said to my children, Don't love me. Don't.'

'GAS!' someone shouts.

'They loved me too much. Don't you see?'

'Paraffin!'

The big beauty Charmayne is stabbing her finger at the roof above the Indian's cage. I smell a petroleum stink. I run back to the tooth-puller, now squeezed into the corner of his cage, his feet tucked under him. Liquid pours from a short pipe high above him, pools on the floor beneath my sneakers. I shove on my intercom, bounce like a boxer, join the others in their frantic mimicry.

'Leaking pipe! Paraffin!' the prisoners shout for me.

'SHIT.' Tamba springs to his feet. He yells into a microphone on his desktop, 'Meirong! Kerosene leak! It's pouring all over number thirteen . . . Yes! . . . Yes!' Tamba turns in wild circles. He mutters to himself, 'Shut. Shut. Shut. Recovery.' His arm swings and falls. 'Ahh.'

The fluid fades to a trickle. The whole hall stares up, watches it drip.

Meirong's voice sounds faintly through the speaker.

Tamba says, 'Okay, I'll rinse him.' He slams a button on his DJ desk. A shower pours down on the tooth puller from his irrigation pipe. He screams and arches, the rungs of his chest a chicken carcass picked clean.

Tamba snaps, 'It's only water, for God's sake. Tell him to relax.' Tamba remembers my disability. He switches his sound off for a second, hammers his forehead with the heel of his hand. He clicks his microphone on again, says more delicately, 'Fuck, Malachi. I think it's time for lunch.'

Shikorina is quiet now, bewildered by the emergency.

The giant speaks to me over the heads of five prisoners. 'Perhaps this is their modus operandi.'

'Malachi?' Tamba urges over my radio, 'Drop what you are doing and come.'

Barry, the fat Australian, asks, 'Do you mean, this is how they will finish us?'

The giant nods. 'It looks like it.'

Someone exclaims, 'Whoaaah.'

Barry points upwards, breathing heavily. 'Each cage has got one. Look.'

The prisoners peer at the transparent tubing running along the roof. Between each shower nozzle is a tiny pipe aiming towards the cages.

Tamba barks, 'Malachi. Get out.' He is pressed hard against his surveillance glass, his nose as bulbous as a gnome's. Is this place about to blow, as they say in those old movies with Leonardo DiCaprio?

'Ohh!' Charmayne gasps. 'Liquid gas for . . .'

'Fire.' Josiah says the word for her.

The word flares, catches alight on the metal wires.

'Fire!'

'Fire!'

Through the glass, Tamba is on his feet, a tall featureless figure, his earpiece pressed to his temple. He is a vulture suddenly, one of the monstrous ones that savaged newborn lions in Krokosoe.

'Malachi!'

I pick up my bucket, my radio still crackling. As I pass Samuel in cage number one, he thrusts his eyebrows high.

'Do you see what I mean?'

I keep my guilty scowl wired to my brow, but my sneakers peel off the floor with soft, sucking clicks, the sound of sycophantic cowardice.

* * *

Janeé dumps our plates piled high with something white. Next to each pale heap is a row of bright orange sticks. She squeezes through the door, disappears.

Tamba turns to me.

'It wasn't your fault, Malachi. That pipe is too high to see a split from the ground.' He evades the question in my eyes, tries to quip, 'Thank God no one smokes in there. One flick and . . .' He flings his hands to the roof like the poor tooth puller who mimed fire for nearly two hours.

Olivia's eyes are huge with fright. 'Why do they need that gas?'

Tamba looks down, shuffles his fish sticks. 'Meirong should tell you. It's not my job.'

'Come on, Tamba.' Olivia won't let go. 'It sounds scary.'

Tamba squirms in his seat. 'Meirong says it's to burn evidence. In, say, a crisis.'

'What evidence?'

'The cages, the cultivation systems . . .' Tamba gestures vaguely.

Olivia chews as if flames are licking the walls of the corridor. 'Meirong said the little lifeboat is for us. What about the prisoners?'

Tamba stabs a fish stick into his white mound, stodgy enough to stifle a small fire. He shrugs uneasily. 'Maybe the big boat Romano sleeps in.' He bites off what might be the head of his fish stick, flips it and does the same with the tail. 'Ask Meirong.'

Olivia succumbs to the potato that now seems designed to induce stupidity. But Samuel's angry eyes still burn into me.

Do you see what I mean?

A figure in a white moon-suit walks past the canteen. It has a padded chest and padded legs, a metal canister on its back. There is a synthetic swish of fattened limbs, the rattle of an ordinary toolbox. The man turns his head, but the reflection from his visor conceals his eyes from us.

Olivia turns too late. 'What was that?'

Meirong bounds into the room as if she might fly into a triple somersault.

'Engineer's oversight,' she declares triumphantly. 'Quenton –' She corrects herself: 'Mr Carreira says it's not Maintenance.' She nods at me. 'You can go in there now, Malachi.' She swings to Olivia, 'Tell Janeé I'll take Romano's lunch up at two.' Meirong vaults after the swishing white figure.

'She's pretty,' Olivia says, as if this is relevant.

I rise just as Janeé lands on the opposite bench. Her side seems to sink. I leave Olivia in suspension, go after the fireproof engineer and the green Chinese nymph, in pursuit of one thing: this day's ending.

* * *

I open the door cautiously. The hall still stinks of flammable gas. As I reach the trolley, a cranking sound starts above me. The man in the white moon-suit is sliding on a harness along the roof. Behind him, a square hatch has opened in the wall next to Tamba's glass station. Meirong crouches in the opening, a trapeze artist about to leap into the voluminous space. But the caged audience are not watching her with bated breath; they are watching the cranking astronaut like their life depends on it. His suit must be fireproof. I glance back, eye the slim opening I have just come through. How many seconds would I take to reach the door? I gather my courage, collect my grooming tools. I ignore Samuel carefully, refuse to look at Vicki. I turn my back on Shikorina, whose children loved her too much, start on the toes of cage number twenty-one. I am relieved to have the prisoners' attention off me, but Meirong is taking this chance to monitor my activities. I clip and clean, meticulous yet nimble. The prisoners give me their extremities absent-mindedly, stare up at their only entertainment since Malachi the tongueless first walked among them. As I work, the engineer tugs a tube from the roof and snips it with his own cutting tool. He fiddles with a wrench, smears on something that may be glue.

After five prisoners, he shuts his toolbox. Every single member of the audience exhales. I even catch a smile from Charmayne, the island beauty.

'Thank God.' The social worker with the silver wings breathes. 'We get a second chance.'

The giant smiles wryly. 'A few more weeks to live.'

I glance up at Meirong's perch, but the trapeze artist has moved to a different stage, perhaps an afternoon matinée in the forbidden wing.

I wash Andride's feet, rub roughly at a beauty spot as the man in the moonsuit cranks back into the tunnel next to Tamba's kiosk. The panel in the wall grinds shut. Tamba's dreadlocks create the silhouette of a rain-spider's hairy legs as he gives me a lazy thumbs-up, smiles a smile as slow as mashed potato.

Did he smoke weed through his raspberry juice? I let the brace drop from Andride's beauty spot.

Is this my second chance? Is God, fireproof and cool in heaven, amusing himself with some cruel symmetry?

The only God I know is the one who cut out my tongue and

said, Look, Malachi. You're the only one who lived to tell the tale.

The only God I know is the God of irony.

It feels like someone has poured liquid lead into me.

If this job is a second chance from some pyromaniac in the sky, I am not interested. Keep your dirty deal! I want to shout at the roof, where the yellow paint has hardened in sloppy creases like the skin of a mammoth, thick and stupid.

I groom a tall man with conjunctivitis, report his infection to Tamba. There is nothing I can do to fix his pigeon chest. I trace the plastic tubes below his cage, winding in, winding out. There will be no leaks because of me. I have come this far without the help of heaven. I will shut up for six months, take my tongue and run, run, run. Escape the bad grace of Jesus or Allah or any of God's favourite sons.

When I reach Charmayne, she whispers to me, 'Just me, Malachi. Leave the others if you have to.' Her angry scar splits her solar plexus, steals beneath one creamy breast. 'Save me, please.' Her pubic bush looks straight at me. Her palm-frond lashes sweep towards the floor, carpet it with luscious grief.

The desert strangler asks, 'Why are you whispering?'

All eyes swing to Charmayne's hunger, her knees spread wide.

She says the words I have heard too many times today: 'I don't want to die like this.'

What's the difference? I want to scream. *What does it matter how you shitting expire?* I throw her towel in the bucket, shut Charmayne's cage. These killers have no right to choose their cause of death. Did their victims get a chance? Did they give them a menu?

Did my classmates raise their hands and ask, Please can you rather do it another way?

I slam my bucket down, start on the next subject. My blood is hot and dark, my skin threatening to split. I work through eight deserving killers, bite on my breath to contain the lava that might escape if I dare to breathe out.

Madame Sophie, on the contrary, is as serene as if she is relaxing at the beautician's. She has no idea she might be buried in position any moment like the people of Pompeii. She doesn't seem to notice that the wrath of Satan is busy trimming her nails. She watches me, says wistfully, 'I did my girls like this. Nails, blusher, lipstick. They loved it . . .'

Josiah throws his head to the enamel heaven, laughs hard enough to let loose all the demons the angels have tied up for centuries.

'Shut up, Josiah!' Madame Sophie kicks at his cage. She turns to me, as spiteful as a child.

'Ask him about the children.'

A snake of fear writhes in Josiah's eyes.

'Not children. Worms.' He rises to his feet. His venom flies from his lips. 'They were *worms*, those Seleka, crawling into us!' He squats in his cage, pulls imaginary strings from between his buttocks.

I hit my switch. *Bring an axe. Light the gas. Chop off the monster's head.*

'What's it?' Tamba says.

I bang my wrists together, mime handcuffs.

Tamba stares down at Josiah. He scoots to the left, lifts his elbow high. A fine spray showers onto Josiah's skin. A strike of electricity cleaves through him. It ricochets in me, finds leftover traces from last night's radio. The monster crashes to his cage floor, his nose slamming onto his excretion plate. The last digits of his fingers hook into the mesh, fuse with the metal. He rises up and slams his face again. He pisses involuntarily. Tamba gives one last jolt so Josiah's fingertips do a double-jointed hook. This time he rips a nail. A bright red drip shocks the yellow floor.

I back away from it.

I will not tend to him, even if his blood is bright red, not black as I imagined. Still vibrating with the electric spillage from the devil's cage, I snatch up my bucket, reel past Eulalie.

The old witch croons softly, 'I hear children, Malachi.'

Her words fire through my crown, detonate in my belly. I stand motionless.

'Are they friends?' She turns a withered ear to me. 'Is it a crèche?'

Panic floods my organs, this time freezing.

'A classroom?'

Streams of ice shaft into my heart, pierce my soft tissue.

'Children?' Vicki's lips part with morbid curiosity. 'Whose children?'

I whirl on the mermaid, pelt her with icy hail.

Vicki shrinks from my silent storm. 'Sorry,' she murmurs.

Eulalie cradles me with gentle sympathy. I tear my eyes from hers, cough up icy pellets, tears ripped from the Arctic of my being. I drop my equipment on the trolley, force my frozen limbs from this ghastly mortuary.

* * *

I tear off my whispering grey outfit, adjust the shower taps to the temperature of blood in a calm, resting state.

105

How dare she?

I stand in the warm rain, begin to shiver. How dare Eulalie? She was taking a clever, cruel guess, surely.

Who did she see?

The ghost of Araba, disgust ruining her flawless face?

Was it Erniel, more furious than when I nearly won the English Olympiad?

Or was it my cousin Kontar, shaking his battered head, disowning me?

What did they want to say to me?

I sink to my knees, raise my face to the shower rose – not a pretty flower, but an ugly plumbing fitting. Josiah and I both on our knees, both made mad by the ghosts of children.

No.

I climb to my feet. The prisoners are the enemy. I am the victim.

I rub my skin hard with a coarse towel. The heat slowly calms my convulsive shaking. I leave enough water for Tamba, should the mood take him to wash his skin. I dress in a pale yellow shirt with khaki trousers. Smart casual, they would say in the fashion magazines. Smart, I suppose, because of the pleats.

Janeé's food tonight is smart casual too. A piece of sirloin steak escorted by a troop of green, rolling peas. They chuckle as they escape the prongs of my fork. Tamba arrives in stiff denim and aftershave as strong as a chemical weapon. He, too, has managed to shower, thanks to me knocking thirty minutes off my clipping time.

'Did you handle the shock treatment?'

I nod, nonchalant.

'They say the Indonesian project had microphones inside the

106

cages. The surveillance man couldn't take it. He had a total nervous breakdown.' Tamba shudders. 'I don't know how you do it, Malachi. You must be a special kind of man.'

Something tells me this is not a compliment.

I jerk my fork from my steak, chase some chuckling peas. After six attempts I manage to catch three.

'Malachi, you're not eating,' Olivia says. 'Are you nauseous or something?'

No, my dear, just in the midst of a total nervous breakdown. Thank you, Tamba, for putting words to it.

'I'll have to tell Meirong you've lost your appetite. We can't have you sick among the prisoners now.'

I shake my head, try to smile.

Yes. Olivia would drop me in the shark pit, wherever it is.

I dive at my sirloin and saw off a piece. Olivia watches as I scoop some mushroom sauce onto it. These mushrooms are no Enid Blyton stalks like the pixies cavorted on in the paper books we got from the Waste to Wonder agency. I part my teeth minimally, force steak into the chasm that Raizier has promised to fill by Christmas.

I see Josiah's blood drip from his torn finger.

I begin to shiver. I should have stayed to cut his claws. I should have reported the injury.

'Malachi, are you okay?' Olivia stands up and puts a hand to my forehead.

'What's wrong with him?' Janeé asks.

'He seems weak.'

Tamba hands me a serviette. I spit my steak into it. The tremors leave me immediately.

I take up a spoon meant for the jelly and custard on the trolley, shovel five hundred peas into my mouth. I munch as if to say, *See? I'm fine. Really.*

But when Janeé starts to hand out the pudding, I scoop my last peas into my cheeks, force myself not to launch off the bench and run. I stand up carefully, rub my stomach in a gesture I have seen among satiated people. I bow slightly to Janeé, a bad actor in a bad sitcom. A flicker of forgiveness softens the cook's surliness.

I weave through the doorway of the canteen.

Outside, I slump in the corridor.

'Dammit, he's cracking up!' Olivia says through the wall. 'He didn't eat his lunch either.'

'He's fine,' Tamba says. 'Leave him for a night. Malachi's not the same as you or me.'

I stare at the yellow paint. Tonight, I see the problem with the interior decorating. The school linoleum was the same yellow, wasn't it?

I rock along the corridor.

I need to speak or I will break down completely.

My peas try to bounce up my throat, but I slam them back with my epiglottis. The ones I hid in my cheeks ping from them like ping-pong balls. I leave a trail of green peas to my room with no sky above and no birds to peck them, like in *Hansel and Gretel*, had they legumes.

I perch on the end of my bed.

I need to draw a line or I will turn into a drooling idiot. I slide my hand into the shadow of the bedside cabinet. Tamba's cell phone is still where he tossed it yesterday. My fingers close on the plastic. If he catches me, I will say I was playing *Fruits against Ghouls*, the game the packers loved to play at lunch break.

I sit down on my pillow. The door seems to shiver in anticipation of Tamba flinging it open. I creep past it to the bathroom, slide the concertina door shut.

*

The bathroom air is still pale with steam. I crouch in the shower, take refuge in the white tiles. The damp wall sticks to my shirt. My spine ticks against the porcelain. My white sneakers grip the slippery floor, still stained with yellow drops of antiseptic fluid. I switch on Tamba's phone, listen to the cheerful Samsung tune. I key in his three stars, press the Glossia icon. A text box opens up, clean and white.

Oh, God. Words. I love them.

I choose cursive to smooth my shocking story. Take a terrible breath.

My fingers are white-tipped and scuffed from their mild detergent burn, but they learn the keyboard arrangement easily.

I had just turned fifteen. We had finished our geometry with Mr Zakari. My father was reading us Elizabethan sonnets, urging us to notice the chauvinism beneath the music of the words. He said it was like a violin playing to a rugby scrum.

The letters take my pain and roll it into mystical shapes. Full bellies and slashing swords, rolling waves peaking, sometimes with pinpricks.

Hamri strained his wiry body towards us. His sheer intensity, as usual, had us listening:
'See how these rhyming couplets hide the fear of women in the sixteenth century.'

A quavering question came from Paulus, the tall one. 'What were they afraid of?'

Hamri smiled mysteriously. 'The richness of their wombs. Perhaps of their love?'

Some of us giggled uncomfortably.

'Look how Wyatt compares the woman he desires to a stag in a hunt . . .'

A face appeared at the door. Noble bones. Not ugly. His eyes were a deep red, a trick of the sun reflecting off the red brick. A man as thin as fish gut stood behind him.

'Shut up!' he growled at us, but our hearts had already flung themselves onto our breathing pipes.

The guerrillas entered gracefully, their movements composed like a brutal sonnet, their rifles like devil birds perched on their shoulders.

For an instant, the men seemed relieved to find shelter in our sunny classroom. They knelt among us, stabbed their AK47s into our ribs. I will never forget the smell of their breath. Fermented pig and death. They had been living on hippo bones from the rubbish dumps.

The thin man crouched in the front, spoke softly in Kapwa, 'Yinawa kani unmiyu.' Eyes front. He put his rifle to my father's knee.

'Carry on teaching.'

Hamri read mellifluously, as he always did, but we heard the terror pushing against it.

'The vain travail hath wearied me so sore, I am of them that farthest cometh behind. Yet may I by no means my wearied mind draw from the deer, but as she flees before, fainting I follow . . .'

Even with the rifle in my ribs, my father's words brought the scent of jasmine that wove between the grass stalks alongside the river.

'There is written her fair neck round about: "Noli me tangere . . ."'

Touch me not.

Templeton Security clattered to the door. Men recruited from the village, many of them fathers of the silent hostages in the classroom.

'Someone saw men on the hill.' Erniel's father inside his bullet-proof vest, a tortoise too small for its shell. His voice was high with fright. 'Any sign of trouble?'

Hamri gazed through the mouth of his cave, the terrified air singeing us still, silent children. The copper eyes of his tribe, the golden sleekness of his shaved cheek as my loquacious father, for once in his life, spoke a single syllable.

'No.'

They rattled away with their machine guns, their illfitting vests squeaking like mice.

The guerrillas rose up and opened fire through the window. The Templeton fathers did not fire a single bullet. Their fingers stayed frozen on their triggers, refusing to risk killing their own daughters and sons.

The guerrillas shot the men to mathematically irregular pieces.

They filled the children with lead, pinned them to the walls as if with the steel pins my father used to stick up his favourite quotations. The demons laughed with the lurid pleasure of killing, the screams of the children feeding their monstrous lust to shatter, annihilate. Our blood was their simplest triumph.

111

I sink to my bum. The water soaks my khaki trousers as the violence, the horror take their place in the sentences, pose as calm fact, as if gently blotting the blood where it pooled on the linoleum and began to grow a skin.

The guerrilla next to me pulled out a machete, shoved the toe of his boot between my teeth. The stink of detritus, the clawing for breath, then the razor tip of his blade across my tongue. He turned me into a fountain of blood.

The scab in my throat tears free and chokes me. I cough and cough.

I stop, touch with my finger where my tongue should be. I see no blood.

I return to my screen, hunt among the memories, find some air to breathe.

The children's teeth flew like corn chopped off the cob. Their stomachs were like soft animals, cowering, bleeding out. The children clasped their bellies as if each were harbouring a vulnerable creature, perhaps a puppy.

Kontar did not even duck. Mouth open, he watched the bullets come. Like Kontar drank his tea, he took the heat. They tore open his chest.

His chest was not metal.

Erniel crouched beneath his desk, his eyes burning above his knees. He was too frightened to move his head but I heard what he said.

'My sisters.'

Their love passed before their eyes. Not their entire life, as some people say. No. Their greatest love, clarified. They died loving the thing they cherished more than anything.

Araba stared past me.

'Mama,' she whispered.

The tears run from my eyes, turn the keys blurry. I open them wide.

A growling cry escapes me, the sound of the dying lioness.

My father fell heavily across my knees. His spine was bare, like the defrosted rats we dissected in Natural Science. This is the effect of the AK47.

My father died reaching up for my mouth.

I drop the phone on my lap, let my hands hang. I am grateful for the lingering steam in the bathroom. The light is nothing like the crispness of a Krokosoe afternoon when the wind blows the factory smoke over the fields towards the hydroelectric plant in Anchi.

I let my head roll from side to side, the neutral white tiles like the blank paper we used before my father arranged second-hand tablets from Kattra. I wipe my eyes, pick up my writing instrument.

I am in two thousand and thirty-five, writing the moments I have hidden from since I was fifteen.

The guerrillas left me to bleed. When my classmates lay drained, I was still a tributary running between them.

Tamba bangs into the bedroom.

'Malachi?'

I jump to my feet, turn on a tap in the basin.

'Malachi, are you all right? You looked shaky at supper.'

I grab my toothbrush and scrub.

'Olivia and I are watching *Apocalypse Three* if you want to come up?'

I spit nothing into the drain. Suck water noisily from the stream.

Tamba slams out again. He has no time for a slow, silent victim of apocalypse.

The chlorine water washes away the fiery crust in my throat. I wait a full seven minutes for the echo of the movie player to start up.

I write easier, breathe easier with a dark, destructive soundtrack somewhere above me.

Templeton called in the army, but they arrived too late. The ANIM burnt the workers on the factory floor and in the packing sheds. They burnt the cornfields with Bayira in his tractor, and then the rest of the labour force. They razed the village, picked off the tottering old women, the angry dogs, the toddlers.

I spent three months in a Kattra hospital waiting to die, trying to sink beneath the lip of consciousness. I tried holding my breath. Be still, I told my lungs. But it was my heart that would not stop beating. It tapped its foot, ticked in time, jerked once every second out of habit.

Sometimes I would wake with a shock that left me wondering if I was dead before the pain brought me to blinding, bellowing wakefulness, whimpering disbelief. Blood spitting, the pain so high and so hot, so utterly embracing it must be that I was being slowroasted, kept alive; or repeatedly murdered, of course with knives.

I do not re-read what I have written. I tap, *Save to audio chip*.

I press on the seam of the built-in ear clip. It snaps off eagerly. I poke the cone into the vee between my first two fingers, flex my hand into a fist.

I snap the furtive little piece back onto its mother ship. I will give it to Samuel, the recorder of facts.

*

I slide Tamba's phone into the shadow where I found it. I crawl into bed naked, too tired to find my sleeping shorts. Dim waves of devastation break from the recreation room, miles above me.

The movies at the refugee centre cured me of diving to the ground at the sound of bullets, and pissing, just pissing. Some children had to be packed into their metal beds with blankets to muffle the sound while the movies played for two hours. It didn't occur to the welfare workers to simply not play films about war and devastation, for goodness' sake.

I expect to lie awake, trying not to wet my bed, but I sleep right through the third act of *Apocalypse Three*. I sleep like a man who did not leave his supper, but ate his fill of sirloin steak. A man who has brokered peace, and will forever live on the seeded side of the unexploded landmines.

MONDAY

I wake to the sound of a bomb counting down. I pull my face off a landmine planted beneath mouthfuls of grass. Tamba has set his timepiece to tick like an old clock. There is a damp patch on my pillow, not from tears but escaped spit, the infantile sign of a deep, innocent sleep. I roll into a sitting position. Tamba's skin has the sheen of someone who has been drinking and dancing until two in the morning. He sleeps with his mouth open, his tongue paralysed.

I pull on my trousers in full view of Tamba's dead eyelids. I wear brown trousers today. Fawn, they call it, but this day is not a day for sweet forest creatures. This brown may as well be military issue. I slip my own rudimentary phone into the cabinet, pick out Tamba's like a practised thief. I drop it in my pocket. Tamba breathes as evenly as if he is on a heart-lung machine. I sling on an olive-green shirt, fasten the cuffs. Tie the laces of my brown suede shoes.

In the bathroom, my hair looks like pigeons have been mating in it. I discourage the fuzz with palmfuls of water. My eyes, I notice, have borrowed a gleam of army green. Camouflage. I am going in.

In the bedroom, Tamba's alarm rips up the quiet. He jerks from the coma induced by too much ping-pong. I hook my intercom to my belt, tramp towards breakfast. In the corridor I tread on three of last night's peas, crushing them.

I burst the skin of my pork sausage without even wincing. I eat it with exaggerated confidence, but there is only Janeé to witness my miraculous healing. Her pumpkin face glows orange in the sun filtering from the two glass eyes above us. If I could make small talk, I would ask her something frivolous like, *How did your parents decide on your name, Janeé?*

Janeé nods.

'It's good that you eat,' she says sincerely. 'You must be strong for Meirong.' She bends her sausage and bites the middle like a papaya. 'The way I stay strong is, I sleep.' She chuckles. 'They can dance on me, I don't wake up. Olivia says she plays music, she keeps the lights on, I only snore louder.'

I don't want to think of Olivia in her panties and bra dancing on Janeé's belly, pummelling it. I smile at the cook. In the quiet before the others come, Janeé and I develop our first friendship.

Meirong arrives, wearing black-and-white checks. What, must she lie flat before Quenton for him to play chess today?

She perches uneasily on the bench. 'Feeling better, Malachi? I hear you aren't eating.'

I nod emphatically, fix my gaze on Meirong's dress, but the chess squares take turns to jut in and out of focus.

'He ate all his sausage,' Janeé tells Meirong proudly. She sends me a secret message over Meirong's head, *Be strong for the lady boss.* I sense it in the careful way she steadies herself to pass me tea.

'Hi guys.' Tamba bounces a sausage onto his plate. 'What's happening?' He seems to have recovered some of the good humour he showed before his sleeping pills were ripped from him. 'Whoa, Meirong, you look stunning today.' But his eyes jitter like mine, trying to still the optical effect of the squares.

Romano enters stealthily. Olivia trails in behind him, still sleepy. 'Mor-ning,' she sings.

I forgive Olivia for her selfish worry last night. This woman has buttery sun stored somewhere in her marrow. When she is happy, Olivia shines like a place that has never seen rain, like the thirty-third clear day at the equator. Araba and I counted during our last summer in Bhajo.

Olivia's two front teeth tease the skin off a sausage like a mother cat with her newborn young.

'I had this lovely dream. We were floating on the sea, me and Timmy. We were on this plastic thing with a little see-through window. You know those old blow-up things? But instead of reefs there were these beautiful flowers growing in the sea.' She giggles. 'Lilies.' Now that the sausage is free of its skin, Olivia nibbles it awake lovingly. 'And the sun!' She stares up at the golden light above us, hushed with reverence for the fire in the sky.

Meirong ignores her completely. 'Romano, still no sign?'

'No.'

'What, the Spanish Armada?' Tamba teases.

Meirong bans all jokes with her tone. 'The tanker convoy passed safely. But we got a report at eleven p.m. of a solo sailor lost at sea.'

'All alone?' Olivia says.

'She was in a yacht race with her father.'

'A girl?' Tamba says.

Meirong nods, nips merciless pieces off her sausage.

'How old is she?' Romano asks.

'Nineteen.'

118

We all stop chewing, all feel the vulnerability of a young girl alone on the hostile sea.

'It's an Éternité Insurance boat. It's absolutely critical we stay out of this. Imagine the search parties.' For a moment Meirong looks utterly desperate. 'Imagine the press. Let's pray she doesn't drift towards us.'

But she would rather kick Buddha's fat arse than ask for help, wouldn't she?

I push my plate away, stand up briskly. I am, after all, the only one in military colours. The only one fighting on the front line. Yes, I took a hit. Last night I stood wavering, choking on a piece of sirloin steak. But I did not fall, did I?

'Already?' Olivia squeaks.

I nod in a manly manner. I have devised a weapon that can defeat forty enemies with a single stroke. I have it primed in my pocket. If it were a time bomb, it would be ticking.

'Um, the bucket's done but it's inside, on the counter . . .'

I put up my hand, invite Olivia to stay and complete her sausage midwifery. I nod politely at the others, cleave briskly from these people weakened by lilo dreams and the petty fears of civilians.

'I'll be there in a minute, Malachi,' Tamba says.

'Now, please,' Meirong orders him.

Tamba gets to his feet. As I reach the corridor, I hear him slur through his baked beans, 'What did I say? I said he'd be okay.'

I open the door to Olivia's laboratory. My bucket of white towels waits on the desk next to a row of transparent sacs draped over the edge. *Testosterone inhibitor*, says a white sticker.

As I pass the canteen, Tamba falls in behind me, my appointed landmine-clearance deputy. But Tamba is not my comrade today. I have stolen from him.

He climbs the spiral stairs to his perch, choking on his toast.

I hesitate at the door, suddenly watery in the area between my shoulder blades. Scapulas, according to *Basic Anatomy*. I pop the ear clip from the body of the Samsung. A mute-speaker sign comes up immediately. I put the clip to my ear, swipe the screen. Who will help me?

Joey. Geraint. Eric. I tap on William.

I type, *Will you speak for me?* Touch the *Talk* icon. William repeats the question into my ear in smooth, sincere American. I hide the audio chip as I practised last night. Make a digital knuckle-duster. I shove open the door like this is a bust.

* * *

My trousers hiss with friction as I collect my cutting tools, walk swiftly towards Samuel, the journalist. I pray to the God of technology, please, please let him recognise what on earth this thing is. I procrastinate, check his piping painstakingly.

Samuel is compassionate on this auspicious day.

'Hey, Malachi. Are you okay?'

Stop with the kindness. This is no way to meet your damned nemesis.

I feel sweat springing between the fingers of my locked fist. Will the moisture wreck the ear clip?

'Yesterday was scary. That fire thing.'

Now I sweat like a hostage with thirty seconds to disarm the explosives sewn into my clothes. I glance up at the surveillance glass. Tamba takes a swig from a plastic bottle, picks his teeth. He rotates his roller chair towards his camera images.

Can he see me on his screens?

I lop off the frighteningly fast growth of Samuel's thumbnail. Relax. The cameras are mounted directly above each subject. They can't see me.

The stump of my tongue begins to weep with fear. I swallow with horrible difficulty.

Do it, Malachi.

I loosen the clip with the tip of my thumb. Samuel's alert eyes catch the movement. I guide the clip between his fore and middle finger, crush them together.

Keep it secret. Please.

Upstairs, Tamba's nostrils are positioned towards me. Fear wells up in me. I have just jumped off this metal planet into the sea. I trim Samuel's hand, neglect his little finger. I stroke the white towel ever so gently across his skin so as not to dislodge the memory chip. Set his hands free like the wings of a carrier pigeon. His eyes dart towards Tamba.

'Check security,' Samuel says softly.

Tamba is lounging back now, gazing into space. His fake cheer at breakfast seems to have turned quickly to melancholy. Good. Let him be self-obsessed.

I nod at Samuel.

The journalist transfers the audio chip to his ear in one smooth movement, buries it in the clever cauliflower of his outer ear. How wonderful is the physiology of the human being.

Focus, Malachi.

I point at Samuel's feet. His smooth testicles swing as he lifts his knees and thrusts his feet through the opening. I slide my free hand in my pocket. Press the *Go* key.

Samuel smiles once, perhaps at the unexpected accent. His lips part to expand his fine Homo sapiens listening ability. He gives himself over to my American ventriloquist. I watch as his eyes glow with interest, darken with dread, widen to show a secret rim of white. He hunches forwards as if to hide his heart from the guerrillas' bullets. Or is it from his own awful memories?

Samuel shuts his eyes, slams his spine against the mesh. Clear water slides down his cheeks. For a second a dumb compassion visits me. But when Samuel opens his eyes, they are flashing emergency lights. Bright yellow. Angry.

'You think I am like them? You do, don't you?'

I glare back at him.

'It takes *courage* to do my work. You try and stand by and watch people being blown up.'

My hands are growing hair, sprouting dirty fingernails like the robot in the Werewolf movies.

'Do you think I'm not haunted?' Samuel plucks the audio chip from his ear and tosses it at my feet.

He pulls his own feet back in. I sweep up the memory chip, slam the metal hatch. But some part of me is kicking for dry ground.

My words were meant to shut the journalist up, not rouse him to fury.

The old witch is squinting at the floor, searching for the plastic chip. 'What is it, Samuel? I can't see.'

'Malachi has written his story for us. And *because* I am honourable, *because* it's my job, I will tell you, Eulalie.' Samuel begins as if he is making a speech at a wedding. 'Eulalie . . . Everyone . . . Malachi wants us to know how he lost his tongue. Listen!'

The whole hall falls silent, ready to hear my first words since two thousand and twenty.

'Malachi was fifteen. He and his class had just finished their maths lesson!'

Samuel roars out sentences he has only heard once. The prisoners gasp as if the guerrillas are trotting down the aisle now, their rifles bristling in the fluorescent light. They fall quiet as Samuel shouts how the guerrillas crouched behind us while our teacher read Thomas Wyatt's sonnet about the king's mistress.

'"Any trouble here?" His friend's father asked. The children held their breath. "No," his father said.'

Samuel's words beat like hooves on my heart.

'The ANIM opened fire on the children . . .'

'Terrible,' someone croaks behind me.

'Children!'

'They burnt the factory and the fields surrounding it. They shot the old people, the animals, the toddlers.'

There is a horrified silence.

Eulalie jerks at her hands, but they are tightly trapped in their leather stocks.

'Good enough, Malachi?' Samuel's fiery eyes burn a hole on each side of my spine.

High above me, Tamba props his chin on his hands; gazes at the greasy paint on the ceiling.

Eulalie searches my face, her eyes a steel scourer. I keep my eyes down, flick a cursory towel across her skin in case Tamba should pull his head out of his blinding self-pity. I lock the witch's cage, hurry to the husband killer.

Vicki is glaring at me as if it was *I* who crept over the copse and sunk my rifle between rows of small, undeveloped ribs.

She jabs her fingers into the leather sheath. 'You know *nothing*, Malachi.'

123

I glimpse the bone between her breasts, more of a secret slope. A fin nudging through a meniscus, too ephemeral to break the surface with a splash.

Vicki leans close, whispers with a muted violence, 'He . . . *he* . . .'

I feel my cheeks go slack with horror.

Rock. Scissors. Fire. Rape. The tools so beloved of Homo sapiens.

Vicki tears her hands free. She huddles over her knees, shows the curved ribs of some marine creature at the museum. I feel a terrible urge to walk my fingers up the rungs, count them. *Sorry Vicki.*

I am so, so sorry.

I groom the Indian with the benzene leak and one more prisoner after him. Lock the leather glove to the cage of the Gadu Yignae.

He shoves his gigantic hands into my taming glove. One hand flutters free from my strap, forms a massive fist. He sinks it between the pectoral muscles on his chest.

'I was a volcano. This thing inside me.' He returns his hand, watches me pit my strength against the hoof-like growths on his fingertips. 'And now, after all this time, do you know what I miss?'

I glance up at him.

'The smell of her hair. She said her conditioner had real geraniums in it. I teased her, I said, Do you really think there are fields of geraniums somewhere?' The giant inhales deeply as if his wife has just shaken her hair free and filled the air with the scent of a thousand tiny flowers. 'And do you know what haunts me more than anything?'

I let his towel drip, wait expectantly.

'Their baby.'

'What baby, Judge James?' asks the Australian.

A sob tears free of the giant's lung cavity. 'They found a foetus during the autopsy.'

'Ah, your brother's child?'

The giant nods his enormous head.

Eulalie's voice arrives like a gentle wind across the plains. 'It was *your* child, Judge James.'

The giant shakes his head, 'No.'

A murmuring takes flight among the cages. 'His child . . .'

His roar rips through the rig, 'NO-O!'

The words flare out of reach, float near the roof, 'It was the judge's son . . .'

The giant pulls them down like a kite. 'My *son* . . .' His sobs are shuddering blasts.

'Poor James,' the Australian murmurs. 'Poor James.'

But the giant is wind through a bombed building, blowing in hollow gusts. Exploding with an emptiness that nothing, not even his thick law books, can ever fill again.

When I reach Lolie the crack killer, she shoots staccato words at me, one after the other in a thudding monologue. I have no idea what language she is firing at me. I tighten my leather strap, stare into her high-tensile eyes. Her skin is the temperature of metal in the middle of a cold, cold night as she waits for her target to leave his warm mistress.

Too many double-o–seven movies, Malachi. My last count was nineteen.

I push the button on my intercom.

Tamba hauls himself out of his gloomy reverie. 'Yes?'

I swipe my forehead, turn my hands up to say, *Check temp.*

Tamba swivels his roller chair, manipulates something that might be a mouse. 'Whoa. It's low. I'll turn up her heat.'

As I clip Lolie's fingers, I feel the quick warmth entering them. Sweat breaks out on her eyebrows. When I unlatch her hands, she wipes her face feverishly, nose, mouth, cheeks, nose, mouth, cheeks, freeing them from whatever they smothered her with. *Was* it plastic?

By the time I reach Shikorina, Lolie is sweating on her arms and her scarred, swollen belly where they are growing not one but two extra spleens.

Shikorina's lap appears empty today. Today she is silent, desolate, like a mother who lost her children in an accident. Her brother would have taken them. What was his name? Kenneth. He was a good man, I could tell by the way she spoke to me yesterday. Why on earth didn't she ask him to take her children?

The giant lets out one last eerie gust behind me.

But it is too late for speaking or shutting up.

Or is it?

My vision fades to a watery whiteness. My eye sockets feel empty. I rub my eyelids, squint behind me. The giant's spine emerges slowly like a rutted road after a flood. He sits utterly still now, a rocky monument to a man who might have lived an honourable life.

Is it too late?

'Let's go for lunch,' Tamba says listlessly.

I leave Shikorina's toenails to flourish one more day. I breathe leftover scraps of breath, force my feeble fingers to fasten the latch.

I have not told the whole truth. I still have a secret in me. It lurches up my throat like undigested meat as I drop my tools on the trolley, stumble from the hall.

I hurry along the corridor, plunge down the three sudden steps, choking on my half a story.

* * *

Janeé drops a plate down in front of me.

'Beef bourguignon,' she says with a French accent.

It seems to be me who gets the gristle. Everything Janeé cooks needs a certain trick, like how to nip off the meat strings and swallow them before they form a sinewy rope that reaches down your oesophagus to hook something up.

Like the whole truth.

Tamba swallows with difficulty. He mutters, 'You're doing better than me.'

Janeé, I see, is very clever. She puts the thick, single strands aside like they might be viable arteries to lie inside her son. Romano stalks in and sits. Meirong whisks in after him.

'I just need a quick bite, Janeé. I'm taking Romano's afternoon shift.'

Optimistic, I think. She will be chewing at this bench for at least two days and two nights.

'I don't need to sleep,' Romano says sullenly.

But Meirong's voice rises to a worried pitch. 'Sorry, Romano, I'm not having you dead on your feet, and this girl sails into us with a whole rescue operation after her.' She sits lightly on the bench, chews her food manically with her tiny, sharp teeth. She rolls a yellow bulb lurking in the gravy. 'Are these onions?'

'French,' Janeé says smugly.

Shallots, I would like to say, the name for baby onions in the country where the onions are very small and the men, some people

127

say, a bit creepy. Speaking of creepy, Meirong's dress is lower in the front than I have yet seen. Above her black-and-white checks a delicate crease hints at the squeeze of her bra against her breasts. I spy like a creepy Frenchman, but don't get me wrong, those silky spheres might as well be flying fish, or giant moths that came to rest on the salt in the centre of the table. Meirong's cleavage turns into a frown line, deeper, more disapproving with every masticating minute. She swallows too early. Her white china face turns the transparent pink of a baby lizard. She dives for the red juice. I watch the obstruction travel down her flawless throat. Is it the bourguignon, or is it the lost girl she is choking on?

Meirong stands unsteadily, hurries out like a black-and-white hologram of a worried woman.

'I can stay awake for five days,' Romano says bitterly.

Tamba yawns, just thinking about the struggle of holding up his eyelids.

'Why not make him a coffee bomb, Janeé? Have you got any?'

Romano shakes his head. 'No need.'

'Can you make one for me?' Tamba asks.

'You're not on night shift.'

'For this afternoon, I mean.'

'Can you not do your job?'

'Janeé. You're starting to sound like a tattle tale.' Tamba pleads, 'I'm just bored. I don't know. Miff.' He drags me into it. 'Malachi's doing such a good job spotting trouble, there's nothing happening.'

Olivia glows at me approvingly.

'I'm like . . .' Tamba's fists clench on the table top, 'battling a bit, Janeé.'

'Okay, Tamba. But I've only got the liquid.'

Tamba's hands go limp. 'Lovely.'

The muscles in Romano's jaw bunch like a chainsaw as he finishes his lunch way before me.

'Bao tarde,' he says dolefully. His canvas clothes seem to sigh as he leaves.

Tamba and I sit and watch Janeé dine like a French princess with Amazon arms and ten-pound teeth.

'Cold milk or hot?' she asks Tamba.

'Hot.'

'Wait here.'

Tamba and I wait in silence for a full five minutes. It is not me who wants the coffee bomb, but I would sit here all day and all night rather than return to the wreckage my half a story has wreaked.

Janeé squeezes through the door again. Tamba jumps up to receive his foaming polystyrene cup. He takes a big swig, gets a bumper of foam on his top lip. He coughs so hard, coffee streams from his nostrils. Cocaine surrogate. Tamba wipes his nose with the back of his hand.

'I love you, Janeé.'

Janeé smiles for the first time, it seems, in her whole pumpkin life. I touch my palms together once, thank her for the difficult beef. Follow Tamba, the coffee charmer, to the place where I least in the world want to be.

Tamba floats up the spiral stairs with his precious liquid. Ebullient, one might say, after a single sip. Heaven help us. He must be sensitive.

I rest my forehead against the metal door. Swallow solid air.

Be strong, Malachi.

The bones in my forehead pick up the ongoing tremors of the tidal wave inside. The prisoners are still stirred up, I can feel it.

I raise my red lanyard, turn the light green.

* * *

The prisoner's beard is prematurely grey, his legs long and skinny. He starts to tell me about something he didn't do, but his words are broken by his chipped teeth. One thing is for sure, Janeé's beef would have killed him. He says the word 'Harare' somewhere in his stream of slurred English.

Ah, a white Zimbabwean, his beard and his teeth ruined by GM corn. I was lucky. My mother grew wild spinach at our doorstep.

I flick my switch.

Tamba is head-banging in his chair, chewing his dreadlocks with his front teeth. He rocks towards the glass. 'What, so quick?'

I mime a shot in the bum.

Tamba squints at my finger squeezing an imaginary syringe. 'Of what?'

I form a vee with my hands, take a chance with the literacy thing.

'Vee . . . vee . . . um. Vitamins?'

Spare me. The two of us are now playing afternoon charades.

'Oh, really? What symptoms, Malachi?'

I swirl my fingers at my chin, knead an invisible beard. I tap my teeth.

'Ah, I see,' Tamba says. 'Good! I'll tell Olivia.' He speaks into a nearby microphone, rolls his chair back to me. 'You're brilliant, Malachi.'

The caffeine has made Tamba horribly hearty. Still, his over-zealous compliment gets me through the next two subjects.

I stall before the social worker and his accusing, grey gaze.

'I thought you were ex-ANIM.'

Your mistake, stupid.

He watches me square off his overgrown fingernails. 'Do you hate me for helping them?'

I can't stop my head from nodding.

'Does that mean you believe I am innocent?'

I falter, bewildered.

He sings joyously to the hall, 'Malachi believes me!'

In the movies they would say, 'Shut up, you fuck.'

Sorry for swearing, Hamri.

My anger burns all the way to Charmayne, the big beauty. I can almost see sparks fly as I slash at her nails. She must know she is a fraction of a millimetre from sudden agony, but still she tries to clear her name with me:

'It was their greed that killed them, Malachi. They both had solar Volvos. Mansions.' She shakes her head. 'If you knew what they spent on their suits.'

Splat, Charmayne. Splat splat. I would love to shut her up with some childish onomatopoeia. Those suits must have split their seams on the concrete. She sees the cynicism in my eyes.

'I grew up wearing other people's clothes from lost property.' Charmayne has dark, soft hairs on her belly, the down on a female doe. 'No children of staff were allowed in our block so I hid all day in the fire escape.' She raises her stair-climbing thighs, gives me her feet. 'I used to sneak into the pool at night and swim up and down the dark side where no one could see me.'

I imagine her broad shoulders rolling through quiet lengths, her breasts swinging up, swinging down the painted line. I clip and clean the long, strong feet that must have kicked underwater so as not to make a splash. I must admit that Charmayne's eccentric hair, her full-cream skin, her eyes gleaming with some mystical mercury must have created a

---

magical sight, even in the dark lane of a locked-up pool.

If I was a normal man I would fall in love, surely, but the only thing that tempts me is Charmayne's beautiful knees. The bones are flat on top like a mesa or a butte, I can't remember which. I drag my eyes from them.

Don't be stupid, Malachi. This woman is an instrument of earth-moving greed with no regard for human life or the flimsiness of suits.

A growl begins to brum at the base of my throat.

'All right, all righ-h-t,' near the end of the row, Madame Sophie soothes sarcastically.

I didn't realise my growl had risen to loud.

Madame Sophie's blonde hair is a blown-out white today, her skin as pale as an albino's. Even her eyes have turned platinum.

Is my mood affecting my eyesight? I see white spots on her nails. Were they there yesterday? I press my switch. How the heck do I mime calcium? The only way to do it is to mime milk.

'And now?' Tamba says.

I pull on imaginary udders. It must be from a cow, though, Tamba. Corn milk only causes further deficiencies. I pinch the teats between thumb and finger, use long strokes. I think those milking machines use grease.

'Milk?' Tamba guesses.

I nod, skim the air in an arc above Madame Sophie's fingertips.

'Ah, calcium.' Tamba is becoming world-class at word association.

I nod at him, bend my tired back over Madame Sophie's fingers.

'Have you heard of euthanasia?' she asks me. 'Do you know that word?'

No, Madame Sophie, I was only the son of an English teacher

who believed that words were life-giving entities.

I loosen her fingers. She hooks them through the mesh.

I straighten up, stare at their half-moons. *Are* there white spots?

'It was euthanasia,' she says. 'Not murder.'

You are too white, Madame Sophie. Overexposed. I drop her towel in the detergent. What of the dark half of the photo negative?

Josiah has had thirty-nine clippings to prepare for my visit. I lock the glove to his cage, but he waves his black talons towards the tiny camera facing it.

'What will happen if Tamba sees these?'

His nails are more than an inch long and knotted like the wood of an ugly tree. I stare up at the surveillance box, but Tamba is still head banging up there, listening to God-knows-what on his speakers. Josiah sighs.

'Useless, that one.'

Josiah's toenails have also gone into their first twist. The trick is to get the clippers beneath the devilish bend.

'A sad story, Malachi. Your cousin was the only one who died with dignity.'

I freeze. Kontar's body on the school-room floor, his shirt hanging in torn strips as if to keep the flies away.

I crunch my blade through Josiah's coiling toenail. It cracks length-wise, rips through the cuticle. Yes.

A sheer accident but painful, surely. Josiah's toe is bleeding. He touches it with interest. I fill my lungs with rumbling breath.

'Are you growling, Malachi?'

I let the roar out of my sternum, 'Haaaghhh!' I don't care who hears it.

'What did you *do*, Malachi?' The dirty flecks in his eyes pull like radioactive magnets. 'What did you do to make them cut off your tongue?'

I crash into his cage. Josiah laughs as if he has ripped out my raw heart. I shove away, rock towards Vicki.

She stares into my open mouth as I gasp for oxygen. 'Malachi?'

I steady myself on her cage, get my bearings.

Upstairs, Tamba chomps down on the split end of a dreadlock.

Floor. Wall. Red hand over red hand I make it to the end of the aisle.

'Your bucket, Malachi,' Vicki hisses.

I force my attention to the floor. One shoe before the other shoe, I retrace my steps. I don't look, but I sense Josiah's pockmarked eyes drawing every last iron filing of courage from me. His laugh is rich with amusement and something more deadly. A terrible satisfaction.

Josiah has given his guilt to me.

It is several kilometres to the door. My legs seem to have lengthened, like the man on stilts outside Eddie's Gas in Nelspruit. The only thing that saves me is the sight of my brown shoes as I follow my stilted course along the floor.

'Josiah, you're such a cunt,' Vicki says behind me.

Josiah's laugh for the first time sounds human. He is finally free. He gave it all to me.

I slam the door shut. I meant for it to be more of a composed click. Another loud thud as I throw my back against it. I crash my bucket to the floor, drop my head between my knees.

What did you do, Malachi?

Is Josiah forever part of me? I watch a string of saliva hanging from my mouth. It is clean, at least. Silver.

What did you do?

'Aaaagh!' I shout to drown out Josiah's chant.

Tamba comes clanging down the spiral stairs. 'Malachi?' He trips the last part, nearly falls onto me. 'What's happening?'

'Aaagh,' I moan.

'Are you sick?' His warm hand touches my back, so gentle I want to rise into it and let Tamba hold me.

Help me.

I want to press my face into his chest, hear his heart beat too fast from his coffee bomb.

I climb slowly to my feet. I lay my back against the door, a metal slab in a parlour for the dead. The floor and the wall have swapped places, that's all.

Tamba steps back. 'What do you need, Malachi?'

Does he expect me to mime some kind of vitamin?

I press my palms against the door behind me. Door. Floor. I push off with my hands, walk along the floor. One brown shoe. Two.

'Okay, just trying to help. I mean, it could have been a heart attack or something.' Tamba touches his heart, the precise place I want to lay my head. 'Jesus.'

He follows me in silence down the corridor.

Walk faster, Malachi. Don't be insipid.

Tamba starts to sing under his breath, his concentration impaired from his caffeine shot. 'Strange day,' his lyrics go. 'Strange day for a break-up. Can we wait till next week?'

I know that song. It's from the Hedonistic Hell Crew, big on the radio before I left, hundreds of years ago. The bastard clicks his fingers. I drop the bucket at the door, turn into our living quarters. Tamba passes by the opening, sings his way to find some sweeter company. He reverses a few steps, pauses in the doorway.

'I won't tell them that you, like, collapsed. But you'd better pull yourself together, dude. I'm not into lying for you. I want to finish this job and get off this ship. Please.' Tamba hangs off the door frame, swings away. I think I hear his fingers clicking further down the passage.

Emotionally strange, the two of us. A strange day for a break-up.

But it can't wait till next week.

* * *

I can't see myself properly in the bathroom mirror. My outline is indistinct. The details of my face have run like watercolours. I point my penis to the toilet. I feel its ditches and its star-shaped scars, the raw welt from my corrective treatment on Sunday. It is ugly, this organ, not accidentally pretty like Vicki with her good, strong ridges. Keloid, not skin. I spit into the toilet, check my sputum. It is still clear and silvery.

This is a sign I can go and have supper with the crew. My fluids are see-through.

No one witnessed my breakdown, other than a self-centred ex-junkie.

I do up my zip, nod to my vague image in the mirror.

Go and eat, Malachi.

Janeé is slopping white sauce onto rice.

'Chicken à la king,' she tells us.

Meirong is the first to break the surface with her fork. For some reason, the afternoon has turned her the precise colour of the creamed chicken.

'That sailing girl is drifting *straight* towards us. Unless the wind

136

or the current swings . . .' Meirong tips the first mouthful in, drops a grain of rice on the table. Everyone stares at it.

My eyesight, I am grateful to realise, is once again crisp.

'Shit,' Olivia swears. Her blue eyes show a rim of cerise. 'We just need three days!'

Meirong turns on her. 'We need two months, actually. We've got to finish three cycles to make it pay. We've got to . . .' She loses two more grains of rice to her terror of failure. She pushes her plate away. 'I'm not hungry, Janeé. I'm going up to tell Romano to switch off the deck lights tonight. We need a total blackout.'

Janeé tries to jump up but her thighs get stuck beneath the table top.

Meirong seizes a covered plate. 'Is this it?'

Her black-and-white squares pull and push through the opening. 'Good luck!' Olivia calls after her.

Near the roof, the two fingers of sun turn pinkish, fade away.

'Christ,' Tamba says morosely. The chicken à la king has pulled him off his caffeine too quickly. 'What if the search party finds us?'

'Meirong won't let them,' Janeé says.

'She's not as perfect as you think, you know, Janeé.' Tamba sips his raspberry juice, stains the chute between his nose and his lips. The green streak in his eye has almost been reabsorbed.

How is Tamba party to secret truths about the bosses?

Your half a story, Tamba. It's a silent scream every time you open your mouth.

He sighs. 'Come, Olivia. Let's go and watch old movies. Let's watch *Tree of Life*. I watched it once when I was h-' He stops.

Only I know he was about to say, 'high'.

'Okay. But there's a good chance I'll fall asleep. Coming Janeé?'

'Yes please,' Janeé says too eagerly. She glances at me. 'What about you, Malachi? Have you seen it?'

I shake my head. I put my hands together, rest my cheek on them. Mime sleepy.

What did you do, Malachi?

My knees have no wish to support me but I scrape through the doorway. My stomach is refusing the food for a noble king. I stagger along the corridor, take the three random steps on my hands and knees. I slam my shoulder against the wall, hurtle through the door of my living quarters. I dive into the bathroom. Bend over the toilet bowl.

Nothing wants to come up.

Nothing.

I shut the toilet seat, sit on it. No. This feels too scatological, like my trousers should be around my ankles. One shoe skids in the shower. I sit in a pool of Tamba's morning water. It wets my buttocks through.

Good. This is appropriate.

For seven months afterwards, I was incontinent.

Truth only.

I pull Tamba's phone from my pocket. The Samsung sign wanes, becomes watery. But I don't need to see.

I feel the truth with my fingertips, let them say what will surely blind me if I look straight at it.

The guerrilla stabbed his rifle barrel into my father's knee.

'Yinawa kani unmiyu.'

My father took a ragged breath. He kept his reading speed measured, but his creamy sonnet was thickened by terror.

'For Caesar's I am, And wild for to hold, though I seem tame.'

The guerrilla's lips were too soft for a killer. They separated with some vile desire as he hitched Araba's skirt up with his bayonet. He made a shallow cut on her thigh. Nothing more than a thin, red stripe, but the blood, or perhaps the sonnet, inspired in him a hunger for her sweet, young beauty. I heard his whispered promise,

'Later, I will love you.'

Araba's brown eyes scorched into mine, begging me to save her. Or were they saying goodbye?

'Any sign of trouble?' Erniel's father asked.

Erniel was sitting two desks to my right, imploring his father behind his thick glasses.

'No.'

Hamri's no was a shield that could wrap the earth and pull it tight, protect it from meteors and stray fire from the sun. Templeton Security clattered away with their machine guns. My words burst from my mouth.

'Yes! They are here!'

A suicide bomber's pin.

Erniel's father stormed through the doorway. Glittering ions spun in orbit around his silhouette as he aimed his rifle at the devil crouched behind his child. But all he could see were his son's desperate eyes. The guerrilla shot him six times in the breast, ripping up his Kevlar vest.

When the fathers were all dead, Araba's guerrilla shot the clothes off her body. In my river of blood, in my halfawake state, I caught a glimpse of one young breast. A taut, tender swelling. Dead. Her scalp had lifted so her braids hung over her face.

I drop the phone on my lap, crash my head from side to side, silent, but the truth burgeons in my heart, incinerates my scar tissue. A soft groan tears from my throat.

I bow my head before the lord of shame in his long, dirty coat.

I killed Araba with my lust.

I thought she belonged to me.

I clasp the phone, write my final line.

I killed them all with my loquaciousness.

It has all come unstuck. The strings, the gristle, the fifteen years of silence that have smothered me. I try to cry, but a strange barking sound comes out. Dry.

I balance the Samsung on the basin, turn on the cold shower tap. I drench my khaki uniform, fight my wet shirt off my skin. I pull off my trousers. Sit naked in my sneakers. This is not a noble image. I hook them off with my big toes, rub my bare feet, rub between the toes like I do with the prisoners. I rub between my fingertips, tear at my nails with my teeth. I bite them to the quick, turn myself into one of them.

A sleepiness comes over me.

I watch the cold rain on the battleground of my flesh, the fires long out. Water runs into the sinkholes where the bomb blasts have changed my landscape. I raise my hand lethargically, turn off the water. I crawl out of the bathroom, onto my mattress. I slip Tamba's phone beneath my pillow, let my body weep gently into my duvet.

I sleep. I sleep even with my shame charged beneath my head, ready to blast through my pillow and kindly shatter my brains.

I sleep until God knows what hour, when Tamba shouts, 'Bloody fuck!'

I bolt into a sitting position.

Tamba crawls out of the bathroom on his hands and knees. I stare stupidly. Is he me?

Am I reliving my last minute of consciousness before I went to bed?

'You wet the floor, you stupid git. I nearly knocked myself out.'

Sorry. A single bird croak comes out.

'Did you say something?' Tamba's eyes jangle with excitement. 'Did you say *sorry*?'

I sink back on the pillow.

He grins. 'Maybe we're making progress.' Tamba pulls on his pyjama shorts, striped pale blue. His skin is smooth for a man so full of prickles. He has funny hairs on his nipples, spring-coiled things from a joke shop. He gets into bed, switches off the light.

'What do you think, buddy?' he asks in the dark.

If you really want to know, Tamba, I think you should pluck your nipples.

I feel for his Samsung, dig my head into the pillow. The last words I hear are Tamba's whisper.

'Christ-mas. I hope I can get to sleep.'

Then Tamba's stolen phone and the whole, untruncated truth chop off my head. I die again to this day, unconscious.

TUESDAY

As I wake, the first thing I feel for is my full story. Smooth plastic with curved edges, strangely warm as if it has been receiving signals from my dream brain. This yellow phone is my friend, my executioner. Today I will be the boy I truly am. Not the baby boy my mother cried over after three miscarriages. Not the one my father stroked in disbelief until the midwife, Granny Beatrice, said, 'Let him sleep.'

I was a little jaundiced, they said. My colour matched my father's in my first few weeks, but soon his hand showed Samwati yellow against my black skin.

Not this boy.

Today I will be the boy who killed his village with a perilous word: *Yes*.

The one who loved Araba like the giant loved his wife.

I lift my head from the pillow. Tamba is nowhere to be seen. It looks like someone has abducted him: there is a tangle of sheets on the floor, a shrunken puddle from my last night's pilgrimage to bed on all fours.

I check my timepiece. 6.57. Late for breakfast! I fly out of bed, kneel at my suitcase. All I have left is a long-sleeved purple shirt.

142

Party purple, for goodness' sake. I throw it on. What trousers? Pale yellow. Even worse.

I drag them on, slip the Samsung into my pocket. I have no time to brush my teeth. I dart into the bathroom and suck on my toothpaste tube, coat my mouth with artificial peppermint. I hope my American ventriloquist has gone to the same lengths.

I am three steps into the corridor when I feel the slap of the cold rig against my bare feet. I scramble back to fetch my sneakers with the yellow detergent drips. Today I will be the boy who went to school with no socks, my bare ankles protruding.

I thud along the corridor with my boy's ankles, man's sneakers, blast into the breakfast room. I glance at the clock. Ten seconds to seven.

'No need to worry,' Olivia says. 'We all slept a little late.'

'What do you mean?' Meirong says sullenly. 'I haven't even been to bed.' She has a delicate smudge beneath each eye. Purple seems to be the theme for this day.

Tamba's spoon stops halfway to his mouth, yellow sweetcorn purée sticking to it.

'Whoa, Malachi. Feeling festive today? I tried everything to wake you up. I tickled your face, but you slapped me away.' He waits, like he expects another crow's croak.

I sit down next to him. No apology from me.

Meirong blurts, 'The sailing girl found us. Just past midnight. She motored right under the rig. Can you believe it?'

The schoolboy in me wants to say, *Wow.*

The buckles on Meirong's shoulders look like epaulettes. She's in a maroon lycra suit tossed with tiny coloured shards like broken windscreen glass. I eat a whole boiled egg. I can't stand egg white,

143

but there is no way I'm going to separate it from the yolk. I will go in today with the whole truth, the white so polished I can see myself in it.

The others gobble their sweetened corn like a group of GM addicts. I leave mine to grow a petulant skin, eat another whole egg. Tamba pours salt onto his plate and rolls his egg round and round, pondering our destiny. He is dressed in dark green jeans and a pink t-shirt. Clubbing colours, if you ask me. That pink would surely glow under strobe lights.

'What's her name?' Tamba asks eventually.

Meirong pulls a perfectly round yolk from its white plastic mould. 'Frances.' A cowlick seems to have lifted from her glossy helmet. She watches me bite into a third whole egg. 'Romano's given her breakfast, but I need you to take her lunch up, Malachi.'

My heart shoots a silly flare. I will see the sun.

Meirong says quickly, 'I'm choosing Malachi because he can't speak.'

'Geez, Meirong. Why don't you rub it in?' Tamba gets up from the table, singles me out with a sympathetic glance. 'See you now, buddy.'

Is this what a strange crow's croak can win? Loyalty?

I swallow a final egg like it is the rubber front of my sneaker. One more yolk for the road.

By the time I reach the hall I am panting with terror. I stick my fingernail into the seam of the ear clip.

I will never again be the boy I was yesterday. But I would rather be Josiah, scratching my arse.

I pin the memory chip between my fore and middle finger, lock it in the crease. Tiny, this explosive, about to blow up the silence

I have cowered inside my whole adult life. No blank façade, no turning the other cheek, no clever plastic-wrapping ten thousand units per second can save me from this. I raise the key card from my heart. Shove the door open.

* * *

Their eyes torch the air like they're wolves at night, waiting to savage my soft underbelly. I want to drop to my knees, crawl towards their eighty eyes, say, *Please take my truth from me.*

Take my father, trying to shut me up.

Take Erniel with no sisters. None. They were gunned down within an hour of him bleeding out.

Take Araba's breasts. Her remaining nipple was like pinched, soft lips. A kiss.

I try to stop my legs from quavering but the ligaments, the tendons around my knees have all turned to weak tea.

God in heaven, hold me up. Please.

The prayer works.

God has not heard my whole story yet. In a few minutes, he will leave me in a dilapidated heap, cross me off his list of holy children, but for now some unseen force lets me collect my cutting tools and walk straight towards Josiah's eyes, driving their greasy drill-bits into me. I swing from him at the last instant, face Samuel, the journalist.

'We were wondering if you were going to come. After yesterday.'

What the heck has happened to his fury?

This time, Samuel is watching my hands, his eyes hunting for the audio chip. I glance up. Tamba is peering through his window straight at me. Another wolf in the night, ready to sink his teeth into the back of my neck. He looks away, suddenly self-conscious about his authority. He rolls his chair sideways, swipes at something on a screen. Good. Let him sneak his surveillance. Hide and seek is the game we will play.

Samuel is actually wriggling his fingers in the leather glove. 'Malachi?'

I make a smooth pickpocketing switch. Samuel draws his hands back carefully, my whole truth hidden in the web between his fingers. He steers my bomb towards his ear. I shove my hand into my pocket, press the manual switch.

It's party time. Let's play.

My heart begins to buck like a panic-stricken beast. A sob rises in me. I clip Samuel's toes through fat, frightened tears. The journalist sits very still, listens in utter silence to William, my American ventriloquist. The subtle lines on the edges of his eyes sweep up, make him seem feminine. He bites on his lips. I wait for Samuel's eyes to catch alight with a raging abhorrence. But his face only softens.

I wipe my tears on the sleeve of my purple shirt, glance up at the glass. Eighty eyes turn upwards, track the predator. Tamba's face is still turned away.

Samuel takes the clip from his ear. His eyes hold one thing. A lion's compassion.

'What do you want me to do with it?' He withdraws his feet, presses them together, toe bone to toe bone. 'Do you want me to tell it?'

My chin falls to my chest. My spinal cord pulls a groan up from my throat.

Samuel frowns. 'Yes?'

I nod three times. My father would have said thrice.

Samuel pulls his lion gaze from me. Every one of my muscles is now the strength of Five Roses tea. My bladder twangs like a guitar string, not from the sounds of guns and war, but from the quantum truth that is about to blast me to pieces.

This is not a party. This is my second death.

Samuel presses the audio chip between his palms. He speaks like Jesus on the mount, without an amplifier:

'While Malachi's father read the poem about the king's mistress, a guerrilla lifted Araba's skirt with his bayonet . . .'

His words, my words keep me moving.

'His blade made a shallow cut . . .'

Eulalie's ancient face threatens to come loose from its skeleton. Her breasts reach down her wrinkled belly. There is something shame-faced about her downward-looking nipples. I get to work clipping, but my heavy, heavy heart is too lightly hooked behind my ribs. If it falls to the floor, this is good, for I will be truly dead and not have to listen to Samuel.

'The words burst from his mouth. Yes! They are here!' Samuel chokes. 'They were a suicide bomber's trigger.'

I wait for Samuel's hatred, but I hear only one emotion soaking his words, my words. Samuel is sad.

'They shot the clothes off Araba's body . . .' He stops, rasps through the smoke fumes in his memory. 'Her braids hung over her face.'

'*Shame*, Malachi,' Vicki whispers.

Shame in South African, which means I pity you? Or shame on you, you murderer in party purple, you demon on two legs?

Samuel chokes, 'He killed them all with his loquaciousness.' He bows his head, keeps his hands pressed together as though asking for consideration from God.

As if he is me.

I no longer exist. I have no hatred, no love. Nothing.

'You had no time to think. It happened too quickly.' Samuel pulls his knees to his chest, hugs them tightly. 'I had three weeks.' He shakes his head, stares at his history. 'My camera gave them courage. I should never have filmed those people.' He cradles his head between his elbows. 'But my father always said, "When will I see your work on AAC?"' Samuel rocks like a baby. 'The film made it to live streaming on Hardnews.com. Over forty million hits –' Samuel begins to cry like a child.

Tamba's face is oriented our way. I can't comfort the lion in cage number one.

Vicki tries to stuff sweet, soft words between Samuel's sobs. 'Samuel, don't cry, please.'

All I want to do is whip out my Samsung and say, *Stop crying, Samuel, stop. You just made a terrible, terrible mistake.*

I bend over my bucket, hang upside down, make like I am scratching for a clean towel. Before I can imagine how funny I must look, I press my fingers to my lips, kiss them. Show them to Samuel.

It works. His crying quietens down.

Vicki, unbelievably, doesn't even snigger.

'See, Samuel,' she says gently. 'Even Malachi forgives you.'

As I snap the witch's tough, old-age nails, she breathes like she is climbing up through rubble.

'I should have said nothing,' she mumbles.

She coughs up small stones as I wash her gnarled feet. A tear falls to her shrivelled thigh, the most enormous tear I have ever seen.

Is she crying for the prime minister's wife?

I stare in amazement as more tears fall. How can one old, dry woman create all that water?

Eulalie's tears flood the cracks of her cheeks, run between her empty breasts. I have no choice but to wash her feet, cover up the natural disaster happening on the factory floor.

Please don't cry, Eulalie. My eyes sting as if I have stuck my face into the antiseptic. I extricate the witch's feet, stumble to Vicki.

I secure the leather sheath, but all I see through my tears is a blur of white fingers. I clutch on to them, try to hold them still. I squeeze my clipper blades, feel a shard of something soft fly from the metal. I stare anxiously. Did I hurt her? But Vicki is watching me with the utmost pity. I tear my eyes back to her hands. It looks like all her blood has rushed from her ventricles into her fingertips. Tears stream down the back of my throat. I sniff.

'You were just a kid, really.'

I shake my head. *Fifteen.*

Vicki frowns. 'Fifteen is the dumbest time.'

I growl a refusal. *No, Vicki. Youth is not an alibi.*

But the mermaid is adamant. 'When you're fifteen you can't think of . . .' she searches her mind for the right word in her thesaurus. 'Consequences.' She gives me her feet. 'I mean, that's when I started cutting. Fifteen.'

My eyes climb the keloid ladder running up her shins.

'How old are you, Malachi?' Vicki asks. 'Thirty?'

I nod, surprised.

'So you lived for fifteen years. Died for fifteen. Am I right?'

Save me. I stare into the sweet, glistening mercy of the mermaid's eyes. The crow's croak, I don't know where it comes from. It nearly sounds like, 'Yes.'

Vicki shrugs. 'I know how it feels. How many times have I

149

thought – I'm not joking, a hundred times a day, a hundred times a night – why didn't I just tell someone?' She stares at her bubble toes. 'Why didn't I just . . . I don't know, *speak*?'

I am very, very careful not to look up, but I feel Tamba's stare hacking into my cheek. What happened to his head-banging to surround-sound music?

I rub the soles of Vicki's feet. *Stop staring, Tamba, please.*

Madame Sophie gasps, 'What's wrong with Eulalie?'

I whirl towards the witch. She is slouched against the mesh, no longer weeping. Her damp-granite eyes have turned to soft rabbit fur, like the one that died of fright when a dump dog chased it into our hut. Eulalie's bony shoulders slump as if her ancestors are whipping her from the roof. Her breathing becomes lighter and lighter until she has no need of it.

Is she still alive?

Her grey eyes are wide open, just like the rabbit after its heart attack.

I hit my button.

'What?'

I bang my heart three times.

'Heart attack?' Tamba jumps up, darts from switch to switch. 'No! We can't afford this. I'm calling the doctor's wing.' He uses an emergency-room tone he might have heard on TV. 'Suspected heart attack. BP eighty over sixty. Pulse fifty-seven.' He loses his professional tone. 'What? Umm . . . She looks kind of sleepy . . . A small one? . . . How much?' Tamba adjusts a setting on his keyboard, touches a switch.

Eulalie's entire body jerks like in a mild car collision. Her head whips forwards, hits the metal. Her chest rises and falls. She is breathing.

I give Tamba the thumbs-up, a crude overstatement of how I am feeling.

'We must investigate this subject. That was really not funny.'

Not funny, no, to live with a regret so deep it can strike you dead just by surfacing.

It might be a muscle spasm, or some aftereffect of the ECG. It might be the electric shock. But Eulalie smiles at me.

The next three prisoners talk in troubled tongues about their deed or mine, I cannot guess. But the yellow man gives me his hands eagerly, grins like I just won a ribbon for his team. He says something earnest in his Sudanese dialect. The desert strangler, it seems, is not in the mood to interpret. He sits with his chin sunken into his chest, his hands turned up on his runner's legs. Has he also had some kind of cardiac trouble?

But as I fasten the glove to his cage, he says quietly, 'Life's a swine.' He watches me lop the nails off his sinewy fingers. He shakes his head gravely. 'I will never forget her.'

Oh, no, please. Not more skeletons.

'Sometimes the soldiers took prostitutes on their trips. Then they drank beer and had sex while they stole our food aid and drove it to Adigral.'

I cut into the hard nail on his wedding finger.

'One time, I killed the driver and took the truck. I left the girl in the desert. The way she died, ahhhh.' His voice is parched, like the poor girl in the desert, half dressed, calling for water. He shoves his broad feet into the sheath. 'What must I do with her, Malachi?' He begs, 'Tell me.'

I stare into his desert-sand eyes.

'Give her water, Gibril.'

Did those words come from me?

'It will make her happy.'

They come from the witch. Eulalie's shock treatment seems to have got her in touch with a thirsty prostitute.

'Water?' The desert strangler scans my face for a more convincing commandment.

Yes, give her water, I urge him silently. *Don't make her wait.*

Slow hope flares in his eyes.

I turn my whole body towards Eulalie. *What about me?* I plead silently. *What must I give? Please, tell me.*

By some alchemy, the old witch hears me. She pulls on her rope of hair like she is ringing a church bell from the twelfth century. 'Give them your love, Malachi. They are not free while you are guilty.'

A wave of ice-cold sea breaks over me.

My father. My school friends. I do love them. I do.

'Malachi,' Tamba speaks sternly. 'Are you feeling faint again?'

I shake my head, somehow pull off a tight-lipped grin.

I love you, Hamri.

It's all I can think through the next few prisoners.

I *will* love them, like Eulalie says. It is easy.

I love Hamri's eyes, their unnatural shine whenever he looked at me. I love Araba's neck, the bones delicate but inseparable as she bent over her maths, digging too hard with her pen. I love Kontar's wild laugh as he tore from my grip, clay covered, his bare heels sprinting through the green grass. I even love Erniel, his timorous smile, his long school socks pulled up too high. Cherishing tears leak from my heart, drip down the seam of my yellow trousers. They leave a trail behind me.

Am I imagining it? I stare at the floor. Yes. I see a damp tread

152

from my sneaker. It is not my penis, surely – it is my heart, over-flowing with the love I have not let myself feel since then.

The tooth-extracting Indian is digging at his bellybutton with a fingernail that must have shot out overnight. His poor umbilicus is red and raw already. It tears me back to the present.

Bullshit, Malachi, those drips are not an overflow of lost love. Your valves are just weak, worn out by too much pressure.

The Indian man gouges at his stomach like he is trying to unbutton it to release the truth. I press my switch, point at the Indian's frenzied fingers.

'Stomach cramps?'

No, he's crazy. A small electric shock would do the trick. Instead, I nod at Tamba.

'Any sign of a loose stool?'

I stare at him, incredulous. *How the heck would I know?*

Tamba gets my message.

'Okay, okay, it's not like you can ask him. I'll get Olivia to check his outflow for pathogens. Let's give him a painkiller.'

Good, Tamba, please. Take his pain from him.

I hear the crackle as Tamba connects with Olivia.

'A painkiller antispasmodic to cage number thirteen. Fast-acting, please. It's that mad Indian dude. Malachi says he's got stomach trouble.'

Well, actually it's his secrets.

'Thanks.' Tamba tips his head to my microphone. 'Tell him to drink from his pipe.'

I point at the Indian's feeding tube. He shakes his head, pokes at his bellybutton.

Tamba touches his torture switch. A fine mist falls over the

153

Indian. Before Tamba can even add violence to it, the Indian sucks frantically on his food pipe.

Almost immediately, he goes loose. A silly smile creeps across his fevered face. I hold out a hand, invite him to give me his feet. He lifts them into the glove, strokes the inflamed skin around his bellybutton as if to say, One more day, then I will undo the knot.

I will have to watch him carefully. It is not an antispasmodic this man needs, but an antipsychotic. But a drug such as this might stop him from remembering.

Let him remember everything, this mad, navel-excavating Indian. Let him remember and die free.

The giant seems to overhear what I am thinking.

'One freedom, please.' He slurs a little, barely moving his lips. 'Just this once, pass me by.'

He is sitting on his hands like a child under rebuke. Has he had a stroke? I stare at his mouth. No. It is not hanging slack. I check his musculature. He still looks like Hercules. I glance up at Tamba.

'Please,' the giant begs. 'I just want some peace.'

It is not like him to plead. And he is in a far better state than he was yesterday. I pretend to fiddle with the latch on his cage.

'Tamba's not watching.'

I glance up. The giant is right. Tamba, thank God, has been lulled by my last few groomings to pull out some chewing gum and play a computer game. I can tell by the rapid action of his thumbs. Yes, he is shooting something.

I skip the mournful giant, move to the fat Australian.

Barry looks strangely stunned, as if suffering some aftershock. Did my confession do this to him?

His voice shakes as he speaks. 'I know how it feels to love a girl like you did. This one girl, Zauna. She really knew me.'

He sounds like he is reciting lyrics from a vintage love song by Justin Bieber. Has he heard of him? Yes, without a doubt Barry had Justin Bieber on his sound system. I trim the Australian's flabby hands, feel his sadness pulsing through his soft fingertips.

But I know what he means. Araba was the only one who understood my twisted humour. She knew of my struggle with my father's poetry, the way it kept surfacing in me. She knew of my yearning for her, so vast I could scoop out the insides of the earth leaving only its porcelain skin, take her hand among the dust and start a new universe.

I cannot bring myself to laugh at the fat Australian.

I work my way to Lolie, the young assassin who could find the nought-point-three-millimetre passage through my brain and stop my heart with a high-pressure hiss. But today, she looks like she has drunk from the Indian's painkiller. She lies back with her black hair tickling her shoulders, pretty. I have not had sex with a woman so I can't say, but rather like a film star in a postcoital scene. Today she is almost making music with her mellifluous Congolese language. I drop her wire hatch, let it hang. A strange admiration shines from her pinpoint pupils as she speaks. She got the wrong message about me, surely. Whoever interpreted for Lolie did a very bad job.

I turn to the social worker. *Put Lolie straight. Quickly.*

Andride misunderstands, translates for me.

'Lolie says she doesn't blame you.' He listens to her lilting speech. 'She says she also killed when she was fifteen.'

I shake my head. *No. Sorry. Forgiveness is not that easy.*

The movement of my head has a shocking effect on Lolie. She

155

buries her face in her hands and makes a high, hissing cry, the sound of a tree through an acoustic sensor as it's being chopped down. She clamps her nose and mouth, smothers herself deliberately.

The prisoners click their tongues. 'Lolie. Lolie.'

'Honey . . .' Madame Sophie calls sweetly.

What if she suffocates herself before my eyes? Above us, Tamba shoves against his back rest, stretches his arms in the air.

Do something, I command the social worker with my eyes.

Andride tries the tone of a terrorist. 'Fight, Lolie. Fight.'

Still she will not breathe.

'Shoot, Lolie! Or they will shoot you.'

Lolie whines like a tree amplified thirty thousand times.

'Lolie?' I try to say. I am surprised by the deepness of the sound that comes out. It is gentle, yet masculine. Lolie drops her hands from her mouth, stares at me. I shine my compassion into her kohl eyes.

Andride is right. They broke you, Lolie.

Lolie's strange chuckle sounds more like a hiccup.

Upstairs, Tamba walks his roller chair to the window, exhausted by the violent coup he has just accomplished with his thumbs. I rap on Lolie's cage, make a soft clang. She catches her erupting laugh, swallows it. I pull on the leather strap, gently tighten it.

Tamba turns a slow, bored circle on his roller wheels. I clip Lolie's nails with the utmost gentleness. She bows her head, hides her smile from Tamba's screen. Her smile is exhausting for her, I think, for it keeps falling to the floor. She picks it up and slings it back on, even sweeter.

What is this? Lolie, the child soldier finding happiness?

Lolie's smile is like a disease. It sets off a whole lot of unpractised smiles among us.

'I've never seen her smile before,' someone murmurs.

'First time.'

'First time.'

Tamba must have caught the contagion of happiness on his screens. He skids back to the glass. 'What's happening, Malachi?'

I glare back at him, fake deep outrage. *These pigs*, I shout silently. 'Are they laughing at you?'

I nod, a ridiculous, huffy figure.

Tamba lynches me with a grin, joins in what he imagines to be crowd mockery. 'Sorry,' he mutters insincerely.

I scowl until he ducks his head and finds something to do on the far side of his DJ desk. I shut Lolie's cage, get away from the lethal weapon of her new, childish smile. I stomp to Shikorina, keep up my façade of fury in case Tamba should come back to double-check on my unhappiness.

Shikorina gives me her long fingers with their circular blue scars.

'We are born from Satan. You and me.'

After the sweet assassin, Shikorina's words are a cruel ambush.

'We come from the place the devil eats bones. The place of graves.'

Maybe, Shikorina, you are right. Or maybe, just maybe, we made a terrible mistake.

Terrible. The intensity catches on my heart like the sharp end of a bone. I try to breathe through it, but it stabs my lungs like pleurisy. Which bone is it?

The blessing bone that says mistakes can be forgiven? Or the curse bone that says sin remains sin; I am spawn of Satan?

Shikorina takes back her hands, lifts her feet like they are water-logged. As I bend over them, Eulalie's words travel slowly down

157

a broken-down telephone of prisoners, 'The children . . . The children . . .'

The words come in wisps, until Lolie speaks in jagged English: 'The children forgive you.'

I jerk up straight. Is the message for me?

But Lolie practises her crazy, crooked smile, holds up three fingers. 'Three.'

The pleurisy pierces my ribs. No. Not for me. I killed more than three.

Shikorina turns her ear to the mesh, like the truth is caught in the wires. 'Is it true, Malachi?'

I shrug. *Maybe.*

But maybe is not enough. Shikorina waits, still watching me. She is asking the wrong person, she should be asking God.

But I have seen Shikorina's gentleness when she touches her ghost children. She took them into the sunshine and stroked them, I know. She held them close at night when the white wolves chased them in their dreams. But her mind cracked down the middle. Broke in half, like Lolie's.

I can't say, but one thing is for sure. Shikorina's children still love the mother she half was.

I hold up two hands, exaggerate. Shove her children towards her, wholeheartedly, not half. *They still love you, Shikorina.*

Shikorina crashes back against the mesh, wraps her octopus arms around the three of them. She is careful not to crush them with a love so powerful it could accelerate the wash-spin cycle of the earth, make plants grow at the rate of three centimetres a second. I free her feet quickly. She murmurs to her children in soft decibels of love as she rolls from side to side, unconscious of the wire cutting into her bony shoulders. I see she has torn a strip of skin from her spine. I will have to keep an eye on the raw spot.

I lock Shikorina's cage with a hope that makes me dizzy. I pick up my bucket, nearly skip a few steps. I stop, compose myself, walk more demurely to the trolley.

What if the witch is more sane than any High Court judge? What if Shikorina's children still love her, all three?

Maybe I just got the lucky bone in my throw. In Bhajo they call it summudiye. Maybe there is a perfect reason to party.

I lift my key card to the door, unlock it.

Manners, Malachi. Hamri had a way of saying it so sweetly.

I turn to face the prisoners. I nod like a manservant, smile my unpractised smile for the second time since I told the whole truth.

Thank you.

* * *

I drink water from the bathroom tap, point my penis gently at the porcelain. I have finally found some friends.

The thought jolts my body. Malachi, are you mad?

I flick my penis roughly back inside my zip. I must be shell-shocked, my limbic brain veering between love and desperation. As moody as a bus driver, my mother used to say. I pull my belt too tight. The prisoners will be back in their old jails in six months. In six months I will have a tongue, dress up in the lie that I never lost it. I will wear it like a cool, classic shirt and tie, buy a matric certificate, get a briefcase like Hamri's, but with new, smooth straps. I will change my name in case my grandfather from Kattra hears I am still living.

I rinse my face. Smother myself briefly with my hand towel. No. I will carry my history like children buried in cement.

Right now, I'd rather die.

This is a sentiment I go to lunch with.

I sit on the bench with Shikorina's children pulling on my ears. This is how audacious my imagination has become. Janeé is slapping down beige soup with shattered bits floating in it. They slip like tiny fish down my throat. I try to catch and chew, but they are too slimy.

'Leek soup,' Janeé explains.

Ah, leeks. Those long pale fingers with hairy ends.

Tamba picks up his spoon, sighs. 'We're lucky to get vegetables this far out.'

I have never knowingly eaten a leek. I have seen them in the mega market, trying to climb off the shelf and scuttle away on legs that look a lot like nasal hairs. As I scoop the swimming pieces into my mouth, Janeé slams down another plate. The first half of lunch is innocent. But this? A chicken's breast with a sprig of parsley tucked like a flower behind a dead woman's ear. The breast is dusted with light brown spice, but is a victim of murder nonetheless.

Olivia notices my consternation. 'Good protein,' she warns me.

There is something of the murderess in Olivia under pressure. I can't suppress a sigh. Smothering child soldiers. Poisoning prime ministers' wives. Torturing chickens for eating pleasure. These are some of the things broken humans get up to.

Stop joking, Malachi. It's really not funny. I am like Shakespeare's Earl of Gloucester, living in a ditch with his eyes plucked out, still making dark jokes. Where will it get me?

I swallow. Some damned relief.

I cut into my breast. Oh, no. I swing my eyes from my plate, fix them on some static lifting Olivia's fringe.

Olivia turns to check the wall behind her head. She hits her fringe like there might be a beetle crawling in it. 'What is it?' she demands.

Tamba saves me from the awkward situation. 'Urgh. I can't eat this. It's still pink.' He pushes his plate away.

I can't help smiling. Yes! My comrade.

My approval lends grist to Tamba's whining. 'I need a microwave.'

Janeé frowns, insulted. 'You're not allowed in that wing.'

'You take it, then.'

Meirong drops her spoon so her leek soup spatters. 'Tamba, there are more important things to worry about right now.' She stands up. 'Malachi. Come with me.' She lifts the solo sailor's lunch from the trolley.

I stand up, sidle away from my plate. Meirong plants the tray in my hands. 'Can you do this without spilling?'

I stare down at it. The solo sailor has survived a storm at sea to eat leek soup. I reach for a clean plate, cover her chicken.

'Wait,' Janeé says. She pours red raspberry juice into a polystyrene cup and fixes on a lid.

I balance the solo sailor's lunch, follow Meirong through the noisy door to the centre of the rig. I pant up the stairs after her. Eight days without working out, and now I must carry leeks to a stowaway up fifty flights of stairs. It's time to start running on the spot. Meirong's bum is beautiful, I know this from the fleshy things that normal men appreciate. Two papayas rubbing together, joined by a bridge of skin. Two halves of the brain, it might as well be, joined by the corpus callosum.

Meirong pulls ahead. 'Malachi, don't tell me you're not fit.'

I give her a disdainful look, skip up the next flight of stairs. Even with her hands free, I breathe against her back, force her to go faster as we climb the steel jungle gym towards the sun. At the door to the deck, I stand casually, as if the sweat is not making dark patches on my purple shirt. Meirong shines delicately, refuses to pant in front of me. She lifts a pink lanyard from her neck. Unlocks the aperture to the sky.

The sun pours through my crown, shines into my eyes like I am its long-lost son. The sea air is lightly salted, cool. Beautiful. It floods my blood vessels, makes them rich, rich, rich as I follow Meirong along the deck. I breathe in, almost dizzy. But as I walk past the helicraft landing pad, the sun starts to beat my head with a stick. I walk after Meirong's papayas swinging one-two, one-two towards a storeroom with three old-fashioned padlocks and a manual key slot.

Meirong unhooks a bunch of metal keys from her waist. 'Lock the door behind you when you go in. Lock every one of these padlocks on the way out.' She points at the old orange lifeboat held by a steel A-frame. 'Hang these keys on the first engine. Do you see it?'

I nod at Meirong, set the tray down at my feet.

She points back at the door to the jungle gym. 'I've left the main entrance open. I'll lock up after you. We can't afford to be sloppy with security.'

Yes, Mrs Hitleress.

I knock on the metal door. Meirong ducks away, darts past the tower towards the management wing. I unlock the padlocks, turn the copper key. I pick up my tray, nudge the door open with the toe of my sneaker.

*

The girl lies uncovered on a metal bed, her body as thin as a torn sheet of canvas. Her eyes are open, the luminous green of underwater algae. She tries to spy past my body.

'Why does she run from me?' Her voice is cracked by sea salt.

The small room is bare, except for her bed and a plastic crate, upended to create a table. On the floor, a scattering of rusted nails and a trampled Texan cigarette packet lie like ghostly remains of the oil-drilling days. I step over a torn weightlifter's magazine. Go closer with my tray. The girl's hair is as white as Madame Sophie's, but it is frayed by deluges of rain and blistering winds. The sun has peeled her nose and cheeks to a deep raw pink; burnt bands of blisters on her forearms and shins. She wears loose boxer shorts that must have belonged to her father. A dirty white shirt hangs open at her neck. The girl has no sign of breasts, as if her fight for survival might have frightened them away. A huge white tooth hangs on a leather strip against her blistered chest.

I put the tray on the crate, kneel next to the bed.

Frances sits up slowly. 'Thanks.' She sounds American. A relative of William, my digital voicebox. 'Are you going to talk to me?'

I stare at her sheepishly.

'Oh no. Not you, too. Romano's very kind, but everything I ask him he says, "I'm sorry I can't say."'

Romano said *sorry* to this little girl who looks like driftwood? I point at my mouth, shake my head stupidly. There is no point in trying to mime, Tongue. Cut.

'That Chinese woman, what is she going to do with me?'

I sigh, get to my feet. She grabs my thumb, pulls at it feebly. 'Do you have a satellite phone?'

Oh no. Not another plea for rescue.

'My black box is under the navigation table.' The sun has polished

163

her eyes to the thickness of a magnifying glass. 'Can you get it from my yacht?'

I point towards the door. *The lady who ran away?* I wag my finger to and fro, mime to Frances: *She's the boss. Sorry.*

'Do you have a cell phone, maybe?' she persists desperately.

I shake my head, deny the thousands of luxurious words hanging in my pocket.

'What about a pen?' She pulls on my hand with her measly strength. 'Please.'

I have no choice but to sink to my knees. Frances drags her leather string through her knotted hair. She writes on the skin of my forearm. *0845691233.* The numbers come up pale from the huge incisor.

'This is my mother's number. Please call her for me.' Frances squeezes my wrist with the little strength she has left. 'Will you?'

I can't bring myself to pull away from her feeble grip. I make a rolling action with my free hand. *Tomorrow, they will call her. Surely.*

Frances tries to smile. 'Tomorrow might not come.'

What does she mean?

She holds out her palm, shows me the serrated tooth. 'It was my father's,' she croaks. 'He got it from a great white.'

I'm afraid I can't share her love for the evil-looking thing.

'I took it off him.' She loops the necklace clumsily over her head. 'I had to roll him into the sea. He was so heavy.' Her arms fall limply, as if remembering the weight of her dead father.

I force myself to my feet, allow myself a small, sorry grunt. My own arms hang from the weight of her mother's phone number. The poor woman must be frantic, her prayers fluttering from her lips like torn strips of spinnaker over thousands of sea miles.

A hoarse, hollow sound issues from the girl's mouth.

'I need my mother, please.'

I don't think the sailor girl can cry. It looks like her tear ducts are too dry. I hunt around, find an empty glass beneath the bed. This child needs water so she can at least weep for her own mother! This is thoroughly inhumane. This ancient rig is not exactly a five-class hotel, but the least they can do is see to her basic needs.

Damn you, Meirong.

I sign for the girl to lift up her torn shirt.

Fear radiates from her glassy eyes. 'Take it off?'

I shake my head, mortified. *Show me your bellybutton*, is all I want to say. I lift my purple shirt and pinch the skin on my stomach, show her how it snaps back.

Frances gets my meaning. She lifts up her shirt, pulls at the skin near her bellybutton. It sinks back very, very slowly. Definite dehydration. The girl needs a drip.

I utter a worried, 'Aah,' like there's going to be trouble unless we fix this. But right now, my only remedy is fake raspberry juice. I put the polystyrene cup in her hands, close her fingers around it. She takes a tiny sip of the syrup. Then she sucks it greedily, leaves a stain of red around her raw lips. Good.

Leek soup? I gesture like an insensitive butler.

Frances turns her face away.

Just try.

I press the soup bowl into her hands, insistent. Frances takes a little sip, then slugs back the glutinous liquid. She closes her eyes with the ecstasy of eating slimy white scraps of a far-fetched vegetable in the middle of the sea. Suddenly she doubles over, convulsing. I grab for a red bucket someone has left for her to do her ablutions in. She retches into it, a pinkish fluid. I shut my eyes, fight the sea-sickness kicking at my oesophagus.

I search the room. The child doesn't even have toilet paper, for goodness' sake. I tear a strip of cloth from the edge of her sheet and wipe her mouth with it. The girl steals a corner of the cloth, wipes her shark tooth clean. I snatch up the lunch tray. A growl starts deep within me, propels me to the door. Whatever happens, Meirong is going to hear about this.

I balance the tray on one hand, turn the copper key, but Frances is clambering to her feet, coming after me. I lock the door again quickly, sweep to the other end of the room, try to draw her from the door. Where the heck is Romano? I am not trained for this. The girl sways against the door, eyes my bunch of keys. Is she going to attack me?

I mime pouring water into the glass, lift it to my lips. I point outside like I was actually just going to look for a garden tap, with a row of impatiens perhaps, those pink-and-white flowers that bloom without thinking twice.

Frances shuffles slowly back to her bed. She lies back, exhausted from her flash of resistance.

'Where's Romano?' she says accusingly. 'At least he speaks to me.' She rolls towards the wall, shows me a raw, emaciated shoulder. Her sigh, I can hear, has not a molecule of moisture in it.

I unlock the door, swing it wide enough to let the sun hunt her down one more time. I want so badly to say sorry. The rattle of the spoon on the soup plate surely won't communicate my apology, but my deep, sorry sigh might.

I shut the heavy door, shut the nineteen-year-old child behind three barbarous steel locks.

I scurry across the deck and cross the little bridge to Romano's lifeboat. I hang the keychain on the first engine, just as Meirong told me to. Romano's snore is loud enough to be considered a serious security threat. He lies fast asleep on a thin mattress, still fully dressed in his Nadras Oil outfit. I stretch into the boat, touch Romano's boot. He is on his knees in a split second, his Kalashnikov pointing straight at my heaving heart. I crash back against a metal mount with my butler's tray, face the deadly glare of the AK97. My lungs have locked shut.

Romano lowers the barrel, flings the rifle beneath a bench.

Finally I wheeze out.

'How is she?' he asks.

I open my mouth, sweep a shaking hand up and out.

'She sicked it up?'

I nod. I stab at a vein on the inside of my arm.

'I know. She needs a drip! I told Meirong, but she's done nothing.' He shakes his head angrily, speaks my mind for me. 'It's not right!'

Romano climbs deeper into the lifeboat and throws out socks, a jersey, two tins of sweetcorn. He releases a long string of Kool-Aid sachets. Then he jerks on a massive drum and carries it to the back of the boat, grunting. He whips the keys off the propeller, shoves them into his pocket. This is Romano's midnight, but he is sacrificing his sleep to help the girl prisoner. I nod at him approvingly. A mutual conspiracy leaps up between the security man and me. Even the sun softens its megalomania, gives us the privacy to agree, without words, that Romano and I must somehow try to save the poor child.

I let myself into the rig, shut the door behind me. The sun was too brutal on the surface, but I miss it, I miss it as soon as I turn my back on it. My heart sinks towards my shoes as I descend the metal stairs, my journey marked by the thousands of rivets I climb past. I pause at the door to the management wing. *Private. Keep Out.*

The door is digitally sealed but I want to shove on it, barge in and shout with my Samsung, 'Look, that girl up there is very sick! She needs fluids. And she needs to go home, she is extremely upset. Can someone see to it?'

Don't blow it, Malachi.

The door to the maintenance wing yowls as I open it.

I pass Olivia in her laboratory, squeezing a drop from a pipette. One fat tear that the solo sailor could not manage. I pass the empty canteen, still jangling with irritation from our lunch, reach the spiral stairs leading up to Tamba's surveillance station. He has put the sound of his overland attack up high. I shut my eyes, steady myself against the stertorous blasts.

Romano nearly shot me up there in the sunshine.

I fumble for my key card, fall through the door, escape the fresh ammo, the flying grit, the stream of machine-gun bullets zinging past my ears.

* * *

They are waiting. The second row of prisoners are clicking their long nails, licking their teeth, loosening their tongues, getting ready to tell me what they think of my truth. But the first row were strangely kind to me. Will these ones hate me?

Number twenty-one is the white Zimbabwean with the vitamin deficiency.

'Junk,' he says with his chipped teeth. He gives me his hands. 'You were junk on love.' The funny thing is he sounds drunk with those teeth. 'I was junk like you . . .' He tries to say something about his felony, but I wish he would shut up. He sounds too absurd for the subject of either murder or love.

I nod politely, check his wires and his pipes.

Was I drunk on teenage love?

As I finish the next prisoner, Tamba must have lost his virtual life up there because he jumps to his feet and roams restlessly around his room. He throws himself in his chair, shows the underside of his shoes as he hitches them onto his control desk. Risky, I think. What if he accidentally kicks a switch and kills off a few precious assets?

As I work down the aisle, the priest killer crouches like he wants to head-butt me to the floor. His teeth are tightly gritted, his demeanour, one might say, nowhere near what one might expect of a lift attendant. The Moroccan looks like he could pounce on his Japanese tourists and rip their McDonald's lunches straight from their stomachs. I put my bucket down a little distance from him.

He shoves his melted hands into the glove. I see they are shaking.

'*I* am the one who hung on.' Cinders crack inside him. The heat bursts his teardrops before they can fall. 'Now he won't let me go,' he rasps. 'I hung on to him. Now he hangs on to me.'

I hold his trembling hands still, clip his melted fingers. I cover his hands with my white cloth, squeeze them as if to starve them of oxygen.

He pulls his fingers from the glove, begs me, 'How can I stop him from coming to me?'

I turn towards the top of the aisle, point towards the old witch. *Ask Eulalie.*

It is Gibril, the desert strangler, who picks up my meaning. He

169

tells the yellow man who tells the prisoner next to him. The priest killer's question lands in Vicki's lap.

She says clearly, 'What do you think, Eulalie? Mohammed, the Muslim oke, he still wants to kill the priest.'

Eulalie gazes down the aisle, finds Mohammed with her smoky eyes. She covers her ears, pulls her senses away from her rowdy friends. The prisoners quieten down.

Her words float down the aisle from the prisoners' mouths.

It is the desert strangler who carries them to us. 'She says you are brothers. You and Father Rayan.'

The priest killer gasps. 'How does she know his name?'

Eulalie taps her fists together. Her words make their way down to us. 'The Christian and the Muslim, they both worshipped the wrong God.'

Did those words come from the tooth-pulling Indian? Surely not. He can't speak English, can he?

Eulalie speaks again, faintly. Charmayne, the big beauty, picks up the phrase from the desert-strangling Ethiopian, 'God is who we are?' Charmayne snorts loudly. 'Did you say that, Eulalie?' She smacks the cage with her huge hands. 'That's rubbish!'

The priest killer slowly unravels his fighting stance. He hangs his head so his shining fringe falls across his face like a curtain. I clip his toes with a lump in my throat the size of a Bible. With each cut it feels like I am ripping out an angry page.

Rubbish. Charmayne is right.

Does he believe that shit?

I clip crudely, shove the priest killer's feet back to him. But my fury is wasted on him. Mohammed wraps his arms around some unseen figure, welds his heart against some imaginary chest. He is busy making friends with a plump Catholic priest. This is way too eerie, even for this cursed, blessed place. The priest has become his invisible friend. The entire hall makes soft sounds of amazement. My hands are shaking. My throat feels ragged, cut by my soundless shout, *God is who we are?*

Never. It can't be.

I am grateful to reach the big beauty, who is as scornful as me. She hugs her muscular thighs, shakes her head bitterly. 'There's no God in *me*, Malachi.'

I lock the glove to her cage.

Charmayne leans closer, hisses, 'Do you want to know the truth?'

Oh, no. Rather keep it. Please.

'They were standing near the parapet. I heard them whispering.' Her hair sticks up like two woollen horns on her head. 'Pete said, "Let's cut Charmayne out." Bongi said, "Yes."' Her lips seem to swell as if the truth is poisoning them. It flies out like a swarm of marauding bees, 'I pushed them.'

Oh God. Here is the God she is not.

'I pushed them. I did!'

Oh, Charmayne. I am so, so sorry. My clippers hang feebly in my fingers. I feel their Versace suits against her skin, the echo of their living breath, the warmth of their living blood as she shoved.

Tamba interrupts, 'Malachi? Is everything okay?'

I nod casually, resume my duties.

'Watch out for that one.'

I glance sharply at him. Is this about Dominic?

'From here, she's a man-eater. I mean, on my monitor.'

I refuse to smile at him, sink to a buddy-buddy kind of sexism. As I start on Charmayne's feet, a strange refrain flutters down the aisle. It starts softly with Eulalie, flits across to Madame Sophie.

'They were gay . . .'

'They were gay . . .'

'The architects, they loved each other,' the desert strangler says clearly.

'Gay, like lovers?' Charmayne shakes her magnificent, horned head. 'Never. Bongi was married.'

I free her feet. Charmayne clambers to her mighty knees.

'Eulalie,' she demands, 'what do you see?'

Eulalie stares at the space above Charmayne's head like she is watching a movie.

'Eulalie?' Madame Sophie prompts.

'They are wearing gold suits. They are very, very happy.'

'Ooh.' Vicki embellishes, 'Glittery, golden suits.'

Charmayne covers her breasts like there are cameras clicking, catching her in a naked act of forgiveness.

Her voice catches with grief, 'You're teasing me.' She turns her smooth, beautiful back on me. But I don't see her expanse of dusky smooth skin. I don't see her vertebrae.

I see Araba's lovely breasts as she bares them to me. Plush they are, perfect cocoa-infused fruits, their silken skin topped by a chocolate ripple, the place to put one's thumb to open it. But these nipples are not torn open by machine guns, they are soft like the ribbon they use to wrap gifts. I blink my eyes, try to refuse Araba's gift of her glorious young breasts. I am thirty years old, please.

But it is the boy before the massacre she is smiling at.

Araba is alive, still flowering. Nothing can touch her, only me, if I want to.

I want to. I want to, but not in the way an ordinary man might. I want to stroke her nipple as soft as a butterfly's wing, press my thumb on it as if I created it. I want to cup her perfect breasts and imagine it was I who healed the blown-apart flesh.

Let me make it better, Araba, please.

Charmayne is digging her thumbs into her eyes, trying to rub out the ghosts in their glittering suits. I leave her to battle with her spirits, float through several groomings in the company of Araba's heavenly breasts.

As I work closer to Madame Sophie, I feel her staring intently, an unflattering platinum strip exposed in her eyes. Can she see Araba's breasts?

By the time I reach her, Madame Sophie's eyes are bulging. I am no doctor, but I have read this could be a sign of a thyroid deficiency. How the heck do I mime popping eyes to Tamba?

I set my bucket on the floor before her. *Stop staring, Madame Sophie.*

Upstairs, Tamba is glancing down at us, starting to pack up. I have no choice but to bow my head, lop off a long white arc she must have cleaned with her teeth.

'Do you see?' Her blue eyes are polar lights from the place where the sun shines all day and all night. She whispers, 'Do you see, Malachi?'

I see what she sees, a row of heroin-fed prostitutes lying on white beds, their transparent drip sacs gleaming above them. A moody golden light caresses the scene, warms my aching elbows, my knees as I rub my white towel across Madame Sophie's photosensitive skin.

She lies back against the mesh, so still it's as if her central nervous system has stopped functioning.

Across the aisle, Eulalie's voice holds a pure, cracked sweetness, 'They are clear, Madame Sophie. As clear as diamonds.'

Madame Sophie moves only her eyes. *Is* she paralysed?

'Your dead girls are free.'

Seriously? Gold suits and sparkling nymphs?

But a blush suffuses Madame Sophie's pale skin. A feathery smile touches her lips.

Josiah laughs as if choking on his own clotted grease. Some of the prisoners cough in strange sympathy.

Josiah snorts, 'You're lying, Eulalie.' But his scarred eyes smoulder with some strange fear.

I squeeze his furry fingers into my glove, punish him gently.

He stares at me, says slyly, 'What of your *mother,* Malachi?'

I clutch my chest, wheeze through the bullet wound.

He hits me while I am still reeling, 'Is she free?'

I sink to my knees, rock like a brain-damaged patient in an asylum. Josiah's words have been hiding in the lining of my brain, malignant as a cancer, corrupting the cells of my interstitial membranes. He found them, the devil, he stitched them together. I rock on the bones of my bum, my only memento of the man who stood here a moment ago.

Eulalie's shout is like a sorcerer's whip. 'Josiah!'

Josiah's laughter crashes to the metal floor.

Eulalie points her crooked finger at him. 'Your mother was Seleka. From the village of Bambari.'

'Oh. Oh. Oh,' Vicki gasps behind me. 'Josiah.'

Josiah's black moustache seems to tear off his lip. His hairy hands fly up to catch it.

The hips of a thin donkey, I rock on them.

Eulalie's tone is calmer now, matter-of-fact as if she is reporting the weather on the day that he did it, 'You sent your soldiers in.'

Josiah rams his forehead into the cruel mesh. Harder and harder, over and over as if he is painting the walls of his cave with red. I shut my eyes. That might be me screaming. Eulalie speaks as if she is describing the strength of the wind, the chances of rain, the size of the hole in the ozone over Antarctica.

'You were a sweet baby, she knows this. He taught you to hate.'

Josiah smashes his face into the floor of the cage, simulating the shock treatment he received on Monday. Eulalie shouts like a thunderclap, 'Josiah!'

Josiah stops.

'Your mother forgives you.'

Josiah breaks his nose on his excretion plate. He smashes his head against the left side, the right side of the cage, like Hellboy the Seventh before he tore free and demolished New Orleans. The five-inch bolts on the floor shiver.

'Malachi, stop him!' Vicki shrieks.

I scramble to my feet, hit the button of my intercom. Tamba appears after a few long moments. Half the prisoner portraits behind him are already black screens. He sounds irritated, like a shopkeeper locking up. 'What?' He watches Josiah batter his head against the mesh. 'Oh-h-h,' he breathes.

'Stop him!' Vicki shouts.

'Blood. Blood. Blood,' Tamba repeats, hunting for the right reflex.

Yes! This is not red paint.

'Fuck. Fuck. Fuck.'

Hurry up!

'What must I do? Shock him?'

Eulalie starts to sing a soothing song to Josiah. 'Sou-al-lé, Souale . . .'

Josiah slows in his effort to smash himself up. Tamba reaches for a switch.

I thrust a hand up to the window. *Wait!*

'Souale-e-e,' Josiah sings a harsh, broken song with Eulalie.

I don't know the language, but I know what it means. It is the unrequited love of a mother for her son.

Tamba is still watching me for an opinion. I conduct him with a reassuring flourish, float my fingers down and out. A gentle ending to a cacophonous climax.

But he remains wary, 'He's going to need an antiseptic.'

I roll my wrist, make a tumbleweed motion that means, *tomorrow*.

Ayenka, they say in Bhajoan.

'You reckon?'

I glance again at Josiah. He is crying some of the blood off his cheeks. I nod like I am absolutely certain.

'Nuh uh, Malachi. You're getting soft.'

I turn up my life-lines to the window. *Please.*

'No. We can't take a chance.'

A rush of water sprays into Josiah's cage. Tamba hits another switch, usurps the role of conductor, but his instruments are not quiet cloth and a pair of nail clippers. They are computer-controlled torture fluids. Antiseptic mist floats off the spray, sears my eyes. I skip out of range. Madame Sophie covers her eyes and whines. Josiah submits to the icy rain pumped from the sea. He turns his face towards the nozzles, lets the red run to pink from his crisscross lacerations. He holds his hands up to the freezing chemical spray. Josiah cries and cries and cries.

Cry, Josiah, cry. Of all people on earth, you have reason to grieve.

Tamba is fascinated by the terrible cleansing. 'Why did he go mad like that?'

Thick oily sobs burgeon inside me.

Mother, how did you die?

The pressure of my sobs is hurting my chest, swelling so huge they could splinter my ribs right before Tamba's eyes. I pick up my bucket, use the compassion on Vicki's face to breathe in through the pain, out.

'Shhh, Josiah. Easy,' she says.

Her compassion, it seems, is not for me.

I stare at the mermaid with what must be wonder in my eyes. You are lovely.

You are lovely, Vicki.

I drop my falconer's glove on the trolley. Lay my clipper carefully next to it. I carry my bucket towards the metal door.

Lovely.

A magic word to smother the volcano in me.

I make it through the door, run down the corridor sloshing antiseptic. I throw the bucket down, swerve into my living quarters. I hide inside the cubicle of white tiles and sob rich mother's milk. Thick, it must be white, for I see no blood, no old engine oil streaking the tiles. It must be milk, for this spring of thick wild comfort, it comes from my mother.

I hope, I only hope it is the milk of forgiveness.

* * *

I pull off my party shirt and my lemon-flavoured trousers. Strip naked.

Tamba shouts through the door, 'Malachi, what happened in there? I need a report!'

I turn on the hot tap, create clouds of steam to say, Sorry. Can't answer.

The steam bumps me like white clouds. I roam the sky, search for my mother's warm breast. Is she up there somewhere above the equator? Does she blame me?

I hold my hands up to the hot, gushing stream, feel the sun peel them like the sailor-girl's skin. I spin the tap off. Turn on the cold, thrust my hands into the ice. This is no soft-breasted cumulonimbus now, just a cruel solution of snow from the North or South Pole, I can only guess. I take the correction just like Josiah did, grateful for the pain.

I dry myself gently, the skin on my fingers purple and stiff. Pull on the party clothes again. I have no choice, these are my cleanest garments. If I am to live another day as the maintenance man, I need to find a way to do my laundry.

Janeé has made us Christmas dinner. I stare at it. Glistening fatty meat the same consistency as hippo, interspersed with yellow chunks that could be tinned pineapple. This is exactly what my mother made for us on Christmas day! She begged my uncle for hippo, harassed him if necessary to feed us real meat on the day the Holy Spirit was born from his mother's hips. But the pineapple always gave me a tingly feeling in my mouth. It was too sweet, too acidic. It made my ears ring.

'I gave them all a shower after you left,' Tamba says quietly. 'It was time, anyway. Their hair especially, so they don't develop nits.' He whispers like the Holy Spirit, harassing me. 'I need to know what happened with number forty. What made that guy flip?'

I stonewall Tamba, chew on a yellow chunk. The pineapple stings my palate, blocks and unblocks my ears. I shove my fork into a piece of pork, but it slides into the gravy river.

Tamba bumps me with his shoulder like a schoolboy bully. 'Tell me.'

I spiral my knife at my ears, mime the sideways horns of a wild goat.

Josiah's crazy, okay? Don't give me grief.

Tamba stares at my purple hands, tries to colour-match them with the rest of me. He can't decide if he is imagining it. 'Okay, cool, don't get defensive.'

Defensive! If only he knew the knives, the fires, the bullets I have had to face while traversing the aisles just below his nostrils. This time, I spike my hippo successfully. Chew it with relish. An unreasonable giggle bubbles up in me. My world is blown open by a plastic Samsung, and here I am sitting in my last clean shirt, eating Christmas dinner with the best appetite I have had since I set foot on this rig.

Janeé is a shipwreck today. She is prodding her pork around her plate, flicking her pineapple chunks and listing, if this is the word for teetering ships. She leans to one side, her weight on one hand. The bench she is sitting on seems to tip.

Meirong slips onto the other side and sighs, a whimsical sound for a woman wearing a shattered windscreen. 'Have you prepared a plate for the girl, Janeé?'

Janeé nods. 'Yes.'

Meirong spoons the gravy like soup. 'Romano will take supper for the two of them.'

I wave at Meirong, capture her tired eyes. She looks up, surprised. I point up, towards the deck. Mime imaginary hair falling in blonde streaks.

'Frances?'

I tap my lips, point at the jug of water on the trolley.

'Thirsty?' Meirong guesses.

This is the first time Meirong and I have tried charades. I dig a nail into a vein inside my elbow.

Meirong sits up straight, snaps a shield over her eyes.

'I know. I know. She needs a drip. We'll fly her out as soon as the search party has passed. Our satellite shield is fifteen miles, but they could spot us from the air or sea. Until then . . .' Fear kidnaps her breath for a second. 'The girl can only see you and Romano.'

Romano appears in the doorway as if Meirong summoned him. She spins guiltily, points at the food trolley. 'There we are, Romano.'

'She's getting worse. She's very sick.'

'Malachi was just saying.'

'It's dangerous.'

'What's *dangerous*, Romano, is what Mr Carreira thinks.' Meirong leaps to her feet, drops some plates in Romano's arms. Romano dances a little, sidesteps.

'Watch out! Hot.' Janeé flicks a dish towel from her shoulder and struggles up. She stuffs it beneath the crockery.

'In two days we operate,' Meirong says, ignoring the fact that she just burnt his wrists.

Romano sucks in a sudden breath. He nods like an obsequious waiter at the Wimpy.

Meirong sits down before her Christmas dinner, turns her small, bossy back on him. Romano shoots me a look over her head that says, *Cruel bitch.* Meirong swings to intercept it, but Romano is gone.

She jabs her spoon at me. 'You and Romano are not here to save lost sailors.'

Too cowardly to confront a war vet, she is taking her shit out on me.

'What exactly are you here for? *What,* Malachi?'

How do you expect me to answer, you shitting idiot?

I lift my bum off my seat, open my mouth wide. 'Uugghh!'

I point inside my mouth, threaten her with the never-before-seen stump of my tongue.

Meirong grabs on to Janeé's shoulder, holds her spoon up like a shield. Tamba begins to laugh, half delighted, half frightened that the lion might ignore the whip and eat the pretty trainer in lycra.

I sit down, shut my mouth. Janeé begins to gurgle, then a hurricane of laughter blows against her huge hull so she tilts alarmingly. The pendulum tips. Janeé snatches at the table, but she misses. I hear the thump of her shoulder as it hits the rig. Her legs try to cartwheel over her head, but their weight drags them back. Her pointed boots with silver buckles sway next to Meirong's head. The table, I am glad to say, conceals the territory beneath her dress. Meirong pins Janeé's knees together – saves her dignity while Tamba and I jump up and lower Janeé's legs to the rig. Meirong falls forward and lands on Janeé's hip, sits there like the cook is a tranquil park bench. Meirong begins to laugh in a high musical trill, the sound of a fairy who has drunk too much nectar. Tamba takes her hand and pulls her to her feet, honking with laughter. A strange sound issues from me. It is deep, yet open-hearted, arrestingly masculine. It is me, Malachi, laughing a mature man's happy laugh, no trace of stones, no grit, no globules of grease caught in it.

I kneel behind Janeé and push with all my might while Meirong and Tamba pull on her hands. Janeé gets her thighs beneath her hips, struggles up. The world is right again.

Janeé sits carefully on the metal bench, holds on tightly this time, smothering her smile. 'Look what you did, Malachi.'

Meirong nods, sniffing. 'Yes, your fault, Malachi.'

Tamba wipes his nose, an old snorter's reflex.

Olivia walks into this aftermath. She stops dead and stares at me, still on my knees. 'What's happening?'

I get up and take my place at the table.

Meirong sniffs up a trickle of happy mucous. 'Uh . . .' she falters.

Tamba says, 'Malachi got angry and he kind of . . . *roared*.'

Olivia's laugh stops at her big bunny teeth. 'Roared?'

Meirong nods. 'And Janeé . . .' She starts to giggle again.

I suppose it's a kind of laughing incontinence. Janeé begins to hoot. 'Whooo . . .' She pats the bench next to her, invites Olivia to sit. Olivia sits down like the bench might be booby-trapped. Janeé gets up and attempts to serve her some supper but a strange whoop keeps blowing from her.

Tamba tries to sound sensible. 'You kind of had to be here.'

'I was getting the antibiotics ready. We're very close, you know.' Olivia stares at me, analysing my chemical consistency. 'Is he okay?'

I nod at Olivia. *Fine.* But I hold up a finger. *Just one thing.* I pinch my purple shirt, mime vigorous hand washing. They all watch me for a few moments, completely astonished.

Meirong guesses, threatening to burst with exuberance. 'Rub a dub dub!' She tries to lock her laugh away, but it trills from her little body.

'Don't start me,' Janeé warns her. 'Don't start me!'

Olivia tells me anxiously, 'There's a clean-dry machine through the recreation lounge. Cycle seven is the quickest. There's a packet of powder next to the plug.'

Olivia's worry shames everyone into a strangled silence.

Meirong shuffles, clears her throat. 'I must go.' She hurries away from the childhood she must have missed in the orphanage.

I sigh. And it all started with a poor girl dying of thirst.

'Malachi, do you want to come and play *Sleeping with the Enemy?*' Tamba asks hopefully.

I hold up my purple hands. *Not me.*

'Olivia? When you've eaten?'

Olivia takes a small nibble of pineapple. She shakes her head. 'Not in the mood.'

'Come on. It's an old one. You probably cracked it when you were ten.' Tamba turns to Janeé. 'Come, Janeé.'

She starts to lumber up. 'I'd love to.'

I make it out before the two of them are even on their feet. Tramp down the passage to fetch my dirty laundry.

I carry my clothes back past the canteen, past the laboratory. I sense rather than see I have dropped a sock. I turn back to search for it, a sudden desperation seizing me.

There it is, black and beaten, lying limp. I pick it up.

How did my mother die? Rock. Scissors. Fire?

I stumble up a staircase that must lead to the recreation centre.

A brown sofa has already closed around Janeé, as if to stop her from toppling again. The War Console controls look tiny in her grip as Tamba explains the weapons, the strategy: 'We've got to infiltrate Syria and get back our VIPs.'

Janeé presses her knees together, breathes hard, her thumbs ready to rescue hostages with a rocket launcher. I hurry through the lounge to the laundry room, employ the same concentration to try and work out the clean-dry machine. Cycle seven, Olivia said. I force the dial. There is an anonymous white powder in a clear plastic sack that stinks of sweet, sweet chemicals. The sound of shooting tears up the sofa behind me. I spin, stare through the door at heads flying, blood hurtling in red orbit around a standing torso. I drop my washing on the floor. Fight not to pee.

'Use your Blind Eye perk!' Tamba shouts.

Janeé's thumbs have the madness of an American General in them. I drop to my knees, shove my clothes into the belly of the clean-dry machine. Scatter some powder on top. Quickly!

Ratatatat. Thump. War comes with its own cartoon sounds. I bang a switch that says, *Start.* Please, God.

The clean-dry machine clicks, contemplates having mercy on me. A red light flashes, then the sound of the sea gushes in.

'Aah,' Janeé exclaims at the catharsis of killing a cybernetic soldier.

I crash out of the recreation room. Tamba and Janeé both turn their heads in time to see me run.

Run.

I run like the humanoid drone on the screen. I bang down the narrow stairs, nearly flatten Olivia as she turns into her laboratory. I rush along the metal corridor to my only safe place.

I catch my penis in my zip, tear through the skin. I pee like Janeé has my bladder between her legs and is squeezing it.

I climb into my bed, still fully dressed. My belt and my buttons dig into my skin but I am a corpse in a field, slain by a laser hip-fire weapon. I roll into a foetal position.

I was a child, Mother. Sorry.

Fifteen is the dumbest time. Is that what Vicki said?

I feel her scarred hands stroke my head, like my mother's, after her night shift.

*

'Me ne hann,' Cecilia murmured.

Light of my life.

I giggled as she kissed me above my ear.

'It feels like a kankabi moth.'

Cecilia laughed.

'No, not a kankabi. A butterfly.'

I sat very still as she pressed her lips delicately, reverently to my skull three times. Not toxic moths, but three genuflections to the God who made this child in his image.

I tried to say the word. 'Flutterby.'

'Mother,' I whisper now without a tongue. I lie curled up, too heavily dressed for the womb. Tamba's phone digs into my thigh, an unlikely thing to be found floating in amniotic fluid.

After a long, long time, the *Sleeping with the Enemy* noises stop. They are replaced by ping-pong.

Is that Janeé returning Tamba's whacking, or did Olivia go upstairs and let herself forget that her child's lungs are so, so close to being carved from a killer?

I am a big breathing baby, lulled by Vicki, the husband killer. I feel a flush of deep self-consciousness. And then I am asleep.

Bayira sings, 'Tra da, tra da . . .'

Even my fingertips vibrate with the fine frequency of his lullaby. His tractor tick-tocks as it threshes through the cornfields, makes patterns like those of alien spaceships. But Bayira is cutting a circle around a sleeping giant in a purple, twisted shirt.

'Nkawe seru, Mbare weh . . .'

Judge James sits up, the size of the Wapakwa Mountains. His sleepy eyes hold the gentle glow of the waking sun. He rises to his feet, lopes after Bayira's tractor to the slate-grey river.

'Makapira, inja fore . . .'

An old man floats on a massive rubber mat woven from strips of car tyre. It is my huge grandfather from Kattra and he is wheezing, wheezing as he paddles his ferry towards the judge.

'Tra da, tra da . . .'

Judge James steps onto the rocking mat, his eyes fixed on the forest where the shadows dance the shutdown dance between the trees. In the middle of the river where the water flows slowly, my grandfather lifts his dripping oar, digs it into the giant's ribs. Judge James crashes into the water. He shoots up, spluttering, his laugh generous and deep, the same handsome laugh that came from my lungs in the canteen.

A loud guffaw destroys my dream.

A woman stands above me with a pile of fake flowers.

No, not a woman. A man with dreadlocks. Tamba carries my folded clothes like a laundry employee.

'Dude, you're singing.' He drops my clothes on the bed. His chuckles pop with glee. I shut my eyes to make him go away. I hear the swipe of his trousers as he drops them from his body.

Tamba throws himself onto his bed in his pink t-shirt, still sniggering. He switches off the light. His horizontal position pours his laughter back in, quietens him. I peep. No, his pink t-shirt is not lumo.

Tamba sighs like an old man with emphysema. 'You don't understand, Malachi. If the search party finds us, Meirong, my . . .' He stops. 'Even Mr Carreira could go to prison.'

He clicks on the bedside light. 'You know the Conscious Clause Movement?' He makes a finger puppet against the wall, two fingers pressed together. 'They're like this with the Free Press. If they find us, we're fucked. Really.' He shakes his head on his pillow. 'That's the real reason why we're hiding. Not corporate secret stuff.' He sits up suddenly. 'That's confidential by the way.' He throws himself back down, snorts with mirth. 'It's not like you're going tell the whole world.' The light clicks off.

Well. I could you know, Tamba. I roll onto my back, relieve the pain of his Samsung digging into me. I smile in the dark. I have a man-made voicebox growing against my skin.

If I didn't get my tongue, Mother, would I die of it?

I am too frightened to consider exactly what I mean by this.

I shut my eyes, hurry towards the cheap refuge of sleep.

WEDNESDAY

I wake to the sound of water showering down. I listen for the cawing of five thousand waking chickens. The rig gives me the near silence of five thousand rivets. I check my timepiece. Fifteen minutes. I hang my legs off the bed in a leisurely manner, but as my feet touch the cold floor I remember last night's embarrassment. Apparently I was singing.

I tug off my party clothes, rub at the indent from my belt buckle. Somehow I slept without disturbing the neat pile of laundry Tamba left for me. I lift the white trousers off the pile, pull them on. They are beautifully smooth, astonishingly white, like the clean-dry machine personally went and swapped them for a brand-new pair. I slip my plastic voicebox into the pocket. Next, my white ball-boy shirt. The sound of falling water stops. I wriggle my feet into my sneakers with the yellow stains, tug my trousers down so the hem covers them. I need to get out before Tamba teases me about my tongueless lullaby. I cup my hand, blow into it. Ooh. Not as pure as my white outfit. Still. I hurry from the room to escape Tamba's dripping smirk and the eyes of my grandfather, his legs bending gently with the to and fro of his ferry.

*

188

Breakfast is melted cheese you could cross a river on. Janeé puts my own rubber mat in front of me. Meirong and Romano are already sitting with their plates, but they have not yet tackled their cheese. There is not a single sign of Meirong's laughter from last night. She is in bright orangey red, like she just fell into a furious sunset.

'You sure you can destroy it?' she asks Romano cryptically.

Romano nods. 'Bring me the right explosive. Trobancubane.'

'We must wait until they're far enough so they don't hear the blast.'

'Wait. Wait,' Romano mutters darkly. 'That's all you ever say.'

'Yes. Wait!' Meirong seizes her knife, saws into her ferry.

There is no water on the table today. Today I will have to be brave. I snatch at the red juice in the jug, pour myself half a glass. I toss it between my lips before I have time to think about the colour of blood. It strips the mucous membranes of my mouth immediately, deodorises my mouth with fake raspberry. I feel an itchy feeling deep in my brain, but there is something exhilarating about the syrupy drink. For a second, my mind is a simple fake fruit, not a tangle of trepidation, a constant jousting between pride and shame.

I take another sip, careful not to drip it on my white angel's outfit.

A happy zing. Mmm. Interesting.

Tamba wafts in, smelling of something that clashes horribly with raspberry. He sits down in a midnight-blue shirt, looks from face to face, confused by the current of anger crisscrossing the room. 'Any news?'

Meirong shakes her head, 'So far, so good.'

Tamba lifts his cheese with his fingers, stares curiously at what lies beneath it. I scoop out some cubes of what might be potato, chew enthusiastically.

189

Meirong blazes right through the middle of hers in her orange sunset. She points her fork at Romano. 'Either eat or get some rest.'

Romano jumps up, as if he might grab Meirong's knife and cut her throat with it.

Luckily for him, Olivia drifts between them. 'Mor-ning,' she chants, like she has decided to beat up her terror with pure optimism. She sits down in her white coat. 'Mm mm, I'm starving. I've been up since five.'

Romano slinks out of the room before he murders his lady boss.

Meirong frowns. 'Take your coat off, Olivia. You smell like a pharmacy.'

Meirong is right. Even the raspberry can't shoot through the stink. Olivia hangs up her white coat on a hook. Beneath it, she wears the crumpled green of a plant that has been trodden on. Next to me, Tamba rolls his rubber ferry and bites into it. Simple, except for the oil drip on his blue shirt.

'Oh shit.' Tamba tries to wipe the oil off with a serviette. 'This shirt is bloody expensive.'

No one finds it in their heart to care about his shirt, but Tamba's first sip of raspberry juice cheers him up. He tucks a serviette into his neck and launches at his roll like he is chewing for charity.

The raspberry juice also gives Olivia extra zing. 'Everything is going well, don't you think? I mean, we're praying the search party misses us, and they will. But the subjects are all healthy. Even number two, her heart is fine now.' Olivia's eyes suck like a tornado in a clear blue sky. 'Please, Meirong, can I ask you something? Please can they start with number twenty and get that lung tissue to Timmy? He's so small, they say he only needs a piece. I'm just so scared something happens and we miss it by a day.'

'Uhh.' Meirong chews. 'Maybe.'

Olivia's green clothes uncrease before my eyes, as if she has had two days of watering and photosynthesis. 'Thank you. Oh, thank you!'

'*Maybe*. I can't say for definite. I'll have to ask Mr Carreira.'

Meirong drops her fork as if the bell has rung for the end of the chewing marathon. She gets to her feet. Olivia grabs Meirong's hand floating near her ear. Meirong pulls free, slips away from Olivia's supplicating spine, her fluttering fingers, her frail green hope that a single day of drought could annihilate.

I finish my red drink, smile at Janeé as if to say, *Thanks for this lovely drink*. It brings a scritchy scratchy sensation but goodness me . . .

Janeé stares at my cheese. 'Malachi?'

I pat my stomach, keep the crazy red smile up, bestow her with fake raspberry happiness.

Tamba tugs the serviette from his neck. 'Me too. My stomach has shrunk.'

Janeé stares suspiciously at the two of us.

'Any chance of a coffee bomb?' Tamba asks.

'No,' Olivia interrupts. 'You're already twitchy, Tamba.'

Tamba shakes his head, lies brazenly. 'Coffee actually calms me.'

'Please, Tamba. Everything's going so nicely.'

But Olivia didn't hear me roar like a lion last night. She didn't see three grown people giggling like they were drunk on Granny Elizabeth's acetati.

'What do you say, Janeé?' Tamba begs shamelessly.

'Sorry. All gone.'

Tamba drops his forehead to the table. 'Arghh.'

He drags his feet from the canteen. Twitchy. Definitely.

Not me. I seem to be on a high induced by the raspberry drink. I have the sudden weird strength to touch Olivia's shoulder, give it a squeeze with my smooth, plastic-wrapped hand. *Three more days, Olivia,* I would dearly love to say. I follow after Tamba's midnight-blue mood.

I swing into our room, scrub my teeth. Rub at the red stain that looks like a damp-lipped woman just kissed me. It won't come off. I smile helplessly in the mirror. My grandfather's eyes smile back at me.

I shrink away from them, hurry down the corridor.

Yesterday was Araba's rubbery breasts. Today my grandfather's eyes are teasing me.

Whatever is haunting me has a gravely stupid sense of humour.

I hesitate at the steel door. I have no words prepared on my plastic voicebox, but I feel light on my feet today. Partly sunny, they might say on one of those vague forecasts. Partly haunted. I make one more attempt to rub my red-stained lips. I raise my key card, turn the red light green. Open the door wide to yesterday's consequences.

* * *

The silence hums like a swarm of bees caught in my cranium. I hear not a cough, not a croak, not a single malicious word spoken about me. I study the air above the mesh. Have they all been accidentally gassed?

No.

Samuel rests his chin on his knees. Charmayne rocks backwards on her buttocks, flicks her thick hair like she is suffering beneath the tropical sun. Even from this distance, Vicki's eyes send me

192

some kind of message as she taps staccato on the ladder climbing her thigh. Is she counting the rungs to reach her vagina?

I pull my gaze from Vicki, drop Samuel's wire hatch almost cheerily. He might get lucky this week. If Olivia gets her way, the surgeons will start at the far end of the aisle and operate on Shikorina instead of him.

'Sad thing, Malachi,' Samuel says to me.

Lighten up, I want to say. How many years has it been raining? Samuel really ought to try Janeé's red syrup.

'It's the judge,' Vicki says softly.

Thirty-nine heads turn towards the giant's cage.

There is something horribly wrong. I crush my leather glove against my chest. I'm afraid there will be blood.

Vicki, tell me.

'It took thirty seconds,' Vicki says.

No. Not dead. Please.

But Vicki nods her head. 'Sorry, Malachi.'

Next to her, Eulalie sighs with a deep, soothing pity.

Run. Save him!

I shunt my feet down the aisle, my heart shrinking from the ghastly sight I am about to see.

The giant has grown even more colossal. He is buckled over one knee, his head bowed to the floor of his prison. One huge arm is trapped beneath him, the other flung against the mesh. One leg is bent at a shocking angle, as if the weight of his torso has popped the rivets in his hip and pulled it right out of its socket. Dislocated, this beautiful man. A gigantic statue the crowd has toppled in a coup.

I sink to my haunches, try to say, 'Judge James?'

There are red raspberry juice drips on the floor beneath him. Three.

I bang on his cage. 'Hey-y.'

I beg him to lift his head, cite some kind of legislation, anything. I duck down to search his eyes. They are wide open, startled. A length of wire loops through his mesh and threads between his big, broken teeth. He has blood on his lips. A cold tremor seizes me. My own stained lips quiver uncontrollably. The giant chewed through two hundred volts to blow himself up. The memory of electric shock rips through my ganglions, but there are no sparks flying from this gigantic body. The blood-drips near my sneakers are already half dry. He has been lying here for hours.

I swing towards Eulalie, beg her with my eyes. *Is he dead?*

Her ancient smile is sorrowful and sweet. 'We must wait three days. Only then can he come to me.'

No. Maybe, just maybe they can resuscitate him. I hit my switch.

Even from up there, Tamba senses me vibrating. 'Oh, Jesus, what's wrong?'

There is no other way. I whip my finger across my throat.

'Dead?'

Maybe they can find breath inside him. I stamp my foot.

A miracle from the doctors. Quickly!

'He can't be! How?'

I jam a finger between my teeth. Bite too hard on it. I flash my fingers, mime a convulsive shock.

'Electric shock? Shit!' Now he touches keys, works his switches. 'I can't get a reading. Fuck, Malachi. He's our best specimen!' Tamba doesn't bother to cut off my intercom. 'Meirong. Suicide!'

'How?'

'Number fifteen. He bit the wires.'

'Pull him up. Pull him up! Your father must save his heart!'

What about his life? And why Tamba's father?

'It's too late,' the Australian says sadly. 'He stopped breathing at about three a.m.'

I challenge him wordlessly, *Where is your timepiece, Barry?*

He shrugs woefully. 'Three is the time we started drilling. Less oil leakage then. Less gas flares.' Barry looks ashamed, as if it was he who chilled the giant's blood at three a.m.

I see the giant's little finger is smeared with red. He must have used it to hook the wire through the mesh.

The prisoners were all complicit, they must have been. He must have been working on the wire for how long?

They are all silent now. Yes. They let the giant die.

Steel cables begin to snake inside the tracks in the roof. A huge metal hook winds down towards me.

'Malachi. Quickly. Unclip the feed pipe,' Tamba says.

I tug the feed pipe clear. The huge hook finds its eye on the top of the giant's cage. The cage begins to quake. There is a catching stutter of metal cogs on metal thread as a motor in the roof begins to winch the toppled statue up, up. I drag my eyes from the giant's thick, clear retinas. Why the surprise? Why?

Did he see his unborn son?

Tamba is operating the motorised winch like he is flying a Boeing. 'I'm doing it. I'm doing it,' he mutters through my intercom as the giant sways above me.

I stare at the giant's penis crushed against the crosswires beneath him. His testicles are imprinted with the gridiron pattern of latitude and longitude, the rational rules the giant loved so much. North and South, left and right – and now so terribly wrong.

I swing towards Barry, the Australian. *Why did you let him die?*

Charmayne feels my accusation across the aisle. 'It was all he wanted, Malachi.' She grips her big toes, her knees pointing out as if her symmetry might save her from culpability. 'When he heard he killed his baby.'

The giant's cage shunts past the glass kiosk where Tamba is concentrating on his flying, not watching me. I run a few steps, thrust at Charmayne's cage.

She recoils, lets go of her big toes. She bangs her knees together, shuts her womb to me. 'We let him, because we loved him.'

Some prisoners nod their heads, murmur words for love.

I smack on Charmayne's cage, refuse her reasoning.

'I'm sorry to say this,' the social worker says gently, 'but you also let him die.'

I wrench my whole body this way and that. *No. Never!*

But Samuel is nodding in cage number one. Vicki's black eyebrows are silent, sorry arcs. My outrage falls off its hinges. I let my arms hang.

They are right. I let the judge sit on his bleeding hands. I ignored his drunken slur and his grisly, gritted teeth. How can I blame them? I loved the giant after knowing him for a few days. These people have lived naked with his grandeur for fourteen weeks. He was a man of honour, Judge James, he deserved to take his own life.

The panel in the wall grinds open next to Tamba's surveillance box. The giant's cage cranks into it. I catch a glimpse of Meirong's orange sunset before it shuts and leaves a façade of melted cheese.

'Malachi?' Tamba says. 'Emergency meeting in the recreation room. Now.'

I shut Samuel's cage. Before I even reach the door, I am rehearsing my alibi for Raizier management. The judge was fine, really. Check the record of his vitals. He showed no sign of injury to his fingers or his teeth.

I don't care that I can't speak one coherent word. I will find a way to protect the giant's beautiful, decisive wish to die.

* * *

I pass the women's living quarters, drag myself up the stairs to the recreation centre.

I take the brown chair with the broken armrest, like someone threw it across the room and didn't bother to reset its limbs. Janeé perches on a puckered beige seat that to me looks a lot like a huge cashew. She glances longingly at the War Console controls at the TV. I know the feeling. I yearn for my own precious keys, sitting so heavily in my pocket. I adjust my leg so it does not show a lump. It's like having an erection in front of people who think I am a eunuch. Tamba sits in the same blue that the dark night of the soul must be. Next to him, Olivia smooths her rumpled green skirt, twitches it. She lifts her bum, plants it again on a green cushion they call a pouffe in the *Good Living* magazine.

'Man, relax,' Tamba murmurs to her.

Olivia sits up as straight as a stick, but her knee jiggles like she swallowed some of the stuff she used to kick-start Eulalie. Meirong pulls up a metal chair and despises it. She balances her tiny bum bones on it, refuses to lean into the back rest.

A tall man comes to a halt before Janeé's *Sleeping with the Enemy* sofa. He has shrieking colour across his cheeks. From here, he has the teeth of a plankton eater, grey and interleaving. His nose is too white, too thin to let in enough oxygen. He waits in silence, creating a gallows by simply not speaking.

A sigh escapes my lips. Is this the only funeral Judge James is going to get?

I let my spine soften into my broken brown chair. A tiny sob escapes me.

I didn't know electricity could tear your ligaments.

I turn my sob into a cough. The giant must have drunk his own blood to hide his wounds from me. The taste of haemoglobin teases the back of my throat. I place my hands on my knees, stare at my little fingers. No blood, see?

Get a grip, Malachi.

Mr Carreira adjusts his feet like he is about to sing. 'I would prefer not to have met any of you.'

Olivia's lips fall away from her bunny teeth. Her knee stops jiggling.

'That way you are less of a threat to our privacy. But this is a special circumstance . . .' Mr Carreira sieves our wriggling fear between his blue-grey teeth.

In the age of clean-dry machines and one-hour veneers, why on earth are this man's teeth so unbecoming?

'Number fifteen was worth over twenty million to us. Hearts are the most difficult of the organs to get right. They need a naturally high supply of iron.'

'The doctor is optimistic he can save the stem-cell heart,' Meirong says.

'That's one out of the six. He had five more cycles.'

Meirong's head hangs like Mr Carreira just broke her neck. A little rash has appeared between her eyebrows which, I notice now, are as finely shaped as a character in Chinese writing. I fix my eyes on the patch of inflamed skin.

'There was a memo from Asia about a suicide.' Mr Carreira asks Tamba: 'Did Meirong not share it?'

Tamba strokes the shirt on his inner arms like his puncture scars are bothering him.

'She did, but she was responsible for training him.'

'Not entirely, Tamba,' Meirong snaps. 'Just his introduction. You were meant to be monitoring him.'

The *him*, I take it, is the mute man in the room.

'I watched him through the glass. I responded to every bloody peep.' Tamba swings to me. 'Didn't I, Malachi?'

I nod at his silent boss.

'So what was the oversight, Malachi?' Mr Carreira asks. 'How did he get it right?'

I glare at him, place my hands on my knees. He did it with the will of an iron giant who hated himself for killing his unborn son.

Mr Carreira sways backwards. He says unexpectedly, 'You can't blame Malachi. He came late in the season.' He swings a finger between Tamba and Meirong. 'I hold you both accountable.'

Tamba's dreadlocks fly up, subside. Meirong bites hard on her lips. She pushes back her hair, sniffs an astoundingly wet sniff.

How is it possible that I am unscathed?

I glance at the clean-dry machine through the doorway. Perhaps it is my white angel's outfit.

A last little sob pushes up, propels me to my feet. Tamba pinches my trousers behind my knee, tries to tug back down. But if I sit, the memory of the giant will tower over me, send strange sounds from my mouth like a man with Tourette's.

'Wait, Malachi.' Mr Carreira is the same height as me. 'We need a midnight inspection. You will need to check their waste plates, check their teeth. We can't have any copycat failures.'

The giant left the earth. It was a resounding success.

199

'How long will it take for you to do a midnight circuit?'

About a minute multiplied by forty subjects. One less. I sign a revolution of the long hand of the clock.

'An hour? Fine. Set your alarm for tonight,' Mr Carreira orders me.

He walks briskly towards the door, determined to leave the meeting before the most menial of his slave force. At the door, he swings to face us. 'If by some terrible luck that search party finds us, and if you speak about anything you have seen or heard on this rig . . .' he glares at each of us, 'you will go straight to one of our asylums in the US. You will be admitted as a delusional schizophrenic. You will stay there indefinitely.'

He sweeps out with a swish of his quality beige cotton. His polished shoes ping down the metal stairs.

I refuse to let my mouth hang like an imbecile's.

'Christ. This is evil,' Tamba breathes.

Meirong unfurls her orange sunset. 'Doctor Mujuru wants to see you straight after the meeting.'

Tamba slumps like she just chop-kicked his neck.

Janeé fights her way to her feet, holds out her hand to Tamba. He takes it, pulls himself up.

'Go ahead, Malachi,' he says. 'I've got to go and have my head bashed in.'

Ah. His father. The doctor. I heard the truth on my two-way radio.

I'm afraid I can't share Janeé's sympathy for the man who is meant to be a poor Zimbabwean, not the son of a top transplant doctor in the Raizier wing. If I'm wrong about Tamba, I will eat my dirty sneakers.

*

My sneakers take me down the metal stairs. I am careful to stay upright, keep moving in case the air in me coalesces into useless sobs.

* * *

I shove on the door, force my eyes to the enormous gap the giant has left in the two rows of metal teeth. The emptiness of the space, the silence of the subjects, rack my heart another notch. I push back the pressure in my sobbing pipes, wheeze like my grandfather on his ferry last night.

I must keep the good air moving, for if it gets stuck behind a rung of bone or cartilage I will fall to the floor and cry for my yellow father who had the courage to read us 'Whoso List to Hunt' to the end without stopping.

I lock my glove to Samuel's cage for the second time today.

'He was a good man, the judge. Deep down he was good.'

I grab Tamba's Samsung from my pocket, type a reply. 'He killed two people.' My American assistant speaks with a deep, sanguine sound.

Samuel licks his lips, checks the surveillance glass. He watches my phone like it is a bomb in a bustling public place. I slip it back into my pocket.

Samuel nods. 'His mind snapped.' His trigger finger jerks inside the glove. 'Boom. Boom. And you can't take bullets back.'

He is right. It is the dumb utterance, the wild mind's decision. The impulse that killed them.

'It's good to hear you talking,' Samuel says tentatively.

I keep my face sombre, but a strange joy tears through my chest. It feels like the giant has crossed my heart wires.

Samuel's eyes are on fire, but he asks casually, 'Where's Tamba?'

I slide out my keypad, type with one thumb. 'Getting into big trouble for letting the judge die.'

'And you?'

'I am mute. They presume I am stupid.'

Samuel chuckles. Vicki's delight warms me from the side. I clip and clean, matter-of-fact, but waves of pride keep heaving against my back teeth. I start on Samuel's toes.

'I see it's a Samsung. Are you using Glossia?' I nod eagerly.

'Do you know there's an African accent in that transposer app? It's very crude. Generic. But it might be better than . . .' He breaks off tactfully.

I check Tamba's glass, slide the stolen phone out. I scroll past *Tone*. Find *Accents*. There it is. Right at the top of the bloody alphabet.

I didn't need to rely on William, the choir-singing baseball player. I select *African*. Type on the keys, 'Thank you, Samuel.'

The voice is almost mine. A little laugh tears free from my secret tsunami. I avert my eyes from Samuel's tiny smile. I lock his cage, move on to Eulalie.

The old witch nods like a priest, declaring me married to my Samsung. 'You have found a way to speak.'

But I am not ready for the commitment! I cut her fingernails, fight the urge to run like hell from what I have just done.

But you can't take bullets back.

Eulalie sighs. 'You were scared to live.'

I glance at her, shocked by her perspicacity.

She says, 'And I was too frightened to love.'

I hide my surprise. This is the first time Eulalie has spoken of her earthly life. It's like Jesus suddenly saying he has Weet-Bix for breakfast.

'There was a man who came to see me about his wife. She was burnt by a shack fire.'

I lift out a towel, wipe her fingers clean.

'After a year, he said he loved me.' Eulalie's despair pierces her voice, carries it to the ceiling. 'But I was married to the spirits!'

I scan Tamba's glass. Still no sign of him. I type one word. It costs me nothing. 'Sorry.'

Eulalie's eyes caress me like a proud grandmother, not like my one with the bleached hands from Kattra. 'You are a good man, Malachi.'

When I lift my white towel, her hands underneath are black velvet.

I hardly need to trim the old crone's feet. Her heart stoppage yesterday seemed to have slowed her nail growth. I wash them gently, release Eulalie to her Valentino memories.

Tamba's antiseptic shower has made Vicki's black hair soft and separated, as they say in shampoo ads. Luscious to the touch. This hair is more befitting a sensuous heroine than a black-hearted mermaid who spends her days blowing sarcastic bubbles from the deep. The web of skin between my fingers tickles. I want to touch her hair.

Vicki smiles shyly at me. 'You look nice in white.'

Is she trying to get me to type?

She tries again. 'Aren't you scared they'll bust you for talking to us?'

I strap her feet in, tap my keys beneath the leather brace. 'I am trusting you to look out for me.'

Vicki looks up, revealing a throat like a waterfall of cream. 'Coast is clear,' she says softly. Almost intimate.

I trim the bubble toes on the cutest pair of feet I have ever seen. Her ankle bones were sculpted by the tools of a genius.

Vicki cocks her head thoughtfully. 'What's the word Madame Sophie says, about helping people to die?'

I think I hear the rustle of her clean hair across her scapulas. It sends a tiny trickle of electricity through the cloth of my white trousers.

'Euthanasia,' I type. But my mind is very far from assisted dying.

Shut up, I tell my penis. Or I will shock you so badly they will harvest the heart that sends blood to you.

'That's what we did with Judge James.'

I shake my head fiercely, press too hard on her fingers with my white towel.

'Eina,' Vicki says indignantly.

I stroke my fingertips across her pink nails, type for the second time, 'Sorry.'

She smiles with teeth so pretty God must have put each one in place with a magnifying glass.

'It's love-hate, isn't it?' she says softly. 'This thing between you and me.'

My fingers grip the cell phone like it is my spokesman's throat. I nod at Vicki, tap one word, the perfect word for us.

'Ambivalence.'

My eyes feel starry bright, heavier to carry now with all the extra glitter.

The rest of the subjects are deathly quiet, perhaps silenced by their ambivalence about the giant. I work through four prisoners, thinking sometimes of the giant's broken finger, sometimes his

204

shattered teeth. Sometimes of the brute force I must use later to kill my admiration for Vicki.

But why must I hurt my penis when all it wants to do is exclaim at a woman's beauty? Why?

I glance back, drop a little kiss on Vicki's collarbone. Her surprised smile is shockingly sensuous.

What is so terrible about hardening at the sight of lips so full they make creases in the middle, eyes so intense they hold a deep purple sheen, ankles so prim, so perfect it can't be they are worn by a woman whose home language is the knife? Vicki is breathtaking now that she is healing. Why must I punish myself for wanting her in my mouth?

I swallow, frightened.

Thankfully the yellow man is too subdued to call me Jesus today. Jesus would never have had to fight off an erection, would he? But perhaps these are the carnal truths the censors burnt.

Jesus, please, please can I perhaps let these feelings grow to a terrible tumescence rather than topple them with a hundred and twenty volts of agony?

As I groom the yellow man, I sense the truth quite clearly.

Yes. Jesus got an erection and he was not ashamed of it. Yes, he fell in love with a fallen woman, like me. It was my father who told me the rumour about Mary Magdalene, who was an ex-prostitute, wasn't she? Hamri might have loved the oppressors' tongue, but he was always wary of their religion.

Next door, the desert strangler nods sagely, like he knows the ancient secrets of all prostitutes.

I smile inwardly. Mary Magdalene was lucky to die a natural death, not be left stranded in the desert by this poor, sorry murderer.

As I clip the glove to Gibril's cage, I sense a shadow high above me. Tamba looks somehow flatter, less three-dimensional than before. Even his dreadlocks lie down as if chastised, creating the beaten silhouette of a bedraggled thief. Like the other man on the cross. What was his name? Barabbas.

Tamba watches me work with a dead, inward-looking expression. What did Doctor Mujuru say to him; 'I'll feed you to Raizier and cut out your heart, if it still works after all that opium?'

I'd like to hit my switch, type to Tamba on his Samsung, 'Hey, Tamba, why don't you try telling the truth? You'd be surprised how high you can get just from confessing.'

I groom two more subjects, approach the cavernous, cold space past the tooth-extracting Indian. The skinny man, I am glad to say, is no longer obsessed with his teeth or his umbilicus. Which is more than I can say about me and my penis. I shut the Indian's cage, take an extra-big breath. The whole hall watches me pass the struts that held the judge's cage. By the time I reach Barry, the fat Australian, my journey through the hallowed space has brought tears to his tiny eyes.

His fingers droop in the sheath. 'Judge James was the best friend I ever had.'

I pause with my clipper, astounded by his statement.

'I mean, he said I was a pig, but . . .' Barry's sobs seem to come from deep below him and shove through his splayed bum. 'I miss him so much.' He weeps uncontrollably. Hysterical, for a man who ran a tight, violent business and got filthy rich.

'The judge always told me, Barry, money is just paper with some ugly president's face on it. It's not like the president's going to jump out and give you a hug . . .' A deep-sea sound blows through his loose mammalian skin.

Above us, Tamba snaps out of his beaten-blue suffering. 'Is that one laughing or blubbering?'

I tip my hand two ways. *Both.*

'What's the problem?'

I point at the terrible, tragic space next to Barry.

Barry rolls onto his back, once more blubbering. I release his feet so he doesn't crack his little ankles. Yes, Barry. We will all miss our Gadu Yignae.

The skinny rapist does not touch his penis today. Angus, I think his name is, mourns for the giant without so much as a mind or muscle spasm. His whole body is an effigy of what is left of a rapist when his madness leaves him. Harmless, he is, a shipwrecked British tourist with not even the will to crack a coconut. Did the judge's death bring him some weird healing?

The microphone crackles. 'How much longer, Malachi? We're going to miss lunch.'

I incline my head towards the last two cages in the row. Can't he see our timetable has been thrown out by the death of a giant? I lock the rapist's cage, move on to Lolie.

She gives me her fingers, sighs like a depressed teenager.

'The judge, he is lucky.' Her English is limited, but her words hold a deep envy. 'So lucky . . .'

Her hands suddenly look too young for someone who has notched fifty kills since she was ten. My fingers itch to grab my cell phone and ask her how old she is, but Tamba sits watching like a schoolchild who has been ordered to stay in the classroom.

It suddenly feels so unfair that Lolie should spend the rest of her life in prison. She deserves to have some teenage fun, style her hair even, drop people with only her deadly beauty. Her eyelashes, for instance, look at them. They have the power to snap people's hearts open and closed, however many times she decides to blink them.

Maybe Lolie and the solo sailor could meet up after this, laugh about the time they were both locked up on the rig.

There is still time to laugh, Lolie. There is time to paint your nails. I trim her toes, will her to live while she wishes herself as stone dead as Judge James.

When I reach Shikorina, she is cradling one of her children again. I can almost see its soft, shining forehead. I stare at the empty space where I thought I caught a glimpse of baby skin. Is it a boy or a girl, I wonder?

Shikorina is a remarkable mime artist. She stops her long strokes, tickles the imaginary child at the nape of its neck.

'The way he did it.' She shakes her head sadly. 'It was terrible.'

I nod imperceptibly. Ask me, I know how it feels for electricity to suck the ions from your blood vessels, crush them.

'I was careful, Malachi.' She leans towards me, whispers as if to prevent the child on her lap from hearing. 'I didn't let the others see.' She rubs her child's spine from its neck to its baby coccyx.

I press Shikorina's towel deeper into the disinfectant, wipe her toes curled up with love for the little ones she drowned so carefully.

High above, Tamba stands up and shuffles some things on his DJ desk, his browbeaten eyes still on me. I lock Shikorina's cage, walk away as if I am not more than tempted to love this crazy mother. The giant's empty space tries to suck me in, but I force myself past his three drops of blood. I feel a flush of heat as I pass Vicki's charming freckles, her seductive smiling mouth. The brace slips from my fingers. I stoop to pick it up. Continue to the trolley, lay down my falcon-taming paraphernalia. A craving tugs at the muscles deep in my belly. I walk to the door with a sullen teenage reluctance. I want to stay.

I want to stay and kiss Vicki.

* * *

Meirong and Janeé have shining lips from something mysterious submerged in gravy. I sit down, strike mine with a spoon, find a hard sunken object. I dredge it to the top. It is a bone with jelly meat clinging to it. I scrape the bottom of my bowl, find another. And another.

'What's wrong, Malachi?' Meirong asks sharply.

I take a noisy sip of the gravy. Delicious. Really. I nibble on a bone. Wonderful. Truly. Not vertebrae, but maybe a tail.

I think of Vicki's pretty coccyx, the place where her tail would have been twenty million years ago, a triangular plate above the soft swelling of her buttocks. Her engineer added two small dimples for sheer sexiness.

I catch a piece of marrow floating with the carrots, gobble it. Delicious. I smile at Janeé.

'Nice, hey, Malachi? I boiled it for three hours.' Janeé grabs the pot, tramps around to my side. 'Have more.'

I lean back to make way for my new mother and her pot of broken bones.

Tamba's sense of humour cracks through his despondency. 'Janeé, you hit the jackpot. Malachi is going to get nice and fat.'

Janeé smiles happily. 'Fat like me.'

Tamba snorts through his stew. Even Meirong's eyes almost smile above the u-shaped bone she is sucking on.

Olivia hurries in. 'I'm so hungry I could eat a horse.'

'Well, you got ox,' Tamba says.

Janeé scoops three spoons of the ox's tail for Olivia.

'Any news?' Olivia asks.

Meirong places a bone on the edge of her plate. Her voice is shaky. 'Three hover-cruisers and a helicraft from –' She stops, refuses to give our location away.

We all wipe our mouths as if Meirong ordered us to. Even Janeé puts down the pot.

'Yes?' Olivia nearly whispers.

'They are heading straight for us.'

Olivia drops her spoon in her food.

'We'll know by tonight. Just, all of you . . .' Meirong glares at each one of us. 'No trouble. *Please.*' She gives up on her oxtail. 'Olivia, Doctor says to add a sedative to their evening feed. We can't take any chances right now.' She drops a bunch of keys on the table, makes me jump. 'The girl. Give her lunch then hang the keys on the engine.' She slings a pink lanyard around my neck, anoints me. 'Now, please.'

Meirong passes me a bowl from the trolley. It looks like we will all be eating waggy tails today.

'She's very weak,' Meirong says grimly. 'You might have to feed her.'

The silence in the canteen simmers with guilt. Meirong claps her hands as if to make the shame of five people fly up and away. 'Come, come. Back to your stations, everyone.'

I hurry on to my horrible afternoon task.

Up, up I climb towards the sun, balancing bits of skeleton. By the time I reach the last flight of stairs, my chest is burning. Surely I could not have lost my fitness this quickly. No, the tightness of my breath must have something to do with a dead judge and a shipwrecked sailor who might be too sick to eat.

I unlock the door to outer space, step through the opening.

The psychopathic sun fires its rays onto the landing pad, strikes at my irises. It turns the sea to a cruel, blue light that houses no life on its skin.

I knock on the door of the storeroom. Knock harder. No answer. I unlock the padlocks, let myself in. Frances is on her back, her arms flung wide. The burn wounds on her shins leak a yellow fluid. She rasps for breath like she is draining the dregs of an oxygen bottle, her face a feverish red. I put her tray on the upturned crate, lay my hand on her cheek. She has a raging temperature. Her eyes prise open. She smiles, delirious.

'Daddy?'

Don't be silly. I am as black as the basalt sands of Bhajo.

'Sit up. Sit up,' I try to say, but all that comes out are dumb-sounding vowels. I dare not use my phone in case she exposes me. I try and lift her against the pillows, but even forty kilos takes some leverage. Frances slides to the side, her forehead banging against the wall. I need to get to her mouth. The marrow will fix her. I drag her straight, grab hold of her chin. I chase a string of marrow, tip it between the girl's blistered lips. She swallows like she has to move a cabinet to let it through.

'Good girl,' I slur in my tongueless language. Still, the sound has love in it. I try again. This time the food hits the cabinet and shoots back up her throat. Frances coughs it out. Fluid trickles from her nostrils. I stretch the neckline of her tattered shirt, wipe her face with it. Why do they not bathe and dress this poor kid? She is dirty and dying.

I haul her up higher. 'Come. Let's try,' I try to say. This time I scoop a tiny sip of gravy. This time it goes in. But Frances's burning head falls back as soon as I release it.

Damn it!

I grab her glass of water, sprinkle some on her forehead. I splash a few drops on her neck, watch it gather in the hollow of her shallow, sucking throat.

She is *dying*, you bastards.

Romano's shadow stretches through the door. I swing towards him.

'She's dying,' I try to sound.

'I haven't slept. I've been watching her. Cooling her like so.' He picks up the weightlifting magazine and flaps it over her face. 'I've just seen Meirong. They're taking her tonight.' He strokes the girl's temples where her hair has saved her white skin. 'Not long, girlie . . .'

I bend over Frances, try to trickle more gravy between her lips. She swallows convulsively.

'Here,' Romano says. 'Let me.' He takes the spoon and dips it into the stew. Feeds her tiny morsels like he is saving a baby bird.

I drop the storeroom keys on the solo sailor's crumpled sheet, walk out of the room with lead in my sneakers. She doesn't have long, I know this in my marrow.

'Drink, girlie,' Romano sings in a high, woman's voice. He hasn't slept since yesterday, but I know he is the best nurse Frances could ever get. I leave the girl to his ministrations, walk into the pounding sun.

Bastards. Profit-driven pigs. I should have known from Susan Bellavista's boots that Raizier would stamp on our faces. Let a young girl bleed pus.

*

I am halfway down the first maze of stairs when I feel Meirong's key card knocking against my chest. I was supposed to hang it on the lifeboat. Romano was supposed to be asleep.

I stop. Consider it.

I will give it to her later. The Meirong bitch can wait.

* * *

I stride into the cultivation hall incensed by the cruelty I have just seen. It makes me prickly with the prisoners. I walk straight past Vicki with her ripe-fig lips. They should harvest those, give them to some old lady in Hollywood.

But the angry thought only hurts my already labouring heart.

If they so much as touch the mermaid, I will kill them.

Janeé's oxtail stew has given me the fierceness of a Maasai warrior, but with no spear and no tongue to take on Raizier. I lock the brace to cage number twenty-one, start on the man's fingers. If the solo sailor dies, Romano and I will be on the war path.

I snort through my nostrils like the ox whose marrow I have just eaten. A mute refugee and a sleepless veteran? I doubt it. The only thing I am sure of is that I could get a mention in the *Guinness Book of World Records* as the fastest nail-clipper ever seen on earth. I half shut my eyes, cut even quicker. The prisoners find it necessary to hold their breaths and keep very, very still as I chop off their new moons.

The social worker is not impressed with my clippers chattering like demented teeth.

'Malachi? Why are you speeding?'

213

I glance at the glass. Tamba is bowed over his lap, his elbow lifted. I don't believe it, he is clipping his own fingers.

I slip the phone beneath my leather glove, type to Andride. 'What are you, a traffic cop?'

The social worker smiles at my stupid quip. I slip my phone back into my white trousers.

Everything, everything is standing on its head. And I have no idea how to save the dead and dying.

Andride tries to interrupt my metal-flashing frenzy, 'What if Eulalie's right?'

I hesitate for a second.

He shrugs. 'What if dying's just like . . .' Andride thinks hard, 'climbing on the roof to watch Foe fetara?'

I know what he means. He means the blinding beauty of gunpowder on New Year's Eve.

A sound clatters down from above. A metal pulley cranks the giant's empty cage towards us. Tamba has abandoned his manicure and is biting on his bottom lip, steering carefully. The cage swings above the empty gap, drops into its cradle. It stinks of disinfectant. Andride and I stare into its emptiness, strain our eyes and our ears for some trace of the giant's spirit.

Satisfied with his pilot skills, Tamba drops down, disappears.

I slip the phone beneath my glove.

Tamba props a bare foot on his DJ desk. He begins to clip his toes.

I type with trembling fingers. 'What if the judge is on the roof drinking a pink drink?'

I wring out a dripping white towel, wipe Andride's hands, smother my crazy smile.

What if the girl with the fever can never burn up, even if the sun takes her right now as firewood?

I drop the towel in my bucket, meet the unearthly light in Andride's eyes.

'Does that man have a fever?' Tamba's feet have disappeared from his desk.

Andride lowers his eyes, hides the lasers of hope I seem to have lit with my African accent.

I jab at my eyes, tell Tamba to see for himself.

Tamba peers at a monitor. 'Temp normal.'

I show him the O for okay, slide the cutting brace from the social worker's feet. I lock his cage, walk away from Andride as if we have not just experienced some kind of earth-defying, light-firing revelation.

The prisoners near us laugh and gabble like they're at a cocktail party. I don't know where that stuff came from, but the prisoners love it. After all, if there is no death then how the heck can there be murder in the first, the second, or the third degree?

I settle down to a less record-breaking clipping speed, curiously exhilarated, but when I reach the priest killer he throws cold water on me.

'It's the people who love them.' He shakes his head. 'I am very sorry for the priest's mother. Very, very sorry. Can you tell her for me? She is Sara Alaoui, from Assilah. Can you write her address?'

Oh no. They're asking favours of my digital tongue.

'She lives at Ali Ibnou Abi Taleb. Please. Tell her I love him now, Father Rayan.' The priest killer's eyes glow like olive oil in the fluorescent light. Healthy he is, even with an extra kidney ripening in him. He shows two fingers glued together like Siamese twins. 'We are together.'

I smile at him. It's going to be the party of the century.

I clip his healthy outgrowths, set his feet free. The priest burner, it turns out, is quite a sweet guy.

The next few prisoners smile dreamily, talk in foreign tongues about eternal life, perhaps.

But when I reach Charmayne, she spits, 'Mohammed's gone mad. It's *rubbish*, Malachi.'

Her hair is madder, more split than it has ever been. One side of her parting looks like she has stuck her finger in a plug, the other half is the good twin, clinging and meek.

'If it's true, why did I bother to kill Bongi and Pete?'

Deep down I want to smile. A murderer's worst dilemma.

'Why?'

I spare a thought for the poor sucker before me who found himself on a sexy, sucking island inside Charmayne's eyes. Tamba is watching us with an unnerving interest, I dare not reply. I turn away from her angry, shaking breasts as fine as midnight sand, work all the way to Madame Sophie.

She smiles at me like Olivia has given her intravenous heroin. Static lifts her hair, creates a blonde halo. Her fingernails are perfectly white-tipped as if she has spent the whole day getting ready for some awards ceremony. She smiles dreamily.

'It makes me want to hurry up and die.'

Me too, Madame Sophie. I would take Janeé's steak knife and sink it between my ribs right now if I knew I would see Cecilia. I would spill my own blood, create a red carpet leading to my mother.

Over the microphone I hear the shuffling of Tamba's fingers. 'Hurry up, Malachi.' He is crumpled up, pressing his penis. 'I need a piss. Number forty is nice and quiet. Is it safe for me to leave?'

I nod at him.

'You sure?' he squeaks.

I roll my eyes. *Go and piss, Tamba.*

He swipes some things from his desk. I give Madame Sophie's nails an extra-tight trim to make sure she can't use them to get to the big, beautiful occasion of death. As I shut her cage, I feel the careless caress of Vicki's eyes behind me.

'If my husband's up there, I'll have to tell him.'

I turn around slowly. Her eyes are the silken inside of an African violet. My body moves closer involuntarily.

Vicki whispers so softly I have to read her lips. 'I love you much more than I hate you, Malachi.'

I stare at her mouth. I want to run my tongue in circles, feel its slippery creases. I drop my eyes, aching with longing. Vicki lifts her knees to protect her heart. She doesn't realise she is showing me the flesh of her sexual parts. She doesn't know how much I want to touch her. But I dare not talk to Vicki. I must save my survival instinct for the worst among us. The one with the biggest, darkest propensity to forget.

Josiah's hairy hands are on his lap, his legs stretched out like he is retired on a beach, simply watching the sea. I switch my phone to *Peremptory*.

'Hands please.'

I swallow my disgust for the knobbed, furry fingers he offers me. His own mother forgives him. Who am I to judge?

Josiah has blue-black bruises on his cheeks and dried blood on his top lip, but the usual cramp of hatred on his forehead has receded. His eyes, I notice, still show their scarring from a lifetime of violent psychosis.

Why are you so calm, you bastard?

A soft metallic music starts up behind me.

Eulalie is running the back of her hands against the mesh, strumming her knuckles like she is playing a strange guitar. She smiles tenderly.

'She stroked your head like this. She kissed you, she said . . .' Eulalie cocks her head to one side, listens. 'These are not poison moths. They are butterflies.'

I suck sharp splinters into my larynx.

'Butterflies?' Vicki breathes.

Some prisoners try the word out. 'Butterflies.'

I shut my eyes. Painted paper wings fly behind my eyelids. When I open them Vicki is smiling like she too saw the picture books from the Waste to Wonder agency. I lift my fingers to the steel squares of Eulalie's prison. She meets them with the pads of her smooth skin.

'Cecilia,' she says.

My mother's name.

I stagger with drunken happiness all the way to the trolley. The prisoners stare like there are extinct butterflies in the air around me. As I float from the hall, the last thing I hear is a giggle from the sweet mermaid, Vicki. The soft, indulgent sound of a woman in love. I shut the door, sorry, so sorry to imprison them.

I glide past the spiral stairs, a smiling idiot.

I don't care what anyone thinks. Cecilia, my mother, has spoken to me.

I forgot to lock the door behind me. I backtrack to the hall, raise the key card, let it click. The peace in me is the exquisite art on a butterfly's wings.

My mother. I think she still loves me.

* * *

I leave my bucket at the door to Olivia's laboratory, whirring and clinking with glass instruments. The canteen is already empty. Only one plate of food waits on the trolley. I lift the cover. Golden, crisped fish. I sniff it. Mmm. There is the delicate scent of silver beneath the greasy batter, nothing like the stink of the fish farms in Zeerust, a thousand miles from the sea. The silver skin is serrated from where Janeé must have torn off the fin. I try a bit of the white flesh underneath. Oh. Succulent. Nothing like the bruised chunks they beat with mechanical mallets in the factories. This is how it should be – fish should be speared from the sea, not bred in gelatinous tanks filled with corn mulch and fish semen.

The fresh fish feeds every cell of my being.

Mother, this is what I have always missed. If only you could taste it.

I stab at the plump, straw-coloured potato. It is soft right through. I cut a deep cross, squeeze both ends so the cross opens up. Stick a block of butter substitute into it. We made the same cross on our mosquito bites, dug our fingernails into it. The absurdity only strikes me now. We made the sign of the Christ.

I take a big buttery bite of my potato. Delicious.

Does Christ see the funny side of our potatoes and our itchy-bites? Or does he only think of the nails and whips and the throbbing blue feet he must have got from hanging so long? I take a big swig of red raspberry juice. I don't know the active evil ingredient, but the juice infuses me with even more joie de vivre than the lovely food. I allow myself a long, happy sigh. I still have Meirong's key card to the deck. I meant to give it to her at supper time. How will I find her?

Janeé fills the doorway. I feel a vacuum in my eardrums before her hips pop through. 'Ah, Malachi. How was your fish?' She frowns at my rumpled batter. 'You don't like your batter?'

I pick on the crust, compose an apology. It is tinted to perfection. Only a magic wand could give it its incandescence. Instead I pick the batter up, take a huge crackling bite.

Janeé takes this as an invitation to warp the bench with her buttocks. 'I made up the recipe. Me. Craymar has been using it for six years already.'

Mother, help me.

Janeé pours herself a glass of raspberry juice. She nods victoriously. 'Have you heard the news? The search party has passed us.' She beams, makes a sawing motion with the back of her hand. 'They're opening them up tomorrow. Meirong says they might take a few arteries from the first ones.'

I try to smile, take another swig of red blood substitute. Immediately my brain itches.

'They will make a little hole in his leg and his neck. Keyhole surgery,' she says proudly. 'They pull the arteries through with a needle.'

Pins and needles attack my scalp. I rub my head frantically.

Janeé checks the canteen clock. 'The surgeons will be here in three hours.'

I bury my fingernails in my hair and scrub, scrub, scrub like I am a victim of head lice.

'Sjoe, what's wrong?' Janeé leans back, stares at me. 'It must be the fish.'

Not the fish. Not the fish. But I nod and cough and scratch – like how many hints do I have to give that I am suffering?

'Shame.' Janeé utters the South African word for sweet pity. But she is not built for emergencies. She heaves to her feet, pours me some water. She stamps around to my side and ruffles the droplets through my roots, rubs it on my temples. 'There. Better?'

The water stings my hot, histamine skin.

Janeé compresses my bench, sticks the glass of water in my clenched paw. 'The funny thing is, my boy doesn't even want to live. He says, "Leave me, Mammie. Heroin is the only thing I want." I say, "Kanya, I will miss you." He says, "Don't worry, Ma, I will see you afterwards."' Her big shoulders shake like an unsound building. Her stomach begins to heave like a bulldozer is ramming it. Janeé lays her huge head on the table next to the raspberry juice and laughs with the mirth of several elephants.

I scratch my scalp frantically.

When she lifts her head, Janeé's face is saturated with tears. She sniffs violently, almost vacuuming the sachets of salt on the table. I offer her my paper serviette. She takes it from me, uses the tiny triangular scrap to blow her nose like a trumpet. Her smile is a child's plump-faced illustration of the sun.

'Tomorrow.' Janeé stands up and crashes my plate onto the tray. 'Do you want to come and play *Sleeping with the Enemy*?'

I stare helplessly.

'You don't know how? I can teach you.'

I scrub at my scalp, use my affliction to turn down her kindness. Allergy is easier to mime anyhow than, Sorry, but if I did I will piss on the sofa every time one of us pulls a trigger.

Just then, we hear a volley of little bombs, muffled by acres of stainless steel. Janeé grins.

'Someone's already up there. It must be Tamba.' She trundles to the door. 'See you tomorrow, Malachi.'

I smile at her wryly. I have two mothers, it seems. Cecilia who gave birth to me, and a big Xhosa cook who would forsake me any day for a War Console game.

I scuttle from the canteen, knock hard on the door of Olivia's laboratory.

'Ja?'

Olivia bends over a long plastic sleeve of pink fluid. Blue bruises of optimism hang beneath her tired eyes. 'Malachi?' she says, surprised.

I hook the top digits of my fingers, scrabble at the air around my head. I touch my bottom lip, show an imaginary pill going in.

'Itchy head?'

I nod, curl my hands into the shape of a dish. Mime the action of eating.

'The fish!'

No, not the fish. But Olivia whips a drawer open, breathing heavily. She digs inside it. 'How is your breathing, Malachi?'

I stroke my throat, put up a hand to reassure her there is no swelling.

'The fish,' she repeats while she fishes in the drawer of glass bottles and silver wrappings. She snaps a yellow pill from its bubble pack. 'Take this. Quickly.'

I drop it in my mouth. Swallow it. I want to explain to Olivia that the fish was mother's milk. It was that stupid red syrup, but Olivia is the last person in the world who should ever see my Samsung.

'Is your throat feeling tight?'

I shake my head. Five plastic sleeves lie on the counter pasted with white stickers, neatly printed, *Zymocticyllin. 200 ml per mouth.*

Olivia is watching me anxiously. 'I think I should call Meirong.'

I wave a casual hand, smiling.

222

'Malachi.' There is a threatening note in Olivia's voice. 'You need to be fine for tomorrow.'

I walk backwards, show Olivia I am perfectly coordinated, thank you. I turn at the door, smiling to quell her worry that I might die of anaphylactic shock and sabotage harvest day. I wave cheerily, glide down the corridor, an old-fashioned actor exiting stage right.

It feels like I have never in my life been so happy. My itch is completely cured by the antihistamine. I whistle in the shower, Bayira's song from Saturday.

I stop suddenly. The warm water pours down. I had no idea I could whistle without a tongue.

I can whistle perfectly, even with water running between my lips. Astonishing. I giggle to myself. Perhaps an unforeseen effect of Janeé's frying grease.

I hide my stolen phone beneath my pillow. Drop both key cards on the cabinet, climb into my sleeping shorts which smell of fake lavender. The antihistamine, I think, has sent me flying. I set my alarm for ten minutes before midnight, put myself to bed among a profusion of purple flowers, humming Bayira's tune.

I will see Vicki at midnight.

My mind travels to her bellybutton. This is safe, isn't it? The bellybutton has nothing to do with the skeleton. It is miles from the saxophonist's knobs of her vertebrae, a different creature entirely from her pretty patella draped in pliant knee-skin. Her bellybutton is just a keepsake, a souvenir from the woman who carried her for nine months, her baby skull knocking against a soft, sloping cervix.

Is a woman's cervix smooth and buttery, or is it spongy, I wonder? I see the dark moss at the entrance to the mermaid's cave. Feel my penis rise up like a medieval weapon. I turn onto my stomach, but it digs into the mattress like it wants to lift me up and go and seek Vicki's pink reproductive parts.

Shame stabs me in the soft centre of my pelvis.

Would my mother be ashamed of me?

I thrash the pillow fiercely. No! Cecilia would want her son to be a full-blooded human, not bomb his manhood out of existence. I stroke my cheek against the pillow, let it comfort me. I slide my hand into my shorts. I want to lick Vicki's bellybutton, thank her mother for carrying her. I want to tickle the globule of skin with my imaginary tongue so she buckles towards me, gives me her breasts. I want to take her nipple between my lips, let the flesh touch the roof of my mouth. I caress my pitted penis, let it grow in response to my delicious gentleness. I want to feed on her unloved abundance, suck her feminine flesh until a surprising richness floods her bony chest, throbs through her guitar frets, passes in ecstatic stop-starts through her knife notches until she is free to be a groaning, grown woman, unharmed by man or metal. I touch my scarred penis, stroke it to shocking rigidity. I want to slip it into her mermaid's cave, feel the slippery velvet swell around it, drive to the edge, sink and lift, sink and lift, rhythmic, until the world cannot hold us and we fall, we fly, we shatter in blazing waves that drown everything we have ever known, our very birth, the fact that we are perfect.

I fall into a blissful, sticky sleep.

I wake still holding her lush hills that guide me back to time. Who am I?

Where do I live?

A helicraft throbs somewhere above me. I am lying in a metal

224

rig beneath a damp, sticky sheet. I smile, wrap myself tightly in it. I am in love with Vicki.

The helicraft engine slows, switches off. The extra surgeons are here. Poor Shikorina. Poor Lolie. I can't bring myself to feel sorry for Angus, the rapist. I listen for the Dragonfly to load up the solo sailor and fly her away to the best medical care on earth. I listen for an hour and ten minutes, but all I hear are muted detonations of outdated war-game weapons. I fall asleep again worrying about the dehydrated sailor.

Why? I ask the giant, who must have a better view than me from my tiny bed. Why have they not left yet?

My alarm plays the violin gracefully in my sleep. I smell the sex on my fingers as I fumble for my timepiece. Tamba mutters in his sleep. I sit up, wide awake. Did they take Frances during my dead delta stage of sleep? Please let her be on a stretcher in the night sky somewhere, please.

I undress quietly, leave a dry snail trail from the first orgasm I have had since I was a teenager.

Thank you, Vicki.

Will the hall be bright or dimly lit at night? Should I wear clean clothes? No, she will notice. She might tease me. I pull on today's white outfit, try to smooth the creases. I love the feel of my own hands on my body.

I love myself, Mother. Now that I love Vicki.

I steal my phone from beneath my pillow, slide my red lanyard over my head. I pick up my shoes and tiptoe to the bathroom. Sneak the light on like a thief. I inspect for sleep in the corner of my eyes. Like a lover before a date, I swallow some toothpaste. I am ready for my midnight inspection.

* * *

The egg-yolk atmosphere of the rig has disappeared. The corridor glows with a ghostly white light, just like in a vampire movie.

I enter the hall, breathless, my hands awkwardly empty. As my eyes get used to the misty white light, I am arrested by the sight of thirty-nine prisoners curled on their sides. Far, far beneath us, I hear the womb-like lap of water against the legs of the rig. As I pad in, my rubber soles make the faintest of squeaks. How do they sleep with that sharp mesh cutting into them? Their snores travel the airspace at different heights, keep careful flightpaths of soft engine sounds. I creep closer. In this light, Vicki's skin glows an opaque white. Her hips sink towards the sea, rise up to the perfect, pale curve of her buttocks. Her long hair falls away from her face, revealing the girlish naiveté of the husband killer. To me she is a sleeping beauty painted in creamy cow's milk.

Samuel sits up slowly, bewildered. 'Is it morning?' He wipes his face with his whole hand as a lion cub might.

I shake my head, protective of the waking cub. I slide out my phone, stroke its volume to soft. 'Just a quick check. Sorry. I need to see your fingers and teeth.'

Samuel gives his head a little shake, like he can't believe he has woken into this grotesque medical nightmare. He flattens his hands against the mesh. I check his fingers. Samuel grimaces obediently, shows me his teeth.

'Thank you,' my African voicebox quotes me in a whisper. I move towards Eulalie's snore.

'Malachi, wait,' Samuel says. 'I've been counting the days. It's harvest time, isn't it?'

'Tomorrow,' I type.

226

There is a plea in his voice. 'Are they starting with me?'

Eulalie stops snoring, half opens her eyelids. I shake my head, happy to reassure him. 'No. With Shikorina. A crew-member needs new lungs for her child.'

I violate confidentiality with every letter I type but *someone* needs to treat these people like humans. Samuel hangs his head in relief. Eulalie stares at me in the horror-movie light, still curled in her foetal position. At this angle, her nose is a long, thin ridge. Her eyes gather up the loose skin beneath them.

Samuel sighs. 'Maybe it's worse to wait. What do you think, Eulalie?'

Eulalie smiles ruefully. I bend quickly, check her teeth. I see only signs of old-age shuffling, no injuries.

The witch sits up slowly, hugs her knees. 'Malachi?' Her old voice cracks the hush of sleep in the room.

Vicki's eyelids flutter. I want to go close and press them shut. Say, *Sshh. Sleep.*

The witch's voice is too hoarse to tame into a whisper. 'I saw a murder tonight.'

The word strikes a gong in the minds of all the sleeping prisoners. Murder is their other name after all, isn't it?

'A girl with hair so white. And she was thirsty. So thirsty.'

The air dries my open mouth.

Eulalie's old skin pleats her forehead. 'Do you know who this is?'

A metal bolt pierces my chest. I type with shaking fingers, 'A sailor girl they picked up. They were meant to fly her out tonight.' I turn to Vicki, type urgently, 'But I haven't heard them leaving.'

A multitude of people shake their sleepy heads.

'Who killed her, Eulalie?' Samuel urges.

Eulalie presses her fingers to the crook of her old, old arm. 'It was a needle. Her father showed me. They put her to sleep.'

I cry out like some wild jungle bird. 'That's not right!' my Samsung bursts out.

Vicki chuckles bitterly. 'What's right on this rig, Malachi?'

Her irises are soft caterpillars, rolling inwards.

My fingers fly faster than my brain can make sense. 'They are murderers. The girl was sick!'

Eulalie shakes her head as if she too saw the girl's sorrow, her third-degree sunburn. 'Poor Frances.'

Suddenly I doubt my confidence in the old hag. 'Definitely dead?'

The truth is a slow, glowing bullet in her grey eyes. She shoots it gently at me. 'Never dead.' She reminds me, 'Remember Cecilia.'

Vicki crosses her arms over her breasts, hides the succulent tips. 'How old was she?'

'Nineteen,' I type.

'Poor thing,' Madame Sophie groans behind me. She is rumpled after four hours of sleep on a wire bed with no blanket, no mattress, no time to comb the knots from her hair.

I type to thirty-nine witnesses, 'Raizier lied to us. I'm going to ask about Frances.' I shove my phone back in my pocket, hurry towards the entrance.

'Malachi! Wait!' Vicki calls after me.

'Watch out, Malachi!' Samuel shouts.

Why these people should care about me is one unfathomable, deep-sea mystery.

I run in my rubber sneakers, crash into our living quarters. I flip the phone into my fingers, jab at the screen: 'Is the solo sailor dead?'

'Huh? What?'

'Did they kill her?'

'What the fuck.' Tamba switches on his lamp, peers at me through swollen eyelids. 'I thought you couldn't write.'

'I lied, like you. Your father is Doctor Mujuru.'

Tamba sounds like he is having an asthma attack. 'Who told you?'

'You did, you idiot.'

'Huh?'

'Your microphone.'

'Jesus.' He presses his fingers into his eye sockets.

'I heard they killed Frances,' I type.

'Fuck. Where did you hear this stuff?'

'One of the prisoners is psychic.'

Tamba stares at me like I am severely mentally handicapped. 'They're lying.'

'What did they do with the giant?'

'What?'

'Number fifteen. His body.'

Tamba sighs, falls back on his bed. He watches water churning somewhere on the ceiling. 'They took out his stem-cell heart. They took out his teeth. They threw him in the shark pit.'

I recoil with horror, force my fingers to ask, 'His teeth for ID?'

Tamba nods. 'In case someone wants proof.'

The giant guessed it! The judge was right.

Tamba jerks up, watches my phone like it is a lethal weapon. His green streak pulses madly in the soft lamplight. 'You've been talking to the subjects?'

I nod my head defiantly.

Tamba springs to his feet. 'You're not supposed to communicate! I'm going to report you.' He snatches for his Samsung.

I swipe it out of reach, swing my back to him. I type quickly, 'You gave me the phone, you showed me the settings.'

I don't get the chance to type the rest. Tamba is backing away, pleading, 'Don't tell Meirong. Please. You don't know anything.'

I jab my keys. 'Tell me.'

Tamba sits down on his bed. 'Six months ago I was in California State Prison for doing coke.' He begs me, 'I had no money to buy safety, no toothpaste . . .'

I stare, incredulous. Does he expect me to care about his teeth?

'I was dead meat. My father pulled me out just in time. They would have raped me.'

I glance involuntarily at his penis. He covers his genitals as if I might bite them.

'I'm going straight back there if I fuck up.' He slumps down on his bed, hangs his dreadlocks. 'My father's sick of me.' He pleads shamelessly, 'Give me the phone, please. I'll shut up about it.'

'I won't use it again,' I type. Toss his phone into his side of the cabinet.

Tamba dives after it, 'Give it!'

I launch at the cabinet, grab my yellow Pep Stores phone I stowed there on Monday. I wave it in the air. Tamba jumps, tries to wrench it from me, but I hang on to it with all my strength. Tamba has the powerful fingers of a computer geek. He tears the phone free and leaps onto his mattress. I flail wildly for it but Tamba bounds to the floor and beats the phone against the metal wall. It shatters easily. He stamps on the pieces with his bare feet, again and again, splintering them.

I shrink away from him. What if he bleeds?

No. The yellow shards of plastic are just a tiny accident at his feet. I see no blood.

I kneel down, pick up the pieces before he can see that he has just wrecked a cheap yellow Nokia, not a ten-thousand-rand Samsung.

Tamba watches me, fascinated. 'You'll never fix it.'

I drop the plastic pieces in the toilet, flush them into the sea.

Tamba sinks onto his bed, rubs his sensitive feet. 'Stupid to do that without shoes,' he says wryly.

I shake out my white duvet, as if this might restore order to the brutal world. Throw myself under it. Tamba is too sorry for himself to notice I'm still wearing my shoes. He switches off the bedside light.

'Aaagh,' he groans in the stainless-steel silence. In the pitch dark, I hear the soft slam of his head against the pillow. 'I wouldn't be surprised if –' A slow wave of grief breaks over him. He sobs almost silently – for himself or for Frances I can't be certain. I lie against the metal wall, wait for Doctor Mujuru's only child to cry himself to sleep.

When Tamba's tonsils start to ululate gently against his tongue, I sit up in tiny increments, slide my hand slowly into the cabinet. My fingers close on Tamba's unblemished Samsung. I slide it out, press my thumb over the tiny glass circle at its snout. Find the torch button on the right. I stifle the light with my thumb, use the skin-coloured glow to find the pink lanyard on the cabinet. I pinch it with my thumb and forefinger, lift it like a sleeping snake. Meirong's key card to the deck.

I stand up in slow motion, my heart banging like a midnight thief's. Tamba whimpers like a puppy chasing dream rabbits. I tiptoe from the room in crumpled white, the Valentino lover of Vicki, the husband killer.

*

I drop down the three unnecessary steps, slink past the canteen, past the atmosphere of two women sleeping. My rubber soles exhale, deliver me with subtle squeaks to the exit of the maintenance wing. The door to the rig's thoroughfare cries like a house cat. I ease it slowly closed. It meows spitefully. I listen for footsteps. Nothing.

This passage is also shrouded in misty white light. I take off on my toes, run up the first flight, spin on the landing. I climb up, up the metal tree. My sense of conviction powers my legs, swells my lung capacity. I race up the stairs, draw oxygen easily. Within minutes I reach the final door to the sea. I lift the pink lanyard, listen for the click.

I step into the gigantic night, broken wide open by a multitude of stars and planets.

The deck lights are all off, as Meirong has ordered. The moon is almost full, only slightly misshapen. It kisses the wings of the sleeping Dragonfly, lights each blade tenderly. It drips golden effulgence down its white walls, strokes the tail of the beast as a cloud moves aside. The moon gazes into the empty windscreen, besotted, watching the creature sleep. Miles above me, the figure of a man stands sentry in the round surveillance tower. Romano.

I peer along the deck towards the girl sailor's makeshift jail. The storeroom door is wide open. I steal along the façade of the building. As I reach the door, the moon reveals the white spectre of the solo sailor's bed. I slip into the room. Her crumpled sheet is twisted like an intestine. Was there a struggle?

The red ablution bucket stands next to the bed. I look inside. Dry. The solo sailor was too dehydrated to even produce urine. Tonight the weightlifting magazine is not a courtier's fan, it is a grotesque anomaly. It curls on the crate, the tanned mammoth on the cover pumping his muscles for no one. It is too dark for me to see but I know his arteries are writhing just beneath his skin, which is that weird chestnut-red that white people go when they roast on a sun machine.

Move it, Malachi.

Stop slipping sideways, like Hamri.

I run back to the Dragonfly, stand on the circle of white paint that demarcates the landing pad. I wave at Romano's silhouette. He paces a few steps, seems to look right through me. I catch a glimpse of a tiny spark on each shoulder. His Nadras Oil epaulettes. I shuffle along the white line towards the Dragonfly's landing struts. I jump up and down, wave like I am trying to hail a taxi from the night sky. Romano gazes past the rotor blades. Am I invisible? I glance down at myself. No, my white Valentino outfit glows in the moonlight reflecting off the Dragonfly. Romano moves out of sight. I run to the base of the surveillance tower, duck through the small door. I climb a flight of stairs as long and steep as the escalator at Home Affairs in Joburg. I push up with my thighs, up, up the dark lighthouse.

Near the top I double over to catch my breath. The barrel of a gun straightens me up. I throw up my hands, feel my eyelids peel with terror. The AK97 expands, fills my vision.

'Malachi!' Romano drops his rifle, lets it swing like an umbrella he might need in inclement weather.

I jab frantically at my screen. 'They killed Frances.'

'What?'

'She's gone.'

Romano shakes his head, 'They took her to the doctor's rooms. Meirong said they were getting her ready to fly out.'

I falter. What if he is right? Who do I trust, the logistics controller or a ninety-year-old witch?

I think of Cecilia's three moth-kisses above my ear.

Flutterbies.

'They killed her with anaesthetic,' I write. 'They're going to throw her in the shark pit.'

Romano raises his barrel again. 'You're lying.'

I stare into the twin steel chutes. A tiny bit of urine leaks down my leg. I type with jittery fingers, 'Why would I lie?'

'When?'

'Some time before midnight.'

'Where's your proof?'

'When do the sharks feed?' I type hastily.

Romano glares at me fiercely. He thinks I am taunting him with a riddle.

I type ferociously, 'When do they drop dead bodies? That suicide.'

Comprehension grows in Romano's eyes. 'Sunrise. The sharks come at sunrise.'

I glance through the door of his glass station. The moon, only slightly handicapped, sinks lower in the sky.

Romano snatches at his face, makes a funny, explosive squeal. 'Motherfuckers. Frances!' He turns ugly. 'I don't believe you.'

'Come!' I beg him. 'Let's go and see.'

We climb down Romano's dark, dark tower in silence and the sweat of two confused men who want more than anything to see Frances alive. For me she is another schoolgirl I have let die. For Romano she is a daughter who clung to him for the simple chance to see the sky, breathe oxygen.

I follow Romano across the deck, glance up once at the splendid white Dragonfly that also let the young girl die.

* * *

Inside the rig, Romano locks the door behind us and takes off down the man-made cliff, lithe on the narrow landings and the steep stairs. He stops halfway down a flight. His eye-line, when he turns, is my sweating bellybutton.

'If they see us, I'll say you broke security. I'll say I was bringing you in.'

He melts down the staircase, his epaulettes glinting like tiny wings in the surreal white light. I pour myself after him, pride myself on my near-silent rubber landings. Romano's boots are huge yet shockingly stealthy. One longer lace clicks as it touches five thousand metal rungs. The tiny sound amplifies as we near the door to the management wing. I seize Romano's shoulder, stop him. He flings me so hard I slam into a railing.

'Aghh!'

The knob on my head swells beneath my fingertips. I jab at Romano's boot, which in this light looks like it is made of crocodile skin. I kneel at his feet, shove the tardy lace into the tongue of his boot. Romano puts a heavy hand on my crown, blesses me with an apology.

I hate this man. I love him.

We tiptoe like midnight children past the door to the right that says, *Private. Keep Out*. Romano stops so my knee bangs into his back. He cocks his head, listens. There is no sound of the Raizier bosses sacrificing their beauty sleep. We steal past the entrance to the maintenance wing on the left. Again, Romano pauses. There is a muffled gushing sound. Is it a toilet flushing?

Romano hurries down a diagonal flight. I pinch the thick cotton of his shirt, hustle after him.

Slowly the vampire light fades until we are suspended in oily blackness. The lights have been snuffed out in this lower chamber. Is it near their graveyard?

There is the jangle of metal keys as Romano fumbles for something. An infrared ray cuts the dark into black chunks, counts the rivets for us as we descend the next ten metres. The roar of a restless liquid beast rises up through our shoes, louder and louder until it echoes through the steel of a heavily reinforced door. Romano lays his head against this final barrier to the sea. I put my ear to the door, listen with him. Millions of tons of sea batter against our dark castle, warning us to not put a single toe out of it. Romano selects a key card from an entire flush. The click is inaudible against the din of the ocean. A tiny red light turns to green.

Romano shoves his shoulder against the door.

The moonlight leaks beneath the metal edifice into a heaving, hungry pit among the shins of the rig. Romano shines his infrared ray into it. Fifeen metres below us, a black wave rolls back, growls a warning, then smashes against the metal stanchions holding us up. It is relentless, this sea, confident that it is only a matter of centuries before the steel gives. The sea air is foetid with salt and some other, organic matter. Romano crosses the platform outside the door, takes off along a narrow ledge above the stormy pit. He turns, beckons to me. My bulging eyes in his torchlight must express my feelings. *You must be crazy.*

Romano shoots the infrared ray at my feet. 'Come.'

I lift up my feet, one by clumsy one, as if learning to walk. My blood swells inside my ears, slaps against my tympanic membranes. I cling tightly to a slim metal railing I pray was welded to last forever, walk the plank above the barbarous sea.

Ahead of me, Romano is digging his fingers into a rectangular seam in the skirt of the rig. 'Help me.'

I see no possibility of it opening, but I stick my smooth fingertips into the seam. The metal sheet shudders and scrapes along its salt-encrusted tracks in the wall of the rig. The moon sweeps into the opening, caresses an intricate-looking engine. On either side is a lateral brace, not meant for men to rest their bums but to hold the huge engine in its storage place.

'Sit,' Romano commands me.

I climb onto the right ledge, he takes the space on the other side.

'Sewage pump,' he says.

I sniff. I smell no odour of excrement. This moon has a definite fondness for machines. She sidles lower in the sky, hesitates on the horizon as if hypnotised by the object of her love. She seems not to be particular about the purpose of the pump. She strokes it with golden light for what might be hours.

After a long, long soiree, the moon turns silver, makes a strange artwork of Romano and the gigantic sewage system. She paints me silver too, irons out my tired creases, then slowly the light turns a soft charcoal pink. It must be close to sunrise. I bend down, peer towards the horizon. The moon turns transparent, exits discreetly, on her way to commit infidelity in another hemisphere.

Now the sky slowly becomes more frivolous. It turns the sea pink, paints the metal pinions with a hue of watermelon. Below us, triangular pink fins appear as if cued by stage lights.

Sharks. I slam my back against the wall. The triangles thrust higher, show a glistening, glutinous coating on their shark-leather skins. The beasts are two metres, three metres long, some of them. Some of them are babies. I see the colossal dorsal fin of an old warrior, pitted and torn in grey and pink. He rolls below us, his jaw crammed with stalagmites thrusting up in razor-sharp disarray. His tiny eyes hook us in our hiding place. I pull my feet up, bang the back of my head on the steel behind me. Romano laughs softly. The rogue shark dives down deep, leaves the seething pit to the juveniles. Just then, the sound of voices falls into the shark pit, bounces back out.

To the left, past the narrow ledge, the door to the rig is open. Two men stand on the platform, dressed in black as if they hoped to cloak themselves in the darkness of the night. They did not expect pink. One is a black man of about fifty, if his grey sideburns are not lying. His face wears an expression of habitual scepticism. Could this be Tamba's father? Yes. He has the same straight shoulders, the same anarchic eyebrows as his rebel son. The other man is plump, as soft as the hake he would become if he fell in. But he says something to Tamba's father, points at the sharks like this is an aquarium. The men disappear through the doorway.

They re-emerge carrying a stretcher. On it is a skeleton, painted pink. Its hipbones are like soup plates, the valley between them grotesquely steep. They must have torn off her shirt after her last breath, dishonoured her by stripping off her father's boxer shorts. The girl was skin and bone beneath her ragged clothing. Her pubic hair is blonde and sparse. Her pale nipples look lifelessly to the side – no flesh to point them heavenward. It is only her eyes that stare towards us. From here I catch a sheen of their arc-eye brilliance.

Oh, Frances.

The plump man loosens the strap around her ankles. Tamba's

father loosens the strap around her sunken solar plexus. Below us, the sharks spin and thrash in grey and black, roll over to get a better view of the skinny offering. Frances' white hair falls back, less frayed in this party light. Tamba's father tips the front end of the stretcher up. The sun arrives above the horizon, turns her sunburnt eyes a turquoise blue.

Is she alive?

But Frances is as stiff as a board as she shoots off the stretcher and slips feet first into the sea. The huge, scarred monster blasts up from the deep. It opens its jaws, engulfs Frances up to her abdomen. Her arms do not flail or fly, she is a rigor-mortis mannequin as the beast lifts her so high she gazes up at us.

Daddy, I hear her say.

The shark plunges into the sea, drags Frances down into its black-and-blue violence. Romano's feet are on the ledge beneath his bum, his head crushed between his knees. A funny sound issues from him, a high-pitched whining. I shove my hand behind a ridged metal pipe, clamp it over Romano's mouth. *Shut up.*

I close my eyes, feel a small desperate relief for the little prick Frances must have felt as they put her to sleep. But my comfort is short-lived. When I open my eyes there is red spilling – bright scarlet in the light, blacker in the shadows. Frances was thirsty but her thin body was filled with blood. My stomach hurls me over my knees. I vomit into the shark pit. A trail of bile sails into the churning sea.

'Stop it,' Romano whispers.

But Tamba's father misses it. He pats his plump colleague on the back. I see his lips, full like Tamba's, form the words, 'Thank you.'

Shitting bastards. Frances wanted to live!

I stare at the red water fading to a less terrible shade. I lock my eyes onto the horizon, where the sun has become a bare, blunt orange.

I am not afraid.

I heard her say, *Daddy*.

Even though they murdered her, I don't care what anyone says. There is no such thing as death.

The doctors pick up their empty stretcher, disappear into the rig. The steel door shuts behind them. Romano is crying openly now.

I set my volume to loud. 'They kill the prisoners. Don't they?'

Romano is rubbing his eyes like he wants to pluck them out. 'I hate them. I hate them.'

'Some of them are innocent.'

'Frances,' he groans. 'She begged me, Malachi.'

'I know. I know. She trusted you.'

'She begged me to get her black box off her boat.'

'Where is the yacht?'

Romano points at the huge metal leg to the right of the shark pit. I make out a dark hatch in the cylinder shafting into the sea. 'I winched it up. Meirong's orders.' Romano snarls, 'I hate her!'

I bend over and vomit again into the pit. Wipe my mouth. I sit with my phone loose on my lap and watch the sun rise in its yellow battle-dress. My heart is emptied out. My mind is very clear as to what I must do next.

'Let's get the black box. Let's call for help.'

Romano shakes his head wildly. 'No. Tomorrow I bomb the boat.' He grabs something from an inside pocket. 'Look.' He thrusts it through the convoluted piping of the pump. It is a glossy photo of a child, her pink dress too loose for her stick figure. 'My baby, Milja.' An ocean of love glows from the eyes in the photograph.

'She calls me Chefe Sol. Sun Chief. She trusts I will save her life.' Romano stares at me through the tangled machinery. 'Meirong says they will send a heart from this harvest.'

'Do you believe her?'

Romano taps the space between his eyes. 'Meirong knows I will put a bullet here if she lies to me. For then I have nothing to live for. *Nothing.*' He climbs out and grabs my hand, jerks me back onto the narrow ledge. My phone flies from my grip. I snatch it from the air, drop it into my pocket. Romano shuts the sliding panel with astonishing strength. He walks the plank above the shark pit, still streaked with hungry fins. I clutch the railing, follow him to the door.

As Romano lifts the key card, the sewage pump starts up. Brownish fluid pours from a round opening below where we were sitting, flies into the shark pit. The anus of the rig. Three sharks rise to receive the prisoners' overnight excrement. The others slash at them with vicious envy.

I hope they shoot me. The thought drills through my head like keyhole surgery.

Let them shoot me rather, if they catch me.

I raise my hand to Romano's neck, as hard as iron. He flinches at my touch. I pull out my Samsung.

'I am sorry about Frances. You tried your best.'

Romano buckles, drops his heavy head to my shoulder. I sling an arm around his back, hold him tight, like a father. Romano begins his terrible, strange keening again. I take the key card from his fingers, turn the light green. I kick the door open and nudge Romano inside the rig. I follow him in, shut the metal door behind us. This time I raise the key card to just below the contact zone. The green light stays on but I sling the lanyard around Romano's neck, usher him into the pitch dark. Romano shrugs me off violently, bounces on the balls of his feet. He snatches for his torch, slices at me with his stream of red light.

'You are not my friend, Malachi!' He stabs two fingers towards his eyes. 'From now on I am watching you.' He bounds up the stairs, powerful, ready to do anything, *anything* to save his daughter's life.

THURSDAY

This time the feline hinges shriek loudly. Twice. I hustle into the maintenance wing, pass the women's quarters, my ears reassured by the engine sound of a snore. Could it be Olivia?

I crash into our bedroom, snap on the light. I haul out my suitcase, try three zips before I find my paper notepad and my old roller-gel plastic pen. I poke Tamba's naked chest with it.

He smacks at the pen, misses. 'Hey!'

I write in large, extravagant letters: *They killed the solo sailor.*

Tamba stares at my dishevelled white outfit. 'Where have you been?'

They threw her in the shark pit.

Daddy, I heard her say.

I tear off the page, write in gigantic letters: THE GIRL SAILOR IS DEAD.

Tamba jerks to a sitting position, gasping. I wait mercilessly. He rubs his knees compulsively, as if this might ease the agony of the truth.

'These people are not human,' he says.

I slay him with my roller-gel weapon: *It was your father.*

'Oh God.' Tamba clutches his head. 'Basta-a-a-rd . . .!' He leaps up and charges at the metal wall, smashes his forehead against it. A red rivulet trickles towards his eyebrows, so very, very much like Doctor Mujuru's.

I tear my eyes from the blood.

It's slaughter. This whole thing.

Tamba shakes his head, paces the tiny room. 'It's not the same, Malachi. That girl was innocent.'

I hold up my white pad, torch him silently. *You are guilty of murder.*

He tears at his dreadlocks like a mad, naked beggar. I stare at his skinny legs, strangely adolescent for his broad chest.

SIT, I command him.

Tamba sits. I perch on the corner of his bed, write quickly, *Some of the prisoners are also innocent.*

Tamba stares at my white pad, distressed.

Help me to free some.

He leaps up. 'Are you fucking crazy?' His torn hair sails from his fingers to the floor. Some kind of vacuum sucks it into the corridor. 'I told you, if I screw up, I go straight back to prison.'

I write desperately: *I will NEVER say you helped me!* I underline *NEVER* three times.

Tamba prowls around my notepad, re-reads my plea. I catch his hand, pull him to sit again. I keep my eyes off the red trickle, for if I look at it I will be sick all over my only writing instruments.

The journalist, Samuel. Sentenced in Algeria. They blamed him for a bomb but all he did was film it.

Tamba leaps up, turns in a circle.

The girl, Lolie. Kidnapped when she was ten. They smothered her with a plastic bag to make her shoot the enemy.

Tamba wipes frantically at his face, claustrophobic. 'Stop!'

I attack him relentlessly. *What did they do to Dominic?*

'Idaho State Penitentiary for Serious Psychiatric Disease.'

How do you live with it?

Tamba hooks his feet on the bed frame and rubs at the punctures. 'I'm *battling*, Malachi.' His voice cracks, lets his tears through. 'He was cool, Dominic.'

I strike while he is vulnerable. *You know how you feel about him?*

Tamba raises his arm, wipes his face with the soft inner flesh of his bicep.

Multiply that by forty. I dare to look him in the eye, now that he has erased the blood. *You will be half a man. Every day hiding from the other half. It's a life sentence.*

Tamba pinches at the needle marks on his arms. 'Better than California State Prison.' He leaps to his feet. 'I can't take the risk!'

Their ghosts will have supper with you, sleep with you, follow you to the toilet. What will you do then, take more drugs?

Tamba crumples onto the cabinet. 'I'm an addict, Malachi . . .' His watery tears don't even have the decency to form droplets.

I crawl on my hands and knees, collect the white pages strewn around the room. I tear them into tiny pieces. They can go to the same place as my shattered Nokia. Let the sharks eat my futile plea. I crush the paper strips between my palms, walk towards the bathroom.

Tamba talks to my hopeless spine, 'The only way is to shut off the power.'

I stop in my tracks.

'You've got three seconds before the second generator kicks in. The cages will unlock for three seconds. All of them.'

I turn slowly to face him.

'The power switch is under my stairs. Second one from the top.

All you have to do is lift the cover.' Tamba stabs a finger at me. 'They'll catch you, Malachi. The whole deck has cameras.'

Uh uh. No. There is one blind spot.

Tamba leaps off the cabinet. 'Romano will kill you.'

I reach for him, still clasping my torn petition, but he dives away from me.

'I don't want to know!' He stops at the concertina door. 'If you tell me, I'll bust you.' He slams the door behind him. I listen to the gushing tap, my hands still in prayer position.

What must I do with my broken words, eat them?

I glance at my timepiece. 6.55 a.m. I drum on the bathroom door. Tamba slides it open, his chin dripping. I thrust our tattered conversation into his wet hands. As he takes the torn paper, I grab hold of his hand and pull it to my lips. Kiss it. Tamba jerks his hands back, his face a mask of wet shock. He drags the door shut.

I smile ruefully to the ancestors who might be watching me. I forced my love onto a single tip of Tamba's thumb.

6.56. No time to get dressed. I lift an arm, sniff. I smell strangely like fish. I glance down at my shabby angel's attire. There is a streak of oil on my shirt from the sewage pump. I rub feebly at it. I have no time to wash or dress like a hero. I must be punctual. Now, more than ever, I must make no mistakes.

I slide Meirong's deck key beneath my mattress, the most original hiding place in human history.

I hurry along the corridor to the canteen. Must I free all of them?

Josiah. The rapist. Must I save them too? They deserve this slow death, surely.

What of Charmayne, and the fat Australian? If I free them, I will be aiding and abetting the life of murderers.

I try to remember the judge's list. Samuel, Andride, Eulalie, Lolie. My darling Vicki. He said any free country would give them asylum. The others would surely go straight back to their old jails. I stumble down the three random steps.

One thing I know is, no matter what happens, they will never be able to scrub off their skins. Josiah's Seleka worms will continue to lay and hatch, lay and hatch inside his anus. The priest-burner's melted fingers will marry him to the priest every time he reaches out to press an elevator button, touch a lover.

Tamba comes thumping after me, his Jesus sandals flapping. He is still zipping up some white jeans, his father's broad chest still bare. He tugs a cream-coloured shirt over his head. We walk one behind the other wrapped in a terse, silent contract that says, The last ten minutes?

They never, ever happened.

Romano is sitting with Meirong at the breakfast table, looking belligerent. The two of us make sure that our eyes don't crash. Meirong is in a tight-fitting white dress, like a nurse in a pornographic movie. Her lipstick is too thick, too red. She chose the colour of the prisoners' blood on cutting day. Insensitive. Her hair has recovered its shining discipline – no more cows have ventured out to sea to lick at her parting.

Meirong has no time for niceties this morning. She thrusts her hand out. 'Key card, Malachi. It's been worrying me all night.'

I let out a dismayed, 'Ah.' I pat my pockets, flutter my fingers near my neck. I hit my head like an under-par, imperfect idiot.

Meirong picks up her fork, impales an unnaturally red vienna. 'Get it straight after breakfast.'

Janeé bounces two of the viennas onto my plate.

Meirong asks me, 'Tamba has told you we're operating today?'

'I told him,' Janeé crows cheerfully. She has a huge white apron tied around her waist like she suspects there might be spatters.

Meirong throws a cutting glance at Tamba. She eats three red viennas in succession, pours herself a second glass of raspberry juice. Is it a boss's thing, this passion for red colourant? She downs half the glass. It makes me itchy just to watch her.

Feeling sweeter, she briefs Tamba about the security status: 'They're motoring in circles, moving very slowly due south. They're almost out of range. To be safe we'll keep security tight for one more day.'

She tells Romano, 'One last double shift.'

Romano crushes his viennas against his palate. He eats his toast more tenderly, gazing into space, honey dripping from his lips. The man will be exhausted by tonight. Surely.

Olivia breezes in wearing her white lab-coat and a long white skirt. Look at us. Did someone put out a memo saying wear white to breakfast?

She shrugs off her coat. Beneath it she is wearing a pleated blouse with fat, pink flowers. Her hair is unbrushed, she looks like a happy hippie. Her blue stains have turned purplish beneath her eyes as if her excitement is beating her up, killing her. She has slapped on some pink lipstick but missed and got her teeth. Olivia's eyes shine weirdly as she boasts, 'If everything works out, Timmy will get his lungs by seven tonight. They say he'll only spend three nights in ICU. Isn't that amazing?'

'Fantastic,' Tamba says sincerely.

'Oh, oh, oh, I wish I was at home –' Olivia stops, recovers her tact. 'But I'm happy to wait here for six months. It's nothing. My granny will take a photo and send it with Mr Rawlins.' Olivia scoops her honey off her toast, sucks her finger noisily.

Did her granny not teach her manners?

I dip my spoon into the cup of honey. Janeé urges me on happily, 'We've got a two-litre jar of it.'

'It's kind of Mr Carreira to share it,' Meirong says primly. 'Susan Bellavista sent it to him as a gift.'

So that was what was in the copper vase with the red ribbon. It looked like an urn for the ashes of forty corpses.

Tamba scoffs, 'Yeah, like a pot of honey can make up for Dominic.'

'Tamba,' Meirong warns.

Tamba shuts up but I know what he means. Idaho State Penitentiary for Serious Psychiatric Disease.

Oh, God.

Will Dominic's fate seem like a funfair compared to the disaster I am about to bring about?

I take a bite of honey toast. Yumm. Bees buzz in my head. Somewhere I think I can hear cuckoos.

Araba's mother kept a blue cuckoo at the door to their hut. I made every excuse to take the footpath past their place in the hope of seeing my love eat her corn porridge or put on her socks and shoes. The cuckoo always burst out laughing and made me hurry past.

Seriously, Malachi. Cuckoos at sea?

Tamba shoves into my daydream. 'Five subjects fewer today. The surgeries come back at . . . What time, Meirong?'

'Eleven thirty.'

'They're too groggy on day one to hurt themselves with their nails.'

Meirong nods sternly. 'Best to leave them to rest.'

It's the kindest thing Meirong has ever said about the prisoners.

She twirls her spoon in the honey. She closes her eyes and sucks like a kitten.

'Meirong?' Romano says.

When she opens her eyes, Meirong looks drunk on honey. She gets clumsily to her feet. 'Malachi, the key.'

I get up, my mind darting like a kankabi moth caught in a gas lamp.

'Meirong,' Romano repeats. She seems not to hear him. Romano jumps to his feet. 'Meirong!'

Meirong swings. 'Sit.'

But Romano towers above her shiny head. 'You made me wait, the last harvest.'

'Mr Carreira is still checking his emergency lists. He says he will try this time to allocate a heart for . . . for . . .'

'Milja!' Romano snarls the name of his reason for living. He sits down grudgingly. In my mind I can hear it, the high-pitched whine of Romano's pain squeezing out, the frequency too fine for our logistics freak.

'It's half past,' Meirong says. 'Come, Tamba, we've got to winch those subjects up.' She stabs her finger at me. 'Give the key to me at lunch.'

She sweeps out in her pornographic white to supervise the winching of Shikorina, Lolie and three other unlucky prisoners through the roof.

Romano's flesh still screams with silent misery, but he arranges his wiry limbs in a dignified exit. Janeé and Olivia get up in unison, bump into each other. Olivia disappears into Janeé's clasp, so all that's left is a thatch of blonde static under Janeé's chin, a scrap of pink flowers under one armpit.

Olivia comes up, suffocated and pink. 'God bless us,' she breathes. She sails from the canteen.

Janeé stays to stack the plates, which stick together as if with glue.

In a little while, Shikorina will present Olivia's baby with a spanking new pair of lungs, and a quiver of blood vessels for Janeé's useless son.

How on earth will the child killer manage to climb from her cage after this, never mind hurry up a thousand metal stairs? What of the fat Australian? Surely he is not fit enough to run for his life?

A sinking feeling bolts me to my seat. It is too much. I am not suited to this heroism.

I ladle two spoonfuls of honey onto my last slice, take a bite. A sweet calm comes over me. The prisoners will have free choice for three seconds. Free will, courtesy of Malachi the mute, the lover of honey.

Thank you to the bees. Even the ones who killed a thief at the off-ramp eatery. I read about it in the taxi.

Thank you to the spring that grew the blossoms the honeybees sucked.

Thank you, Susan, for the gift. I am so sorry to ruin your career, but it might pay you back for all those chocolate-flavoured farts.

I take another bite. Delicious.

Thank you for the taste buds I still have in my cheeks. And for my beating heart, leading me inexorably towards the sea.

I collect my white towels for the very last time.

At the door to the hall, I let my key card do its magic. Open the door to my second chance.

* * *

The last five cages are already missing. Their cradles lie empty, their feed pipes hang uselessly. The prisoners are all craning their necks, gazing up at a cage swinging by its thick chain near Tamba's surveillance glass.

'Help me . . .' a girl's voice drifts from the roof, 'Ple-e-ase.'

'Be calm, Lolie!' the desert strangler soothes.

Through the glass, Meirong is standing over Tamba, prodding at something on his DJ desk. She steps back, exasperated, flings a few words at his dreadlocks. She disappears. Tamba sits hypnotised by the tears glittering on Lolie's cheeks, her kohl eyes terrified.

Her cage is stuck.

'Don't worry, you're safe, Lolie!' the social worker shouts. 'They have too much to lose.'

Andride is right. If the chain snaps, they will risk three priceless GM spleens.

'Help me-e,' she cries.

'Close your eyes!' Madame Sophie shouts.

Lolie shuts her eyes tightly. Madame Sophie begins to sing, 'Rocka-bye baby on the tree top . . .'

'Oh, God, Sophie,' Vicki groans.

Tamba is watching this fascinating movie without sound. He squeaks through my device, 'The engineer is coming. Bear with me, Malachi.'

But what the heck is he doing besides staring at Lolie? I glare up at Tamba, send him a silent message. *That's the girl they tortured with the plastic bag.*

It's as if Tamba hears me. He swivels on his chair, scoots far away from the beautiful, distressed assassin. I hurry to Samuel's cage. He senses my urgency, shoves his hands into the sheath.

I bow over them, type beneath the leather shield. 'Tonight. Get ready. I am going to switch the power off. Your cages will unlock for three seconds.'

Samuel's fingers curl with shock. The prisoners near us gasp, strain their ears to hear my spokesman over Madame Sophie's singing.

'There's a search going on for Frances –' I stop. It's too complicated. 'We can try to catch up with them.'

Samuel's eyes glow with courage. 'When?'

'I will come in at midnight.'

'When the wind blows . . .'

Lolie's eyes are closed, she's clinging to Madame Sophie's tender soprano.

'. . . the cradle will rock.' Madame Sophie leaves out the last, catastrophic lyrics.

Above us, Tamba is still cowering from his conscience, out of sight.

I type quickly, 'We can try to launch the lifeboat.'

'Do you know how?'

I shake my head.

Samuel says, 'I filmed a launch once from a container ship. I was doing a feature on piracy.'

Across the aisle, Josiah shuffles out of his lethargy. He sits up straight, his scarred eyes slowly letting in light.

I type to Samuel, 'We might get shot. There's a soldier on deck with an AK97.'

Samuel nods. 'Romano.'

I glance at him, astonished.

'Dominic told us,' Vicki murmurs.

I have a vision of Vicki's lungs exploding before Romano's machine gun. I dare not look at her face or her breasts in case it comes again. I look down, type fervently, 'If you don't want to take the risk, just stay in your cage.'

But Vicki's dark eyes grab hold of me, press my breath from me. 'I want to.'

The old witch nods and smiles. 'Let's go and see the sun rise.' She sounds like a young heroine in a *Grave Escape* TV show.

The information travels down the aisles in short, sharp sentences. 'Three seconds . . . Midnight . . . Malachi . . .'

I clean Samuel's feet gently. Please God let them hold him upright for the first time in fourteen weeks. I hit the buckle, set them free.

'Thank you,' Samuel says simply, the look in his eyes like the dying lioness when we saved her cubs.

As I clip the witch's fingers, they say my name down the aisle, achingly pretty. I drop the clippers on my sneaker, pick them up. They think I am a hero but I am a fumbling idiot. And Madame Sophie's incessant singing is driving me insane.

Vicki slips her crooked, cute toes into the brace. 'Why are you risking your life for us?'

Her question tugs at my vocal chords. I glance up. Tamba is sitting with his back to Lolie, staring at his wall of computer portraits. Is he watching Vicki? I catch her baby toe between my fingers, squeeze it. Point up at Tamba, put my finger to my lips. I press each of Vicki's funny, swollen toes one by one. I can't help it. There is something about sex and death. I feel my penis come alive, remember the love I showed it last night. All I want to do is take Vicki's sweet, clean toes into my mouth.

Vicki suppresses a giggle. The purple vortex of her eyes does some weird tantric trick.

'Ticklish,' she breathes.

I see a flash of Meirong's white outfit high above us. I slip my phone back in my trousers. It knocks my penis, tells it to go to sleep. I hurry through Vicki's feet, that today seem dangerously sexy.

A metallic grating sound rattles the air above us. The hatch slides open next to the surveillance station. A thin man appears in the rectangular space, a torch shining from his forehead. He wears loose white overalls, like he too got the memo. Is this snail the same man inside the fire suit on Sunday? He shines his headlight to the roof, his eyes ghoulish below the beam. His fingers are long protuberances poking a spanner into the machinery above him. Is he going to cut the chain and let Lolie crash to her death?

We listen to the clank of his metal tool, the click, click of some stubborn ratchet. Tamba's fingers are poised on his table top as if he is about to play a piano piece. He refuses to look at Lolie, but Meirong's eyes are stripping the poor girl's bare skin inch by inch. I think I hear her snort.

The engineer raises his radio to his mouth. Tamba presses a switch.

Lolie's cage sways wildly, shunts towards the shadowy opening.

'Good luck, Lolie,' someone says dolefully.

Meirong watches us with her hands on her hips. Some kind of silence thickens in the glass box, I can almost see it.

I keep my eyes down for five more prisoners. When I get to the desert strangler, he says urgently, 'I worked for three months on an oil rig off Eritrea. They taught us the lifeboats.' He frowns anxiously. 'I will try to remember, Malachi.'

Try, Gibril, try.

I glance up. Meirong gives me a wisp of a smile. She gives Tamba's shoulder the ghost of a stroke, perhaps some kind of frail apology. Then she turns on her heel and departs with just a shimmer of her pale thigh.

I cleanse the strangler's sinful hands for the last time in my life. I thought he was from the desert. How the heck did he end up working offshore? Perhaps he will regale me with his story while we die slowly of thirst on a mysterious sea.

The tooth-extracting Indian whoops with joy as I catch his hands, then frets compulsively in Hindi or some dialect. Will he cooperate tonight, or will he make a big noise and sabotage the mission? I cross the space the good giant inhabited. Sneak my Samsung beneath my brace, type to the Australian, 'Can you keep him quiet tonight?'

'I can try.' Barry scratches behind his ear. 'Maybe we should leave him.'

Upstairs, Tamba is tapping the screen of an app. Is he playing *Fruits against Ghouls*?

'We can't. It's all or nothing. There's only one power switch.'

The skinny rapist nods, incredulous. 'They're not even leaving *me*.'

Barry gives me his flabby fingers. 'Do you think we have a chance?'

I hide my terror, type, 'No clue.'

'One thing I can do is swim. My father let me eat as much KFC as I wanted, but he made me go to swimming lessons.' Barry gives me his soft feet. 'I loved it once I was in. But it's a long way from the changing rooms in your speedo when you're a fat kid.' He laughs, asks desperately, 'Do you think we'll have to swim?'

I type beneath the brace, 'We will have to see.' This is all I have to offer him.

The skinny rapist bestows an awed gratitude on me, but he and Josiah are the ones I would leave behind. If the rapist survives this crazy mission, I must personally make sure that someone, somewhere takes him into custody. Josiah too. And the Australian. They should never be released into society.

I finish the rapist's feet, bury his towel in the disinfectant. I sigh, exhausted by the terrible responsibility.

As Hamri used to say, I will have to cross that bridge.

The next few prisoners thank me in languages I can't even guess at. *Stop*, I want to say. *The chances are you will drown or be shot down by a desperately tired war vet.*

I am relieved to reach Andride, my fellow Bhajoan. As I lop off his nails, he picks up my secret tremors. 'Are you scared, Malachi?'

Tamba's knees are up, his chin digging into his chest. His shoulders twitch with the ecstasy of killing ghouls with his thumbs. If I didn't know better, I'd say he was masturbating.

I shrug. 'My life is not worth living if I turn a blind eye.'

But my fear keeps hitting me in sickening waves. Am I about to orchestrate another massacre?

'I'm scared too.' Andride laughs feverishly. 'I can't swim.'

'Oh, shit.'

Sorry Hamri.

I say nothing to Andride about the size of the sharks' teeth. I wipe his hands gently, hope he knows to keep his fingers pressed together while he is scratching towards the surface of the sea.

When I reach the priest killer, he interrogates me. 'I worked on the docks in Larache in the winter. Does the lifeboat have an electric winch? I knew those ones from the big ships.'

I think of the metal mount near Romano's lifeboat. Is that it? I nod uncertainly.

'What is the distance to the water? Maybe fifty metres?'

I nod. At least.

The priest killer sighs. 'It's not as easy as you think.' He watches me work on his feet. 'Do you have a radio to call for help if we get onto the sea?'

I glance up at the glass. Tamba is still smashing ghouls with pieces of fruit.

'Maybe.' I type quickly. 'Do you know anything about yacht radio systems?'

The priest burner shakes his head. He translates my question into Arabic. Andride translates into what must be French. There is a thoughtful, frightened silence.

I try the magic concept. 'Does anyone know how to work a black box?'

The tooth-pulling Indian starts to chatter. I turn his way. He is tapping at his head with a good, short nail that I have just clipped.

'What's he saying?' the priest killer asks. 'Does anyone know Hindi?'

Charmayne snaps at the Indian, 'Speak English, Vihaan.'

The Indian stares at Charmayne, taps his head manically, 'In the navy. In the navy.'

Oh, please. A crazy man as my communications assistant. I cast around, plead wordlessly, *Can anyone else help me?*

'Leave it, Malachi,' Charmayne warns me. 'Tamba's watching.'

Tamba stands up, kneads his eyes with his knuckles like a tired child.

He announces through my intercom, 'Time to eat.' His microphone clicks off. He disappears from the window.

Down the aisle, Madame Sophie says tremulously, 'I'm *so* scared of big waves.'

Big waves? I want to laugh. Is this what Madame Sophie thinks of the mountainous sea thrashing with a species of shark that chopped Frances in two pieces?

Sorry, Frances. I am so, so sorry.

The same sea that drank the solo sailor's blood will hold us up to the vicious sun, let it peel our skin then fill our lungs, forty of us, with the tiniest of gestures.

But Vicki says kindly, 'Come on, Sophie, after what we've been through, the sea is nothing.' She grins. 'The only thing is, you're going to have to mess up your hair.'

'Man, Vicki!'

Their sweet laughter bruises my intestines.

Am I making the same mistake? Am I murdering my classmates?

Their laughter trails into silence as I hurry past them, crash my tools on the trolley. I feel a feather of consternation floating from Vicki but I let it fall to the floor, almost run from the hall.

I stare up the spiral stairs, try to make out the cover of the power switch Tamba spoke of. The handle of the surveillance door twists. I scurry on, my heart stampeding. And I have not done one single heroic thing.

* * *

I take a leak, as they say, in the privacy of the concertina bathroom. Listen to my musical pee.

259

I've got to do something drastic to hold on to the deck key.

I try to visualise the locking system, a mixture of digital and old-fashioned penetration. Piston into cylinder. My brain tries to push through nerve ends that never did grow dendrites. I was not born with my mother's good reason. I am a hopeless dreamer, I realise now, like Hamri.

Hopeless.

But my eyes in the mirror are a strange golden hue, cleansed by the tears and the trauma of the last week. I smile tentatively. I like the look of me.

I wash my armpits in the basin. Wipe at the oil stain from the sewage pump, rub green soap into it. I scratch the black mark with my nails, which seem to have grown quicker than usual in this place. I go to lunch with a big wet patch on my chest.

Tamba's knife and fork are suspended in the air as he stares into his plate, fascinated. 'What is it?'

'At home, we call it tomato bredie.' Janeé slaps down a pastry. 'And steak and kidney pie.' She must have pulled the pie from the Ice Age, then abused it with her microwaves.

Meirong arrives and takes her place next to Olivia. We all watch her with an air of tight expectancy. She spoons in tomato stew so fast, it's like she has a secret proboscis. Meirong's hair has become slightly stringy since this morning. She is sweating a bit. Did she hold a scalpel in the doctor's rooms? No. Her white dress is quite unblemished.

She knocks back a tall glass of colourant, smiles suddenly. 'It's looking good. No losses so far. We've got five organs safely in the incubators.'

Olivia and Janeé burst into delighted laughter. I pick at my pastry while the three women across from me guzzle their tomato bredie like vampire bats. I expect them to tip over any minute and hang by their tails.

Tamba scoops out the insides of his kidney pie. 'Freaky, wasn't it, that prisoner hanging from the roof?'

If I survive, I will use the word 'freaky'.

'I thought it was you, jamming the system,' Meirong says.

Tamba nods self-righteously. 'You know what thought did.'

Planted a kidney and thought a prisoner would grow.

The three women stare at their pastry. Janeé says, 'I know what we need.' She teeters backwards, stretches for the trolley. Olivia and Meirong lean forward instinctively. Janeé snatches a huge bottle of tomato sauce and pops off the lid. She shakes it too hard. Plop. Plop. It lands like a hippo's shit hitting the earth. I pull flakes off my incinerated pastry, suck on them.

'Malachi?' Olivia says worriedly.

I stab a kidney, blow on it.

'Is there another pie for me?' Tamba asks.

Janeé stares at the shattered pastry on his plate.

'I like the insides,' Tamba says defensively.

I push my pie across to Tamba. He pushes it back to me. I shove it his way. *Take it.* The three vampire bats pause in their feeding.

'You haven't eaten!' Tamba snaps.

What he is saying is, Fuck you, Malachi, for making me feel guilty.

A short, harsh grunt issues from my throat. Not a single soul has mentioned the solo sailor. Not once.

I impale a kidney, thrust my fork at Tamba. He surrenders, takes it between his teeth like he knows he's going to need the haemoglobin.

Meirong has made tomato-sauce patterns on her plate, somewhat curved and chaotic for a meticulous woman. In a few seconds she will ask me for her key to the deck. It is time to put myself at risk.

I pour myself a glass of the juice. Slug it down. The stump of my tongue prickles, then stings. The membranes of my mouth catch alight. The fire spreads beneath my cheekbones, even my eyes itch. My scalp tries to lift up and fly towards the portholes above us. A hundred bees bite into it. I scratch it with my hands, scratch, scratch, scratch, but my hands are afflicted too. Tiny eruptions appear on them, red blisters that make my fingers go stiff. I stare at my hands, watch them popping up like tiny volcanoes.

Olivia's eyes go as wide as a bush baby's.

'Oh, no. Allergy. Quick!'

She grasps my wrist with shocking strength, drags me to my feet. I collide with Meirong's elbow so red juice spills on the table, drips to the floor. Olivia pulls like a steam train as I scratch at my eyes, add a tight little cough to my symptom picture.

She drags me through the door of her laboratory, rips a drawer open. The little plastic sacs are still draped on the counter, waiting. Antibiotics, must be, to stop infection in the cells of my evil friends once the doctors have hacked their treasures from them. Olivia drops a clutch of tiny bottles on the counter, flicks through them with a finger, muttering, 'Anti– Anti– Anti–' She falls on a brown bottle with a trampoline top. She fits a hypodermic needle into a syringe, stabs her needle into the rubber lid.

In the tiny mirror above the basin, I see Meirong hurry in. 'How bad?'

Olivia narrows her eyes, draws the fluid up.

'Must I call Doctor Mujuru?' Meirong asks.

Olivia shakes her head, doesn't bother with conversation. She raises the syringe to the light, presses out a pustule of air. It pre-ejaculates onto her flowery sleeve. A hippie with a hypodermic. God help me.

Olivia undoes my belt buckle.

Meirong steps back, darts her eyes to the wall of the laboratory. She thrusts out a hand. 'Malachi. I need that key.'

Olivia struggles to undo my zip. 'Not now. Please.'

I pull my zip down with stinging fingers, drop my trousers to my feet. Shove my boxer shorts past my knees.

In the mirror, Meirong stares at my bare bum like it is a wild animal on the loose in the city. Olivia stabs the needle into my flesh. It bites like a knife tip. I think I hear the surface cells of my skin pop. Meirong watches her squeeze the fluid slowly in.

Olivia rubs the site of the injury. 'There,' she breathes.

I deliberately leave my white trousers at my feet. Meirong keeps staring at my black arse, not with revulsion, not with lust. But something close to it.

She is ashamed of my beauty.

'Get the key, Olivia. Keep it for me.' Meirong disappears from the mirror.

Olivia stares at my good buttocks, thanks to my years of running on the spot. 'Can you feel it working?'

I feel it. A relaxed sensation is coming over me, spreading from my hypothalamus all the way to my knees. My stomach feels fluttery. It feels just like love.

Olivia's yellow tinge returns to her cheeks. She announces happily, 'Metorizine.' She smiles like she and I share the same blood-stream. 'A very powerful antihistamine.'

263

I bend towards my dropped trousers, give Olivia a deliberate, clear view of my swinging testicles.

She stares at my penis, backlit by the laboratory light. 'God in heaven!'

It is not my stallion anatomy that is taking her breath away. It is the lightning strikes on the loose tissue of my genitals. I turn as I pull up my boxer shorts, give her a full-frontal view.

Olivia swivels towards the wall, grants me my dignity. 'Who did that to you?'

I watch her in the mirror, slide two plastic sacs off the counter. Shove them into my shorts.

Olivia keeps her back to me, chokes with pity. 'I'm so *sorry*, Malachi.'

I snatch the other three sacs, stuff them in. Pull up my white trousers, do up my zip.

'Was it torture?'

Of course I remain mute. I thread my belt buckle, tighten it.

'Oh, Malachi.' Olivia peeps to check that I am decent. She makes a feverish promise: 'When I get home I'm never *ever* going to let my little boy out of my sight.' She shakes her head, forever haunted by the sight of my private parts. 'It's *terrible*, what people do.'

Olivia forgets to ask me for my key.

I hurry away with my stolen goods, pass the empty canteen. The table is clean and tidy, the sachets of salt pointing up to the roof. A few drops of red juice still stick to the floor where Meirong was sitting. It's just a matter of time and she will come for me. I've got to think of something more practical than drinking poison.

I'll have to switch keys. But how do I give up my key card to the prisoners?

I stop in my tracks.

Salt.

I backtrack along the corridor, slip into the canteen. I grab a sachet of salt, drop it in my pocket.

A slim extract of the sea, a slim chance of succeeding, but I have no choice but to clutch at straws. Or should I say, sachets of sodium.

I swing into the bedroom, peel the antibiotics from my skin. I pack them inside my pillowcase, flip the pillow, plump it.

Sorry, Cecilia. Sorry, Hamri. I know how hard you tried to teach me honesty.

The antihistamine blesses me with their forgiveness, carries me to the dead-end door. I raise the key card, open the door a tiny bit. I prod my fingers into the metal pocket that receives the latch, explore the depth of it. It is exactly as I thought.

I shut the door behind me.

* * *

Tamba is waiting at his window for me. His eye sockets seem deeper, giving him a zombie look.

'Are you sorted, Malachi? Did Olivia give you something?'

I nod serenely, collect my cutting tools from the trolley. Despite all the organs that he ate, the poor man is clearly suffering from severe anxiety. Welcome to the truth, dear Tamba. No coffee, no codeine. Just damn consequences.

He watches me walk towards the prisoners. I dare not smile at Vicki sitting so shamelessly, her knife notches adorning her cow's-milk skin. It was *she* who gave me the strength to show my scars to those women. I stroke her violet eyes with mine, thank her silently as I go past her gorgeous knees. Perhaps Vicki and I could get naked one day and laugh about it, compare our scars. It might be a simple effect of the Metorizine, but as I walk down the aisle I feel Vicki's swollen lips press against the top two of my thoracic vertebrae.

I don't know what happened to Charmayne over lunch but she seems to have lost her big-match temperament.

'It's risky, Malachi. It's stupid.' She gives me her hands moodily.

Tamba's eyes are still on me. I strap her fingers in, work slowly, as if Olivia performed a lunchtime lobotomy on me.

'We're all going to die tonight.'

My heart jerks from its restraints. Charmayne is right.

Her hibiscus lips pull down sulkily. 'I don't believe that shit about souls and cocktails on the rooftop.'

I remember now; she did her terrible deed on the roof of a high rise.

Sorry, Charmayne.

It must be hell when heaven makes you think of two flying men in suits. But all I can do to show my sympathy is wipe her toes clean.

As I lock Charmayne's cage, a grating sound jars the frightened peace among us. All of us look up. The panel in the wall next to Tamba's kiosk grinds open once more. A cage sways and judders along the roof. Another one cranks behind it, followed by another, until five cages form a broken train, hammering our ears with metallic echoes. As they shunt closer, my eyes catalogue a swathe of red, raised edges, hundreds of black stitches. One of the patients is wheezing. Is it Shikorina?

The cages hang suspended while Tamba calibrates his switches.

266

He sweeps two hands down his desk, plays his climax. The cages descend in unison. Moments before they crash to the floor, Tamba slows them. We hold our breaths as they land gently on their metal cradles.

Nice flying, I would say if the pilot was my friend.

Shikorina is breathing like the doctors have punctured something. I stare into her cage. The colour pink is weeping from her solar plexus. Oh, no.

I clap my hand over my mouth. Something comes up. There is a pea up my nose, I can feel it, even though I haven't eaten any since Friday. I press my switch, flutter my fingers to show fluid dripping.

Tamba guesses my affliction. 'Pull yourself together, Malachi. You've got to get used to blood. We rinse them twice a day when they're post-operative. Watch.'

A white spray thrusts from the nozzles above the last five cages. Shikorina shrieks.

I cover my ears. I don't care if Tamba thinks I'm useless. The rapist hunches his hands into bony fists, but not a sound comes out of his mouth. The spray must be ice cold, straight from the sea, but Angus endures it as if he is glad of the extra punishment. Shikorina shreds the air with high-pitched screams.

'Easy, Shikorina, easy,' the social worker soothes. His tender tone brings her shrieks down to a whimper.

Tamba looks shamefaced after his show of strength. 'That one always reacts badly to anaesthetics.'

The anaesthetic? Really? Not the sixty-seven stitches cutting a jagged line from her collarbone to her hip?

Andride shakes his head. 'No. They broke her ribs again. She doesn't scream for nothing.'

Of course Tamba doesn't hear this minor detail. He orders over his radio, 'Connect their feed pipes, Malachi. And check their cuts. Sometimes they open up in transit.'

But there is no way in hell or heaven I can go closer. I turn away from Shikorina's wound, which has delivered lovely new lungs for Olivia's little Timmy.

'Malachi, do you need to debrief?'

What does he want me to do, climb up his spiral and chat about my fear of blood?

But I must pull myself together, as Tamba says. I must rehearse for tonight. I turn back, take a few tentative steps towards Lolie. Her face is as transparent as the waning moon last night. Her jaw ripples with the same striations as the metal wires of her prison. This young girl is in pain. I press my button, touch my lips, mime a sip of something.

'Painkillers?'

Clever Tamba.

'Dammit,' he mutters. He leaves his microphone on. 'Olivia, did number nineteen . . . No, number twenty's looking good . . . Olivia . . . Listen! Did number nineteen get painkillers? You sure? . . . Look, it's just freaky to watch. Can you ask for extra? . . . Thanks.'

The radio play ends. I feel a rush of gratitude for Tamba who is nothing like his father who cuts and sews people like he is upholstering lounge suites. I force myself to inspect the other two prisoners. Those careless black stitches are grotesque, but they seem to have survived the cable-car trip.

Oh no. What of the sharks tonight? They will surely smell the blood on these prisoners, who really should be in ICU. As Charmayne says, it's a hopeless, mad mission. I have no nautical skills, no idea how I will hustle all these people into an escape vessel, lower it sixty metres and start the engines.

Something unravels in me. All I know is, in terms of logistics, God is our only hope.

I do what Tamba says, clip the feed pipes to the mesh. Then I clip and clean the rest of the prisoners, with that strange calm that comes before death. I remember it.

By the time I reach Madame Sophie, she looks like she has already been through a terror at sea. Her hair is clumped and clinging, her nails oddly tatty.

'I'm scared, Malachi. What if we die tonight?'

That's strange. Yesterday, Madame Sophie was fantasising about death. I check Tamba's window. He has finally relaxed his guard after hours of stalking me. He slouches in his roller chair, doodling with what looks like a digital pen.

I pull my phone from my pocket, type beneath the leather, 'There's a good chance of it.'

'Don't talk like that, Malachi,' Vicki says in a low voice behind me. Damn it, she sounds sexy.

'What if I see my mother?' Madame Sophie frets. 'What if she's angry with me?'

'Ask Eulalie,' I type. I add, very sincerely, 'Or die and find out.'

'Malachi. You're not helping.'

'Leave him, Sophie,' Josiah growls.

'I'm *scared*, Josiah.'

'Well, stay behind, you silly thing.'

The bickering pair sound gentler than they have all week.

'Stop,' I type. 'We don't have time for this.'

Strangely, I feel no revulsion for Josiah's hands today. I tighten the glove, use two thumbs on the clipper to split the knots in his nails. This is, after all, my very last job as a manicurist.

Josiah ventures, 'I know about boat engines. I used to fix them on Lake Chad before my father made me officer in the Anti-Balaka.'

Engines! I want to laugh down the rig and the sky above it. No wonder the grease.

A swarthy blush creeps beneath his scarred skin. 'I'm just saying, engines, I know them.'

I incline my head. *Thank you, Josiah.*

'What about worms?'

The evil Vicki can't help herself.

Josiah narrows his eyes. 'What do you mean?'

Samuel intercedes. 'Vicki, leave it. We need to stick together, like Malachi said.'

I nod emphatically. And God only knows where bickering could lead, once all these killers are free.

Upstairs, Tamba is considering his doodles, twiddling his pen like a drum majorette. I throw down my last towel, soiled by Josiah's feet. I lift my chin, hope my profile looks heroic from Vicki's point of view as I walk towards the trolley for the last time in my life.

Josiah starts again behind me. 'What do you mean?'

Vicki is incredulous. 'You're really asking?'

'Shut up, you two,' Samuel says. 'Please.'

Shut up. I love you, is what I would love to say. I want to slide my volume to maximum, shout out before I die, 'I LOVE YOU VICKI!'

Instead I touch the button on my intercom.

'Yes?'

I lay my cheek on my hands, mime a sweet, sexless afternoon sleep.

Tamba sighs. 'I'm tired too. *Someone* woke me up at sparrow's fart.'

I stare at him innocently.

'Go so long. I've got to monitor the surgeries and send their stats through at five thirty.'

I nod at Tamba, lay my clipper on the trolley. Lay my leather brace for raptor taming next to it. I open the door, carry my bucket of towels over the threshold. I swing the door slowly closed, leave it open a crack. Feel in my pocket for my single sachet of salt, bend it in the middle. I fit it gently in the tiny hatch inside the door frame.

Please don't break.

I shut the metal door gently. This time the click is a faint hiss, the miniature version of hitting a pillow. The light goes red for security observed, restraints in place.

Please let the light be telling a lie.

There is a scattering of white salt on the floor. The bolt has punctured it. I sink to my hands and knees, blow the grains under the door.

Don't be an idiot. Who on earth would notice a tiny spill of white powder?

Tamba the ex-addict might, actually. He might want to fall to the floor and sniff it up his nostrils.

I stand quickly, glance up at Tamba's shut door. He said five thirty. I climb the spiral stairs quietly. Near the top I drop to my knees, hunt for the cover of the shutdown switch.

No sign of it. I feel in the shadow beneath the second step. My fingers hit a slightly protruding plate. Yes.

I press my forehead against the step, peer into the shadow beneath it. The plate is the same yellow as the rest of the rig, almost invisible. I dig my fingers under the bottom edge. There is a shuffle and a scrape on the other side of the door. I shoot to my feet, but one heel slips off the stair. I flail my arms to stop myself from toppling.

Tamba's door swings open. 'Malachi, what . . .?'

I clutch the railing, my eyes too wide. I pat my cheek hard, mime a rough revival from sleep. I toss invisible food into my mouth, chew double-speed like a cartoon squirrel.

'I must wake you for supper?' Tamba wants to laugh, but he has a greater need. He presses on his penis like a small boy on a long bus journey. 'Okay, Malachi.'

He pushes past and trots down the stairs ahead of me.

I dare not stay to inspect the switch, in case Tamba glances back and sees me through the haze induced by too much urine.

I lie on my bed in filthy white, thirsty. The sound of Tamba urinating only makes it worse.

Tamba comes out buttoning his trousers. 'Got to get back. Meirong's so paranoid, I can't even piss.' He surveys me on the bed. 'Lucky fish.'

I smile at him. Lucky fish is something a kid might say when his friend gets a bigger slice of chocolate cake. Tamba hurries off to record blood pressure, pulse rate, temp for the five surgeries who will be lucky to get within sniffing distance of the sharks tonight. I feel inside my pillowcase, touch the plastic sacs of antibiotics. Then I take my chocolate cake, drop into a desperate sleep made sweet by the terror of what comes after it.

* * *

Someone sinks a fist into my ribs, jiggles it. I jerk awake, grab the wrist with steel fingers. It wrestles free.

'Geez, Malachi!'

I stare at his nostrils, try to remember who he is.

'Remind me not to surprise *you* in the middle of the night!' Tamba says.

I smile a sleepy apology.

'Supper, dude. Five minutes.' Tamba is gone, his dreadlocks leaving last.

The fist in my ribs calls me to combat. I spring to my feet, throw off my crushed angel outfit. I am about to save thirty-nine lives, or be the cause of their violent ending. Either way, I must prepare myself for murder and mayhem.

I adjust the shower to temperate, rub my hands over my skin. I knead my shoulder bones, my pectoral muscles, stroke my long forearms. The water falls warmly, a consistent lover. I stroke my thighs firmly, beg them to have the strength to bound up three hundred metal stairs. My feet, I rub them, pinch on my toes. Stay with me, please. Press me upright.

I rub the edges of my ears, the sweet, sensitive cartilage.

Will I soon be dead?

I massage my scalp with my fingertips. It's okay, it's okay. If they blow me up, there is something in me that has no need of neurons shaped like tadpoles with preposterously long tails. There is my living spirit.

I bang the heels of both hands against my heart. Keep beating, please, until I tell you to stop.

I open my eyes in the falling water, rinse them. Next, I stroke my pitted penis. Forgive me for hating you when you are so beauteous. My penis rises up in my hands. I smile at its one eye gazing up at me. I pull the skin down gently. Groan softly. Soon, if I live. I will give you pleasure.

273

But tonight I need it begging to be touched. I need it urging me to save Vicki. I would so love to enter her fig lips gently, have her suck me. Feel the spongy floor of her tongue curling around me, sliding in, sliding out. My erection is so enormous I could hang my towel on it. I take a moment to gape at it. I tear my eyes from the mirror. This is serious.

I dry my skin gently. Tonight I must be a silent shadow herding them up to the stars.

I dress in black chinos and a black t-shirt. I nod to the mirror now, a dark pastor. I tuck my stiff penis into my Sunday best.

I lift my mattress and pull out the key to the deck. I swap the lanyards, clip the hall key to the pink strap, clip the deck key to the red. I pour the red strap onto the cabinet, let it take the form of a beaten snake.

As I enter the canteen, Meirong leaps to her feet like she wants to punch me. She thrusts out an open palm. 'Key.'

I smile obligingly, unravel the pink lanyard from my pocket. Meirong snatches it and loops it around her neck. I try not to look at it dangling between her breasts. Not because of the soft, swollen place where it is nestling, but because I have just played a trick on a very dangerous woman. The weight of the key seems to relax her.

But something has lit the green fuse in Tamba's right eye. 'You look smart, Malachi. You going somewhere special?'

I smile and shrug, mime a shower. I uncurl my fingers, show the opening of the petals of a sweet-smelling flower. I sit down, turn the tables on Tamba. I point a finger at him, pinch my nose as if to say, *Dude, you're stinky.*

Tamba lifts an arm, smells himself. Janeé giggles.

'Mmm. Sweet Tempest,' Tamba says.

I can't help but let out a deep laugh. Sweet Tempest, the perfect deodorant for being lost at sea. I watched the making of their ad on TV once – they spent two million dollars on a mechanical seagull the size of a pterodactyl. The sky, I remember, was not the pale, punished blue I have seen above the rig. It was the luminous blue of brake fluid. I start to hum the song from the Sweet Tempest TV ad.

Janeé shrieks with delight. 'Malachi's singing!'

Tamba grins, lifts his arms to fly, gives us a whiff of chemical sweat. I have managed to distract him from me dressing like James Bond, but I am appalled at my own stupidity. Nice, Malachi. Have a shower and dress like a cat burglar with your roommate watching your every move.

Isn't this why there was such a bloody, bloody ending to Thomas Wyatt's sonnet?

A deep despondency settles over me. These could be my last moments on earth, and here I am humming advertising jingles.

Olivia traipses into the canteen, her white skirt rolled up like she has been leaping for joy across green grass. I am the only one who notices that she is barefoot. She sits down, beaming. There are pink smudges on her hippie shirt like she has been eating ice cream. But the fluids in her lab are mostly pink. Possibly from the preservative.

Janeé serves us our supper, a whole baby chicken each, but in South Africa they don't call it that, they call it a flatty. A chicken pressed flat, its tendons stretched to make it lie low. This one is dusted with something that smells like Aromat.

Olivia pricks her flatty with her fork. 'Looks lovely, Janeé.'

'Delicious,' Janeé agrees, like someone else cooked it.

My last supper, and I am eating what I could have bought in a Nando's budget box for eighty bucks in Nelspruit. New Nation supplies the franchise with fast-growing hybrid fowl, those creatures with no wings, no beaks, no feathers, no feet.

I mean, no *feet*.

I stare at my golden thighs that end at the knee. This poor thing didn't even get to stand up.

I nip the end off a sachet of salt. Sprinkle it on my chips. Will a sachet of salt take us to the sea? If it wasn't so pathetic, it would be funny.

Funny like dropping my trousers before the Asian beauty before me. Meirong catches my eye, blushes a becoming pale pink. She was thinking of my bum. Definitely.

What is wrong with me? I can't stop thinking like a man. Pornographically.

Sex and death. Non-identical twins.

Now that Meirong has seen my bum, she seems to consider me a human being. 'It won't be long, Malachi. Six months will go quickly.'

I nod amicably at her.

'We're thinking of using that subject with no teeth? He keeps pulling them out, the idiot.'

Tamba says, 'Number thirteen.'

The Indian. They were going to use him to grow my tongue! Ironic, very ironic that he is the only one who can help me with the black box. My laugh erupts as a hiccup.

What black box?

Get real, Malachi. Six hours to go and the precious object is nothing more than a mention from a dead young woman.

As Olivia tucks into her chicken, she tells me her news. 'Timmy's in theatre right now, Malachi. They're busy with the transplant.'

I grin at her. *Wow. Wonderful!*

'I'm not worried, really,' she assures me passionately. 'I prayed the whole of last night.' But tears dampen the smudges beneath her eyes.

Janeé hugs Olivia with a huge arm. 'My boy, too. They're fixing him tomorrow,' she tells me.

Lovely.

I exude genuine happiness for both of them. Inaudible sounds tease my mind for the second time today. First Romano's pain, now Janeé and Olivia – they are ululating, aren't they?

Something odd is happening to me. It's like I can hear people's sound effects. Am I becoming schizophrenic?

I stare at my footless flatty, feel a terrible yearning for sand and grass and trees. Let me walk again on solid land, please. I will eat the earth if necessary to show how grateful I am to be delivered to it. God only knows how. Lifeboat. Black box. Outboard engines. These are not things I am familiar with, other than from my compulsive reading of discarded magazines. The fluid in my body dives towards my feet. I am frightened, so frightened of the monster sea waiting to unleash its hatred of the human race with its cruel fish-finders, its oozing oil, its fishing nets as long as the Nile River.

I stare down at my plate. And I can't eat a chicken that may never have stood on the earth. This flatty is too flat.

'Malachi? Don't you like your chicken?' It is Tamba this time who busts me.

I take a nibble. My last supper. I must eat.

Frances slipped into the water like a carcass.

Across from me, Olivia chews on her chicken that looks like Oscar Pistorius, the guy with the metal legs who nearly won the Olympics, then shot his model girlfriend dead. Raizier should have stolen him from prison and made him grow beautiful new hearts, one after another.

277

My mind keeps slipping sideways into fiction. Flighty, like Hamri.

That's when it hits me. Romano's daughter. What about her heart?

I wave at Meirong, pull her attention from her chicken. I pat my shoulders, indicate Romano's epaulettes.

Meirong frowns. I aim an automatic rifle at her, pull the trigger.

'Romano?' Olivia guesses.

I nod eagerly.

'What about Romano?' Meirong asks warily.

I thrust out my hand below shoulder height, sweep the air on both sides of my head. Plaits. Hair. Feminine. Have they not seen his heartbreaking photograph?

Janeé is the one who gets it. 'His little girl.'

I tap at my heart, throw open both palms to ask clearly, *Where is it?*

'It's sorted,' Meirong says.

Tamba becomes steely next to me. 'Have you sent it?'

'Tamba,' Meirong warns.

'Have you?'

'It's . . . earmarked.'

Olivia and Janeé's smiles flap like wings. They dive back into their chicken. Tamba and I both glare at Meirong. Earmarked, like a notch in the ear of a cow? I take a bite of my Oscar Pistorius. Something in my heart rips.

Will a little girl die because of me?

The Aromat makes me thirsty, but I dare not take a drink. There is only fatal raspberry on the table today.

Olivia sniffs up her happy tears. 'I'm never going to get to sleep tonight. Should we play Remote-Mo badminton later, Janeé?'

'Ah, no,' Tamba groans. 'I hate that game.'

'Okay then, Remote-Mo knitting,' Olivia teases.

Tamba's look of despair makes Janeé giggle. 'Table tennis,' he bargains. 'The real thing.'

Meirong glances up at the orange glow shining through the portholes. She shakes her head. 'Blackout again tonight. The rec room has windows. You can't switch on that light.'

'There are blinds on those windows,' Tamba argues.

'We'll shut them,' Olivia pleads.

'No. No games tonight.'

Tamba holds up a finger, 'One game.' He forgets his fury about Romano's daughter. 'Come and play, Meirong. I need you on my team.'

Meirong laughs. 'Okay. One game. I'll come up to make sure those windows are sealed.'

'Do you want to come, Malachi?' Janeé asks me kindly.

I shake my head ruefully. Not me. I would love to watch Meirong playing table tennis in her white minidress, but I have some slightly more important things to do this evening.

I would love to give them all a big hug, stretch my arms around Janeé, send love to their loved ones and say, *Thank you, thank you for this nightmare week.*

I turn at the door, my imaginary tongue itching to speak. But they are scraping their chicken bones into a shallow grave, all of them helping so they can go and play ping-pong.

Next time, I tell them silently before I leave. We will play ping-pong in heaven. The real thing.

When I reach the bedroom, the sight of my soft pillow slaughters the tiny hero in me. Thousands of tons of sea smash me into a foetal position. I desperately want to sleep and let this last chance drift past. Instead I force my eyes open. Listen.

Four-way ping-pong taps at my cranium.

* * *

I roll off the bed, land on my feet like a panther. I flick off my shoes, peel off my socks. Barefoot, I pad silently down the corridor. The sudden three steps, I glide down them. The LED globes shine their dim, deathly light, sealed from the sea by the brutal design of the rig. I flit past the two fingers of moonlight poking near the canteen roof, past Olivia's laboratory. I hurry past the women's room with its smell of chemical perfume. Did Janeé spray her underarms before the ping-pong foursome? Is someone still in there?

The perfume tickles my nostrils. I want to sneeze. Here it comes. I pinch my nose, use fifteen years of practice to stifle my sound. A muted explosion detonates in my sinuses. I break into a run in case another sneeze attacks me. I shove on the door to the central stairwell. It howls like an unneutered cat fed on chicken intestines. It shrieks louder as I shut it.

I drop down the spine of the rig on the pads of my feet, which seem to have developed extra cushioning. The growing darkness finally presses me to stillness. I fumble for my cell phone, find the torch switch. Ah. A ray of clear, white light. I shine it down the stairs as I climb down, down, follow the echo of the eternal war between water and metal.

My torch finally finds the steel door to the shark pit.

Yes! The green light is still glowing on the door lock. I kill the torch on my Samsung, bury it in my pocket. I dare not use it outside in case Romano is patrolling up there and spots the pinprick of light. I seize the steel handle. The heavy door opens like a dream.

I step onto the platform above the shark pit. White foam flies up from the black morass, but the moon is out of sight, perhaps seducing some rusted machinery higher up on the rig. Are the sharks sleeping?

I sidle onto the narrow ledge that runs past the sewage pump. Dark water rushes up to try and smash me off my perch but I grasp the flimsy railing, creep like a fugitive along a high city roof. I shuffle all the way to the massive column Romano pointed to. I grab at the edge of the shadowy opening, swing myself away from the sadistic sea.

I grip my phone, shine my white beam inside the huge, hollow cylinder. A chain thicker than my body plunges through the middle of a chasm, about ten metres across. I shine my torch upwards. The chain is wound around a massive winch. My light catches a thin ladder running up the wall of the cylinder. I aim my light down. The ladder plunges into eternal darkness. I put one foot on a rung. The metal is slimy from decades of darkness and salty sea mist. I need my sneakers. I cling like I have suction pads on my fingers and my feet.

I have got to save Vicki from dying like a lab rat.

The breath in my hollow body matches the rush and the roar of the insomniac sea. I climb down, down fifty-seven rungs that I pray someone has welded with obsessive care.

I hang on with one hand, shine my light down. My torch finds a splintered curve hanging five metres below me. A shattered hull, it must be. A snapped metal beam swings at ninety degrees.

281

A ragged canvas hangs off it. The boom of a boat, what else could it be? It looks like the mast is entirely missing. The yacht is pointing directly up, its bow lifted clear of the water while the sea chews mercilessly on its back end. The massive chain drifts sideways, tightens, suspends the yacht in the middle of the column.

Help me, I plead to the ghost of the girl sailor. Help me to find your precious communication device.

I climb the ladder past an expanse of broken deck. Past a jagged hole in the hull smashed by a container of corn submerged in the sea, or car engine parts on their way from Africa. I stop at the place where the boom and the amputated mast meet, shine my light on some letters painted in cursive. *Sea Sprite RF547*. She must be about twelve metres.

BANG. The boom swings towards me.

'Arggh!' I duck just in time. It jerks, hangs like a torn limb.

Who is stronger, the malevolent sea or the spirit of Frances?

I take three convulsive breaths, watch the boom as if it is a striking snake. The sea stops gnawing on the tail of the boat for a moment. I stretch my hand to the snapped railing. Where to put my feet? I shine my torch on a silver winch the size of a tortoise. Measure the distance. I secure my phone between my teeth.

I kick for the silver fitting. Find it.

I am part of this yacht.

I grab on to the splintered hatch, swing a leg inside it. Beautiful, beautiful strong body.

I shine my torch inside the waterlogged yacht. My brain makes a frightened inventory. Sea water, lapping five metres below me. Soggy beds, upended. Floating orange life jackets, a tin that says, *TEA*. The wooden walls of the yacht are bowed and smooth.

Beneath the navigation table, Frances said. Where would I find such a thing?

Ah, a board with switches to the right, three metres above the water line. A table top tilted vertical. I hang by my fingers in the dark cavity. One big toe is all that can reach. I hang on with one hand, shine my torch down. If I fall I will plunge into a black, wet chasm deep enough to drown me. The plastic cover of a paper book floats beneath me. *The Rime of the Ancient Mariner.*

Is that supposed to be funny?

My fingers must be bleeding. I am not, after all, a red-haired orangutan. I use my throbbing arms to pull myself back out.

Oh, God, what's the time?

Think, Malachi. You have promised thirty-nine prisoners the chance to live with their dead albatrosses slung around their necks.

That's it.

I drag at a thick wet rope wound around the winch. I haul out five metres, tie a double knot on the fitting. As I tie the free end of the rope around my chest I taste the unmistakeable flavour of blood. My lips are bleeding from their desperate grip on my only communication device. My sun, my moon, my tongue.

I snarl deep in my trachea, slither into the hatch. This time I get a foot to the navigation table, let myself fall. I land across the thin edge of the desk, utter a ghostly scream. Someone has lit a fire in my left lung. I shriek with each breath, keep rhythm with the rocking sea.

Come on, Malachi. You have survived worse than a cracked rib in your uncharmed life.

I slide down the table top. Please. My toes hit something solid. I feel with my bare feet. Is it a treasure chest?

I shine my light. It is grey, not black. And it is certainly not a box. It has a lower edge and a raised face with empty cable inlets. A padded black case is taped to it with silver duct tape. I pull my phone from my mouth, read the lettering along the bottom edge. *Garmin 1000945 Voyage Data Recorder plus Very High Frequency Radio.*

'Bayunga na.' My father's voice comes to me.

Good boy.

Now how the heck do I get it up? The black box weighs the same as a two-kilogram chicken, I remember the weight from the millions of mistakes I stopped on their way to China. I press it into my broken rib. I have survived self-inflicted mutilation, I can handle a sore rib. I release the noose from beneath my arms, tie the black box up like a parcel for the post. I clamber onto it, stand up.

I kick off the table, swing. The black box hits something glass. A microwave perhaps. On the return swing my toes find a metal object, perhaps a tap. I thrust off it, reach for the faint reprieve in the darkness above me.

'Agh!' My ribs spit and crackle like burning kindling as I pull my torso through the opening. 'Thank you-u-u,' I groan through my clamped teeth. I mean it.

I pull the black box up, untie it.

BANG. I duck the evil boom. I haul myself back on to the ladder. My tears do nothing to put the fire out in my ribs. I climb the slippery rungs in searing agony. I bite on my Samsung, hang onto my black box, the only two things that make my life worth living.

Thank you, thank you for the book about the albatross. I might have been swimming in circles until Romano blasted the yacht to smithereens with Trobancubane. Is that the name of it?

Climb, Malachi. Stop with your loquaciousness.

I clamber from the steel column with my torch switched off.

The sea is no longer my enemy. The smashing waves in the shark pit are white signs of welcome erupting for me. I smile at the stars swimming in the purple water. The pain in my rib separates from my body and suspends next to me as I walk along the narrow ledge.

I shut the heavy door behind me. I wipe my cell phone on my trousers, try the menu button. The screen responds beautifully. Thank you.

I climb up, up the spine with the solo sailor's treasure chest. What will I say if someone catches me? Can you believe, I stumbled on this black box while strolling around on a sky-facing yacht?

The stairs lighten gradually. I switch off my torch, pass the maintenance door. I climb twelve more stairs, searching. At the foot of the next flight I drop to my haunches, fit the black box into a shadow that seems specially made for it.

I let out a long sigh. *Now* my rib hurts.

I wind slowly back down.

I open the maintenance door. The rogue cat screams a call to war. I have no choice but to let it scream twice, shut the damn door. Listen.

My heart starts again at the soft, soft sound of tired ping-pong.

I creep along the corridor, let my feet take my dead weight on their pillowy flesh. There is a long pause in the collisions of plastic bat and plastic ball.

The tapping starts again, desultory. The fire in my ribs takes me down the passage to my bedroom. I enter in darkness.

'Aaaagh.' I lay myself down on my feather duvet.

I set my alarm in the dark. Double-check. Yes. Beethoven will play at fifteen minutes to midnight. I need to rest my broken bones for what might be the last sleeping hour of my life. I sink into the middle of the smouldering flames. Sleep immediately.

*

Who comes to me? Not Cecilia, not Hamri. Not even Vicki to bring me a blessed wet dream. It is Romano's daughter who visits me. She looks like she did in the photo. Her eyes are torch lights, but they are laughing, not pleading for oxygen. Milja is sprinkling salt onto a woman's head, creating a streak of white from her forehead to her crown. The moon strokes the path with a golden beam, lights it like Midas. The woman smiles at me.

'Tell Eulalie to marry him.'

The salt forms a moon path across the sea.

'Who?' I ask the moonbeam sleepily.

'The man with the wife in ashes,' the moon answers me. I try to follow it with my dreamy eyes, but a loud bang cuts off my pathway to heaven.

'Shit!' someone says.

The first feeling comes from my burning rib. I am not in heaven yet.

Tamba switches on his lamp, rubs his head. 'Fuck it.'

Well, if that is his bedtime prayer, I wish him good luck.

Tamba wrestles out of his clothes, kicks them to the floor. He lies down on his bed, ill tempered. I check the time. 11.26.

I lie stiff like a corpse, pray that Tamba stops cursing and goes to sleep. He pulls the covers up, tosses towards the wall. He flips to the other side.

'Malachi?' he whispers.

Sleep, I urge him fiercely.

He says louder, 'Malachi.'

I fake deep, slow breathing. Tamba breathes deeper, slower in

286

sympathy. After eleven minutes he makes a funny little rattle in the pit of his throat. I watch his body ease. His dreadlocks fall away from his face, show a finer, more breakable jaw than the one I stare up at from the factory floor. His ear is almost without an earlobe. Delicate.

I hang my feet off the bed. The pain attacks me viciously. Get thee hence.

Help me, Hamri.

It separates again, floats next to me as I sit up slowly. My mattress creaks. One knee makes a tiny crack as I stand up. It is the same knee Hamri flung himself onto to try and silence me. I switch off the alarm before Beethoven sabotages me. Slide my hand into my pillow, steal the plastic sacs of medicine one by one. I pull my stomach in and pack them beneath my belt. The rig is cool at almost midnight, but I begin to sweat under the plastic.

Who is the woman with the silver streak? I begin to feel feverish. Why did my ancestors not come to guide me?

11.41.

If I can open the door because of a stupid sachet of salt, I will take this as a sign that heaven is on our side.

I unravel the lanyard in slow motion. Tamba rubs his nose with the back of his hand. I practise my deep, peaceful breathing. Tamba breathes slower, falls back to sleep. I want to kiss his forehead. He is sweet, this man, especially when his wicked green streak is covered by his eyelids.

I pick up my sneakers with my fingertips. This time I will take them for better grip. My thighs are more prepared than me. They know the word 'escape', they have been waiting. The door creaks like it has a horrible sense of humour.

'Malachi?'

My heart bangs like a bird flying into glass.

Tamba sits up, stares blindly at me. 'Oh.' He lies back heavily. 'Midnight shift.'

I am a mere black shadow someone painted in the doorway. Tamba farts. He chuckles and rolls towards the wall.

11.50.

The fart seems to put Tamba swiftly to sleep. I shut the door to a crack, listen. A soft snore rasps from his voicebox. Like a baby that has been burped, he sleeps blissfully. I squeeze the door shut behind me.

I tiptoe down the corridor to the cultivation hall. I sit on the first spiral stair, panting for no reason other than I am about to commit mass suicide. I pull on my sneakers, gaze at the door in the white nightmare light. A big obstruction has appeared in my throat, soft but intractable, like a lump of Janeé's batter. Air sneaks through my nostrils, keeps me living. I walk to the door.

'Na me sahn,' Cecilia called me. Light of my life.

* * *

The door swings open as if on a spring. Salt sprays on my black trousers, scatters on the floor. It can't be true.

I stare at the torn paper hanging from the latch. It worked!

The prisoners are jerking from their wombs, teetering on their buttocks, their eyelids torn open. I leave the door ajar, set my cell phone to *Whisper*. Josiah is staring, the scars in his eyes as thick as keloid tissue. He committed mass murder, my mind

288

howls at me. How can you free him?

No. The sachet of salt is all I must think of.

I must not judge.

Samuel is crouching as if at a starter block. Vicki is on her hands and knees, gazing at me. Eulalie's hands are flat against the door of her cage, ready to shove. Sweat trickles from the plastic sacs against my belly-button. I must do what the dream woman said, in case this is the last time we ever speak. I go close to the witch, type in the open.

My African translator whispers, 'I dreamed of a woman with a white streak in her hair.'

Eulalie's breath rasps in.

'She said you must marry the man with the wife in ashes.'

Eulalie groans. She nods, her grey eyes smouldering in the eerie dimness. 'The man who loves me.' She touches her crown. 'His wife was struck by lightning when she was three.'

Of course! The man with the wife in ashes.

Vicki brings us back to terrifying reality. 'Malachi?'

I check my timepiece. 'Eleven fifty-eight. At midnight I will cut the power off. You only have three seconds to open up.'

The whisper flies down the aisles as if on a bird's wings. The wings shut to stillness. We wait, all of us, barely breathing.

I check my wrist. 'One minute,' I type.

I watch the numbers switch to 11.59. Hold up one finger. Vicki whispers for me:

'One.'

The prisoners take up the count. 'Two. Three. Four . . .' Eulalie counts too, her eyes curiously happy. I turn my back on Vicki's frightened, counting mouth.

'Twelve. Thirteen. Fourteen . . .'

I run from the hall.

I fly up the spiral stairs, crouch on the second-highest step. My fingers find the metal flap easily. I shine my cell phone light onto it. It is striated, covered with greasy paint. I can't get the damn thing up.

Twenty-eight. Twenty-nine . . . Thirty seconds to get it open.

I dig my sore fingers into the seam, pull hard on it. My fingers slip. I do a crooked backward somersault down three stairs. My head hits the metal. Something trickles down my temple. Blood.

I shudder, check the time. Nineteen seconds. I launch at the metal plate again, croak softly, 'Please!'

My scrabbling fingertips sink into a slit along the top edge. It flicks down easily.

Down, not up, Tamba!

11.59.51. I have nine seconds.

I peer into the opening. A bulbous switch, good for the fingers of an extraterrestrial.

Fifty-three. Fifty-four . . .

Down or up? I wiggle it. It won't budge.

Five seconds. Help me!

A strange calm soaks my nerves in gentle sunlight. It sinks into my muscles, sends signals to my brain. I explore the centimetres around the switch. Yes. There is a tiny track to the left. This is a sideways switch.

Fifty-nine . . .

I jam my hand against it.

Sudden shocking darkness. The silence of a sleeping whale. I count. One. Two.

Do I hear the soft sound of thirty-nine simultaneous clicks?

The whirring, the clicking of machines returns to the metal arachnid. The misty lights flicker like birthday candles above me.

Happy birthday, Malachi.

The rig did nothing more than hold its breath for three seconds. Electricity hums through its steel skin, its heart beats relentlessly. I smile like a man who has suffered damage to his amygdala, the part of the brain that receives lethal danger signals. One breath gets my sneakers all the way down the spiral.

As I burst through the door of the cultivation hall, I am met by a straggling line of creatures who have only just evolved into Homo erectus. They rock sideways on their spines, unsteady on their legs. They cling to their cages, shuffle towards me.

I blow air between my teeth.

'Shhh.' I press my finger to my lips. One silly word makes me their leader.

The prisoners let go of their cages, stumble towards the one who has promised them a chance to do something other than shit liquid and suffer recurring, live autopsies. These people are too frail to reach the deck, surely. Still, I beckon wildly. *Come. Quickly!*

Vicki thrusts her long legs forward like a newborn foal. She buckles. Samuel pulls her up, his hips more powerful than they seemed when he was caged. His penis looks longer than it did when he was sitting. Eulalie collapses to her hands and knees, smiling like this is a party game. The yellow man grabs her shoulders, wrenches her from the floor. Where is the Indian? Eulalie might be excellent at communicating with spirits, but she is useless with satellite technology.

There he is. Barry, the fat Australian, is holding on to Vihaan as he grunts and grinds down the aisle. Barry falls to his knees, but he keeps a stubborn grip on the Indian. Vihaan topples onto him. I thrust my palms towards the roof. *Get up! Bring him!* I turn towards the door, fling my arm forwards, mime to everyone. *Follow me!*

The desert runner overtakes the other prisoners, trotting like his legs work on some wind-up mechanism. Charmayne catches up with Madame Sophie, drags her like a beloved rag doll she can't bear to part with. She claps her free hand on Lolie's back and gives her a powerful push towards the door. I wait outside the hall. Vicki hangs on to the door frame behind Charmayne, her face drained of life. She is corpse-like, a bare mannequin in a night window.

I urge her without words, *Come, my love.* I smile a tender smile I have been hiding for decades.

Vicki forces her pale thighs through the opening. As she brushes past me, her silky hair slides across the nodules of her spine. I raise a hand, touch it. Vicki stops, stares at my mouth as if she is afraid of my eyes. I take her hand, weave my fingers between hers, weld our panic-stricken electricity into one. Vicki's soft, sweaty hand feels like the long, wet kiss I have never had.

Behind me, the desert runner yanks the stragglers over the threshold. I give him a thumbs-up with my free hand. I think I have finally become a Valentino hero.

In the snuffling, shambling silence, the prisoners follow Vicki and me. I catch a glimpse of Shikorina and the priest killer shoulder to shoulder, sharing the odd experience of walking on wasted legs. Lolie, the skinny rapist and the other three post-operative prisoners are still among us. The skinny rapist, I see, has a raw, red wound over his heart, but his stitches seem to be strong, however shoddy the workmanship. He slips through the door before Josiah, who takes the last place in the naked pack.

'She's bleeding,' someone whispers.

The crowd makes a space around Shikorina past the spiral stairs. I refuse to look at the site of her incision. I jab my finger towards my bedroom door. Gesture wildly, *Be silent. There's someone in there!*

The priest killer grabs Shikorina's hand and pulls her along the corridor. I tug Vicki with me.

Please, please if Tamba hears us, let him think he is dreaming.

Some prisoners creep, some shuffle past the glorious thrum of Tamba's epiglottis. God *must* be with us.

It is Vicki and me and Charmayne in the lead, pulling Madame Sophie who is much, much tinier than she was in captivity. Samuel and the social worker walk abreast now, linking arms like new best friends.

Tamba's snore breaks off.

Andride falters against the wall. Samuel plucks at him gently.

The door swings open behind them.

'Jesus Christ!' Tamba is stark naked. 'Go back! Go back!'

He makes a cross with his fingers, exorcising the ghouls. 'They will kill you!' he shrieks.

The red-haired prisoner totters backwards, his freckles colliding in the garish light. He turns and shambles the way that we came. A tiny Chinese man, quite sprightly, overtakes him. A black man as elongated as an afternoon shadow whispers, 'Espere por mim.'

I don't know what it means but he slides sideways towards the hall, his hands high on the wall like a reflection, flung there.

'Wait,' Samuel hisses, but they hurry back to their cages, choosing euthanasia on a stretcher over a slaughter at sea.

'Go back, Malachi,' Tamba pleads. He could be one of us with his heaving lungs, the puncture marks on his arms. I shove past some prisoners, take hold of his shoulders. March him backwards like I am teaching him to dance. Tamba wrests this way and that, scrambles onto his mattress.

Lolie darts in front of me. I pluck at her elbow but she hunts him with her lethal, black-lined eyes.

'I helped you,' he pleads. 'Ask Malachi.'

Still, Lolie stalks him.

'Lolie!' he shouts.

She hesitates at her name. Tamba dives into his storage hatch and pulls his knees up. He curls on his side among his clothes and his Red Riding Hood Kindle.

'Lock me in,' he begs me. 'Quickly.'

I shove past Lolie, slide the hatch shut on Tamba.

He panics immediately, choking. 'Wait. Malachi! . . . I can't breathe.'

I turn the rusted key. Lolie falls back, scrapes a difficult breath in sympathy. I pull the key out, give Tamba air to breathe.

'Please. Fucking *please* . . .'

I leave him to swear in his steel uterus, drop the key on the bed. The Volkswagen keyring is stark against the white sheet. An upside-down peace sign.

As I shut the door to our living quarters, Tamba starts to hammer at the hatch. 'Malachi-i-i!' His scream is muted by two layers of metal.

I take Vicki's shaking fingers, lead her past the canteen. Behind us comes the fat Australian, almost suffocating the Indian. Beyond them I catch sight of Shikorina's eyes, dazed with bewilderment as she clings to Mohammed's forearm like an octopus. He could surely twist from her cloying fingers but he lets her hang on, perhaps remembering the priest.

Outside the women's living quarters, there is still a trace of factory-made jasmine. My nostrils tickle slightly. I hear the sound of an indrawn breath. A strangled sneeze explodes behind me.

Oh no!

Another sneeze explodes in the skinny rapist's fists. There is a thudding sound inside, a clumsy landing. The door to the women's room opens slowly. Olivia stares out, her sleepy eyes growing huge with incredulity. Her fringe is pinned to one side with a big, gold clip.

I scramble back through the prisoners, type feverishly, 'Let them go.'

The white bunnies on her shining vest are doing karate kicks.

'Timmy has his lungs,' I type desperately. 'Go to sleep. Please.'

Olivia stares at the gathering, considers my bizarre plea. Vicki brushes against my back, creates a shield of female electricity.

I type to Olivia, 'You know they're going to kill them.'

She shakes her head violently. 'They're going back to prison.'

'You know it's a lie.'

Guilt stains her blue eyes like nicotine. She spins towards the ungainly shape on the bed. 'Janeé!'

'Mm?' Janeé is curiously sweet-tempered in her sleep.

A terrible brutality comes over me. I grab Olivia's arm, slam her spine into my belly. I clamp a hand over her mouth. Olivia's big teeth bite into my good hand.

'Agh!' I grunt.

Lolie ducks past me, snatches at a huge white dressing gown hanging on a hook. Vicki tears off Olivia's bunny shorts. She tugs my stinging fingers from Olivia's mouth and stuffs the silky shorts between her teeth. Olivia bucks against me, tries a muffled shout.

Inside the living quarters, I hear Janeé reply, 'Huh?' as if the two friends are miscommunicating in a deep, bewildered dream.

Lolie jerks the furry belt from the dressing gown. Her little hands fly as she ties tight knots around Olivia's wrists. Olivia lifts her legs, kicks wildly at the crowd. The desert strangler's head snaps back. He dives at Olivia's legs and drags her to the ground. He takes over from Lolie, binds Olivia's wrists to her feet.

'Don't hurt her,' Vicki whispers.

We all gape at Olivia in a foetal position, her pubic hair reddish in the steamy light. I float Janeé's huge dressing gown over her white buttocks, make her decent. I grab Vicki's wrist, haul her towards the maintenance door.

Behind us, Lolie crouches down and strokes Olivia's cheek. 'Sorry,' she whispers.

Angus, the skinny rapist, steps carefully over Olivia. 'Sorry,' he echoes Lolie.

Samuel picks Angus up, almost tosses him after us. Vicki throws her white thighs forwards, grips my hand like we have been lovers for far longer than eleven minutes. Her trust turns my stomach to steel, powers my courage to lead this party. By some freaky miracle the cat-mating door opens soundlessly.

I draw Vicki into the steep stairwell dividing the rig, pull her up the first twelve stairs.

'Vihaan,' I type. 'Where is he?' My spokesman whispers the words to Vicki, who whispers them to Samuel. The words drop down the staircase, snake through the door to the prisoners still emerging from it.

Barry almost carries the Indian over the threshold. The others flatten against the wall to make way for them to climb the stairs to us. I pick up the black box from its perfect shadow, show it to the panting little man. Vihaan squints at it. He nods, grins a gap-toothed grin. The relief hits me like a fever. I press the black box into my broken bones, grab Vicki's hand and pull her up the next flight. The prisoners behind us catch my happy delirium. They find new strength in their atrophied limbs, grasp the railing, shunt their bodies after us. Two by two they climb the ark to start a colony of sinners who, if they live, will spend their days and their nights asking for forgiveness from their beloved dead.

So be it.

Vicki's legs are stronger now. She breathes against my back, the scent of something dark and sweet. Is it liquorice? She keeps a tight hand on Vihaan while Barry pants heavily, flagging behind us. The desert runner catches up, gets a shoulder beneath Barry's bum and heaves him up. A stifled cry comes from somewhere below us.

Eulalie has collapsed to her hands and knees. Charmayne lets go of Madame Sophie. She slings Eulalie's withered arm around her neck and lifts her easily up the next ladder of steps. I peer down the twisted metal cliff. From this height I see it clearly. Shikorina has left a trail of bloody footprints. The murky light paints her thighs a deep red.

My legs buckle towards the floor. I grip the railing, hang on to the black box. Vihaan babbles something, tears it away from me.

Josiah climbs lethargically in Shikorina's red footprints.

Vicki hooks her arms beneath my armpits. 'Up, Malachi!'

I press my face into her stomach, a silken, pungent pillow of strong, striped skin. I thrust my feet into the rig, rise up against her full-cream breasts. I extricate myself from Vicki's delicious breath, watch Samuel far below us, trying to persuade Josiah to keep climbing. Josiah is shaking his head hopelessly. Samuel smacks him hard on the back of his head. Is he mad? Josiah will crush his skull out of mere reflex.

'We need Josiah for the engines. Tell him,' I type.

The words start with Vicki, tumble down from the prisoners' mouths.

They land in Josiah's fleshy ears.

He stares up at me from beneath his oily eyebrows. A slow pride seems to infuse him, the little boy who loves engines. Josiah places a hairy hand on each railing, swings himself over Shikorina's bloody footprints.

I give Samuel a quick smile. Thank him.

Vicki and I reach the door to the rest of the universe. She waits one step below me, breathing heavily, whiter than the pages of a paper book. The prisoners gather below us, rasping through rusty lungs, exhausted from carrying the organs Raizier has smuggled in their bodies like drugs. I raise the key card from my heart.

God help us.

A bolt of terror strikes me down. I slump in the shadows of the top stair. Vicki touches my knee. I grab her hand and pull her to me. I kiss her, fold into her fig lips. I suck their plush sweetness, feel the terribly loud ticking of both our hearts, out of time. I kiss Vicki hard with the inside of my lips until our heartbeats synchronise. I will take a bullet right now for this brave, man-killing beauty. I want to kiss deeper, touch her taste buds, but I have no tongue to reach her. I stroke my hand gently between her legs, touch the velvet of her vaginal lips. I do this instead of a tongue kiss.

'Hurry,' Samuel whispers somewhere below us.

Vicki does not flinch. She stares into my eyes with a mixture of desire and fear. I use my lips to try to mime my infinite gratitude. *Thank you.*

This is the first time I have ever kissed a woman.

Now I raise the stolen key card, unlock the door to the night sky.

* * *

The rig lights are all off. A golden moon path sweeps across the sea, as broad as a triple-lane highway. It is bright, as if lit by LED street lights. Just as Romano's daughter showed me in my sleep.

The Dragonfly is parked in its white circle for the night, waiting for Mr Rawlins to wake up and flick his silver fringe, play Hollywood pilots again. It glows above me, flirting with the moon for the second night in a row. At the edge of the deck, Romano's lifeboat hangs off the rig, its tarpaulin breathing in the soft breeze. Where is he?

The curve of the security tower glitters in the moonlight, but the glass circle at the top is blind and dark. I glimpse a movement behind the reflective glass. The moonlight touches Romano's profile. I shrink into the rig, shut the door, leave a fist-wide opening to spy through. Romano's rifle pricks from his shoulder, breaks his silhouette as he turns towards me. I sink out of sight, slide my volume up a little.

'Go straight to the helicraft ring. Stand on the semi-circle closest to us. It is a blind spot.'

'What?' someone mutters.

I will them to believe my preposterous words. 'You will be invisible.'

'Ha!' Charmayne scoffs.

I scorch her mutinous eyes, rebuke her for her lack of faith. The big beauty bows her head sullenly.

Romano swings slowly the other way. Only his forehead shows as he stares out to sea. I grab Vicki's hand, savour the memory of the feline, furry softness between her thighs. The clouds rush across the moon, conspire with us as we take off towards the helicopter ring: me, Vicki, Vihaan with the black box and Barry the Australian. A clutch of others scramble after us. The prisoners press together, plant their perfectly groomed feet on the white landing ring. Eulalie, Madame Sophie and Gibril the desert runner lead another frightened rush. The clouds pass by, curse Josiah with sudden, bright moonlight. He blocks the doorway, refuses to move. Samuel doubles back and hauls Josiah to his place on the white line. Again the clouds cover the moon. Another sweep of prisoners launches towards us, then Charmayne leads Shikorina onto the white ring. I dare not look at her smeared legs. The last group of prisoners stumbles across the space. The skinny rapist is the last of the prisoners to take his position on the white paint. We form a human curve around the tail of the huge metal bird, desperately trusting the magic of Romano's blind spot.

Inside the lookout tower, Romano strolls towards the window, stretches and yawns. For a moment the moon turns him into a little god in epaulettes. Some prisoners suck a scared breath as he faces the blades of the Dragonfly. He turns his back on us. I squeeze Vicki's hand with all my might.

'RUN,' Vicki gasps for me.

Barry finds some metaphysical strength, blunders forwards half carrying the Indian. He clambers aboard the life boat, pulls him into it. Yassir, Mohammed and Gibril are the next ones in. By the time Vicki and I throw ourselves over the edge, Vihaan is already tearing the duct tape off the waterproof case with his few remaining teeth. I think I see him grin in the gloom of the orange tarpaulin. Samuel crawls with Josiah to the back of the boat and stations him at the engines. Josiah immediately pulls up a cap and checks a dipstick. He unscrews something, lets a dark fluid bleed. He pumps and locks a handle. The night breeze blows his greasy hair back, exposes the noble profile of a dark Viking, not a sadistic murderer. I sit down with Vicki, hold her like she is all I have left in my life. The priest killer and Samuel are hunting on the bottom of the boat like someone has dropped a wedding ring. Samuel falls to the floor, thrusts a black disc into an opening. He twists it to lock it. Oh, God. The bath plug.

The priest killer calls out softly to the desert runner, 'Untie, untie!', then releases a rope attached to the A-frame above us. The desert runner darts from hook to hook, frees more ropes as the prisoners keep staggering across the deck and throwing themselves into the boat.

A siren screams from the tower, piercing us with panic-stricken peals of sound. I let go of Vicki, dive towards the last steel hook, haul on it. I can't untie it. The desert runner shoves me aside, engages the muscles in his hands, releases it. A volley of shots blast out, makes shrieking pings. But this is not the sound of table tennis, it is the screech of copper bullets ricocheting off the deck. Angus the skinny rapist runs towards us, screaming like a woman. He leaps into the boat and rolls up like a hedgehog. There is a pause in the pinging while the rest of the prisoners fall and crawl, fling their weak bodies into the lifeboat. I catch sight of Lolie darting behind a huge steel pillar.

'Push the red button! Start the winch!' the priest killer shouts.

Samuel dives towards the metal mount at the railing of the rig.

He leans out of the boat, shoves on the red power switch. Nothing happens.

Romano sprints from the tower towards us. He swipes at the skinny rapist below the lip of the lifeboat. He grabs his straw hair, drags him back onto the deck. Angus fights back with startling violence. He snatches Romano's feet from under him and pins him to the floor. Romano wrestles free, flings the rapist three metres through the air. Angus lands on his head with a crack that splits the night with a single syllable. He rolls to his hands and knees, his heart, miraculously, still sewn up. It is his head that is bleeding.

'Pull the brake handle!' the priest killer screams.

I swing my eyes from the red mask dripping through Angus's eyebrows, grab for the brake lever on the metal mount. I pull with Samuel. The brake suddenly gives, snatches at my sore hand. Pain rips away all sensible thought as I stand there, stuck in a beehive, stopping us from reaching the sea. Samuel heaves the handle up while I drag my hand out. I glance at my crushed fingers. The boat jitters and sways as the gigantic winch wakes up but Romano is running towards us, his Kalashnikov raised. As he passes the pillar, Lolie slips from her hiding place and rips the machine gun off his body. Romano snatches at her but she skips over the skinny rapist and runs towards the lifeboat, her bare breasts on each side of the machine gun.

'Lolie!' I scream. I have no need of a tongue.

There is the scream of metal cable unravelling under hydraulic pressure as the winch lowers the boat towards the ocean. Romano flies beneath a canvas cover, throws up a hatch near the Dragonfly. He pulls out a second rifle. Lolie swings and shoots a burst of bullets at him. Romano's Kalashnikov catapults through the air, detonates three times by accident. Romano hurls himself after it,

302

rolling like a soldier across a killing field. The lifeboat is shunting down without Lolie.

'Wait!' I try to shout, but Josiah is already gunning the engines, preparing them for full speed. Lolie leaps towards the sea, lands lightly in the bow of the boat. Above us, Angus launches off the railing of the rig. As he jumps, Romano grabs hold of one flying wing. The skinny rapist twists off course and falls down, down, down past us.

Angus lands with the smallest of disturbances in the monster sea. He rolls slowly to the surface and floats lopsided, his mouth wide, gasping. A dark shadow browses past him, vanishes. Then the moon catches an enormous fin. The beast races towards Angus, rams his thin body, propels him forwards half a metre deep. I think I see his bulging eyes, his mouth crying out. Then the rapist is gone.

The lifeboat's backside dips violently. We wrap our arms and legs around the benches as the boat stops. It rocks back, swings, filled with soft, naked targets in the traitorous moonlight. Gibril, the desert runner, hurls himself at a pulley on the bow. He heaves at it, every sinew stretched to snapping point. Above us, Romano aims his shattered Kalashnikov at him. *DTT DTT DTT*. Out of the corner of my eye I see Lolie rise up from the bow. *DFF DFF DFF*. The fabric on Romano's shoulders rips. Something shiny flies up and tinkles on the metal deck. Lolie has shot off his epaulettes.

Romano drops to his haunches, crawls out of sight of Lolie's crack fire. He shoots from his hiding place. *DTT DTT*.

'Barry!' the social worker screams.

'Ugh. Ugh. Ugh.' Barry is on the floor of the boat fighting for each breath as he watches the blood pool around his buttocks. More blasts from the rig. The bald man next to Barry folds on impact. He stares at his toes like a puppet on a shelf. Three holes between his nipples bubble with blood. His eyes flare like stars, then turn to green glass. Next to him, red fills Barry's folds, runs down his hips. Romano has shot him in the stomach.

He smiles a weird smile, some kind of horrible reflex. 'Oh. Shit.'

High above us, I catch sight of Mr Rawlins' silver hair and Meirong's pale face at the railing of the rig. Romano rises up behind them, hurls them down on the deck. The wind tosses his scream towards us. 'They're shooting!'

Lolie shatters a railing to confirm his words. Romano aims his disembodied weapon over the edge of the deck. His bullets shatter the steering wheel right next to Gibril.

'Keep them alive!' I hear Mr Carreira's unmistakeable bellow. I might be imagining it, but I think I see a glimpse of his grey teeth. The desert runner wraps his whole wiry body around the pulley, pits every quivering strand of muscle against it. Suddenly the jammed wire screams out. The strangler has restarted the orbit of our earth.

As the lifeboat tilts down at the bow, Barry's blood streams towards Vicki and me. I lift my feet, clap my hands over my eyes like a refugee child. When I look again, Barry is staring up at Romano taking aim at our engines.

'Shoot him, Lolie!' someone screams.

Lolie shatters the air next to Romano's head. She could put a copper pellet through the cubic millimetre of his brain that tells him to breathe, but somehow I know, Lolie is desperate not to kill again.

The lifeboat lands with a sickening violence, hurling bone against bone, cracking our faces against the fibreglass.

'Pull the pins!' Mohammed screams. His candle-wax hands drag at the steel tackle hooking us to the winch. A metal pin comes free. 'Help me!'

Samuel leaps up and fumbles with a catch, but Gibril moves like the wind, pops three pins in quick succession with his strong hands. The old boat is in the water, gunning through the waves, the rig a devouring shadow above us.

Behind me, I hear Vihaan saying in perfect English, 'Mayday, mayday, mayday. This is Sea Sprite, Sea Sprite . . .' A screen illuminates his face as he reads off the solo sailor's monitor. 'This is Sea Sprite, RF, five four seven. Over.'

White foam flies up behind us, creates a parting as we roar through the sea. This close, the ocean is our friend, dark and deathless, filled with ramming sharks to terrify our enemies. The moon path dissolves behind us, lets the vastness of the night cover us. The sea wind follows politely, escorting us. The broken wheel on the helm twists as if a ghost is steering the boat but it is Josiah, working the tiller under cover of the tarpaulin.

I type on my phone, slide the volume to *Shout*, 'Josiah. Due south!'

He crawls to peer at an instrument. He eases the tiller, corrects our course. Vihaan persists in clear, confident English, 'Mayday, mayday.'

Samuel sits close to him, holds the black box steady on Vihaan's knees. I don't bother to tell them the radio will be useless for another fifteen sea miles. I stand up to get a glimpse of Barry, the Australian. He is a pale, inert form made of undulating clay, an unfinished figure, not yet smoothed by the fingertips of the creator. Someone has stuffed a sponge into his stomach. But Barry has already bled to death.

* * *

The Dragonfly shatters the beautiful synchronicity of fleeing prisoners, courteous wind, moonlit sea. The machine knocks its massive metal cogs, hammers at the sky. It strips the sea naked with its floodlights as it slices towards us. I shield my eyes against the cruel, white light. Romano is positioned at a gap in the door. Meirong is kneeling on the seat behind him, her face a white orchid blooming in the midst of metal death. Romano's automatic weapon slides through the opening. I throw myself at Vicki, hurl her to the floor as bullets tear apart the air molecules surrounding us. The light bounces off the sea, bares the vulnerable belly of the Dragonfly as Lolie takes aim, returns fire. The helicraft roars away, advances again. More ear-splitting explosions. Romano is shooting at the hull of our escape vessel, not at our fragile skulls or our soft parts. Lolie, too, is shooting at their machine, not their mortal bodies.

She puts a bullet through a spinning blade. Mr Rawlins jerks the Dragonfly sideways, swoops out of range. He charges at us again. Romano lets loose another volley of bullets suffocated by water. This time the lifeboat jolts, sends a shudder through our skeletons. Water washes beneath our seats.

Vicki panics. 'We'll drown!'

I crouch against her, squeeze her tightly. No. I will never let her. I can swim right across the Tantwa River.

Lolie shoots the tail of the Dragonfly this time. The white beast simply shivers and flies straight up. Samuel crawls to the edge of the lifeboat, wrests open a sluice in the boat lining. Barry's pink water drains. Fresh water runs in to take its place.

Eulalie shouts hoarsely near the bow, 'Milja Mongoose is dead!'

Her words thread between the sounds of splintering fibreglass. She is standing now, thrusting her hands at me, 'Tell him! Her heart stopped last week!'

I tear my phone from my pocket, stab at the screen. I tap *Megaphone Mode*, watch the speaker sound amplify a hundred times. I type the terrible news. My digital voice bounces off the sky, returns to us. It is not strong enough.

The Indian stabs at his black box, shouts something.

'What, Vihaan? Tell me!' Samuel puts his ear to the Indian's mouth. 'Malachi!' Samuel leaps up and grabs my phone from me. He jams a cable into it, lets Vihaan plug it into his communication system. The Dragonfly is plunging towards us for another hit on our hull. Samuel swipes the screen, pokes at a setting.

My spokesman is no longer African. He is simply BOOMING. He shouts the terrible news of Milja Mongoose like the riot police before a crowd of angry thousands. 'MILJA MONGOOSE IS DEAD! HER HEART STOPPED LAST WEEK!'

Romano hears it through the metal casing. His bullets cease. The Dragonfly veers aimlessly. Romano is on his knees in the doorway, clutching his rifle to his breast. He cannot question the truth of Eulalie's message.

Mr Rawlins' mouth barks something cruel at him. Meirong crouches behind Romano, tugs at the ripped fabric on his shoulders. She is trying to resurrect him, get her war vet to shoot.

Josiah jams the engine to full speed. The waterlogged boat grinds slowly through the ocean. We strain towards the lightening skyline, stagger towards freedom. Behind us, the clatter of the helicraft sounds the savage grief of a bereaved father.

There is a reckoning happening up there in the Dragonfly. The wind brings us wisps of a man's roar, a woman's shout. I think I can see Mr Rawlins, thin-lipped, glaring towards us. They dare not come close without the cover of Romano's machine gun.

Suddenly Lolie shrieks. 'Josiah!'

Josiah has left his engines and crawled to the bow. He is playing tug-of-war with Lolie's rifle.

'No-o-o!' Lolie screams, but Josiah rips the weapon from her and gives her a vicious kick. Lolie smashes back against Shikorina. When she stands up, her back is smeared with red. Josiah is aiming for Mr Rawlins. *DTT DTT DTT!*

Immediately the engine lowers its pitch. The flying creature loses velocity. Its tail dips then lifts, as if in a last desperate mating ritual. It tips onto its side, wallows in the night air. Something explodes. The Dragonfly plunges head first into the water fifty metres from us.

White foam boils all around the crash site. Slowly the air bubble in the front lifts the cockpit. The machine sinks again, then finds its equilibrium. It floats, half buried in the purple sea.

'Romano! Romano!' I try to scream. 'Meirong!'

My enemies. My friends!

A black head bursts to the surface. It is him! I can see from the gold streaming off his dark skin. Romano swims straight towards us, his arms cleaving through the heaving, shining sea. I stumble towards Samuel. He almost throws my phone to me.

'Josiah. Cut the engines!' The voice blasts from my Samsung, deafening.

Josiah stares defiantly at me, his machine gun hanging in his hairy fist. I stand up, lurch for the engines. Josiah scrambles along the port side. He snatches my fingers from the engine, twists them violently. I howl with fresh pain, tear them free.

I switch my settings to normal, top volume. 'Let Romano live!'

'Listen to him!' Samuel shouts at Josiah.

Josiah stares at us both with contempt. He reaches up reluctantly, kills a switch.

The heavy boat rocks in limbo. Romano swims to the side. It is Charmayne who reaches down to clasp his wrists. The priest killer throws his arms around her waist, helps her haul Romano into our watery vessel. The sea is lapping at our shins now. Romano sits in his sodden clothes like he is seated in a grassy graveyard. He hangs his head as if he's praying. I hear it before anyone else does. Romano's sorrow escapes in that high, tearing whine. Lolie shifts close to him. Charmayne kneels before him, unlaces his boots.

'Sorry Romano,' I type. 'I am so, so sorry about Milja.'

It only makes his keening louder.

The desert runner clips open a hatch somewhere near the back of the boat. He hands out five bright orange buckets on ropes. He scoops a load of water, pours it into the ocean. While Romano cries, some prisoners take up his respectful, careful movement. Vicki dips her orange bucket, pours water into the sea. The wind blows softly at our backs now that we are not moving.

Something white floats towards us, lifting and dipping in the golden water. It is Mr Rawlins in a white vest and white boxer shorts, floating on his back like he is on vacation. His hair is swept to one side, just as he likes it, his complexion smooth in the fading moonlight. As the current pulls him close, I see that he has shaven legs. He must have been a cyclist. Or perhaps a cross dresser. Either way, Mr Rawlins is dead.

A black shining ball bobs past him. Meirong shoots up, sucks a breath, sinks again. She is swimming the breaststroke. A tiny wave swamps her. She thrashes up, gasping, her nose streaming with mucous.

I can't watch her drown. 'Josiah. Fetch Meirong!' I thrust out an arm like a pirate captain.

Strangely, Josiah obeys me. He switches on the engine, turns the tiller. We churn through the water, an overcrowded refugee ferry sinking at sea. Josiah ploughs towards Meirong's little head. She raises a diminutive hand above the waves.

'Malachi,' she chokes.

Josiah swings to miss her. I hang off the railing, reach down with my crushed fingers. Something hits me hard from the side, rams me from the railing.

'Let her drown!' Romano bellows.

He picks me up like I am a matchstick, flings me to the floor at the social worker's feet. Andride does something odd. He leans forwards, pats my head like I am a spaniel looking for affection. I grab my phone from my pocket before the water reaches it.

I crouch, type quickly. 'It is murder, Romano!'

Romano blocks my way to the sinking, swimming woman. 'She murdered Milja. She made her wait.'

I shake my head. 'Milja is watching you right now.'

Romano stares at me, terrible hope flaring in his sodden eyes.

'She doesn't want you to live with a dead woman around your neck,' I type desperately.

Romano clenches his huge hands. 'I will kill you, Malachi!' He guards the side where Meirong is sinking and surfacing, scratching at the hull with what sounds like her fingernails.

'Malachi is right,' Eulalie shouts. She shakes her silver head, her crone's face miraculously smoothed in the moonlight. 'You are still her Sun Chief.'

I gasp in surprise. This is what his daughter calls him.

Romano crumples to the floor of the lifeboat. He sits with

straight legs, his head sagging back like he is in a warm bath. He stares up at the stars, showing him home movies of his sweet Milja.

Vicki acts quickly. She grabs the lifebelt off its hook and flings it towards Meirong's submerged head. But it is too late, Meirong is sinking. I rip up my shirt, peel off the plastic sacs grafted onto my skin. I drop them on the bench, thrust my Samsung at Vicki. She clutches it against her breasts as if I have entrusted her with my tongue. I climb onto the railing of the lifeboat. I take a deep breath, ready to race across the crocodile pit. I dive through the air, cleave through the sea.

It is icy. The crack in my rib feels like a savage bite. The sharks, the cold sea, they will tear out my insides. I have never in my life swum in the ocean but I dive down deep, flailing. I feel slippery skin. I lock my arms around Meirong's thighs, thrust her up like a rogue great white, my eyes wide open. Her one tiny hand grips the lifebelt. Then another.

I break the surface. Meirong pulls her head from whatever sea we are in, lays her cheek against the lifebelt like it is a pillow. She seems to fall asleep. Strong arms pull on the rope that ties the lifebelt to the boat. Who is it?

There are three of them forming a chain gang, Charmayne, Andride, Gibril. Gibril grabs Meirong's small hands, hauls her up the side of the boat while Vicki throws the lifebelt back to me. The other two get behind her, drag me into our flooded vessel. Near me, some prisoners scoop slow, futile buckets of water into the sea.

Meirong is shivering as if she has touched a live wire. 'Malachi?' she whispers.

I bend close, listen attentively. She tries to say something, but she is too weak. Meirong is wearing a pale pink onesie. I think she is

311

dying. I sink down next to her in the shallow water, begin to tremble.

'What is she saying?' Romano growls. He slouches in the shallow water, his hands hanging off his knees. 'Bitch killer.'

I look around for Vicki. She splashes over a bench, lets me dry my fingers on her soft stomach. She gives my Samsung to me.

I take the liberty of writing Meirong's silent truth for her. 'She says her parents should have kept her.'

Meirong begins to splutter.

'Not left her in an orphanage.'

Meirong cries uncontrollably. Josiah starts the engines, forces the broken boat through the water. Now that their adrenalin has subsided, a fever of cold spreads through the prisoners. They huddle and shiver, their teeth chattering.

But near the bow, Eulalie seems to have a secret fire smouldering inside her. Her smoky eyes drift to me. I smell a fleeting fragrance of burning wild thyme. 'Love. And the cry for love,' she says.

'What do you mean?' I type urgently.

Eulalie shrugs her bony shoulders, swathes me with her gentle smoke. 'That is all there is.'

I get it. The simplicity of it.

The rape, the abuse, the mutilation. They are all acts of self-hatred. A cry for love.

I stroke the ridges on Vicki's thighs. I slide my volume to *Whisper*. 'I love these.' I put the phone to Vicki's ear.

She grabs my sore hand and squeezes. I want to extricate it but she is loving me.

'Ouch,' I type.

Vicki giggles, lets go of my hand. She runs her thumb along the fine scar on my cheek, laughs that dark, perverse laugh only I can see through. She is still wicked, this beautiful, ruined woman, but I am in love with her spirit, shining beneath her cruel sarcasm. I will wait forever, if necessary, for glimpses of it. Vicki lays her head against me, shivers against my skin. I kiss her temple with my soft, virgin lips. Bless her.

We churn slowly through the water, only half afloat. Vihaan still worries at the black box like he did with his poor unfortunate teeth. 'Mayday, mayday, mayday . . .'

We must be out of the satellite shield now. I keep a watch on the sky, still strewn with tiny fires in star patterns. The moon is weary of our drama but it hangs near the horizon, waits patiently.

A voice crackles then clears on the black box. 'Copy Sea Sprite. This is Saint Helena Rescue Vessel, SH three four seven six two. Fifteen degrees, forty-two minutes south, five degrees, thirty-three minutes west. We have been searching for you. Over.' The accent is French.

'Yes, yes, yes!' Vihaan nods and spits. He bangs on the black box like it is a bongo drum.

'Answer him,' Samuel hisses.

Vihaan adjusts a dial, presses a switch. 'Where are we?' he asks sincerely.

There is a stunned incomprehension on the other side. The man murmurs, 'Are you kidding me?' Then he says officiously, 'Repeat your question, Sea Sprite. Over.'

I leap up, crush myself onto the bench next to Vihaan. He digs his elbow into my cracked rib, shouts in a foreign, angry language. The black box is *his* business. Instinctively I throw my arm around his shoulders, hug him tightly. I stroke his head, hum to him.

Love and the cry for love. That is all there is. Vihaan goes pliant. He kisses my wet sleeve, shifts the black box onto my lap.

I type quickly. 'Nadras Oil lifeboat here. This is Malachi Dakwaa. We're in terrible trouble about fifteen miles south of a Nadras Oil rig. Have you seen this rig?'

'Confirm. Our vessels passed it on Wednesday night. Are you with Frances Shaw of Sea Sprite? Over.'

Something tells me the solo sailor is our only hope.

'We have her black box.'

'Where is she? Over.'

'We have sustained serious damage to our lifeboat. The water is flooding in. How long will it take for you to get to us?'

There is an awkward silence from the black box.

'We are only authorised to rescue Frances. Is she with you? Over.'

'She's dead.'

'I'm sorry. Race insurance won't pay. Over.'

'Free Press,' Samuel urges me fiercely.

'If you don't rescue us we will call the Free Press.'

There is a crackle, some muffled dialogue. A woman answers through the black box. This one sounds Russian. 'This is Angelika Pasha. I'm a Free Press journalist. I am with them.'

I switch my Samsung tone to *Emphasis*. 'They're coming back. We are under attack from the same party who murdered Frances.'

There is the sound of a muted argument. Angelika speaks tersely, 'Are you moving?'

'Very slowly, south.'

'How many on board?'

I minus the three deserters, minus the dead. 'Thirty-seven.'

I hear the Frenchman's muffled growl, 'Angelika, we are not allowed . . .'

'I will try,' she promises me.

The Frenchman chops off our communication like a guillotine. 'Over and out.'

Samuel stands up, whoops with euphoria. Madame Sophie titters. She asks no one in particular, 'Will they come?'

'We're going to live,' Andride says uncertainly.

Charmayne scans the silent sky. 'Raizier will kill us.' She shrugs her shoulders, tries for nonchalance. 'And if we live they will send us home to our prisons.' She breaks into massive sobs. Eulalie strokes Charmayne's powerful thigh with her maiden's fingers. In some strange way she is younger than the big beauty, as if the sea air and the prospect of a lover have stripped off a lifetime. Charmayne raises Eulalie's hand to her eyes, wipes her eyes like it's a tissue.

Please, Angelika Pasha. Make them come. *Please*.

I stare down at my attire. I am dressed in sodden, suave black. I even brought my sneakers. It is God-smoothed, this path, surely. I am dressed for the press.

FRIDAY

The moon turns surreptitiously silver. It fades discreetly, begins to rub itself out. The sun hides below the horizon, stains the sea charcoal grey. Inspired now, the prisoners take turns to bail water from our leaky boat. Even Shikorina tries to help. Red swills in the water like a skirt around her shins, follows her everywhere.

I slide my volume to medium distance. 'Shikorina. Be still. Please.'

She sinks obediently onto a bench.

I find the antibiotics floating in the corner near where I left them. I hand four to Samuel to send down the aisle. 'One for each surgery. They must drink it.'

'Is it not intravenous?' Samuel asks.

I shake my head. 'It was meant for their feeding tubes. Make sure they finish it.'

I pull my feet up in case the lifeboat pours Shikorina's blood my way. I bail a few buckets of what I hope is simply sea water.

Meirong stirs for the first time. She pushes back her wet hair, which, astoundingly, is still a neat, shining helmet like an anime heroine's. 'Quenton has weapons in Saint Helena.' But this is not a warrior vixen. She hugs herself in her pink onesie, wipes her nose on her sleeve. 'If the press get here first, I'm going straight to jail.'

Romano is still sitting in the bath, his legs outstretched as if the news of his daughter has stopped his own heart. He lifts his chin off his chest, nods. 'Yes.'

'Conscious Clause is global,' Meirong intones hopelessly. 'They will get me.'

'I hope you go to jail forever, Meirong. You lied to me.'

'I promise you, Romano, I was going to tell you.'

Romano shakes his head. 'You killed Milja.'

Meirong flashes sharp canines. 'You killed many, Romano, before you had a daughter.' She spins towards us, lashes at the prisoners, 'All of you are killers!'

We are a silent, dead weight beneath our dead, wet albatrosses.

The engines cut off. There is a movement at the back of the boat. Josiah picks his way from the engines towards the port side. His hairy knees brush my trousers. His thick fingers brush my cheek by accident. He falls over Samuel's feet. Samuel draws them up beneath his buttocks.

'Easy,' Samuel warns him. 'Where are you going, Josiah?'

Josiah snatches at the railing, hooks his hairy feet onto a rung.

'Josiah!' Samuel shouts.

Josiah's buttocks are flat and shockingly furry. They clench together, prepare to leap. I lunge for him but Josiah kicks from the top, dives into the glittering sea.

Madame Sophie thrusts out her arm, commands me, 'Throw the lifebelt!'

'No!' Vicki screams. 'Leave him!'

We stand up, some of us, watch Josiah swimming freestyle with a funny, stylish flourish of his fingers. He is a beautiful swimmer. His arms cleave close to his ears, the water swills over his greasy head, runs off immediately. Oil and water don't mix.

'Save him, Malachi!' Madame Sophie begs me.

Vicki argues, 'No!'

'Malachi!' Madame Sophie shouts.

I shake my head, type on my Samsung, 'It's easier for him to drown than to carry on living.'

Madame Sophie clings to the rail, watches Josiah travel the vanishing moon path with his funny, extravagant flick. The lifeboat is silent for long, long minutes as we watch Josiah swim almost out of sight. Vicki picks her way to the edge, peers into the fading night. She climbs the railing as if Josiah's freestyle is towing her towards the horizon.

'NO!' I try to shout. I scramble after her, gather her tangled hair in my fist. I haul her down like a caveman.

Vicki arches, strains against my grip. 'Let go-o-o!' she shrieks.

I throw an arm around her belly, drag her from the railing. I lock her wrists with one hand, snatch at my Samsung. 'You deserve to live.'

'I don't want to.'

'Your husband has forgiven you.'

I glance desperately at Eulalie. *Help me.*

'I can't forgive myself,' Vicki shouts tearfully.

'It is braver to live and face it.'

'I want to die.'

'No. I need you!'

Vicki searches my eyes frantically, left to right, reads the love letter written in them. Her body softens, her wrists go loose. She bows her head gracefully. I lead her to our bench. She weaves her cool, smooth fingers tightly between mine. I sit down next to her, kiss the fingertips I cut every day for a week.

God help me. I am in love with a suicidal mermaid.

*

A whirring sound rides on the sea breeze.

Lolie scrambles along the starboard side, squeezes behind the engines. We throw ourselves into the shallow water beneath our benches, spy a metal object flying through the grey dawn towards us. It looks like a flattened beetle with flaps and apertures, sucking in and spitting air at a shocking velocity. I hunt frantically for Vicki. Her hand snakes out, grabs on to my sneaker.

The thing looks like a US military tank in Syria – as small as a toy at Planet Kids. A lightning bolt shreds the water six metres from us. The second bolt strikes a railing above our heads.

The violence of electric air. A burning stink.

A laser drone. Flown out by Raizier.

A streak of fire rips into an engine. The shock kick starts a fresh panic in all of us.

'Malachi!' Lolie shouts. 'Spin us! Spin!' She jabs at the engines.

Even as I am moving, I see Lolie's stitches are pulling loose in her abdomen. Red runs like perfect tears from each perforation. Flames spit from the engine that has been hit. It could blow up any second but I dive towards the other engine, punch every switch I can set my eyes on.

Where is Josiah? We need him!

The engine snarls savagely. I grab hold of the tiller I saw Josiah steering. Jam it hard to the left.

Help us, Josiah, please.

The boat churns in a tight circle. I shove my weight against the tiller, snatch at an orange bucket, scoop water from the floor and throw it at the burning engine. The flames suffocate to black smoke. Lolie crouches down, slots the rifle between the two machines. She tracks the drone, waiting for a cunning moment to release

319

her bullets. The swirling stars, the spinning drone make me dizzy. I want to lie down next to Lolie, let the steel engines protect my heart, my intestines. But I hang on to the tiller. An infra red strike slices a bench near the engines. Oh, God, no. They are firing to kill. Sacrificing their organs.

Another streak of light sears what could be human tissue. A woman screams.

Vicki!

I jam the tiller in position, crawl towards the stink of burning flesh. I shove past Samuel, get caught against his bristly cheek. We breathe into each other's nostrils, two animals close to death. I scrape past him.

Vicki. I know those bubble toes. I grab onto them, draw my torso over hers.

Her body still throbs with life. Was she hit?

No, but the yellow man lies loosely, like someone cut him from a cross. A blistering, black wound on his temple emits a thin red stream. I shut my eyes, lay my head precisely above Vicki's so they must sear through my skull before they can hurt hers.

Yassir is dead. And the funny thing is, he looks just like Jesus Christ.

I breathe in my own tears, bury my head in Vicki's hair to escape the smell of his death.

It *is* the scent of liquorice. Vicki smells like the wild fennel that grew at our village tap, feathery and green, but touch it and it pricks you like a knife. I bunch Vicki's fingers, wrap them in my fists.

The scent of liquorice mixed with salt, a mermaid's hair at night as lasers strike the benches to our right. Lolie returns fire, forces the drone to dart away, fly erratic zigzags. It swoops back again, a terrible insect, ready to fight to the death. Lolie's bullets spit behind us, stertorous.

There is a shift in the whirring, a self-pitying whine from the drone's motor. It dips above us as we spin like a playground roundabout. A new motor kicks in. The deadly beetle whirrs up in a smooth arc again.

Near the bow, Shikorina sits up carelessly, staggers to her feet.

'Shikorina!' Andride shouts.

Shikorina is climbing up the railing, her legs a dark red. The sun creeps up gently on this war scene. It catches her legs from the front, turns them orange. The colour of emergency.

'Get down!' Andride screams.

Shikorina's legs buckle and sway but she clings to the railing. She shakes her fist at the toy machine. 'My children! My children!'

Beyond the drone, the sky is a gigantic flower blossoming. Shikorina jerks as a laser rips into her chest. She slides slowly from the railing, as if exhausted by her furious gesturing. Shikorina curls up on the ledge, tucks her hands beneath her cheek. She sleeps.

Lolie lets seven bullets fly in succession, shreds the drone's steel skin. A return strike splinters the bench behind me. I feel a blast in my calf muscle. A quantum delay.

How strange. Like thunder and lightning. Then, the pain.

'Malachi! Are you hit?'

I shake my head, lie to Vicki. But my blood makes clouds in the water beneath us. I roll onto my back but the red floods my throat, suffocates me. I cough, but more blood shoots up.

Vicki struggles from under me, throws herself across my knees. She grabs my jaw, wrenches it to the side. 'Malachi! Breathe!'

I gag on the liquid, find a thread of oxygen. More precious air streams in.

This is what Hamri was doing! He was trying to turn my head. He was trying to save my life, not shut me up.

Father.

There is a pause in the deadly hum above us.

I wipe my mouth with the back of my hand, stare at it. No blood, silly.

I watch the pink sky flowering above me. Vicki prods my calf, tries to feel the extent of my injury.

'Aah,' I grunt.

'It's nothing, Malachi. It's just a shallow cut.'

I want to giggle. Nothing compared to the wounds she received in the medical wing. As the boat spins, the blood from my shallow cut gathers around us. I shut my eyes. It's fine. It's fine. It's just raspberry juice.

The drone spins again, whirrs towards us once more. I crawl back onto my Cleopatra, cover her carefully, bathe her not in milk but red raspberry juice.

The sound of a huge engine hacks up the morning sky.

A black craft charges towards us, short blades thrashing inside a wheel on the roof. The front is tattooed with a pirate's face, grinning with white teeth. A dark-skinned pilot sits inside the pirate's good eye. Inside the red eye patch a woman with long black hair aims a huge camera at our broken, spinning planet.

Angelika.

Her shining lens throws a shield of truth around blood, water, buckets. The dead among us.

The rotorcraft sinks closer, visits a gale force on us. A pirate galleon sails across the body and tail. *Brave Heart Rum*, it says in white lettering. *Rescue SB6*. Silhouettes press against the tinted glass, their seeing eyes our precious, wonderful protection. The scarred metal beetle hovers in the distance, paralysed by the camera's eye. It swivels in the sky, drifts towards where Saint Helena might be. I roll off Vicki's body, crawl to the engines. Lolie is crouched between them, nothing more than two traumatised eyes. The sky paints their dark mirrors with pink streaks. I flick the switches. Cut the engine. The spinning slows.

Our world stands still, rocking with the rhythm of the sea. Lolie seems unharmed. The only wound I can see is the one made by Tamba's father or one of his clumsy team. It has torn apart a little more, so blood streaks from the stitches like red eyelashes. I crawl between the engines. Kiss her on the forehead.

Angelika's camera is still rolling, enforcing the ceasefire, recording this atrocity of human nature.

Not love. But a cry for it.

The priest killer stumbles from the bow to find Lolie among the engines. He clutches her hands with his melted fingers, kisses them.

'Thank you.'

Madame Sophie's mind snaps loose from reality. 'Smile!' She fixes her hair, fluffs it out.

Vicki laughs with an unfettered, rare happiness.

I make my way over the benches to sit next to Shikorina. I don't care about the colour red. I stroke her head like she is my daughter in a deep, deep sleep. She is cold already.

I love you, Shikorina, I tell her spirit.

There is an explosion far away on the rig. Two, three massive blasts. Have they sprayed their benzene, flung a spark into it?

Oh, God, Tamba! Did his father find him?

And the three deserters?

Eulalie struggles to her feet, raises her face to the breeze. She lets the rising sun drench her withered skin. She waves a silken hand at me, smiles like we are all at a cocktail party.

I shut my eyes. Tamba is fine. Dead or alive.

Another detonation from the rig. But it is too late for secrecy. The prisoners are here. They still have their teeth. And I have a mouth to speak.

I smile to myself. No one can silence me and my Glossia.

A loving presence visits my heart suddenly. It expands and aches like Tamba's cocaine high. Grace, I think it is.

Vicki is sitting on the bench, her thighs slightly apart. The flames from the far-away rig flicker in her purple eyes. She is watching me now with unbelievable tenderness.

She will get asylum, I know this in my heart. And Grace will be the name of our first daughter.

ACKNOWLEDGEMENTS

Thank you to David for floating our boat while I was on the rig, and to all my beautiful children for always, always calling me back to land.

Thank you to my agent, Isobel, for loving Malachi, and to Henrietta, my editor, for not shutting him up.

Thank you to Sophie at Titan Books for taking this story across the sea.

T.C. Farren is a novelist, prize-winning screenwriter and former journalist. Her work has been shortlisted for the *Sunday Times* (SA) Fiction Prize, adapted into the feature films, and received numerous film festival awards.

@TraceyFarren
traceyfarren.com

For more fantastic fiction, author events, exclusive excerpts,
competitions, limited editions and more

VISIT OUR WEBSITE
titanbooks.com

LIKE US ON FACEBOOK
facebook.com/titanbooks

FOLLOW US ON TWITTER
@TitanBooks

EMAIL US
readerfeedback@titanemail.com